Mothers, Sisters & Other Lovers

Simone Mondesir

Copyright © 2016 Simone Mondesir

All rights reserved, including the right to reproduce this book, or portions thereof in any form. No part of this text may be reproduced, transmitted, downloaded, decompiled, reverse engineered, or stored, in any form or introduced into any information storage and retrieval system, in any form or by any means, whether electronic or mechanical without the express written permission of the author.

This is a work of fiction. Names and characters are the product of the author's imagination and any resemblance to actual persons, living or dead, is entirely coincidental.

The views expressed in this work are solely those of the author and do not necessarily reflect the views of the publisher, and the publisher hereby disclaims any responsibility for them.

Cover design by Ana Grigoriou www.books-design.com

ISBN: 978-1-326-51433-4

PublishNation
www.publishnation.co.uk

Also by Simone Mondesir

Acquired Tastes
Coming Up For Air

'…you should see the landscape of Greece – it would break your heart.'
Lawrence Durrell

ONE

DARLING CHILD COME IMMEDIATELY ABSOLUTELY <u>DESPERATE</u>

Grace read the six words scrawled in block capitals on the postcard in her hand for perhaps the thousandth time. The word 'desperate' was underlined so heavily that the pen had almost pierced the card. There was no signature, but Grace did not need one. Even if she had not recognised the handwriting, the lack of punctuation and extravagant exaggeration meant only one thing - it was from her mother.

Grace dropped the postcard onto her lap and turned to look out of the cabin window. The cheery pilot, who had sounded all of fourteen years old, had promised good weather all the way and the aeroplane had indeed been cruising through a cloudless blue sky for at least two hours. Grace closed her eyes. Back in London it had been grey and wet, and once again she wished, as she had regularly wished almost every minute of those two hours, that she was back in her cramped office just off Gower Street, watching the rain trace muddy rivulets down the window. The last place she wanted to be was on a plane heading towards her mother.

What had possessed her to obey her mother's summons yet again? Whenever there was a problem, her mother expected her to come running, and, like a dutiful daughter, she always did. Why, Grace did not know. It was not as though Marjorie was a dutiful parent, far from it. She had spent most of her life running as far away as possible from the responsibilities of motherhood. Grace became her 'darling child' only when her mother wanted something.

She looked down at the postcard again. There was no address as to just *where* Grace should come to find her mother. When it first arrived, Grace was tempted to throw it away. But, try as she might, she had been unable to dismiss the nagging feeling that what if, this time, her mother really *was* in trouble?

She had not seen Marjorie for nearly four months. For all she knew, her mother could have been lying in a hospital bed swathed in bloodied bandages for weeks or even worse... As the images took shape in her mind, Grace squeezed her eyes tight shut, but, after a moment or two, she opened them and forced herself to take several deep breaths. She was being over-dramatic, just like her mother.

Before the post card, the last time she had heard from her mother was in April when she received a letter with an Athens postmark, but that had been nearly ten weeks ago. In the letter, her mother had extolled the glories of Greece, which, contrary to the Guide Bleu and Baedeker, seemed to consist largely of the considerable beauty of Greek men and the perfect size and firmness of their buttocks. According to Marjorie, this physical perfection was attributed to generations of Greek fishermen rowing their boats while standing upright. Only her mother would remember a fact like this while ignoring the splendours of ancient Greece all around her.

Grace now wished she hadn't shown the letter to Roger. She had thought it would amuse him, but it hadn't, and, when the postcard arrived and she said that she thought she really ought to try and find her mother, it had caused a terrible argument. Roger had virtually forbade her to go to Greece. Not that he used quite such words - even he wouldn't dare to do that - but nearly as good as. Grace had never seen him quite so adamant before.

She hated it when they argued. They had been together for three years and the only disagreements they ever had were about her mother. The subject always made Roger see red, and when he read the postcard, he had seen scarlet. Her attempts to reason with him, pointing out that her mother might be ill or even in some terrible Greek jail, merely caused him to declare that a spell of prison discipline would do Marjorie nothing but good.

Realising further argument was useless, she said no more. However, during her lunch hour the next day, she closed the door to her office and began to make phone calls to airlines. It took a little time, but Grace finally tracked down the one charter airline that flew to the island from the UK and even then only once a week. She booked a seat on the next flight.

She had felt rather like a naughty schoolgirl waiting until Roger had left for his chambers that morning and then hurriedly packing. She would only be for away for a week. He could cope without her for that long. She had left a note saying that she loved him, but her mother needed her, and that she would call once she had booked into a hotel.

Grace knew leaving a note was a cowardly thing to do, but she hoped that Roger would understand that she needed to make sure her mother was okay. For all he said about Marjorie, his relationship with his own mother was equally difficult, or at least, Grace found it difficult. Roger was still living at home when they first met and would probably have still been there if his mother, Phyllis, could have her way. As it was, he continued to spend the occasional night there, just to keep the 'old thing' happy, as he put it. Grace had a strong feeling that he would probably move back in with his mother while she was away, so at least she would succeed in making his mother happy - something Grace did not often succeed in doing.

Roger's father had died when he was young and his mother never remarried. She owned a large barn of a house in West Kensington where she lived on the ground floor together with her companion, an elderly and malodorous Chihuahua called Fifi. Having lost most of its teeth, it emitted strangulated chirruping noises rather than barks, but its lack of teeth did not prevent it trying to gnaw Grace's ankles whenever she visited. Fifi was not only partially blind and wholly incontinent but constantly had what Phyllis laughingly called her 'little accidents' which were not the least funny when inadvertently stepped in. The housekeeper who came in every day kept a saucepan simmering on the cooker into which all food scraps were put. Fifi was fed from this, noisily relishing the foul smelling, but presumably soft and easily digested, mess.

Grace had tried very hard to get on with Roger's mother, obeying her weekly command to go to West Kensington for Sunday lunch and afternoon tea without complaint. But Phyllis still talked about Roger as though he lived upstairs, whilst his rooms remained just as though he still did, despite Grace pointing out that it would be better all round if he moved all his things into her house. Even the announcement six months ago that they intended to get married had not brought about any alteration in Phyllis's attitude. She continued to act as though Roger was still at school and Grace was a six-year-old friend who had come round for tea. It was irritating, but at least it was better than the way in which her mother had greeted the news of their impending marriage.

'Have you taken leave of your senses?' She spoke so loudly that she caused other lunchers to look in their direction.

'I know you don't like Roger very much,' began Grace.

'And the sentiment is mutual,' interrupted Marjorie. 'He's a pompous, arrogant, mummy's boy with political views which would put Genghiz Khan to shame. If you really intend to marry him *please* don't ask for my blessing nor expect me to come to the wedding.'

'Actually mother, I'm not asking for either your blessing or your permission,' retorted Grace. 'I'm thirty-six and I will be thirty-seven by the time I get married, so I rather think that I have no need of your approval. As to whether you choose to come to the wedding, that is entirely up to you. I will naturally be very disappointed if you don't come, because despite all signs to the contrary, you are my mother. However, if you do come, don't even *think* of causing a scene.'

'Me? Cause a scene?'

Grace could have kicked herself. Although her mother had sounded indignant, her mother's eyes had lit up at the idea of causing a scene - an idea that Grace had planted in her mind. As she signalled to the waiter for the bill and reached for her credit card, Grace had a strong feeling that whatever her mother said about not coming, Marjorie loved dressing up, and, as Roger planned a grand wedding, at the very least she would attempt to upstage all the other women with her outfit.

'Don't send her an invitation if you think she's going to be bloody stupid,' was Roger's retort that night when she told him about lunch with her mother. 'It's your day, so if you don't want your mother embarrassing you in front of our guests don't invite her. It's as simple as that.'

But it wasn't as simple as that, was it? Roger said it was going to be 'her' day however, if she was honest, she would prefer a small, informal wedding in a registry office. Roger and his mother were planning a guest list of several hundred, most of whom she had never met and some of whom were more his political contacts than real friends. She could understand Roger's wish not to be embarrassed in front of them, but to describe them as 'our' guests was rather stretching the point, they were his guests, not hers.

Yet she had said nothing at the time because she had found herself uncomfortably close to tears and she did not want Roger to see how upset she was. It would be yet another thing he would hold against her mother. Grace found the animosity between Roger and her mother very difficult. She had hoped that, with time, they would grow to like each other, but the opposite seemed to be happening. No-one knew better than she just how badly behaved and infuriating her mother could be, but no matter what Marjorie wore, or what she did, Grace did not want to get married without her mother being there.

Grace had begun to consider the likelihood of marriage was receding as she got into her mid-thirties, so it had been wonderful when Roger came along. Maybe he wasn't the great, all-consuming passion of her life, but that sort of love was for adolescents and romantic novels. It was also true that, at times, his manner and outlook could be more in keeping with 1955 than 1995, but she found that both endearing and sweetly eccentric. Perhaps it was his old-fashioned ways that made her feel secure as she could see herself growing old and grey with him, surely the best test of a relationship. Grace just wished she could make her mother see that her feelings for Roger were the kind that lasted a lot longer than just mere lust.

She sighed and, loosening her seatbelt, reached under the seat in front of her for her handbag, then sat back and fastened her belt again. Although the fasten seatbelt signs had been turned off two hours ago, passengers had been requested to keep their seatbelts on while in their seats. She carefully stowed the postcard away and then found the guidebook to Greece she had bought at the airport.

Alongside her, a middle-aged couple dressed in shorts and T-shirts ordered gin and tonics from a flight attendant. Grace had noticed while queuing at the check-in desk that everyone else on her flight was dressed equally casually. Her tailored skirt-suit and expensive high-heeled sandals had made her feel conspicuous, but then, she was going on business, not on holiday, and did not intend to stay in Greece for one moment longer than it took to sort out whatever trouble her mother had got herself into. For Grace had no doubt that any trouble her mother was in was of her own making - it always was.

Grace caught the flight attendant's glazed eye and bought some mineral water. As the woman next to her passed it over, she gave Grace a cheerful smile that threatened the opening of conversation. Grace waved at the attendant again and requested a pair of earphones. She immediately plugged them in. There was not much choice of music, but Grace was not in the mood for exchanging small talk with strangers.

As the tinny strains of the popular classics channel played into her ears, she traced her forefinger down the contents page of the guidebook, looking for some reference to the island where she was heading. It was not particularly encouraging. According to the book, it was not a noted holiday destination. Until recently, there had not even been any direct flights from England. Unlike other islands like Corfu, Rhodes and Mykonos, which occupied pages of purple prose, the entire island merited only a few paragraphs of uninformative description. It seemed that there were a few small resorts that were attempting to attract the booming 1990s Greek package tour trade, but clearly the village where Marjorie had posted the card was not one of them. The few lines about it read:

"An unspoiled fishing village, off the normal tourist track. The lack of hotels, shops, banks, discotheques and other tourist amenities makes this a spot strictly for the hardy Grecophile few who still like to experience Greek life in the raw. But for those adventurous enough, the village offers a meze of surprises."

It did not sound promising.

Along with the guide to Greece, Grace had brought a novel she had long been intending to read, but it was in her flight bag in the locker above her head and she would have to ask the couple beside her to move in order to get it. For want of anything else to do, she turned to the front of the guidebook and began to read it section by section until *The March of the Toreadors,* playing for the sixth time in her earphones, was interrupted by the voice of the Captain announcing their imminent descent.

She looked out of the window. Down below she could see what looked like a mountainous, desolate landscape, with few forgiving features, and, as they banked, a single runway. It looked both too short and too near the sea for safety. Grace closed her eyes as the plane made a rather bumpy landing.

Whether in gratitude for their safe landing or in delight at reaching their holiday destination, a smattering of applause ran through the cabin. Several of Grace's fellow travellers launched into a spirited, if unsuitable, rendition of *Y Viva España* that seemed to be the signal for everyone to ignore the flight attendant's pleas for them to remain seated until the plane had safely come to a halt. Instead, they leapt to their feet and tore open the overhead lockers, bringing beach umbrellas, coats, bags and bottles of duty free alcohol tumbling down onto unwary heads.

Grace waited until nearly everyone had left the cabin before collecting her bag and walking down the steps onto a runway sticky with heat. Inside the small airport building, immigration control was a silent uniformed man wearing mirrored aviator glasses leaning against a desk. An almost imperceptible nod indicated that dutifully held out passports had passed scrutiny.

Once through immigration, all semblance of order vanished as the passengers stampeded towards the baggage carousel where they stood looking ferociously from side to side, their elbows out at angles, ready to defend their position against all comers, seemingly prepared to trample small children and the elderly underfoot in their scramble to be first to retrieve their suitcase.

Grace waited to one side. She had a feeling that few, if any, of her fellow passengers would be heading for the same place as her. They did not have the look of tourists who liked their holidays dished up raw.

Her assumption soon proved correct. Through the dirty plate glass windows she could see a small parking area where several coaches were lined up, each with its hotel destination emblazoned on its windscreen. Suitcases began to move jerkily round the carousel and they were seized with much groaning and grunting before being trundled to the exit where tour reps clutching clipboards advanced. With fixed white smiles, they rounded up their perspiring clients, herding them to their respective coaches before returning with practised efficiency to collect stragglers who had been seeking relief in the toilets. Grace watched as one by one, the coaches roared away in a cloud of dust like some sort of latter-day wagon train.

With their departure, the airport lapsed into a lethargic stillness. Minutes before, it had been busy with officious looking men in white, short-sleeved shirts and dark blue trousers, gazing at the milling tourists from behind their uniform mirrored aviator sunglasses. Now it was deserted.

Grasping her suitcase in one hand and her flight bag in the other, Grace made for a sign proclaiming: Car Hire, Taxis and Information. The hatch to the office was firmly closed although a sign written in Greek and English said it was open. She pressed the button on the desk and waited. There was no response. She pressed it again and this time, she kept her finger on the button. After about thirty seconds the hatch was inched up, revealing a young Greek woman.

'My name is Hamilton. I have a hire car booked.'

The woman looked blank.

'Do you understand English?' asked Grace.

'Yes. But no car. They went this morning.' The woman reached up to pull the hatch down.

'That's impossible. A firm booking was made from London. Please check again, my name is Hamilton.' Grace helpfully spelt it out.

The woman looked at a list of names and shrugged. 'Yes, it is here, but no car. One has accident, poof...' she threw up her hands in illustration, 'so no car today.'

They gazed at each other for a few moments. The Greek woman looked away first, shrugging her shoulders.

Scenting victory, Grace squared her shoulders. 'Then you will order a taxi for me, *now*, and you can deliver a car to me tomorrow.'

The woman shook her head. The battle had not yet been won and she still had some ammunition left. 'No taxi. Today English come, so no taxi. Yesterday, plane from Athens, so plenty taxi. English no take taxi.' To emphasise her point, she gesticulated at where the row of coaches had been parked and then, her explanation over, she started to pull the hatch down.

Fighting a rearguard action, Grace foiled the manoeuvre by swiftly placing her flight bag on the counter. The hatch was grudgingly lifted back up.

'But *I* am English,' she said rather too loudly, her voice now tinged with desperation, 'and *I* arrived today and *I* want a taxi to go to this village,' she pointed to the name in her guidebook.

Grace's exasperation was made worse by her awareness that she was beginning to sound like a Joyce Grenfell impression of an Englishwoman abroad.

The woman followed Grace's pointing finger and then shrugged.

'You can call but I don't think they come. Too hot,' she fanned her face, 'and is veerry long way. No good.'

'But there must be a way to get to this village.' In the face of the implacable shrugs, Grace's voice began to quaver in a most un-Grenfell like manner.

'Bus.'

Acknowledging defeat, Grace removed her bag from the counter. 'What time does it leave?' she asked wearily.

The woman looked pityingly at her for a moment and then leaned through the hatch and yelled in Greek. There was the sound of scraping chairs and another aviator-glassed wearing man emerged from another office and ambled over. What to Grace sounded like a heated debate ensued. Finally the woman looked back at her. She jerked her head at the man.

'He say, maybe one hour, maybe sooner.'

Grace took a deep breath. 'How long will it take?'

Another loud discussion ensued.

'Three, maybe four hours. Long time.' The woman had won and she knew it.

Grace avoided her eyes. 'Where can I catch this bus?'

The woman's expression seemed to indicate that Grace had overstepped all the normal boundaries of tourist enquiries, but the man put a damp hand on Grace's elbow.

'Come, I show you.'

Grace waited for him to pick up her suitcase but he merely gripped her elbow more tightly. She settled her flight bag onto her shoulder and grasped her suitcase with the other hand. Behind her, the hatch slammed down with a loud bang.

As they emerged into the glaring sunlight, Grace was forced to screw up her eyes. The intense noonday heat had squeezed the life out of the landscape. Nothing moved apart from the heat eddies which shimmered and danced above the surface of the potholed road. Her moist-handed guide pointed wordlessly into the distance.

Grace squinted looking for something resembling a bus stop. She could see nothing, not even a house.

She turned to the man. 'How far?'

The man shrugged and held up a finger, then he gave her arm one more damp squeeze and retreated into the cool of the building.

Aware of his eyes watching her, Grace straightened her back, clasped her flight bag firmly to her side and marched smartly down the road. Within yards, perspiration began to trickle down her forehead, as the unsuitability of her close-fitting jacket and skirt and high-heeled strappy sandals became painfully obvious.

She trudged along, head down, concentrating on trying to avoid the largest potholes, oblivious to what was going on around her. Suddenly, the sound of a raucous klaxon just behind her startled her into an unwisely athletic leap to the side of the road. One foot twisted awkwardly under her as the strap on her sandal snapped.

Looking up to see the cause of her agony, Grace saw the back of a bus. Abandoning dignity along with her suitcase, she hopped and skipped after it, waving her arms in the air and yelling for it to stop.

Grace's actions, if not her language, were international, and the bus creaked to a halt. She hobbled back to retrieve her suitcase and then limped to the bus as fast as her ankle would allow.

Willing hands helped her on board and stowed her suitcase and flight bag on a rack occupied by some loudly clucking crates. In the timeless gesture of all travellers in a foreign country, she pointed wordlessly to the name of the village in her guidebook and proffered a hand full of Greek bank notes to the driver.

He read the name aloud and it was picked up and repeated like a chorus by all the other passengers. Then he twisted round in his seat and seemed to consult with several of the passengers who gesticulated at Grace. Eventually the driver seemed satisfied, and he took several notes from Grace's hand and gave her some change and a ticket. He then grasped the gear stick with both hands, and with scant use of the clutch, thrust the engine into first gear. With a sudden lurch the bus sprang back into life and Grace was propelled into an empty seat half way down the bus.

Had this been an English country bus, everyone would have reverted to their own private worlds, but Grace found herself the focus of a circle of bright-eyed attention. Disconcerted, she tried to ignore them by bending down to massage her swelling ankle.

There was a collective intake of breath and a general concerned sound of 'po-po-po'. A middle-aged man, whose lack of hair on his head was more than compensated for by the luxuriance of his moustache, held up a length of string and gestured at Grace's sandal. After a moment's hesitation she took it off and handed it to him. He deftly tied the broken strap into place and offered the sandal back.

Smiling and nodding, Grace fumbled through her guidebook for the section headed 'Useful Greek Phrases'. 'Thank you' came after how to order cold beer, ask for the toilet and demand an English speaking doctor. Holiday makers were urged to think of 'old Harry' as a means of remembering 'thank you' in Greek which was pronounced 'Efharrysto'.

Grace repeated the phrase, hoping it sounded right, and was rewarded with a broad smile.

A woman seated beside a mountain of bulging carrier bags, which occasionally parted to reveal a small boy contentedly munching his way through a packet of sweets, produced a large handkerchief which she proceeded to dampen with water from a bottle in one of her bags. She made tying motions with it and pointed at Grace's foot.

Another woman seized the handkerchief and pressed it into Grace's hands. With the loud, though incomprehensible, guidance of both women and of several other passengers who were standing and leaning across their seats so they could see what was happening, Grace clumsily tied the handkerchief around her ankle. When the bandage had finally met with a chorus of 'bravos', the woman to whom the handkerchief belonged gave Grace a satisfied nod and handed her the bottle of water indicating that she should drink.

Someone else promptly produced a plastic cup, and Grace was watched with proprietorial concern as she drank two cups in quick succession. This seemed to satisfy everyone and after someone else had pressed a large peach into her hand and Grace had practised her one halting Greek word several more times, the other passengers settled back into their seats leaving Grace to contemplate the passing countryside.

The bus rattled through the outskirts of the island's main town. Once elegant neo-classical Italianate mansions, their stuccoed facades ravaged by age, and their gardens choked with weeds, stood as mute reminders of a more leisurely past among squat modern concrete apartment blocks. Grace glimpsed a large bustling harbour, and then the busy streets gave way to smoke-leafed olive groves, where an occasional donkey stood tethered in their shade like a sad-eyed sentinel.

After about half an hour, the trees thinned out, and the bus descended onto a wide, shimmering plain with dazzling white, salt flats where it bordered the sea. Here the heat was so intense, Grace could hardly breathe. When she closed her eyes against the glare, her eyelids felt like sandpaper and the backs of her thighs felt as though they had been welded to the plastic seat.

After an hour, the road swung inland and began to climb into the mountains, turning into a narrow, twisting snake of hairpin bends and blind corners. At first, Grace breathed a sigh of relief as the air grew cooler, but as the bus swung round yet another corner, its gears grating loudly as its tyres sought terra firma, she was forced to cling to the seat in front of her, her palms sweating and stomach heaving. The other passengers seemed unconcerned as the gears gave a metallic growl of triumph and the bus negotiated yet another bend before attempting a shuddering crawl up to the next one.

Closing her eyes made it worse. Grace's stomach had been left several bends behind, and her head was spinning. She took a deep breath and prayed that she could control her digestive system at least until she got off the bus. Whether it was her prayer or just the thought of her humiliation if she threw up, the moment passed and the bus climbed even higher, into air that was cool and pungent with the scent of pine trees.

Grace began to lose all sense of time. Although her watch told her otherwise, she felt as though she had been on the bus for an eternity. Occasionally, the bus passed through a small village. Every time the bus stopped to let off a passenger, Grace stood up but the driver motioned her to sit back down again. Eventually the only other passenger left on the bus, was an elderly priest dressed in dusty black robes. His long grey beard was spread over his chest like a bib, and rose and fell in time with his snores.

Grace became aware that the landscape was changing again. They had left the treeline behind and entered a desolate, red-brown moonscape. It was hard to believe that anything could grow in this inhospitable terrain, but the air was fresh with the smell of wild herbs, and now and then, in the jagged valleys below, she caught unexpected glimpses of dark green foliage encrusted with starry, flamingo-pink oleander blooms.

Suddenly the bus began to descend and its engine stopped complaining, perhaps sensing the end was in sight. It began to take bends at a speed that Grace thought excessive for the age of its brakes. By now, hypersensitive to every change in the atmosphere, she felt the air change again. Soon she could see why - it was blowing off a midnight blue sea far below. She craned her neck and saw that the road ended at a tiny village of whitewashed houses clustering round a small harbour.

The bus took the last mile along the flat, coastal road at a cheerful rattle and then came to a gasping halt, its engine shuddering like an overtaxed muscle for a moment or two after it had been switched off. The driver turned round and signalled to Grace that they had at last arrived. The priest continued to snore. The driver smiled indulgently and shrugged his shoulders before lighting a cigarette and inhaling deeply.

Grace climbed stiffly to her feet and lifted her suitcase down. Then she loosened her skirt, which had become firmly stuck to the back of her legs. The priest gave a loud grunt and woke up. Gathering his skirts around him, with a backwards benedictory wave, he nimbly got off the bus. The driver watched amused as

Grace clambered awkwardly down the steep steps, then he slammed the engine into gear and sounded the klaxon deafeningly.

A woman clutching a large drum of olive oil came rushing down the street screeching loudly, almost knocking Grace down as she climbed onto the bus. It gave a loud belch of diesel fumes and wheezed slowly away, its gears grinding painfully as it disappeared around a bend in the road. Squinting against the metallic glare of the sun, Grace watched it go, suppressing an impulse to run after it.

It was at moments like this she hated her mother.

TWO

Grace looked around despairingly. According to her guidebook, travellers to Greece need not worry about finding accommodation. It would come to them in the shape of the hordes of small boys who greet new arrivals to every village, anxious to show them to mama's nice clean rooms. However, it seemed that small boys and their mamas in this village had not read her guidebook. Apart from an unfortunate-looking brown and white dog of uncertain parentage that lay asleep in the middle of the dusty square, its short, splayed, legs twitching as it pursued a cat in its dreams; the village appeared deserted.

On one side of the square, stood a large, forbidding, church that dwarfed the surrounding buildings. To its right were the remains of a building which was either half-built or half-demolished, but whichever, it had long since been abandoned. Next door was a taverna, the wooden chairs and tables lined up outside bleached grey by the sun. Opposite the church was a small kiosk plastered with lurid film posters. A few postcards, curled almost double, clung to a wire holder beside its firmly closed shutters. Next door to it was a small kafenion. The chairs and tables outside were empty, but through its dusty plate glass windows, a few elderly men were visible sitting motionless, hunched over a board game, long-empty coffee cups at their elbows.

A line of feathery tamarind trees bordered the other side of the square, shading the coast road that ended at the small harbour Grace had seen from the bus. Small fishing boats bobbed listlessly at their moorings, an assortment of plastic bottles and dead fish lapping round their hulls.

She heard a mewing sound and looked around for its source. A skeletal kitten gazed wide-eyed at her from behind a crumbling wall. It looked neglected and motherless. Feeling a sharp pang of kinship, Grace stretched out a comforting hand but hastily withdrew it as the kitten arched its back and hissed its rejection before running away as swiftly as its spindly limbs would allow.

Abandoned even by a stray kitten, Grace closed her eyes for a moment. The intensity of the light dazzled her. She fumbled in her bag for her sunglasses, but even as she did, she realised that in her rush to get to the airport that morning, she had left them lying on the dining room table, together with her untouched breakfast and the note for Roger. The memory of Roger caused her to square her shoulders resolutely. She had to find her mother and get back to London as quickly as possible, but where on earth should she start looking in this god-forsaken place?

She picked up her suitcase and cautiously put her weight onto her twisted ankle. It made her wince, but it was bearable. She limped slowly up what she hoped was the main street of the village. It was barely wide enough for a car and was rutted and uneven, but the other paths leading from the square were even narrower and little more than donkey tracks. A shuttered general store and post office seemed to suggest she had made the right choice, but as the road got steeper, her steps shortened and her shoulders ached with the weight of her suitcase.

Glancing down an alleyway that led off the road, she spotted some chairs and tables shaded by a green canopy of vines and decided that she could go no further without a cold drink. Dropping her suitcase beside a table, Grace collapsed gratefully onto a chair and sat patting her face with the shredded remains of a tissue.

A young boy materialised silently from the dark interior of a kafenion behind her. He was about fourteen or fifteen, the first dark fluff of manhood on his upper lip. He was dressed in the regulation black trousers and white shirt of Greek waiters everywhere. He gave Grace a quick, white-toothed smile and stood waiting for her order.

Flustered by his unexpected appearance, Grace reached for her guidebook and opened it at the useful phrases section. She read out the first request: 'Mia birra parakalo.'

'Beer, hokay,' replied the boy and disappeared back into the depths of the shop.

Grace removed her crumpled linen jacket that now looked like little more than a rag, and dropped it on the chair beside her, then sat flapping her blouse away from her body. Little rays of sunshine pierced the green canopy and made dappled patterns on the plastic tablecloth. A breeze that hinted at coolness blew from some hidden place.

The boy reappeared with the largest bottle of beer Grace had ever seen. He placed a tall glass on the table and with a majestic flourish, opened the bottle and placed it beside the glass. He then sat down at a neighbouring table and watched.

The bottle was ice-cold to the touch, beads of condensation trickled down its surface. Grace poured beer into the glass and creamy-coloured foam rose and brimmed over onto the table. Heedless of the drips on her blouse, she drank deeply and then refilled her glass. It tasted better than vintage champagne.

The boy grinned at Grace. Despite herself, she smiled back and then hastily wiped her mouth as a cold prickle on her upper lip told her that she had a foamy moustache. They sat in companionable silence for a few minutes. Then the boy gestured at her suitcase.

'Room?'

Grace could have cried with relief. 'Yes please.'

'Wait. I come.'

He disappeared into the interior of the kafenion once again. A woman's voice answered his and after a short conversation, he emerged holding some keys. He picked up Grace's suitcase and trotted off up the street.

'Wait,' she called trying to catch up with him, 'birra, how much?'

He waved his hand dismissively. 'Welcome,' he said and kept walking.

'Thank you...efharisto,' Grace said rather breathlessly as she tried to keep up with him.

He turned off the high street and began to climb a narrow flight of steps which seemed to lead forever upwards. The steps turned into a stony, unmade track with high-walled houses on either side. The boy was now far ahead. He turned a corner and disappeared from sight.

Grace made a desperate effort to catch up with him, but when she turned the corner, he was nowhere to be seen. She put out a hand and leant against the nearest wall. Her ankle throbbed and she felt dizzy. Her breath was coming in short gasps, and her heart was thumping alarmingly.

A voice from nowhere beckoned: 'Come.'

Bewildered, Grace looked around. The voice beckoned her again, and this time she looked up. The boy was gazing down at her from the top of a flight of steps that led up the side of the house against which she was leaning.

Grace looked at the steps. They may as well have been Mount Everest. She sank dejectedly onto the bottom step, her chest heaving and her head lowered in defeat.

The boy was beside her with a glass of water.

'Hot,' he said rather unnecessarily as she gulped the water.

'Engleesh?'

'Yes,' Grace held out the empty glass.

'Hokay now?' he asked looking concerned.

'Yes, hokay now.' Grace managed a feeble smile as she struggled to her feet. She climbed slowly up the steps and followed him through a door.

After the intense sunlight, she could see nothing in the gloom and stood blinded on the threshold. The boy crossed the room, opened some shutters and instantly saturated the room with light. Grace blinked.

The room had whitewashed walls that were bare apart from a picture of a doe-eyed, Greek icon cut from a magazine and pasted into a plastic frame. A large, rough-hewn, pine bed draped with a cream lace bedspread stood against one wall, beside it a table and two chairs. A chipped vase filled with faded, plastic flowers stood in the middle of the table. Separated from the main room by a wooden partition was a tiny kitchen dominated by a monstrous, old-fashioned refrigerator nearly six feet high, which alternately shuddered and purred. On the cupboard beside the fridge was a tiny, two-ring cooker with a grill underneath.

'Come,' the boy called.

Grace turned to see he had opened another door.

'Bath,' he gestured proudly.

Grace peered round the door. Her heart sank. There was no bath in evidence, only a small sink, a toilet, and a hand-held shower that drained directly onto the sloping red-tiled floor into a small hole. She turned intending to complain that this was not what she understood as a bathroom, but the boy's proud smile and her exhaustion made her decide it could wait until the next day.

'Clothes?' Grace asked miming hanging up her jacket.

The boy pulled a curtain aside revealing a small alcove with a rail and some ancient misshapen wire hangers. 'Hokay, good?' he inquired.

Grace nodded wearily. 'Fine.'

The boy looked uncertain.

'Hokay, yes?' he asked again.

Grace looked blankly at him and then comprehension dawned. 'How much?'

'Verry cheap, only 5,000 drachmas. Special price for you.'

'I'll take it,' Grace said reaching for her purse.

The boy looked crestfallen. 'Verry cheap,' he repeated wistfully as he realised that he could have asked for much more.

Realising she had disappointed him, Grace consulted her Greek phrases again. 'What is your name? Pos sas lene?' she repeated in halting Greek, pointing at him just in case he hadn't understood.

'Adonis,' he replied proudly, his face lit up by a white-toothed grin.

Grace waved at the room. 'Efharisto Adonis. I like *verry* much,' she added in pigeon English.

Honour satisfied, with another wide grin Adonis left.

Grace hobbled across the room after him.

'Don't you want some money in advance?' she called leaning over the top of the stairs waving her purse to emphasise her point.

In reply, Adonis gave a dismissive wave and yet another grin then disappeared round the corner.

Grace went back into the room, undoing her clothes and stepping out of them as she headed for the bathroom. The shower worked in lukewarm fits and starts, but she was beyond caring. She luxuriated in the sensation of water on her skin even when it stung her blistered feet. Someone had left a small bottle of bath foam from the Bali Hai hotel in Goa on the sink. She emptied it gratefully over her body and after a final rinse, reached for a towel. A small, thin square, barely larger than a hand towel, hung from a hook behind the door.

She padded across the floor that was awash with water, and into the other room. Dripping, she heaved her suitcase onto the bed and tossed her carefully packed clothes aside until she found her towelling robe. After a cursory rub down she slipped it on. It was only then that she noticed the motif embroidered across the left breast. It read 'HIS'.

The image of the expression on Roger's face when he discovered that he would have to wear a bathrobe saying 'HERS' flashed into Grace's head and she felt an absurd desire to laugh, but instead her throat constricted and an odd, strangled sound like a sob emerged. She sat heavily on the bed. Poor Roger, he would be so upset when he came home and discovered where she had gone. His face would get that tight, controlled look, expressing a combination of indignation and martyrdom that was becoming almost habitual of late. He was right. He should come first on her list of priorities. However, her mother had no one else to look after her, she couldn't abandon her.

Grace stood up and tied the belt of the robe firmly around her waist. Feeling sorry for herself would get her nowhere. She sorted through her case and hung up as many of her clothes as would fit on the few hangers and draped the rest over a chair. In her hurry to pack that morning she had brought far too many clothes and from the look of the place, her neat tailored suits were not exactly suitable wear. But then again, she hadn't known where she was going or what she would have to deal with and a suit always made her feel more in control.

At the bottom of her suitcase was the cause of its extra weight - two thick manuscripts. She was officially on a week's holiday from the publishers where she worked, but she had brought the manuscripts along because there was no-one else to work on them and they were already behind their deadlines for submission to their publishing houses.

Like most of the few small independent publishing houses left in London, hers was struggling to stay in business. Grace had worked there for nearly ten years and loved it. She had always wanted to work with books and liked the eclectic mix of fiction, poetry, memoirs and academic books it published. It was an old family business run by two brothers, Bartle and Duncan Burgess, whose eclectic and somewhat eccentric tastes were reflected in their publishing lists. But the international conglomerates which now dominated the publishing world, combined with the large advances demanded by agents and expected by writers, was making it increasingly difficult for small companies like theirs to survive. Even when they recognised and nurtured a talented writer, once the writer became successful, too often they were lured away by the offer of large advances from the very same big publishing houses that refused to take a chance with them when they were starting out.

This outraged Grace, but Bartle and Duncan seemed unconcerned. According to them writing and books should not be seen as a source of wealth but of pleasure, and if writers could bring pleasure to a greater number of people by moving to another publisher, who were they to stand in their way?

However, they had recently lost two good editors to headhunters from large publishing houses and editors were almost as hard to replace as good writers, particularly at the salaries that Burgess & Burgess could afford to pay. Grace had been approached by headhunters several times, but she had rejected their blandishments. She liked the unpredictability of her work, of never knowing what she would find each time she opened a large brown envelope containing an unsolicited manuscript. More often than not, she would put it down within the first few pages, but just occasionally, she would find herself reading something that made her fingers tingle with excitement as she turned the pages, and that was one of the best feelings in the world. However, since the loss of the other two editors, staying with Burgess & Burgess meant an increase in her already heavy workload and less and less time to read unsolicited manuscripts.

It would help if Roger was more sympathetic. When they first met he had seemed to like her independence. Her salary was small, but a legacy from her grandfather had enabled her to buy a small terraced house near the river in Putney as well as providing her with enough to live comfortably if she wasn't too extravagant, which she wasn't. However, since they had decided to get married, Roger had started to complain about her working long hours and he absolutely hated her bringing work home.

Every time she did, he pointed out, yet again, that he earned more than enough for the two of them, so why did she persist in working so hard for such a small salary? He had recently decided to seek selection to stand as a Conservative MP and since then, his occasional hints that she should give up work once they were married had become less of a hint and more of a lengthy argument he might make in court in order to win his case. According to him, the Tory shires were still very old-fashioned when it came to women, even more so when they were the wives of prospective parliamentary candidates.

Grace fully supported Roger's ambitions, although not in a political sense as she had never held any particular political views, but because she loved him and he was going to be her husband. However, there were times when she wished he could be more supportive of her ambitions in return.

She placed the two manuscripts on the table and then arranged the yellow lined notebook she liked to use for making notes and half a dozen sharpened HB pencils beside them. She intended to get down to work as soon as possible, but first she needed some more air. Adonis had only opened one set of shutters so she went over to the others and drew back the bolts. They opened onto a balcony. She stepped outside.

The house was at the top of the village and below her feet, burnt-orange and umber tiled roofs jostled their way untidily down to the cobalt blue Aegean. The whitewashed walls of the houses were chequered with wooden shutters painted in every conceivable shade of blue and green, shut firmly against the heat of the late afternoon sun. And everywhere, on windowsills, in hanging pots, in courtyard gardens, in pots on front door steps, there were brilliant splashes of pink and red geraniums.

An ancient fort, its once impregnable walls crumbling under the twin enemies of time and weeds, still guarded the entrance to the harbour. Just offshore, two long, undulating islands, that to Grace's squinting eyes looked liked cats stretched out in the sun, almost turned the harbour into a lagoon.

In other circumstances she might have appreciated the beauty of what lay before her, but all Grace could feel was a sudden and overwhelming desire to sleep. She yawned. A little nap would not hurt. Her mother as well as her work would just have to wait a while.

THREE

Although the warmth on her skin and the golden light filtering through her eyelids told her it was morning, Grace kept her eyes resolutely closed. Since Roger had moved into her house, she was rarely able to enjoy the luxury of a peaceful and unhurried awakening.

Roger set the alarm clock for 5.45 am and he let it sound, even though he always woke before it was set to go off. According to him, its clarion call heralded the start of the day, like a cock crowing, and not until the final piercing trill sounded did he throw back the covers. He then proceeded to the bathroom where, to the accompaniment of Farming Today on Radio 4 and a reverberating basso profundo hum, he completed what he called his ablutions.

However, despite the alarm clock, Grace had to admit that there was something soothing about Roger's predictability. Radio 4 could suddenly break into its programming to announce that Armageddon was due that day, but Roger would still refuse to vary his routine. Grace could even forecast what kind of day lay ahead from the sounds emanating from the bathroom. Roger had a limited, though eclectic, musical repertoire. If he hummed a jolly little ditty from Gilbert and Sullivan, like 'Three Little Maids', it usually meant he was prosecuting a juicy murder, whilst the death knell of one of Puccini's more unfortunate heroines like Tosca, was usually occasioned by a more mundane case, like shoplifting.

Quite why he chose to accompany his arias with the price of pork and the weather forecast for farmers, she could not understand. If there was an archetypal urban man it was Roger. If the soles of his hand-made shoes were not walking on pavements or tarmac, he felt faintly queasy. In his opinion, the countryside existed merely in order that motorways could be built through it, so enabling civilised people to drive between cities with more ease and speed. On days when he was prosecuting motorway protesters, he could get through almost the entire score of 'The Pirates of Penzance' before he sat down to his bowl of All-Bran and the Daily Telegraph editorial.

His decision to act as Counsel for the engineering contractors in a public enquiry about the building of a motorway through a Site of Special Scientific Importance earlier that year caused yet another heated argument between him and Marjorie. It ended only when Marjorie marched out of the house vowing never to cross the threshold again while Roger was living there.

As the door slammed behind her, Roger picked up his spoon and applied himself to finishing his dessert - bread and butter pudding - one of his favourites, but after several mouthfuls, he suddenly banged his spoon down and looked across at Grace.

'If I could believe that woman would keep her promise and never darken out doorstep again I would die a happy man, but she'll be back if only to annoy me.'

Grace took a deep breath before she spoke. She didn't want to argue with Roger if only because she knew her mother would be pleased if she did. 'Can't we forget about my mother and finish our meal in peace?'

'Forget about her, your mother?' Roger snorted loudly. 'That's like saying can you forget that the pope's a catholic? She only does it to provoke me you know.'

Grace knew she would regret asking, but she asked anyway. 'What does she do that provokes you?'

'She espouses causes that she knows will annoy me. Marjorie doesn't give a damn about the environment and wouldn't know a water meadow or an ancient woodland if they leapt up and bit her on the nose, but because I'm appearing for the engineering contractors, she suddenly becomes a tree-hugger.'

'I think that's a little unfair,' as soon as the words were out of her mouth Grace wished she hadn't said them. 'You only agreed to take the brief for the public enquiry last week and I haven't mentioned it to my mother. So how could she have decided to join the 'tree-huggers' as you call them just in order to provoke you? She annoys me too, but I don't doubt she cares about the environment.'

What followed had not been their first argument, but it had been their worst, and things had not been the same since. They hadn't quarrelled again, at least not until the arrival of her mother's postcard, in fact quite the opposite - they had both made a studious effort to be nice to each other. However, rather than improve things between them, not quarrelling made matters worse. When things were left unsaid, they didn't go away but instead hang around in corners smelling badly like something long-past its sell-by date pushed to the back of the fridge.

As she replayed the things she and Roger has said to each other, the feeling of well-being Grace had awakened with ebbed away. Why did emotions have to be so messy? Roger was right, she ought to get her priorities sorted out but that put her into a difficult position. Maybe if she talked to her mother, explained the situation and how it was affecting her relationship with Roger...

Grace opened her eyes. If she even so much as hinted that she was having problems with Roger, far from being sympathetic, her mother would crow with pleasure and possibly behave even worse the next time she saw Roger. No, what she must do was to find her mother as quickly as possible, sort out whatever trouble it was she had got into, and get back to England and to Roger.

She glanced at her watch. It was seven thirty in the morning. From somewhere down below in the village, a cockerel was loudly asserting its masculine supremacy, while in the eaves outside, a family of sparrows were noisily engaged in a domestic dispute. Grace sat up and swung her legs over the side of the bed. She felt stiff. She had intended only to take a ten-minute catnap, but she had slept nearly fourteen hours. She had not even got into bed, sleeping curled up on the bedspread. Pulling Roger's bathrobe around her, she opened the balcony doors and stepped outside.

The silent, deserted village of the afternoon before had disappeared. The morning was noisy with the sound of neighbours greeting each other and loud, though half-hearted, reproaches at the squealing children who darted everywhere and into everyone's way. Flat roofs and courtyards fluttered with washing, and doors and windows were wide open as women swept and scrubbed, shaking the bedclothes clean of the musty night and draping them over balconies to air in the sun.

Grace stepped back inside, and after a cursory wash, searched for her flattest shoes and something more suitable to wear than the suit in which she had arrived. She finally settled on a sleeveless white silk top and a black skirt. As she savagely pulled a brush through her hair, wincing at the tangles, Grace went over what she knew about her mother's trip to Greece to see if she could remember a clue that might help to find her, but she did not have a lot to go on. Past experience suggested that if her mother was in trouble, it was likely to involve a man, and given Marjorie's tastes of late, it would probably be some handsome Greek fisherman, many years younger than her.

The first she had known of her mother's decision to go to Greece was a telephone call early one Sunday morning at the beginning of April. Roger answered the phone and handed it over to her without saying anything, mouthing 'your mother' and pulling a face at her as he headed to the bathroom.

Marjorie was in the departure lounge at Gatwick Airport and sleepily struggling to sit up, the first thing Grace heard as she put the phone to her ear was the sound of a flight being called.

'Where are you?' she demanded.

'At Gatwick, waiting for my flight to Athens. I just called to let you know I'll be away for a little while.'

This took a moment or two for Grace to digest. 'Athens? Why Athens?'

'I just thought I needed a change of scenery for a while.'

'Are you going with that Italian artist? I'm afraid I can't remember his name.'

There was a long silence, then: 'If you mean Annunzio, no. He left.'

Grace was just about to say she was sorry that her mother's relationship had broken up, but then she realised she wasn't. Annunzio had been completely unsuitable for her mother. Instead, she began to list all the reasons why Marjorie should not get on the next plane to Athens just because her latest affair had come to an end. When Grace finished, her mother's voice sounded plaintive.

'Why do I always detect a note of criticism in your voice whenever I decide to do something that I know is right for me?

26

These days we never seem to be able to talk without you finding fault. You never used to be like this before you met Roger.'

Grace found it hard to contain her irritation. Roger had nothing to do with her attitude and her mother was well aware of it. Even before she met Roger they had never had one of those cosy mother-daughter relationships apart from in Marjorie's imagination. In her view, her mother had an unerring capacity to choose the wrong type of man and to make matters worse, the gap between Marjorie's age and that of her much younger lovers had been growing at an alarming rate of late. But Grace's attempts to point out that the age difference might have something to do with the increasing rapidity at which her mother's affairs ended always met with stubborn, if not angry, resistance.

'Age is just a number on a bit of paper which can be torn up,' retorted Marjorie the last time Grace brought the subject up. 'If *I* say I'm twenty-five, I *am* twenty-five. I live for today, yesterday is dead and gone. I refuse to live in the past like some people I could name.'

However, it wasn't just the age of her mother's lovers that worried Grace, or even their number. Her problem was the aftermath of her mother's affairs. While Marjorie was having an affair it was as though Grace did not exist; she never heard from her mother. But when the affair ended - as they inevitably did - so did Grace's well ordered life, at least until the next so-called greatest love of her mother's life came along.

When she was upset, Marjorie believed she had first call on Grace, no matter what time of the day or night. It was not a view that Roger shared. He was also resolutely unhelpful in his comments when Grace fretted about her mother taking up with a new and even more unsuitable lover. As far as he was concerned, it did not matter with whom Marjorie was involved, as long as she wasn't telephoning them at three o'clock in the morning. Grace could see his point, but she felt he could have been just a little more sympathetic. Still, that didn't stop her defending him to her mother, just as she defended her mother to him, even if her words sounded hollow in her own ears.

'Roger is just as concerned about your happiness as I am. I just don't want to see you rushing off again. Why can't you just settle down for a while?' The moment the well-worn phrase was out of her mouth Grace regretted it. Her mother had an unerring way of making her feel and sound middle-aged.

'With some nice elderly man? Is that what you mean?' Marjorie's voice was tart. 'How on earth did I manage to raise such a conventional daughter?'

Grace suppressed the impulse to point out that her mother had precious little to do with her upbringing. That had been left to Grace's grandparents and boarding school. She tried another tack.

'So, what went wrong with Annunzio?'

Annunzio was an Italian artist who had inspired Marjorie to become a patron of the arts, although up until that point, she had not been a noted lover of fine paintings. To support her mother, Grace had convinced Roger to attend Annunzio's first exhibition. It had taken place in a gallery, or a space as Marjorie called it, in a large warehouse in Clerkenwell. To find it, they were forced to leave the car and walk down a maze of muddy, rubbish strewn alleyways. By the time they eventually found the entrance, Roger was not in the best of moods, especially when they were greeted by loud pulsating rap music and flashing neon lights.

Grace had decided to make the best of it. Taking two large glasses of red wine from the tray offered by a purple-haired waitress at the door, she pressed one into Roger's hand and then put her arm through his and guided him towards the first of the vast canvases which lined the walls. She knew that Roger rather prided himself on being a good judge of art, and stood beside him sipping her wine as he considered the first painting. It appeared to be an abstract swirl of clashing colours.

Roger waved his glass at it. 'The usual five-year-old's hand painting job I see,' then he stopped and looked harder. *'Good god!'* His ejaculation could be heard over the rap music and several heads turned in their direction. 'Do you see what I see?' he demanded, 'it's a painting of of...' words failed him.

Grace looked at the canvas. At first she couldn't see see anything in particular but just then the lights changed yet again and she stepped back. It was quite clearly a painting of male and female genitalia in enormous close-up and in a state of arousal. She swung round to look at the other paintings and instantly realised they all had the same subject matter. Red-faced, Roger grabbed her by the arm and marched her out of the gallery, setting his wine glass down with such force on the tray held by the purple-haired waitress that several glasses fell onto the floor in a Niagara Falls of red wine. Grace had barely had time to call out 'sorry', as Roger pulled her out the door.

Now her question about Annunzio was greeted by another long silence on the other end of the line. Grace could hear a flight delay being announced.

'He had to return to Italy. He said he couldn't paint in England. The weather was too depressing and who am I to stand in the way of his talent?' There was a tremor in Marjorie's voice.

Grace relented. 'I'm sorry to hear that mother, but he was a *little* young.'

Her attempted kindness did not have the desired effect.

'Twenty years is nothing, we were twin souls, but you'd never understand. That's why I have to go to Greece. It's my spiritual home and I need to commune with the gods,' she ended dramatically.

Before Grace could enquire as to which gods and where exactly she was going, Marjorie had rung off.

As she scraped her hair back into some semblance of tidiness, wincing as she pulled a brush through its tangled mess, Grace looked at herself in the cracked mirror. Could she have been the result of an affair her mother had with another Annunzio a long time ago? It would account for her olive skin, dark hair and almost black eyes, so unlike her mother's pale colouring. However, despite her mother's boast that no subject was taboo, any questions on the subject had always been met with evasions or even tears. Grace's birth certificate merely stated that her father was 'unknown'.

As the years passed, the large, father-shaped gap in her life shrunk until it was only a small, empty space somewhere in the corner of her mind. Nowadays, Grace rarely thought about her missing father until suddenly, something - usually something as insignificant as the tangles in her hair - made it important again, like now. It was at moments like this that the face that looked back at her in the mirror seemed to belong to a stranger although she could not explain why. For a long moment she stared at herself and then turned resolutely away. It was her mother rather than her father that should concern her.

Outside, the sun was already hot. Grace gingerly tested her ankle. It appeared to be holding up, so she set out to retrace her steps back to the kafenion where she had met Adonis. She needed some strong coffee to help her think.

The contrast with the afternoon before could not have been greater. The narrow alleyways and streets were now busy with people and almost everyone Grace passed nodded and greeted her with a 'yassou' or a 'kalimera' even though she was a stranger. Women bustled down the street, arms straining at the weight of bulging shopping bags. Small boys pedalled furiously up and down, perilously ignoring their handlebars, one hand clutching a large golden oval of sweet smelling bread still warm from the bakery, the other raised in greeting to some friend. Music blared discordantly from the loud speaker of a small pick-up truck piled high with fruit and vegetables bursting with ripeness. Women prodded and squeezed the bulbous tomatoes and aubergines, loudly disparaging their quality before overfilling plastic bags that were then weighed on large silver scales perched on the tailgate of the truck.

Further down the street another van blared even louder music declaring its wares which this time were clothes. Three old women, nearly as wide as they were tall, and dressed in black from their headscarves to their toes, laughed toothlessly as they held up brightly patterned dresses against each other, covering their eyes coyly, and shaking their heads like young girls when urged to buy.

All along the street, men sat or stood, talking importantly, their fingers busy with clicking worry beads, their eyes alert for any diversion. Everyone seemed to have one arm raised in permanent greeting.

Grace spotted Adonis leaning against the corner of the kafenion talking to several other adolescent boys, their air of careless arrogance mimicking that of the older men. Adonis grinned broadly as he caught sight of Grace coming down the street and he lifted his arm in greeting. Grace smiled back as she walked into the welcome shade of his small terrace.

Adonis's companions turned and appraised her with already expert eyes. One of them said something and they all grinned in her direction. Grace was disconcerted to feel her cheeks burning. She opened her guidebook and pretended to read.

Adonis came over. 'Breakfast?'

'Coffee?'

'Nescafe?'

Grace nodded. 'Toast?' Then she had an idea, this was Greece after all. 'Yoghurt?'

Adonis smiled and was gone.

Grace settled back to wait, watching the ceaseless parade of people going past, then she noticed two figures who seemed out of place. They walked down the street as though they had an invisible cage around them. No-one greeted them and in their turn, they acknowledged no-one.

They were both women and had almost identical cropped, spiky hair; one bleached white-blond and the other hennaed red. They were deeply tanned, although the blond girl's shoulders were blistered and pinkly peeling. They were dressed almost identically: skimpy singlets, rolled-up army surplus shorts, and Doc Marten boots. Both wore several pairs of silver earrings in their pierced ears and black imitation Ray Bans. Grace would not have given them a second glance in London or even in a more cosmopolitan holiday place, but here they seemed like an alien presence.

Adonis reappeared with a tray and interrupted her study. 'Breakfast,' he announced proudly.

The coffee was black and very strong. Grace declined an offer of condensed milk. Toast was several slabs of cake-like bread nearly an inch thick, lightly singed on one side only. There was no butter but a bowl of honey. Grace ladled several spoonfuls of honey onto a slice of bread and added even more to the large bowl of rich, creamy yoghurt before breaking through its thick, butter-yellow crust.

Adonis trotted off down the street only to return almost immediately with a plate of golden apricots that he set down on the table. Grace wolfed down the toast and the yoghurt. She had not realised she was so hungry, but she had not eaten for over twenty four hours, having refused the meal of tired-looking coronation chicken and square of sponge cake coated with artifical cream masquerading as 'gateau' offered on the flight.

Barely pausing for breath, she reached for an apricot. Unlike the pale yellow apricots with dry skins and a slightly sour taste that she was accustomed to buying in London, these tasted as though the sun had been concentrated in their sweet flesh and their delicate fragrance lingered on her fingers.

She sat back finally replete. Unbidden, Adonis refilled her coffee cup and she sipped pensively, the sounds from the street filtering through a pleasant, almost happy haze.

'Ena kilo mila,' a voice said loudly, 'that's right isn't it? One kilo of apples.'

Grace put her cup down, slopping coffee into the saucer. Her mother's voice was unmistakable. She scrabbled for her bag and beckoned to Adonis, gesturing at the table.

'How much?'

'Five hundred,' he held up five fingers.

Grace counted out the notes and offered him a further fifty drachmas, but he waved them away.

With a hurried thank you, she almost ran into the street. Shading her eyes with her hand, she looked around. Her mother, or at least the woman she thought was her mother, was already at the bottom of the street walking down towards the harbour.

Grace strode after her, not wanting to call out. Although she was certain she had heard her mother's voice, the figure in front of her bore little resemblance to the woman she had last seen some four months ago.

FOUR

Grace had long since given up expecting to recognise her mother when she saw her. Marjorie transformed her appearance with such chameleon-like regularity that there were times when Grace could not swear to remembering what her mother really looked like. She even seemed to adopt a new personality along with her new clothes and hair colour.

Marjorie's constant changes of appearance were not a recent phenomenon. When Grace was growing up in her grandparent's house, she had looked forward to her mother's infrequent visits even though they usually ended in an argument between her mother and grandmother and Marjorie storming out in tears. In anticipation of her mother's visits, Grace played a secret guessing game as to whether she would arrive as a blonde, a brunette, a redhead, or, as on at least one occasion - a variation on all three. It was like having many different mothers and seemed to compensate for not having just one.

But what seemed like a game of dressing up in the eyes of a small child, became painfully embarrassing when seen through the critical eyes of an adolescent, especially when other peoples' mothers who came to the strict boarding school Grace attended in the 1960s were uniformly neat in their twin-set and pearls with handbags which matched their court shoes. Halter-neck, thigh-high, crochet dresses and white patent leather boots were not approved wear for pupils, and they were most definitely not considered suitable for visiting mothers, but Marjorie seemed to revel in the fuss she created.

When monochrome Mary Quant fashions dissolved into a hippy haze of patchouli and incense, and Marjorie appeared at the school in a multi-coloured kaftan and bare feet painted with flowers, Grace was summoned to the headmistress's study. There she was told to inform her mother, that unless she was prepared to dress in an acceptable manner, she could no longer visit Grace during term-time, as she was having a bad influence on the other girls. As this edict coincided with Marjorie setting off on the hippy trail to an Ashram in India, her visits ceased to be a problem. Grace left school eighteen months later, just as her mother was repatriated, penniless, and with a dose of dysentery, from India.

The last time Grace had seen Marjorie before she left for Greece, she had looked much younger than her fifty-two years. Her then honey-blonde hair was cut in a short, flattering bob, and she had been trim enough to wear the kind of body hugging clothes that would not have looked out of place on someone half her age. But the figure now walking ahead of Grace down the dusty road had generous hips encased in a long, crumpled, peasant-style skirt which swayed exaggeratedly from side to side as she walked flat-footed in thick-soled sandals. An unkempt cloud of greying hair and plump, brown wrists, heavy with silver bangles, carrying several plastic shopping bags, almost convinced Grace that she had mistaken the voice she had heard buying fruit. However, as the figure turned the corner into the village square, Grace caught a glimpse of her mother's familiar profile and quickened her pace.

Reaching the corner, she hesitated, but a flash of an ankle and a frilly hem going into the taverna near the church drew her across the square. She paused in the doorway of the taverna, unable to distinguish anything in the gloomy interior after the brightness outside. The clink of bracelets drew her attention to a figure seated at a table, fanning herself with her hand, shopping bags spilling their contents around her feet.

'Mother!' said Grace.

Marjorie jumped guiltily and looked suspiciously around the empty taverna for the source of the accusation. She spotted Grace and her eyes widened in surprise, then she held out her arms. 'Darling...'

Grace picked her way around the shopping bags and touched her lips to Marjorie's plump cheeks. Her mother's face was sunburnt and bare of makeup. Her tan unkindly emphasised lines around her eyes and mouth that Grace had not noticed before. Thin white bands of untanned skin cruelly ringed her now fleshy neck. With a sudden sense of shock, Grace realised that her mother was growing older.

Marjorie sensed her critical gaze and tried to push her hair back from her face, but it fell forward again in greying strands. 'I didn't think you would come, at least not quite so quickly.'

The note of petulance in her mother's voice irritated Grace. 'Your postcard did seem to indicate you needed me urgently.'

'Well sit down, sit down,' Marjorie tinkled her wrist at Grace. 'You make me feel hot standing there like that.'

Grace sat down. She knew her mother well enough not to expect gratitude for obeying her summons, but she felt she at least deserved a slightly warmer welcome.

Her mother waved an arm at no-one in particular. 'Aliki, thio lemonades parakalo, and make sure they are very cold - *poli* krio.'

The lemonades arrived almost immediately, borne by a silent unsmiling woman whom Grace assumed to be Aliki. Marjorie downed her drink in one thirsty gulp. Some of it escaped and dribbled down her chin. She wiped it away with a grubby hand.

Grace sipped slowly, still gazing at her mother. Marjorie looked down and started to twist one of the dozen or so cheap silver bangles she wore. Grace noticed her mother's usually expensively manicured nails were bitten and unvarnished.

'Well?' she demanded at last. 'I've come a long way to see you at very short notice, the least you could do is to tell me why. You couldn't have chosen a more inconvenient time. My coming here has caused no end of trouble with Roger.'

As the words came out of her mouth Grace wished she hadn't said them. Was it her imagination, or could she see a triumphant light in her mother's eyes?

'And how is *dear* Roger?'

Grace looked sharply at her mother, but Marjorie gazed innocently back.

'He sends his best wishes,' Grace lied.

'Really?' her mother's unplucked eyebrows indicated her disbelief. 'How *very* sweet of him.'

'Mother, can we please get back to the point of all this.'

Marjorie reached over and placed her hand over Grace's. 'Before we do, I think there's something you ought to know. I've changed my name.'

Grace stared at her. 'Have you got married?'

'No, not quite...that is...well, I'll explain that bit later...' Marjorie began twisting her bracelets again. 'The thing is... I'm now called Gaia.'

'Gaia?'

'That's right dear, Gaia. It's a beautiful name don't you think? I never liked Marjorie. It's not really me - so staid and old-fashioned sounding. It belongs to a woman who crochets tea-cosies and makes chutney for the church bazaar, don't you think? Gaia is so much nicer.'

The urge to shake her mother grew. Grace tried to keep her voice down. 'You mean I've travelled thousands of miles to this awful place in the middle of nowhere just because you decided to adopt some ridiculous name?'

Her mother looked hurt. 'Well, if that's how you feel, I'm glad I didn't invite you to my naming ceremony. Lilith said I should, but I said you wouldn't be interested. Anyway, it's not a ridiculous name, it's the name of the Great Earth Goddess, or Mother of Mothers if you prefer.'

Grace wanted to tell her that she preferred neither, but her mother was not to be interrupted. She waved her arm expansively.

'Gaia is the source of everything, even the gods themselves. One always thinks of Zeus as being the god of gods so to speak, but Gaia came first. Patriarchal men created Zeus in their own image in order to displace the one true religion, the worship of Gaia...' Marjorie paused.

Grace opened her mouth to speak but nothing came out. She kept on trying to convince herself that there was nothing her mother could do that could surprise her anymore, but once again, she had succeeded.

'Men have always tried to control women,' Marjorie continued, 'because they know we are far more powerful than them because we control the mysteries of birth, and therefore life itself. So they have used religion to try and control us by always making sure that there is a male god on top, if you know what I mean.' Marjorie waited for Grace to smile at her joke, however, none was forthcoming. 'But the Earth Mother keeps coming back in one form or another. Look at

Catholics and the Virgin Mary. Anyway, the girls - or rather the women - say I am like an earth mother, so they decided I should be called Gaia. You see, we have all taken the names of goddesses because our Christian names were given to us by a male religion.' Marjorie looked thoughtful for a moment. 'Except for Killili of course. I think she was originally Hindu or something like that, so she wouldn't have a Christian name, would she?'

Grace suddenly realised that her mother was waiting for her to respond. She took a deep breath. There was no point in getting angry. This time it was some nonsense about Greek goddesses, but she had heard it all before - her mother fired up by some cause that she would discard the next day like a used tissue.

'No, I don't suppose she would,' she replied wearily.

'So that's why from now on you must call me Gaia or mother, of course. Lots of the other gir...women just call me mother. They say they are reclaiming the role and putting it back in its rightful place at the centre of our being. I think that's rather nice don't you?'

'Nice?' Grace repeated.

Marjorie leant back in her chair and signalled to the silent Aliki. 'Shall I order some more lemonade? I don't know about you, but all this talking has made me rather thirsty.'

'Let me try and get this straight, mother,' said Grace slowly. 'You've hit the hippy trail again, but this time you've changed your name?'

Marjorie looked hurt. 'It's different this time. All that Sixties hippy stuff was just a chance to indulge in some rather jolly sex and get high. This is about the New Age - the rebirth of the Golden Age of the True Religion. First, we women had to reclaim the present, now we must reclaim the past.'

Grace stared at her. One phrase Marjorie used kept repeating on her like something unpleasant she had eaten. 'And you've been named after the great earth mother? *You*? An earth mother? Do these girls or whoever they are know that you abandoned your baby at birth and left her to be brought up by someone else?'

Marjorie paled beneath her tan. Her eyes filled with tears and her jaw wobbled slightly as she fought to stop them rolling down her face.

'You're never going to let me forget, are you?' she said in an unsteady voice. A tear escaped and trickled down her cheek. 'Things were different then, you don't understand...' her voice trailed off and another tear followed the first.

Marjorie hunted for a handkerchief. Grace watched, unmoved. She was used to her mother resorting to tears when faced with something unpleasant. Then Marjorie sniffed rather too loudly and like a mother to a recalcitrant child, Grace wordlessly offered her a linen handkerchief. Marjorie blew her nose.

'I wanted to be a good mother...'

Grace sighed. This was a path they had gone down so often that they both knew every step. She also knew that it led nowhere so there was no point in going further.

'So what's this oh so urgent problem you want me to help you with?' she asked wearily.

Marjorie tucked Grace's handkerchief into her pocket and then leant across the table and patted her hand. 'I knew you would help, you always do in the end.'

She bent down and rescued some runaway apples, then stood up.

'Pay Aliki for me will you,' she commanded over her shoulder as she headed for the door, 'and then we'll make some plans.'

Her tears had magically vanished.

FIVE

Anxious not to lose her mother now that she had found her, Grace thrust several bank notes at the morose woman who had served them lemonade, and hurried out into the village square. However, she needn't have worried, Marjorie was waiting for her, juggling her shopping bags from hand to hand.

The sight made Grace realise that she had never seen her mother looking like an ordinary housewife before - returning home, loaded down with shopping. Shopping for Marjorie had always been about clothes - food was something selected from a menu in a restaurant.

Grace held out a hand. 'Can I help you with your shopping? We can talk as we walk to your rooms, or are you staying in a hotel? I couldn't find one.'

'That's because there isn't one here. It's not that kind of place. I'm staying with...with...' Marjorie seemed to be searching for a difficult word, '...friends,' she said finally. 'They're not really expecting visitors at the moment, so why don't you amuse yourself for a couple of hours? We can meet this evening and talk some more.' She swopped her shopping bags over again. 'You could go for a swim. You need to relax and get London and all that stress out of your system.'

Grace felt a familiar knot of resentment growing inside her chest. 'I didn't bring a swimming costume and I don't want to relax. This isn't a holiday for me. I came because I thought you were in some sort of trouble...'

'Swimming costume?' Marjorie interrupted her, 'good heavens! You don't need a swimming costume. Nobody bothers with that sort of thing here.'

Forgetting her shopping, Marjorie tried to wave her arm to dismiss the idea of swimming costumes. Several large tomatoes fell out of her bag, splattering their juicy ripeness on the ground.

Grace and her mother stared at the mess for a moment. A large black ant, nearly an inch long, its antennae frenziedly twitching, rushed forward to claim the feast.

'Mum...'

Marjorie looked up at Grace, alert to the change in her voice and this rarely used endearment.

'Please, I *really* can't afford the time. I must get back to London. Can't you just tell me what the problem is so I can pay or do whatever is necessary so that we can both go home?' Perhaps if she had stopped there it would have been all right. But in her attempt to win her mother's sympathy, Grace added the one phrase that was guaranteed to lose it: 'Roger says...'

'Roger!' snorted Marjorie derisively. 'How my own flesh and blood could consider marrying that self-opinionated, pompous, male chauvinist... Just the thought of making love to that...that...' She illustrated her words with a theatrical shudder.

'Better Roger than some of the underage schoolboys you chase after,' Grace snapped back, stung into abandoning her earlier restraint. 'It's not what you see in them that puzzles me, but what they see in you other than a free meal ticket. Have you taken a look in the mirror lately?'

She saw her mother flinch. For a moment Grace felt a sense of triumph - she had finally got through to her. However, the next instant she hated herself. Why did she let her mother goad her? Sometimes it seemed they were like two punch-drunk fighters, condemned to remain circling endlessly round and round each other, waiting for the other to let down their guard so they could land a well-placed punch, opening an old wound.

Heedless of the marching columns of ants now winding backwards and forwards from the fallen tomatoes, Marjorie dropped her shopping bags. She put her hands on her hips, her face flushed.

'Well at least if *I've* made mistakes, I've made them for love. I sometimes wonder if you know what the word means. Love should sweep you along like a raging force, so that you neither know nor care what you're doing.' She waved her arms wildly as she spoke and then stopped and pointed an accusatory finger at Grace. '*You* intend to marry Roger not only to irritate me, but to avoid being in love. Love means taking chances and making mistakes, but you're such a little Miss Perfect that you just can't allow yourself to do either can you? Well I've taken chances and I've had to live with the consequences, but much better that way than to live in fear of making mistakes and so not live at all.' She drew herself up to her full height, which was a good three inches shorter than Grace. 'And just in case you've forgotten, I *am* your mother and I neither want nor need your approval or your morality lectures.'

'*I'm* not the one who keeps on trying to forget our relationship, much as I'd like to sometimes.' Grace's voice had an irritating tremor which she fought to keep under control. 'And since you clearly don't need me, I will be on the first plane out of here.'

She turned on her heel and stalked away.

A small voice followed her across the square. 'Yanni's taverna, tonight, eight thirty. It's the last taverna on the coast road out of town. You can't miss it.'

By the time Grace reached her room, the heat had burned the anger out of her. Feeling hot and sticky, and wishing yet again that she had packed more suitable clothes, she stripped off and stood under the shower. Was her mother right? Had she subconsciously agreed to marry Roger just in order to get back at her?

Grace lifted her head up and let the water cool her face. It was a ridiculous idea. Just the kind of popular cod-psychology peddled to women in certain types of newspapers and magazines that she disliked. Nevertheless, she could not deny that when she first met Roger, she had not been very impressed by him. However, the circumstances had not been auspicious as they were the only two single people at a dinner party thrown by a mutual friend and had clearly been invited in the hope that they would match up – a ploy Grace hated and normally avoided if she got wind of it.

As a single woman, Grace knew that she was a bit of a challenge when it came to dinner parties. Most of her friends had paired off at university, and those who had not, were in pairs by the time they reached their thirties. Nobody liked having an odd number sitting down to dinner, but according to Grace's married women friends - and it was inevitably the women who always organised dinner parties - while they knew many single presentable women, single presentable men were much harder to find.

There were of course, divorced men. However, if they were too newly divorced, they tended to either leap on any available woman they met, or bore them to death by endlessly retelling the tale of their marriage break-up, sometimes while weeping into their wine glass at the same time. Whichever of these tacks they chose, neither made for much of a jolly evening even if experience suggested that men were much more likely to want to pair up again without waiting for the decree absolute to arrive.

Roger was considered a rare creature among givers of dinner parties who needed to make up numbers. He was in his forties and had never been married, yet was both sociable and presentable. Most men who got into their forties and remained single so meriting the description 'bachelor', were usually single for very good reasons, according to Marian, the friend who invited Grace to the dinner where she met Roger. At best the forty-something bachelor often looked a bit dusty whilst their clothes often had an odour, if not of uncleanliness, but of spending too long in a musty cupboard about them.

'And at worst, please don't tempt me to go there apart from saying the words "underwear" and "unwashed",' Marian laughed. 'However, I give you my word – cross my heart and hope to die - that Roger is *not* one of those sorts of bachelors.'

And he wasn't, although at their first meeting, he had not made much of an impression either good or bad on Grace. She noticed that he was quite distinguished looking in the way that men who go grey when they are young often are, but while he engaged her in the usual social chit-chat of establishing where she worked and how she knew their hostess, most of his conversation was directed at a fellow barrister. Once or twice she sensed that he was staring at her, but when she turned to speak to him, he looked away. So she had been taken aback when he rang her the following week and suggested they go to the theatre together.

'Marian thought you wouldn't mind her giving me your phone number,' he said. Then added quickly: 'But I quite understand if you think I'm being a bit forward.'

Grace found herself smiling at his use of the word 'forward', it was quaintly old-fashioned. 'No, I don't mind you calling at all,' she assured him. 'I've been meaning to get tickets for that play for weeks. How clever of you to choose a play I want to see.'

It was only later that she remembered that she had told Marian how much she wanted to see the play. She had been set up once again.

However, Grace found that she enjoyed Roger's not too demanding company, and, after that, they just seemed to fall into step with each other. He proved the perfect partner when she needed someone to accompany her to a book launch or a party, as he was adept at providing just the right kind of amusing small talk needed at these occasions. She also appreciated the regularity with which he rang to suggest going to the theatre or the opera, usually to a new and much-vaunted production that she had read about in the Sunday supplements and wanted to see. After a while, their respective friends began to invite them as a couple, although at what point they had become one, Grace was not sure, only that by some unspoken process they had.

It might have been the night that they finally had sex. This was not until they had been going out for nearly three months, and only then at her instigation. She had a feeling that Roger would have left it even longer before suggesting they went to bed together, but by this time, she wanted to know if they were going to be just friends or something more. If she had been younger, she would have taken a man's lack of attempt to get her into bed on their first or at least second date as a sign he wasn't attracted to her, but she knew it was different with Roger.

He was ten years older than her, but experience had taught Grace that age rarely had any restraining effect on men when it came to sex. She had been out with men in their late fifties who had tried to get her into bed within minutes, let alone waiting until after dinner. When Marian had pressed her on how their relationship was progressing on this front and Grace had admitted the lack of sex, Marian had described Roger as the kind of man who was born middle-aged, citing a photograph of him as a student showing him wearing a three-piece pin-striped suit. Grace had bridled at this, but even as she defended him, it dawned on her that that was precisely why she liked him. Roger had always been sure of who he was and where he was going. He was, to use his own terminology - solid.

Once she had inititated sex and Roger had proved more than obliging if - like in the rest of his life - a little old-fashioned, Grace reluctantly decided that it was time he met her mother. Her mother was the test of whether a relationship had any chance of surviving, and, long ago, Grace had decided that if both she and the man she was dating could survive a meeting with her mother, it suggested the relationship might also have a chance of survival.

When Grace was younger, Marjorie had flirted outrageously with men she was dating, acting as though she was Grace's sister. The men subjected to this display had either thought Marjorie wonderful and had fallen in love with her or, terrified, had run away. Whichever way they reacted, Grace had just wanted to curl up and die with embarrassment. For many years, she had avoided any contact between her mother and men she was dating, partly because she had dated a lot less in her thirties and partly because none of them had meant very much to her. However, now that Roger had become such an important part of her life, Grace decided that a meeting could no longer be postponed.

Once a date was agreed, all she could do was pray that her mother would wear something suitable and not turn up with one of her toyboys. As fate would have it, at least part of her prayer was answered as Marjorie had just broken up with her latest boyfriend - an Australian personal trainer called Grant. However, Marjorie's legacy from this relationship was an extremely slim and well-exercised body that she liked to show off in revealingly tight-fitting outfits, one of which she wore to her first meeting with Roger in a discreet little restaurant in Kensington. Grace knew that battle lines had been drawn when she saw the look on Roger's face as her mother teetered through the front door on the highest of high heels and imperiously ordered Grace to pay her taxi driver.

That first meeting set the tone for the relationship between Roger and her mother. Far from swapping flirtatious repartee, Marjorie and Roger had bristled at each other like two porcupines, swapping comments each more barbed than the last. So, when Grace announced her engagement to Roger, she should not have been surprised by the virulence of her mother's opposition, but she could not help it. Her mother could not - or would not - understand that wanting to be with someone who made you feel comfortable and secure was more important than being swept along by some great uncontrollable passion. Lack of control almost inevitably led to a crash where someone got hurt.

Grace resolutely wrapped herself in Roger's towelling robe. Her mother was wrong, of that she was certain. While she may not have fallen madly in love with Roger at first sight, their love had grown with time as it did with any mature relationship. They did not have to swing from chandeliers to prove they were in love. From now on, her mother would just have to accept that Roger came first in her life, something Grace intended to make clear in no uncertain terms tonight at the taverna. If her mother chose not to come back to England with her, then she would just have to sort out her own problems.

Feeling resolute, Grace decided to make a start on editing the first of the manuscripts. She carried a chair out onto the balcony and sat down with her manuscript in her lap. Below, the village had already turned silently in on itself as protection against the afternoon sun, and, although she was sitting in the shade, the heat made her feel drowsy. She let the towelling robe slip off her shoulders and closed her eyes. A few moments rest before she got down to some work could do no harm.

Two hours later, Grace woke up to find that she was no longer in the shade and the sun had done its worst while she was sleeping. She gazed at the mirror in despair at her face. It not so much glowed as pulsated after its unaccustomed exposure to the sun. She winced as she touched her shoulders. Mindful of her mother's weathered skin, she gingerly applied a liberal coat of moisturiser.

Seeing her mother's face stripped of its usual artifice that morning had reminded her yet again how unalike they were, and how much of an outsider she had always felt in the Hamilton family. Her dark, Mediterranean looks had no precedent in the Hamilton family photograph albums, in which generation after generation of short, stockily built, pale-skinned and pale-eyed Hamiltons gazed sternly back at the camera lens.

Wedding pictures occasionally revealed that an unusually adventurous Hamilton had chosen a spouse who did not possess the Hamilton colouring. However, the christening pictures which marked the conjoining of two bloodlines showed that this aberration had been quickly put to rights, as somehow or other, the offspring always reverted to type. At least until Grace had arrived.

Nor was she possessed of the other distinctive Hamilton feature: the family nose. They all had it in larger or smaller versions. It was long and thin and curving, causing even the least supercilious Hamilton to look as though they were looking down their nose at the world. Grace's nose had neither the Hamilton curve, nor its prominence. It was both small and neat. Marjorie's nose was also small, but that was only because she had employed a plastic surgeon to make it that way.

Grace knew about her mother's real nose. She had seen pictures of Marjorie when she was much younger. The photographs documented Marjorie's life from lace-bedecked babyhood, through a stiff-petticoated childhood, to a pretty and sophisticated fifteen-year-old, wearing, according to the careful italic inscription, her first long dress. However, this was the last picture in a photographic record of the Hamiltons which stretched back to Victorian days, and which was contained in leather-bound albums that had lined her grandfather's study wall.

After that, it was as though the Hamiltons had ceased to exist. There were no photographs to record Grace's arrival in the world, or her progress through it. For a family hitherto obsessed with recording its existence, the omission was marked. Grace's grandmother, Eleanor, was the keeper of the family flame and the arbiter of who appeared in the family albums, and it was she, rather than Marjorie, who omitted Grace.

Eleanor was not an unkind woman in the sense that she consciously chose to hurt Grace's feelings. After all, she had taken Grace into her house and raised her at an age when most women feel they should be past caring for the needs of small children. This was especially true of Eleanor who felt that she had already done more than her duty by raising Marjorie, who was a late and unexpected baby, arriving when Eleanor was forty-one and considered herself past the polite age for childbearing. However, Eleanor was bred of the school that could not turn their back on their duty. They stiffened their spine and got on with it, however irksome.

When Marjorie produced an illegitimate child at the age of sixteen, duty demanded Grace be accepted into the house and raised properly - if only to try and prevent her from repeating the sins of her mother. However, it did not call for her to be accepted into the family. That honour had to be earned legitimately, and only then was it duly recorded by inclusion in the family photograph albums. Eleanor was a firm believer that if you refused to acknowledge the existence of something unpleasant and resolutely ignored it, it would go away and simply cease to exist. Unfortunately for her, although no pictorial record of Grace's existence marred the family albums, Grace was the living, breathing, three-dimensional, proof that something unpleasant and outside Eleanor's control had happened.

Logic dictated that as Grace did not resemble any known Hamilton, she must look like her father, and that somewhere, there was another collection of family photograph albums in whose pages her features were mirrored, but Grace had never found out where. For while Eleanor was not a Roman Catholic - a religion she deemed as foreign and as morally reprehensible as Hinduism - she chose to believe that Grace's birth was the result of an immaculate conception and was never to be mentioned. And, when it came to enforcing a vow of silence on a family, Eleanor could teach the Mafia a thing or two.

Grace never asked where the family photographs that contained her likeness were, at least not directly. As a small child, she had not even realised she was missing a father because of her beloved grandfather. She called him papa, and despite the age difference, most people had assumed he was her father, an assumption her grandmother had encouraged for the sake of appearances.

Grace led a rather solitary childhood. Eleanor had discouraged her from bringing friends home, and was so strict about whose house she could visit, invitations to other people's houses were scarce. Looking back, this was probably a good thing as Grace thought households like hers were normal as she had no experience of any others, and as long as she had books to read and her papa, she was happy. His death of a heart attack when she was ten, rendering her fatherless again, was a shattering blow.

Whether or not it affected her grandmother the same way, Grace never knew. Grief, like other emotions, was never discussed or displayed in the Hamilton house, and Grace retreated further into the solace of books. Soon after her grandfather's death she was sent away to boarding school.

Grace learned young that her grandmother did not take kindly to unwelcome questions. By the time she felt at last able to talk to her grandmother on a woman to woman basis, it was too late. When Grace was eighteen, Eleanor suffered a stroke from which she never recovered. She died when Grace was twenty. Although they had not been close, Grace felt like an orphan, even though she had a mother, and possibly a father, still living. She had always thought of her grandparents as her parents, which, to all intents they had been. Her adored grandfather had provided the love and warmth she craved, and while Eleanor may not have been the easiest of women, Grace knew that in her own way, she had done her best.

Grace smiled grimly at herself in the mirror as she dabbed powder on her nose in an ineffectual attempt to stop it shining. Marjorie claimed she hated Eleanor and had spent her life trying to be as unlike her as possible. However, in one respect, her mother and grandmother were exactly alike. Both believed that unpleasant facts would go away if they either ignored them or said they weren't true, and while just a warning glance from Eleanor could cause unwelcome questions to be stillborn, her mother had other, equally effective ways to avoiding answering them.

On one occasion, at the age of fourteen, when Grace timidly raised the subject of her possibly having another family containing aunts and uncles and cousins whom she would like to know, her mother's eyes filled with accusing tears.

'You hate me, don't you? You think I'm a terrible mother. If you loved me you wouldn't want to know who your father was.'

Upset that she had caused her mother to cry, Grace instantly declared that she loved her and that she didn't care who her father was, but by this time her mother was sobbing into her handkerchief. 'You just don't understand! Nobody can.'

And Grace couldn't, because no-one would tell her what there was to understand.

She inspected her face in the mirror. She was lucky. Unlike her mother, her skin tanned quickly and easily, so the red would quickly fade, but she would have to be more cautious of the sun. Her mother's sun-ravaged complexion had shocked her as she had always been sensitive about her age, going to great lengths to conceal it. Marjorie was fifty-two but answered to only thirty-nine. She had even succeeded in getting the wrong date of birth in her passport. Until that morning, Grace would have said that her mother could have passed for someone in her early forties, but the woman she had seen in the taverna looked her age and more.

Grace gently eased a long-sleeved blouse over her shoulders. Now she had decided to tell her mother that, from now on, even though she would always be prepared to help her, Roger was going to come first in her life, perhaps she should also confront her mother about her father and demand to know who he was. She had a right to know.

Oddly enough, not knowing the identity of her father was the only subject on which her mother and Roger agreed. Grace had hesitated before telling Roger the truth about her parentage as he could trace his lineage back to the time of the Norman conquest of England. However, for once he had confounded her expectations and had merely shrugged.

'Does it really matter to you now? I know who you are which is all that matters to me, so it should be all that matters to you. 'Anyway,' he had added, 'knowing your mother, chances are he's a bit of a no hoper which is why he hasn't come looking for you. Do you really think the sort of man who abandons their child is the kind of man you want as a father?'

Maybe Roger was right, Grace thought as she buttoned her blouse, but somehow, without knowing who her father was, she felt she could never be really sure of who she was. It was the missing piece of the jigsaw - not large, but vital to see the complete picture.

She sat down at the table and stared at the first page of the manuscript not seeing the words. It was unfair, but it had crossed her mind that maybe Roger would prefer not to know the truth as her mother had always shown a total lack of discrimination when it came to her lovers. Grace willed herself to concentrate on the manuscript. It was entitled: *The Myth of Love or an Anatomy of Desire*. It was a book arguing that there was no such thing as love, merely a response to biological imperatives. Her mother would hate it.

Grace began to read. She had a feeling she was going to enjoy it.

SIX

The fierce afternoon sun was only a hazy golden memory on the horizon by the time Grace set off to walk down to the harbour. An evening mantle of muted blues and greys lay across the surrounding hills, softening their stark outlines.

Women sat on low chairs or the stone steps outside their houses, their hands busy with lace work or sewing. As Grace walked past they looked up, nodding or smiling, wishing her 'kalispera', hardly pausing in their conversations. For a precious hour or two as the shadows deepened, and before they had to return to their kitchens to prepare yet another meal for their families, this time was sacred to women. The only males allowed were small boys and the occasional old man, his gnarled hands fingering worry beads, his eyes cloudy with memories that he could no longer share.

When she reached the coast road, Grace paused. Some small fishing boats were setting out from the harbour. Their put-putting engines sounded frail, but they swiftly made headway, their lone occupants fleetingly silhouetted against the now violet twilight before being swallowed by the inky black immensity of the sea. Soon, only a small light in their bows was visible from the shore, forming a necklace of sparkling lights across the horizon.

Grace began walking towards a place about two hundred yards ahead, where lights spilled across the road. She was hoping it was the taverna her mother had mentioned, as beyond it was only darkness. She glanced at the luminous face of her watch. It was after eight thirty but she knew her mother would not be on time. Marjorie considered punctuality the province of small-minded people, and now that she had been transformed into a goddess, no doubt her time-keeping would be even worse. If Grace remembered her Greek mythology correctly, one of the ancient gods' favourite games was causing mortals to lose all sense of time.

When she reached the taverna she hesitated. It was a balmy evening and it would have been nice to sit outside, but the terrace was already merrily and noisily occupied by several generations of the same Greek family seated at four tables pushed together. Deciding that she and her mother would find it hard to have a serious conversation, Grace went inside. The taverna's neon lit interior was empty apart from two young Greek men sprawled indolently in one corner, their table littered with beer bottles and an overflowing ashtray. Their eyes ran appraisingly over her figure and one smiled hopefully in her direction. Grace made for a table on the far side of the room beside some large windows that were open to the sea breeze. Choosing a chair with her back to the two men in order that they received the message she was not interested in them, she sat looking out of the window as the twilight deepened to indigo and finally to a velvet black.

'Parakalo, ti tha parete?'

The request for her order was spoken softly in Greek and startled Grace out of her reverie. She had not heard anyone approaching the table.

'I'm waiting for someone...' she replied and then stopped. She had left her guidebook with its handy Greek phrases in her room.

'I'm sorry, forgive me. You look Greek, I thought...' the man gestured with his right hand and smiled.

'I'm English,' said Grace unnecessarily.

The man smiled again. Grace guessed him to be somewhere in his late twenties and, while it was evident that she did not conform to his image of a typical Englishwoman, neither did he conform to her image of a typical Greek. His thick curly light brown hair was streaked blond by the sun, and his eyes, which for a disconcerting moment looked directly into hers, were green flecked with gold. He was not dressed as a waiter but wore faded blue denims and a T-shirt.

'Would you like something to drink?' His voice when he spoke English had a rasp like a lion's purr.

'I'd prefer to wait. Perhaps I can look at a menu?'

'A menu...? Of course.'

Grace thought she glimpsed an ironic smile, but the man bowed his head solemnly before returning with a menu that he presented to her with another bow before walking away. While his manner was deferential like that of a waiter, he gave the impression that deference did not come naturally to him.

She was studying the menu with more attention than it merited when a loud voice made her look up. 'What are you reading that for? You're in Greece. You don't look at menus here, you look in the kitchen.' Marjorie enveloped Grace in a bracelet-tinkling hug. The large fringed shawl she wore smelt overpoweringly of patchouli.

For a moment Grace felt disoriented. It was not just the musky scent that possessed an almost hallucinatory quality, but also her mother's unusually enthusiastic greeting. It was only after Marjorie released her that Grace realised that her performance of maternal affection was intended for an audience rather than her. Watching them from the doorway was a tall, slim woman.

Marjorie turned and beckoned her over. 'Lilith, I'd like you to meet my daughter Grace.'

Lilith put out a hand. 'Hi.' The handshake was firm, the accent American. Unlike Marjorie's multi-coloured, gypsy-like outfit, she was dressed in black denims and a black vest.

Grace smiled politely at her, trying hard to conceal her irritation that her mother was not alone. Her smile was not returned as Lilith slumped into a chair and crossed her arms. Marjorie sat down beside her and smiled encouragingly across at Grace.

'This is absolutely the *best* taverna in town. Yanni serves the best fish and of course, vegetables, for miles.' She put a hand on Lilith's arm when she said vegetables, then she looked back at Grace, an expression of mock repentance on her face. 'I'm trying to be a vegetarian although I haven't quite gone all the way yet because Yanni keeps tempting me, don't you Yanni?' She dimpled flirtatiously as the man who had spoken to Grace earlier came to the table.

'Kalispera Miss Hamilton. What would you like to drink?'

'My usual Retsina please Yanni, and I've told you before, you must call me Gaia.' Marjorie tapped him playfully on his arm.

He looked at Lilith.

'Amstell.'

Grace sensed Yanni stiffen at Lilith's curt order for beer, but he merely inclined his head in acknowledgement and then looked questioningly at her.

'Do you have a wine list please?'

Lilith snorted.

Marjorie put a hand on Lilith's arm again. 'Perhaps a bottle of that nice local white wine for my daughter Yanni?'

'Your daughter?' the surprise was genuine.

'Oh I know I don't look old enough, but I was a child bride...' Marjorie began, but her voice trailed off as Grace gave her a warning look.

'Only such a beautiful mother could have had such a beautiful daughter.'

Yanni's words were practised, as though he knew what women tourists expected of a Greek waiter. However, although the flattery was directed at Marjorie, his gaze was on Grace. She looked away. Her mother might think it fun to flirt with a waiter but she did not.

'Would you like to order something to eat?'

Yanni's question was directed at Marjorie, but Grace could still feel his gaze on her.

'We'll take a look in a minute dear, after we've had a drink.' Marjorie waved him away and then looked from Grace to Lilith. 'Isn't this nice? All of us together.'

Grace did not think it was nice, and she was not too sure what her mother meant by her use of the term 'us'. However, politeness dictated she should make an effort with Lilith, although why, she did not know. Lilith was the intruder in what should have been a family occasion, yet she was giving a very good impression that it was Grace who not welcome.

As Lilith was rather rudely gazing out of the window, Grace took the opportunity to study her. Her initial impression had been that Lilith was much younger than her because of the way she was dressed and her short, boyish hair, but now she looked more closely, Grace guessed they were about the same age. However, her impression of severity was confirmed. There was something almost of the ascetic about Lilith's appearance. Thin yet wiry, she was darkly suntanned and wore no jewellery, not even a watch. Her square jaw suggested a forthright character, an impression heightened by her thick, dark eyebrows that almost formed a straight line above her grey eyes, eyes which Grace suddenly realised were now looking directly at her.

Grace felt her cheeks grow hot. She searched for a suitably neutral topic of conversation. 'Is this your first visit to Greece?'

Lilith shook her head then looked away again.

Grace looked across at her mother, but no help was forthcoming. Exasperated, she gave up and lapsed into silence until Yanni returned with their drinks. He opened the beer, but before he could pour it into a glass, Lilith seized it. Putting one foot on a spare chair, she leant back and drank straight from the bottle. As she raised her arm, Grace noticed the black, luxuriant growth of hair in her underarm. She stared, embarrassed that she found something so natural, so alien.

As though challenging Grace to look, Lilith kept her arm raised and tipping her head back, drank until the the bottle was almost drained dry, then she banged the bottle back down on the table and wiped her mouth with the back of her hand in a gesture Grace could not help feeling was aimed at her.

Marjorie gave her a reproachful look before raising her glass. 'Welcome to the birthplace of the women's movement, Grace darling.'

Lilith picked up her beer bottle and waved it at Grace. 'Yeah, welcome.'

Grace ignored her and looked at her mother. 'I think your history is a little bit shaky. I can't remember either Emmeline Pankhurst or Betty Friedan taking package holidays to Greece.'

Lilith's chair crashed back down onto four legs. She looked across at Grace and snorted derisively. 'Somehow you not knowing this is the birthplace of Sappho comes as no great surprise to me. Now let me give *you* a history lesson...'

But before she could begin, Marjorie yet again put a restraining hand on her arm. 'We'll explain everything in good time, Lilith. Grace has only just arrived. She needs to relax a little before we get down to business.'

'You'll have to excuse my lack of knowledge of ancient Greek history. My mother forgot to tell me I needed to do my homework before coming,' said Grace dryly.

An awkward silence descended on the table and Grace sipped her wine. It was not as bad she expected. It did not have much depth but it was light and slightly floral without being sweet. Grace put her glass down. She was getting as bad as Roger. She looked across the table at her mother only to see her gazing intently over the rim of her glass at Lilith. Grace felt an unexpected jolt of jealousy. Her mother seemed to reserve all her affection for the waifs and strays she was so fond of adopting, and this ill-mannered American woman was clearly the latest.

When she spoke, her voice was sharp. 'I think it's time for you to explain what's going on, mother. I haven't come here to have a holiday as I have a lot of work on and I need to get back to London as soon as possible.'

Marjorie poured herself another glass of Retsina. 'If you insist,' she sounded pained. 'Now, where shall I begin?' She held her glass up and gazed at it as though it could provide her with the answer. 'There are these turtles which live in these big pools by the beach...' she hesitated, 'well, they're terrapins really, but never mind. There are tortoises too, although they don't go in the water and there are so few of them left, poor things, and all because we wanted them as pets. My Percy cost one and six pence. Your grandfather bought him for me when your grandmother said I couldn't have a kitten. I cried for a week when Percy died. He unfortunately decided to hibernate in a bonfire, before it was lit of course, and when it was... Anyway, there's this Australian... Well, he's really from this village, or at least his parents were I think... He's called Aristotle and he wants to build a hotel on the turtle beach which will completely destroy it and we intend to stop him.'

Grace listened to her mother's rambling explanation with growing impatience. Her voice was sardonic. 'We? Do you mean you and Lilith?'

Lilith leant forward and jabbed a finger at Grace. 'What Gaia, your mother, is trying to say, is that we *women* intend to stop him destroying the terrapin pools. It's environmental rape but no-one in the village seems to care. That's because like everywhere else, everything here is controlled by men. Rape of the environment and rape of women is all one and the same thing in the patriarchal system. What men can't control they try to destroy.'

'I think there are a lot of people who would take issue with your analysis of rape,' said Grace coolly. Her earlier instinct to dislike the woman was now taking tangible form. She looked at her mother. 'What other women? I haven't noticed many other tourists here.'

'Tourists! We're not *tourists*,' Lilith managed to make the word sound obscene. 'Tourists don't give a fuck about the environment. What do they care as long as they have their twenty-storey, concrete blocks which flush untreated shit...'

'Now now, Lilith,' Marjorie chided.

To Grace's astonishment, Lilith suddenly smiled and tenderly touched her mother's cheek. 'Okay, okay, I stand corrected. No more talk of shit over dinner.' She turned back to Grace. 'I wasn't talking about tourists but about the women who come here every year from all over the world and set up the Sappho camp just outside the village.'

Grace felt her heart sink at the thought of another women's camp. The last time it was the women's camp protesting against nuclear weapons at Greenham Common. She had hoped her mother had learned her lesson after. Marjorie had gone there 'just to take a look', according to her, but had ended up being arrested and spending a night in jail after kicking an American colonel during a demonstration.

It was a long time ago, but Grace could still remember the awfulness of having to lie to her grandparents in order to borrow enough money to bail her mother out of the police station as Marjorie made her swear she would not tell them where she was. What made it worse was that Marjorie immediately abandoned all her pacifist principles and dated the American colonel, declaring he was too good looking to be a total fascist.

'As you constantly keep reminding me, mother, it's your life and you can do whatever you please with it. All I want to know is, what do turtles - or whatever they are - and some Australian philosopher, have to do with you asking me to come to Greece?'

Her mother looked at Grace as though she was a backward child. 'But you know lots of journalists and we need publicity, so I've told everyone that you will help us to get the media to sit up and take notice.'

'Me? Help you get some news coverage...?' began Grace and then stopped.

Words momentarily failed her. She was furious. How could she have fooled herself into thinking her mother was in danger and actually needed her? Her mother only needed her when she was useful in some way, the rest of the time she forgot about her existence. Grace spread her hands palm down on the table and looked at them as she carefully composed her reply. If she dared look at her mother, she might say something she would regret.

'First of all, the journalists I know write for the literary pages of newspapers and magazines and are unlikely to be interested in turtles. Secondly, *if* these animals are a threatened species, you should contact one of the wildlife conservation organisations. They would be able to help you as they are geared up for campaigns like this.'

'So, it's only after we've brought something to the point of extinction that its worth saving and even then it's not worth your time and trouble?' Lilith's voice was heavy with sarcasm.

Grace flushed. 'That's not what I meant at all. It just so happens I *do* care about environmental issues, but I don't see how I can help you, and frankly mother, I feel I have been brought here under false pretences.'

Lilith pushed her chair back and stood up. 'I'm sorry Gaia, but women like your daughter,' she jerked her head in Grace's direction, 'piss me off. They keep their heads down and let other women fight their battles for them, but they are only too happy to take their share of the spoils once the war's been won.'

'Now stop it!' Marjorie commanded, 'both of you, and Lilith, *sit down.*'

To Grace's surprise, Lilith meekly sat down.

Marjorie placed a hand on Grace's arm. 'Grace dear, I'm not going to apologise for what Lilith said, although her language was perhaps a little direct. She's right, you know, there's a point when you have to stand up and be counted. We women have got to be prepared to unite and fight together or else nothing will ever change.'

Grace struggled to control her temper again. It seemed to her that it was Lilith who was behaving badly. 'Strange as it may seem to you mother, I have a lot of sympathy with what you say. However, I think it's about time we moved on from all this "women together" talk. We're in the 1990s now, not the 1960s. I've never asked anyone to fight my battles for me, and whatever I've achieved, I've achieved for myself by hard work out in the real world.'

Lilith flushed, but before she could deliver the angry reply that was clearly on her lips, Marjorie stood up. 'Enough! I think we could all do with some nice food. I always find it helps. I'm going into the kitchen to see what fish Yanni has tonight and I'll order for all of us,' she put a hand on Lilith's shoulder, 'even for you dear. Vegetables are all very well, but a bit of fish won't hurt, and we should support the local fishermen, that way they won't need to build a hotel and become waiters will they?' She gave Grace as near a look commanding obedience as she could ever remember receiving. 'And while I'm in the kitchen, I expect you two to get to know each other better. I want you to be friends.' She swept off in a jangle of bracelets.

Grace glanced at Lilith but she was studiously looking in the opposite direction, her arms crossed across her chest. Grace opened her mouth to say something but stopped. What was the point? They had absolutely nothing in common and she had no wish to exchange pointless small talk. If Lilith wanted to be rude and not talk, it suited her. Grace turned away and stared out of the window into the dark.

Marjorie returned a little while later, followed by Yanni, who was laden with dishes of salad and stuffed vegetables. She began piling food onto plates, all the while chattering away as though they were on a family outing. Grace looked at the food and felt faintly nauseous, as though she had eaten something particularly sour which was fermenting in her stomach. She picked listlessly at some salad, her loss of appetite not helped by the sight of Marjorie and Lilith eating heartily. When Yanni returned with a large plate of grilled red mullet, they fell on them, sucking the fishbones clean of flesh and mopping up every bit of sauce and olive oil with large chunks of bread. They chattered as they ate, but Grace made no effort to join in. Eventually, Marjorie patted her mouth with a napkin and sat back with a sigh.

'That was absolutely heavenly! Yanni's mother cooks like an angel, not one of my accomplishments.' She dimpled at Lilith and then raised her arm, 'Yanni dear, the bill please.'

She reached over and patted Grace's hand. 'Now, I know you've had rather a lot to take in, but please reconsider about helping us, it would mean so much to me.'

'I'll give it some thought but I really can't make any promises,' said Grace wishing she had the courage just to say no.

Marjorie nodded. 'Good. Oh...just one more thing, you know how it is with foreign banks. There seems to be some problem with transferring money from my London account, so I was wondering...' Marjorie indicated the bill Yanni had placed on the table.

Grace wordlessly picked it up and counted some notes onto the table.

'Is there a problem?'

Grace looked up at Yanni.

'A problem?' she repeated.

He indicated her plate. 'The fish...was it not good?'

'I wasn't hungry.'

For the first time her mother noticed that she hadn't eaten. 'Is there something wrong?'

Grace shook her head. There was, but right at that moment, she could not trust herself to speak. She stood up, and with a curt nod in their direction, left the taverna, overwhelmed with the desire to put as much distance between herself and her mother as possible.

She strode swiftly along the coast road, heading back towards the light of the village, but after about a hundred yards, she stopped and took a deep breath. She had been clenching her jaw so hard it hurt and her nails were cutting into her palms where she had been holding them balled up into fists. She stood still, letting the night air cool her cheeks. Out in the bay a large fishing vessel was returning to port. It was lit from stem to stern with lights and trailing behind in its wake, was what looked to be a shimmering bridal veil.

Fascinated despite her anger, Grace watched. As it neared the shore, a hoarse clamour revealed the cause of the apparition. Like poor relations falling on the buffet at a wedding feast, hundreds of seagulls were swooping and fighting over the remains of the catch that were being thrown overboard, their white wings illuminated by the lights on the stern of the boat.

SEVEN

By the time she reached the village square, Grace felt calmer, although it was a calm edged with quiet fury. How many times had she sworn to herself that she would not come running when her mother wanted, only to give in worried that something might happen to Marjorie if she didn't? Well, this really *was* the last time. Next time Marjorie demanded she do something, she would refuse. Roger was right; her mother was like a fourteen-year-old, complete with the self-centred adolescent capacity to believe that they and their problems were the centre of the universe.

At the thought of Roger, Grace felt a sudden rush of guilt and contrition. She had been so concerned with her mother that she had not yet called him. He would be frantic with worry by now. Grace wished she had brought her mobile phone with her. She had only recently bought it and then, only because she had had lunch with an editor at one of the major publishing houses who assured her that soon, business would be impossible without one. When she brought it home, Roger had accused her of being over-impressionable and said that they were overpriced useless gadgets that would go the way of all gadgets - forgotten at the back of a cupboard. Experience had taught Grace that when Roger got a bee in his bonnet about something it was impossible to argue with him, so she kept her phone at work, only carrying it with her when she had to be out of the office for any time. Her bosses, Bartle and Duncan, were also technophobes and refused to have mobile phones themselves, but they liked the idea of being able to reach her if needed.

Earlier, Grace had noticed what looked like a telephone kiosk opposite Adonis's kafenion, now she hurried across the square, fishing in her bag for her purse. Reaching the kiosk, she placed her bag on top of the telephone and then stood in the street straining by the light from the kafenion to see what change she had.

'I'm afraid you won't have much luck with the phone tonight, something's wrong with the line again.'

The voice startled Grace and she dropped her purse, her change rolling in a dozen different directions. She knelt down to pick it up but the woman who had spoken was there first. For a few moments they scrabbled around in the dust then Grace shook her head.

'It doesn't matter. It was only a few coins.'

'You're *English!*' The woman sat back on her haunches and gazed at Grace with what seemed to her to be unwarranted delight.

Grace nodded. 'Yes.'

The woman clasped her hands together as though she had just been awarded a prize. 'I'm *so* thrilled. You've just *got* to allow me to buy you a drink.'

Grace got to her feet. The conversation was odd enough without it taking place with both of them kneeling in the dust. The woman followed suit.

'You see I'm Australian,' the woman announced as though it explained everything.

Grace was unsure how to respond as it explained nothing to her. She put her purse back into her bag. 'It's been very nice meeting you,' she said uncertainly, 'but I must be going...'

'Oh but you can't,' pleaded the woman, 'not now we've met, and the phone might be okay in a little while so you can make your call later. Sometimes it's just a question of which way the wind is blowing...'

Grace settled the strap of her bag on her shoulder, indicating her intention to leave, but the woman put a hand on her arm to stay her. 'My name is Kelly and I've been simply *dying* to meet someone who speaks English. We've been in the village for what seems like forever. My husband, Ari, is Australian too, but he speaks Greek because he was born here so it's all right for him...'

Although she was tired, and the last thing she wanted was another drink, Grace hesitated and the woman seized her chance. Almost before she knew where she was, Grace found herself standing inside the kafenion which was crowded and noisy, both things she hated. As she looked around, she became sharply aware that they were the only women in the place and that they were being stared at and appraised with a frankness that made the blood rush to her cheeks, although it appeared to have little or no effect on her companion.

Now she could see her in the light, Grace understood why. Kelly was not only a woman used to being the centre of male attention - she actively sought it.

Three-inch high stilettos and a fearsomely back-combed Ivana Trump blond beehive gave her a stature that she otherwise lacked. Taut breasts, that were improbably large for her small, slim frame, were barely held in check by a tiny fuschia pink bandeau masquerading as a top. Between the top and a pair of white, skin-tight lycra pedal-pushers, was an expanse of taut stomach whose colour owed more to year-round tanning-beds, than the sun.

She hailed a busy-looking Adonis. 'Adonis, honey! How is the handsomest boy in the village this evening?'

He came to greet them and was clasped tightly against her breasts, a sheepish expression on his face. Kelly released him and turned her attention to the rest of the kafenion, bathing everyone in the brightness of her smile, a brightness that was only outshone by the gold jewellery that adorned her neck, ears, arms and even one ankle. Although she could have been imagining it, Grace sensed that the friendliness of the woman's smile had caused a general air of disapproval and most of the men turned their attention back to their cards or their Tavli boards.

'Kalispera, Adonis,' a voice boomed from behind Grace making her start yet again. 'I hope you haven't been flirting with my little sugar plum again. She's got a spot for you that's just a little too soft for my liking.'

Adonis retreated hurriedly behind the counter as the newcomer walked past Grace hand outstretched. 'Us Greek men have to stick together when it comes to women. We don't want them getting out of order do we?' The speaker was rewarded with a playful slap on the arm from Kelly. Adonis smiled weakly and shook the proffered hand, but kept the counter safely between them.

The newcomer turned and surveyed the room as though it were his private kingdom. To Grace's eyes, he looked Greek, but her ears said he could be nothing other than Australian. He was short, and stockily built, with wiry black hair streaked with grey, and a heavy five o'clock shadow on his fleshy jawline. He was dressed in matching Hawaiian shirt and shorts that nearly equalled Kelly's outfit for brightness. He, too, wore the equivalent of a small country's gold reserves round his neck and wrists. Grace felt his interested gaze come to rest on her. Kelly let out another little squeak.

'Oh, silly me! Honey, this is my friend..?' She looked enquiringly at Grace.

'Grace Hamilton.'

'From England,' added Kelly.

'Kalispera. My name's Aristotle, Ari for short, like Onassis, only not quite as rich yet,' he gave a loud bark of laughter.

Grace reluctantly took the large slightly sweaty paw that was thrust at her and shook hands. Ari's eyes made her feel uncomfortable. She suddenly wanted to look down and check that all the buttons on her blouse were securely fastened.

'Grace is going to join us for a drink, aren't you?' said Kelly.

It was now the very last thing that Grace wanted to do. 'Perhaps another time, anyway, there are no tables free,' she said.

'That's no problem,' said Ari. He snapped his fingers at Adonis and pointing at two tables occupied by three men playing cards.

Adonis went over, and after an animated conversation occasioning much shrugging of shoulders, he removed one of the tables. The men turned and glared angrily at Ari before returning to their game.

Ari put a moist hand on Grace's back and propelled her towards the table. He pulled a chair unnecessarily close to hers and sat down without waiting for Kelly. 'So, how do you like our little village? It's a bit primitive, but it has its charms, or so Kelly keeps telling me, although I suspect they have more to do with young Adonis here than the scenery, eh?'

Adonis, who was waiting for their order, looked uncomfortable. Ari's tone was jocular but his words had a perceptible edge to them.

Kelly smiled and placed a reassuring hand on Adonis's arm. 'Stop teasing poor Adonis, Ari darling. He's only a young boy and I'm sure he doesn't know what you're talking about, do you Adonis?'

Adonis vigorously nodded his agreement.

'When it comes to women, Greek men are dangerous at any age. I was about the same age as Adonis when I had my first woman and she was twenty-four, so you'd better watch your step around here Grace. A pretty woman like you could get herself into a lot of trouble, unless that's what you're looking for?' He winked lasciviously. 'We Greeks keep our own women locked up, but other women are fair game, eh Adonis?'

'Look, it's late. I really must...' began Grace.

Ari put a hand on her arm. 'Get this little lady a Metaxa, Adonis,' he commanded, 'and I'll have one too. Be sure to make that five star Metaxa, with ice, and a Tia Maria and Coke for my sugar plum, no ice.'

Adonis scurried thankfully away.

Grace pulled her arm away from Ari's grip as politely as she was able. 'It's very kind of you to offer Mr...Ari, but I don't drink spirits.'

'I won't take no for an answer. It's a sacred duty for us Greeks to offer hospitality to strangers, particularly when they're as pretty as you. Take my advice, relax a little. You Brits are so tight-ar...' he corrected himself with another knowing grin, '...buttoned up. It's no use being in a hurry around here, everything's done in Greek time.'

'Oh yes, please do stay,' urged Kelly. 'We've been here for nearly three weeks and I haven't had anyone to talk to. It's alright for Ari, his parents came from this village so he's been visiting all his relatives, but I don't speak Greek, and I've had to sit still for hours on end drinking awful coffee. It would be so nice to have someone to chat to.' From under their starkly black mascared fringe, Kelly's eyes appealed to Grace.

Ari patted Kelly on the knee. 'Sitting still and looking gorgeous is what you're best at.' He waved at the men at the other tables. 'I like watching them eat their hearts out with jealousy. But if you want to spend more time on the beach...'

'No, of course not Ari sweetie, I know how important family is to you. It's only, well...' she looked across at Grace again. 'Ari's first wife was Greek, and she came from this village. I get the feeling that some of the women here don't approve of me. They really don't like their men marrying out so to speak.'

'Nonsense, you women are all the same - too bloody sensitive for your own good. It's nothing to do with you not being Greek, they're just plain jealous. Now let's wish Grace here welcome.' Ari raised the large glass of brandy that Adonis had just brought to the table. 'Stin iyia sas! Your health and welcome to Greece.'

Grace raised her glass to her lips but did not drink, wondering how soon she could escape. If Ari had been alone, she would have rebuffed him without a second thought, but despite Kelly's brazen appearance, there was a vulnerability about her that made Grace hesitate about getting up and leaving immediately.

She looked at Kelly. 'I would imagine that being a second wife is always difficult, no matter what the circumstances, and in a conservative society like this, divorce is probably still unusual.'

'Is that why you're on holiday by yourself? Are you divorced?' asked Kelly.

Grace immediately regretted her earlier sympathy. The last thing she wanted to do was to discuss her private life with strangers. 'No, I'm not married, that is, not yet. I'm engaged. My mother is here on holiday and I've just come to join her for a few days.'

'Oh, but where is she? You must introduce us. We could make up a foursome for dinner. Wouldn't that be fun Ari?'

Ari's expression did not suggest it would be.

Kelly turned back to Grace. 'Are you from London? I'm simply *dying* to go there, but Ari won't take me. He went there once and he hated it, didn't you honey? Ari says that the English act like they've got something stuck up their you know what,' she giggled. 'You should hear him whoop when we beat you at cricket. He even got into a fight with some English people in a restaurant once over cricket. It was so embarrassing, I nearly died.'

'And I beat them too, just like we do at cricket. They still think we're some little backward colony and that we have to curtsey to them and their tin pot queen. Well let me tell you,' he jabbed a stubby finger at Grace. 'If it wasn't for the new immigrants, people like us Greeks who have given the Anglos a much-needed shot in the arm, that's what Australia would still be - a backward colony. The Asians have helped too. They know how to do a day's graft, not like the Poms who are a load of bludgers. They really jack me off. They won't lower themselves to get some honest sweat on their brow and then they have the cheek to winge about the Japs coming! The Japs bring big money with them and that speaks good business in any language, particularly in mine.'

'And what kind of business are you in?' asked Grace for politeness sake, although she would rather have not heard anything more the loud Australian had to say.

'Real estate, mostly residential, but I'm thinking of moving into the hotel business.'

'Ari's had such a good idea, haven't you darling?' Kelly draped a forearm over his shoulder and began to play with one of the heavy gold chains around his thick neck. 'He thinks they ought to build a hotel here. It would be so nice. A proper hotel with proper showers and air-conditioning, and perhaps a beauty salon, because everyone likes getting their nails done and having a facial when they're on holiday don't they? It could have a swimming pool too. I do *so* hate getting sand all over me when I go to the beach, and a gym, it simply *must* have a gym. I really hate missing my daily workout - don't you?'

Ari feigned a hurt look and placed a hand on her thigh. 'But I thought the twice daily workout I've been giving you was enough to burn up all those calories, honeybun.'

Kelly blushed in spite of her tan and gave him a playful slap on the arm. 'You are naughty, Ari and you're embarrassing Grace.'

However, Grace had not been listening to this last exchange. She was still digesting the fact that she was sitting with the man who, albeit unwittingly, was the cause of her coming to Greece. The knowledge had caused her to drink her brandy without noticing it.

'Where exactly are you planning to build this hotel?'

'I've seen the perfect piece of land to the north of the village, right beside a beach. It's ripe for development. There's nothing there, only a few fields. It will have to go the village council, but no worries about that. The President of the Council - that's the Mayor to you and me - is a second cousin on my father's side.' Ari became increasingly expansive. 'Of course it takes someone like me drag a backward place like this into the twentieth century. They're still living in the dark ages here. The height of their ambition is to own a few goats.'

'You don't seem to have much of a high regard for your fellow Greeks. From my observation, everyone here seems perfectly happy. They have their fishing, a few tourists...' Grace found herself defending the village she had been so disparaging about earlier.

Ari jabbed a stubby finger at her again. It was a gesture Grace was beginning to dislike almost as much as she disliked the man itself. 'A *few* tourists. That's just it. They rent out the odd room, all quaintly decorated and no mod-cons, and think they're making a living. What they don't realise is that if they got organised, they could be bringing tourists in here by the coach load, and then they could be taking *their* holidays abroad in luxury hotels. They just don't think big enough. This place has got potential and I'm going to show it to them.' He drained his brandy and waved his glass at Adonis.

'He's so dynamic, isn't he? That's why I married him.' Kelly twisted the large diamond and emerald engagement ring that encrusted her third finger. 'The first time I saw him, I said to myself, Kelly, that man is going to be your husband, and very soon he was!'

Ari chucked her under the chin. 'And that's why I married my sweet little sugar plum. She's a woman after my own heart. She saw something she wanted and didn't stop until she got it, even though I was married. Now that's what I call guts.' He turned Kelly's head and kissed her wetly on the lips.

Grace scooped up her bag and rose to her feet. She had suddenly had enough of Greeks, sugar plums, and terrapins for one evening. 'I'm afraid I must be going, my mother will be wondering where I am. Thank you for the drink.'

Before either of them could react, she was gone, fleeing into the darkness for the second time that night.

EIGHT

Grace tried to lift her head from the pillow. She failed and fell back, groaning faintly. She did not usually drink very much, but last night she had drunk nearly a bottle of wine in the taverna, followed by the large brandy in the kafenion, and all this having eaten barely a few mouthfuls of salad and a little fish. She had not had any experience of hangovers, but she had the feeling that she was experiencing one now. The hammering sound in her ears was getting louder. She buried her face in the pillow, but the noise continued. Grace gingerly turned her head to one side and experimentally opened one eye. It was still dark, but she could just distinguish the faint outline of the furniture in her room. She opened her other eye. It was odd, but the hammering no longer seemed to be inside her head. She tried to focus. There was someone at the door.

Grace sat up rather unsteadily and reached for Roger's bathrobe. Pulling it tightly around her, she stumbled across the room.

'Who is it?'

'Me!'

Grace opened the door. Outside her mother stood looking ghostlike in a long, white shift.

'Trying to wake you up is like trying to rouse the dead. Hurry up and get dressed or we'll be late.' Marjorie walked uninvited into the room.

'Late? Late for what? What time is it?' Grace stood bewildered at the door, still talking to the space where her mother had been standing.

'Late for the dawn. We've got to be there for the first rays of the sun. If you hadn't been in such a bad temper last night, I would have told you.' Marjorie began rifling through Grace's clothes. 'Haven't you brought anything white with you?' she demanded.

Grace shook her head. Her mother continued throwing clothes onto the floor. Then she made a triumphal exclamation. 'These will do!' She held up some cream linen trousers and a white T-shirt. She thrust them into Grace's hands. 'Hurry up, put them on.'

The urgency in her mother's voice made Grace obey. Marjorie watched impatiently and then, as though Grace were a child, she bade her sit down and then brushed her hair. When Marjorie had finished, Grace automatically reached up to tie it back, but her mother pushed her hands away.

'Leave it loose, it looks much better. You're beginning to look positively middle-aged with that silly bun thing you insist on wearing. Now hurry up, or we'll be late.'

Before Grace could object, her mother was out of the door. Grabbing the jacket that matched the trousers and hopping on one foot as she pulled on her shoes, Grace followed.

Marjorie led the way along a rocky path that skirted the village. She was surprisingly sure-footed, even in the gloom, leaving Grace to stumble blearily behind her. She would have demanded to know where they were going if she could have caught up with her mother, but Marjorie was several yards ahead and getting farther away all the time.

The village was soon behind them as they followed a rough track that ran along a valley between some low hills. The stars were still bright in the sky but grey streaks along the horizon suggested that dawn was not far away.

Marjorie's voice floated back to Grace: 'Do hurry up, we haven't got much time.'

Feeling like Alice in Wonderland following the White Rabbit, Grace hurried. When Marjorie at last stopped, she heaved a sigh of relief, but it was short-lived. Marjorie had only paused long enough to gather her long skirt above her knees so she could climb over a rusty wire fence. Gritting her teeth, Grace followed as carefully as she could. Her suit had not been designed for cross-country rambles. By the time she had negotiated the fence, Marjorie was already scrambling up a hillside a hundred yards ahead. Grace quickened her pace but then stopped. The ground was covered with clumps of low spiky bushes that tore at her very expensive trouser legs. She stood, wavering between her desire to protect her suit or follow her mother, whose ghostly white figure was beckoning to her from the crest of the hill. Deciding it would be easier to repair the damage to her legs than to her suit, Grace rolled her trousers up over her knees, then toiled up the hill as fast as she could, wincing as thorns plucked at her skin.

As she reached the top of the hill, she paused to draw breath. The air was cool and salty. Down below was a long curving bay, made visible in the pre-dawn light by the white fringe of waves breaking against the shore. A pale figure, which Grace assumed to be that of her mother, was already walking along the beach.

She cupped her hands in front of her mouth in order to call to her mother to wait, but then thought better of it. There were other figures on the beach, although it was impossible to distinguish how many. Wondering what she had got herself involved with this time, Grace scrambled down the hill, grazing her shins against the rocks that littered the hillside. She gathered momentum as she descended, almost falling the last few metres onto the beach.

Cursing her mother under her breath, Grace dusted herself down and removed her shoes. Holding them in one hand, she set off after her, her feet sinking into the wet, cold sand that made walking slow and uncomfortable. Ahead she could now see about twenty or thirty women. She had not been able to see them before as most of them were sitting on the ground, silent and unmoving, almost melting into the boulder-strewn landscape that bordered the beach. A small group of about a dozen women, all dressed in long white robes like her mother, stood apart with a purposeful air. One of them was drawing something in the sand with a stick while the others watched.

When she saw Grace approaching, her mother detached herself from the group. 'Just sit over there out of the way and don't say anything unless asked,' she whispered, pointing to the women sitting among the boulders.

'I don't see why...' began Grace loudly, but then lowered her voice as several heads turned indignantly in her direction. 'I don't see why I should go along with your nonsense, Mother. What on earth are you playing at this time - Druids or the Ku Klux Klan?'

'I told you not to bring her along,' hissed a voice at Grace's elbow.

Grace turned. It was Lilith. Grace had not recognised her. She was completely transformed by the long white robe she was wearing and the band of small, star-shaped, white flowers which crowned her hair. Although not conventionally pretty - her eyes were far too fierce for that - Grace was forced to concede that Lilith was a strikingly handsome woman. However, that in no way mitigated her rudeness, and Grace was about to tell her so in no uncertain terms, but before she could say anything, the woman who had been drawing in the sand straightened up and held her arms aloft. There was a sudden hush.

She was the kind of woman who in any circumstances commanded attention - tall and imposing. Grace could imagine her as the headmistress of a girls' school, dressed in a tweed suit and sensible shoes, her grey and white streaked hair drawn tightly into a French pleat. However, at that moment her hair looked distinctly unheadmistress-like. It was woven into tiny plaits that snaked down her shoulders almost to her waist and a star-like white flower had been tucked behind each of her ears. The feet peeping out from under her flowing robe were naked, and to Grace's critical eyes, distinctly grubby.

'Daughters of Demeter and Virgin sisters, it is the hour,' she declared in a deep, ringing voice which echoed in the chill morning air.

Grace shivered and wrapped her arms around herself. She was glad she had thought to bring her jacket. She felt cold and the cold served to sharpen her anger. Dawn or no dawn, she intended to go back to her room and finish her interrupted sleep. She looked round for her mother, but Marjorie had rejoined the other white-robed women who were forming a circle around the tall woman. Ignoring the hostile looks cast in her direction, Grace walked over. As she reached the circle, she caught sight of what had been drawn in the sand. It was a pentangle.

Grace grabbed her mother's arm. 'If this is some kind of coven...'

Marjorie prised her fingers open and pushed her gently but firmly away. 'It's not what you think. The pentangle is a sign even older than the Old Religion. It's the sign of the Goddess and it's sacred to all women. Now just keep quiet and watch from over there. I had to beg for a special dispensation for you to come along at all, not all the initiates like outsiders being present,' she whispered impatiently.

Grace reluctantly retreated. She could not leave now. While she was convinced that the whole thing was just some form of silly theatrics, she had to be certain. Her mother could be very naive. She looked round for somewhere to sit. There was a ragged half circle of women sitting on the ground a little way away. They were dressed in white too, although not in the flowing garments worn by the women in the circle. These were obviously reserved for the chosen few, everyone else had been forced to make do with what they had brought with them, resulting in an eclectic mixture of styles.

Grace reluctantly went to join them, but felt unwelcome here too. Nobody looked in her direction. It was almost as though she did not exist. The sensation that she was dreaming, or even a figment in somebody else's dream, began to take hold. However, just at that moment, a woman at the edge of the circle gave her a cheerful grin and patted the ground beside her. Grateful for what seemed like the first human contact that morning, Grace sat down, wishing there was something between her trousers and the damp sand.

A second glance confirmed that her neighbour looked reassuringly normal. Something about her demeanour suggested she was not taking the proceedings quite as seriously as the other participants. Russet-coloured hair framed a freckled face and amused green eyes. She wore a thick white cotton sweater and faded jeans. Grace guessed her to be about thirty.

Grace drew her knees up to her chin and hugged her jacket round her body. The chill air seemed to have penetrated her bones. If something was going to happen, she prayed that it would happen soon. As she tried to control her chattering teeth, a wraith-like figure standing apart from everyone else caught her eye.

The girl - she looked no more than sixteen - was anorexically thin. Nervously twisting strands of her wispy, fair hair, she was staring fixedly at the women in the middle who were now seated in a circle, their legs stretched out in front of them and apart, so that their feet touched their neighbours' to form a star shape in the centre of the circle. Grace followed her gaze as they joined hands and bowed towards the centre. After a moment's silence, they began to hum, almost imperceptibly at first, but growing louder and louder as they uncurled their bodies, slowly straightening their backs and lifting their arms and faces skywards.

A high, clear voice began to chant:
'Like a flower opening,
To welcome the wind and the rain and the sun.
Let us open our hearts and our minds and ourselves,
To welcome the Great She, the Mother of us all.
Her body is the earth that gives us life,
Her breath is the air that gives us wisdom,
Her spirit is the fire that gives us warmth,
Her womb holds the fertile waters that sustain us.
She is us, we are she.'

The rest of the women repeated the last line three times, exaggerating the sibilance of the 'she'. As the last syllable was carried away by the breeze, the first faint glow of dawn appeared on the horizon.

Despite herself, Grace felt the hairs on the back of her neck rise.

'She might be crackers but she sure knows how to put on a show,' murmured her russet-haired neighbour.

Grace looked enquiringly at her.

'Hecate,' the woman nodded towards the circle, 'the one with the hair. Reckons herself to be a High Priestess.'

Grace would have liked to ask more but the women were getting to their feet. Hecate held up her arms and raised her face to where the sun had just begun to rise in a milky pink glow. Her voice rang out again.

'The birth of a new day heralds new life for all. Come, let us return to the sacred waters so that we can be born again.' She led the women down to the edge of the sea.

Grace became aware that the wraith-like girl-woman had gone. All that remained where she had been standing was pile of discarded clothes. Grace looked along the beach. About fifty yards away, she was wading naked into the sea. Grace felt a faint prickle of apprehension. She had looked neurotic, could she be suicidal too?

Grace tapped her neighbour on the shoulder and gestured at the now half-submerged woman. 'Do you think we ought to do something? She might be about to do something silly.'

The other woman grinned. 'Don't worry. It's all part of the show. Watch.'

With their backs to the sea, the initiates had formed a line that began in the shallows, and led out of the water and up the beach to where Hecate stood facing the sea. The thin woman began to swim strongly towards them as Hecate raised her arms heavenwards yet again.

'Come forth and be born again of the Goddess,' she cried loudly.

At this, all the women lifted their skirts and parted their legs. Behind them, the woman took a deep breath and then dived under water. A few moments later she surfaced a few yards to the right of the woman in the shallows. She took another breath and dived again, this time coming up successfully between the woman's legs. She then began to crawl between the legs of the other women up onto the beach.

'Lucky this one's so small. You should have seen it when Big Bertha there tried it,' Grace's neighbour whispered, nodding at an extremely large woman with body builder's shoulders and an aggressive razor-cut hairdo. 'She knocked them over like nine-pins. It was a painful birth, should have been a Caesarean. Still, it makes you think what it must have been like for her real mother - ouch!' She began to laugh, but put a hand over her mouth as one of the women in their group turned and made a loud shushing noise.

Grace wanted to giggle at the absurdity of the women standing bow-legged as a naked woman crawled between them. Surely no-one could be taking it seriously? However, the expressions on the women's faces, including that of her mother, suggested that they did. Grace coughed to smother the laughter welling up inside her and earned herself a fierce look from Hecate. Once again she was reminded of a headmistress, although Hecate had a curiously young looking face despite her mane of greying hair.

Having struggled through the last set of legs, the naked woman now crouched in a foetal position. Hecate held out her hands.

'Those reborn of the Goddess are no longer bound by the rules of the usurper gods created by men in their own image. Cast off your man-given name and from henceforth be known by your Goddess-chosen name. Psyche is born!'

And with that, the newly-named Psyche uncurled her body and stood upright.

'Christ - Psyche! I might have guessed,' muttered the woman beside Grace, 'neurotic by name and neurotic by nature.'

Still naked, Psyche now began a slow dance, weaving in and out of the women who were still standing in line. Grace felt vaguely embarrassed.

As though sensing her thoughts, the woman at her side whispered in her ear. 'Hecate wanted everyone at these ceremonies to be naked so that they would all be equal, but she was outvoted so I guess we can consider ourselves lucky. By the way, I like your outfit. I bet it didn't come from Marks and Spencer.'

Grace smiled her thanks.

The woman held out her hand, 'I'm Sîan by the way.'

'Grace. How do you do?'

'Better if I don't have to get up at the crack of dawn.'

Grace was just about to ask her why she had, when she realised that Psyche had finished her dance. The line of women broke ranks and surged around her, hugging and kissing her. The large woman with the razor hair cut produced a towel and vigorously began to rub her dry, while another woman combed her tangled hair and a third retrieved her robe.

Marjorie came over to where Grace and Sîan were sitting. She wiped a tear away.

'Wasn't it just wonderful? When it happened to me, it felt, well...it felt like I was really being born again.'

Grace looked incredulously up at her mother. 'You crawled *naked* through those women's legs?'

'You should try it. It was as though the past with all its mistakes and problems was another life that I was discarding like an old skin. It was utterly blissful.'

Grace gritted her teeth and swallowed the retort that rose to her lips. Her mother had spent a whole lifetime discarding her responsibilities. She had no need to crawl through anyone's legs to do it.

'Looks like Juno the warrior queen is staking her claim,' said Sîan scornfully as Psyche obediently held up her arms and the large woman slipped her robe over her head, 'and I don't think she'll meet with much resistance.'

'Now, now Sîan,' Marjorie chided. 'You know we don't allow that sort of thing here.'

'What sort of thing?' Grace looked from one to the other.

'A woman's body is hers to give, not someone else's to take,' replied Marjorie.

'Why is it that everyone wants to take the fun out of sex? The chase is half the pleasure,' retorted Sîan.

'But they're both women,' said Grace.

Sîan raised an interrogative eyebrow at Marjorie. 'Where did you find your friend?'

'She's not a friend,' replied Marjorie. 'She's my daughter.'

It was Sîan's turn to look incredulous. 'Your daughter! I thought...' she shrugged, 'well, never mind what I thought.' She smiled wrily at Grace, then got to her feet and went to join the main body of women.

Grace struggled stiffly to her feet, trying to dust off the sand that was damply encrusted to her trousers. 'Can we go now?' she demanded. 'I think it's about time you and I had a long talk.'

'Oh but Lilith and I were hoping you would come to the camp and have lunch with us, weren't we Lilith?' asked Marjorie as Lilith joined them.

Lilith's expression suggested she was hoping nothing of the sort.

'I would like to speak to you *alone*,' said Grace stubbornly.

Lilith put a protective arm around Marjorie and stared fiercely at Grace. 'Anything you want to say to Gaia can be said to me as well.'

'I don't think you quite understand,' said Grace. 'I'm Marjorie's daughter and I think that gives me a right to speak to her where and when I choose, and what I have to say is between us. I'm not prepared to talk in front of some casual acquaintance.'

'*Casual* acquaintance! Is that what you think I am? Tell her, Gaia, or shall I?'

'Tell me *what*, Mother?' demanded Grace, although even as she said it, she had a feeling that she did not want to hear.

Marjorie twisted her bracelets. 'This isn't how we agreed we would tell you Grace, but I suppose you had to know sooner or later. It's just that...'

'Gaia and I are lovers,' finished Lilith.

Grace flinched as though she had been struck on the face. She stared at Lilith. For a long moment their eyes met and then Lilith looked away. Grace turned to her mother.

'Are you telling me you are in love with her?' She pointed at Lilith. She could not bring herself to say her name.

'Yes, but let me explain...' Her mother tried to put a hand on her arm, but Grace shook it away. She turned and stumbled blindly off across the beach.

Her mother's voice called shakily after her, 'Grace...*please*...'

NINE

It was a long walk back to the village. Even if she had wanted to, which she did not, Grace could not have found her way back by the route her mother had brought her, so she took the road. However, the term 'road' was a misnomer. It was a rutted, dusty track that forked several times, and each time she took the wrong direction, she was forced to retrace her weary steps. By the time she eventually saw Yanni's taverna up ahead and knew she was not far from the village, it was after ten o'clock and the sun was high, and she was both hot and exhausted. To make matters worse, her feet had blistered in several places and were bleeding, as her shoes were unsuitable for rough walking.

Not that Grace had noticed the pain, or anything else for that matter. She had walked in a daze of confused emotions. What was the right way to feel when your mother announced she was in love with a woman?

Women fell in love with each other all the time - there was nothing wrong with it - but it happened to other people, not to her mother. And if she was going to fall in love with a woman, why couldn't her mother fall in love with someone nearer her own age - someone she could settle down with? That would have been acceptable - almost appealing - but not Lilith. It was one thing to have affairs with younger men, but with a woman who was the same age as your own daughter? As if that were not enough, Lilith had used the word 'lovers'. Not that she and Marjorie were 'in love', but they were 'lovers'. It was a word that spoke actively of sex.

As she neared the taverna, Grace made an effort to pull herself together, pushing her hair off her face. Despite her blisters, she quickened her pace. She did not want anyone to see her in such a state. However, as she tried to hurry past, her face averted, a cheerful Australian voice hailed her.

'Honey, you look as though you could do with a long, cool drink. That must have been one *hell* of a party you went to after you left us last night. Now I know why you were in such a hurry to get away.'

It was Kelly. She was sitting at a table outside Yanni's taverna sipping a drink, dressed in turquoise palazzo pants and a matching haltertop, looking as though she was lounging on a yacht in St Tropez.

Grace stopped. She felt acutely embarrassed. 'It's not what it looks like,' she began gesturing at her crumpled clothes. 'I haven't been out all night. I've just been...'

Kelly patted the chair beside hers. 'Sit down, honey. No need to explain. I'm just glad someone round here has been having a good time. We're meant to be on holiday, but Ari is up half the night on the phone to Sydney or out drinking with the Mayor and his buddies hatching up plans for the hotel.'

Grace was about to refuse, but then changed her mind. She was exhausted and her hangover had returned to haunt her. She sat down and closed her eyes for a second.

Kelly removed her saucer-like sunglasses and studied her closely. 'Is there something wrong, honey?' She lowered her voice, 'I mean, nobody's done anything to you have they? The men around here...' Her concern hung in the air.

Grace opened her eyes and attempted a weak smile. 'No, really. There's nothing wrong. I just decided to take an early morning walk and stupidly got lost. I was forced to scramble through a fence and up and down a few hills...'

Kelly's expression showed that even she did not believe people wore expensive suits to go early morning hill climbing, but instead of questioning her further, she put a sympathetic hand on Grace's arm. 'What would you like to drink? I've just had some of Yanni's mother's homemade lemonade. It's not only delicious, but it's great for the complexion. It cleanses the system and helps to get rid of all those nasty little impurities.'

Grace nodded. 'That sounds nice.'

Kelly twisted in her chair and called Yanni. After a moment or two, he appeared in the doorway. Much to her annoyance, Grace found herself instinctively reaching to tidy her hair again.

Seeing him again, she realised he was not as tall as she had first thought, but even though he was wearing a faded T-shirt and scruffy shorts, and looked thoroughly dishevelled, if anything, he was more attractive than she remembered.

He stood in the doorway, a packet of American cigarettes in his hand. Putting one between his lips, he bowed his head towards his cupped hand then flared his lighter. His eyes half closed, he hungrily sucked in a lung-full of smoke. It was only after he had exhaled a long stream of smoke that he acknowledged Grace's presence.

'Kalimera, Miss Hamilton.'

Grace nodded curtly. Although she knew it was irrational, the time he had taken to acknowledge her presence almost felt like a deliberate slight. Not that she cared. She loathed people who smoked.

'Oh, you've already met. Isn't he just the cutest man in the village?' Kelly giggled. 'But don't tell Ari I said that as he's very possessive. If I so much as look at another man he goes wild with jealousy. Is your fiancé like that?'

Grace glanced towards Yanni. Not that it mattered, but she wanted to see whether he had heard the reference to Roger.

'Roger is not the jealous kind but he doesn't need to be, and I certainly don't need to worry about him and other women. He's incredibly loyal.'

'Ari says that Englishmen are cold fish because they don't really like women, not like Greeks who are very passionate as well as jealous.'

'I'm sure that there are just as many passionate and jealous Englishmen per head of the population as there are in either Greece or Australia,' retorted Grace.

'But don't you like it when men get jealous? It makes me feel kind of wanted.' Kelly's voice was wistful.

Had a man ever been jealous of her, Grace wondered? If they had, she had not been aware of it and she had a strong feeling jealousy was not part of Roger's emotional makeup, it certainly was not part of hers. 'I don't think jealousy necessarily proves that you're wanted. Jealousy is about possession, not love. Mutual respect for each other's feelings should preclude any need for jealousy in a relationship.'

Yanni had been leaning against the door listening. Now he straightened up, dropped his cigarette on the floor and extinguished it with his shoe. 'Then I cannot think you know love.' He came and stood beside Grace. 'Have you never seen someone...in a crowd perhaps, you do not know their name, perhaps you see this person only once, never again. But you see each other,' he gestured at his eyes for emphasis, 'and you are filled with...' He searched for the right word, '...a hunger to have them? You are...how do you say...strangers, and yet, in that one look, you see into each other's very soul?'

Her chin resting on her hands, Kelly gazed enraptured up at Yanni. She let out a long sigh. 'Isn't he romantic? Did you know he's the village poet Grace?'

'Really?' Grace sat back and looked at Yanni. 'Shall I tell you what I think happens after these so-called lovers' eyes meet across a crowded room and they rush into each others' arms? She discovers that he cuts his toenails in bed and only wants sex after his favourite football team wins, and he complains that she can't cook like his mother and won't let him go out drinking with the boys every night. That kind of romance never lasts, it can't. You have to get to know someone properly before you can love them and that takes time and effort.'

Yanni shrugged his shoulders. 'Most people, they are blind, both with their heart and their eyes. They only see and feel what they want to. Love cannot be made by men. It is the gift of the gods.'

'The gods!' snapped Grace. 'I've heard enough superstitious nonsense about the gods this morning to last me a lifetime. It seems to me that men and women make their gods in whatever shape and form they want them.'

Kelly looked shocked and crossed herself. 'You shouldn't say things like that Grace honey, it's bad luck.'

The incongruity of Kelly making the sign of the cross made Grace want to throw back her head and laugh, but all that came out was a harsh croak. She covered her face with her hands.

'I'm sorry,' she managed after a moment or two, 'I'm afraid it's been one of those mornings.'

Kelly patted her leg. 'Don't you worry about it honey, take your time. Yanni will bring you a nice glass of lemonade, won't you Yanni?'

He nodded and went inside the taverna. Kelly produced a packet of tissues from her copious beach bag and handed one to Grace, who gratefully wiped her face. Yanni returned with three glasses of lemonade and sat down. Grace thirstily gulped hers.

Kelly waited until she had finished and then leant across the table. 'Now, you're among friends - tell us what happened.'

Grace considered this for a moment or two. Perhaps because she had been an only child in a household in which the emphasis - at least by her grandmother, Eleanor - had been on self-reliance, she had never been one for sharing confidences. Even at school she had not made any close friends of the kind who shared secrets. Problems were for solving, not sharing. However, right at that moment her world - the rational world back in London, a world over which she had some control - seemed a long way away. She put her glass down on the table and gazed at it for a moment or two, then looked up.

'I went to the women's camp this morning. My mother appears to be involved with a woman.'

Kelly's eyes grew wide. 'You mean...*involved* with a woman?'

Grace nodded.

'But how can your mother be a...one of those? I mean, she's your mother...she's had you...your father...'

'Having children does not preclude a woman being a lesbian,' said Grace a little dryly.

Kelly's pink-lipsticked mouth made a little 'o' shape at this revelation.

'I came here because she wrote to say she was in some kind of trouble. I assumed it was a man, it usually is.' Grace tried to smile, but her lips refused to co-operate.

'But how could she...? I mean, if she likes men...?' Kelly's eyes looked ready to pop out of her head.

'My mother is very easily led,' said Grace.

'This other woman, she is very strong. I can feel it,' said Yanni. 'Your mother is lonely, she meets this other one...' he shrugged, 'it is not good for a woman to be alone.'

Kelly nodded vigorously. 'Yanni's right you know. I couldn't bear to be without a man, not for a minute. Perhaps it would help if you found her a nice man?'

'My mother is perfectly capable of finding herself a man and they're not always nice,' said Grace. 'A man was the reason she came here in the first place; she was trying to get over yet another broken love affair.'

Kelly's smooth brow wrinkled earnestly. 'Since your fiancé isn't here, do you want me to ask Ari to have a word with your mother? He's very good at sorting things out. People listen to him.'

Despite herself, the thought of Ari talking to her mother made Grace smile. 'That's very kind of you Kelly, but I can sort this out by myself, really. In fact, I'd be grateful if you didn't mention this to your husband. The fewer people who know about it the better.'

'Oh but everyone knows, at least about the camp. People have even been talking about getting rid of them. Some of the men in the village say that they are giving Greek women ideas.' Kelly giggled. 'The men are jealous. They think tourist women coming here should only fancy them. Ari says they ought to evict them as they give the place a bad name.'

'Evict, what does this mean, evict?' asked Yanni.

'Get rid of them, send them away,' explained Grace.

'But they are not bad. I do not much like women together with women,' Yanni shrugged, 'but people should do what they want.'

'Well, Ari's been talking to his cousin Taki, the village President about it, but nobody is quite sure who owns the land beside the beach. Ari says...'

'Do I hear my name being taken in vain?' Ari's voice interrupted loudly.

Kelly's lips parted in a wide smile as she greeted her husband, but Grace saw a momentary look of anxiety in her eyes or was it fear? 'Ari, darling, I was just telling them about the camp and your plans for getting rid of the women.'

Ari sat down and put a muscular arm around Kelly's neck. 'Now, what have I told my little sugar plum about talking about my business when I'm not around? Anyway, I'm sure Grace isn't interested.'

Yanni stood up and walked away. The two men had not acknowledged each other.

Ari called after him: 'Coffee, and make it snappy.'

For a moment, Grace wondered whether Yanni would ignore this rude order, but he turned back, his face was expressionless.

'Greek or Nescafe?'

'Real coffee,' snapped Ari. 'That Greek stuff tastes like powdered mud. And milk and two sugars,' he called after Yanni's retreating back.

'Ari dear, you promised. Where are your sweeteners?' Kelly began to hunt around in her bag again.

'I don't care what the damn doctors say. I need sugar first thing in the morning to get the adrenalin going. Stop fussing woman.'

'He really is a very naughty man,' Kelly looked appealingly across to Grace. 'He's been told so many times that he has to cut down on sugar and fat.'

'Have you ever seen a finer figure of a man, Grace?' demanded Ari, thumping his chest. 'I've never felt better in my life and I'm fitter than a man half my age.' He fondled Kelly's thigh. 'If you come back to the villa, I'll prove it to you right now.'

Kelly went red under her tan and pushed his hand away.

Grace stood up. 'I think I'll be going. Thanks for the drink, Kelly. It was very kind of you.'

Kelly looked up. 'Oh, but I'd hoped we might go to the beach together today. You wouldn't mind would you, sweetie pie?' she appealed to Ari. 'You said you had some business to attend to. You're always telling me to go and enjoy myself.'

Ari's expression was anything but sweet, but he waved a dismissive hand at them. 'You girls go and have fun, but keep out of mischief.'

Kelly jumped to her feet and almost pulled Grace away. Once they were out of earshot she giggled with relief.

'Thank goodness you were there. He was in one of his moods this morning, and I hate it when he gets like that. You don't mind do you, Grace? It would be so nice to have a girlie gossip about men and things. You haven't got anything else planned have you?'

Grace wearily shook her head. What was the point of her having any plans? Everyone else seemed to have already made them for her.

TEN

'I do wish you hadn't been quite so frank last night Lilith darling. Grace looked awfully upset.' Marjorie bit into a slice of watermelon and leant back against the trunk of the small pine tree in whose shade they had pitched their tent.

She waved her handkerchief futilely in front of her face. It was mid-afternoon, and the heat was intense. If she craned her neck, she could glimpse the shimmering cobalt blue sea through a gap in the tents pitched in front of them. She considered going for a swim, but the thought of walking even a few steps in the heat made her feel faint. Instead, she closed her eyes and indulged herself in a fantasy that had come to obsess her of late. Unlike her usual fantasies, it featured neither sex nor food, but a cool, marble-floored hotel room, with a large, comfortable bed, crisp white linen sheets that were changed every day, and an enormous tiled bathroom, with hot and cold running water and an endless supply of fluffy towels. Had it really been *only* three months since she had been in a hotel like that in Athens? Her pleasant reverie was interrupted by a large fly buzzing around her head, causing Marjorie to open her eyes and flail wildly at it.

Lilith, who was sitting cross-legged beside her on the ground, slicing the melon, stopped what she was doing for a moment. 'It's only a fly for chrissakes, it won't hurt you. It has as much right to live as you have. Just ignore it.' She finished cutting a slice of melon and bit hungrily into it. As she ate, she spat the seeds onto the ground. She wiped her mouth with the back of her hand. 'I don't know why you're worried about your daughter. She's a grown woman. You don't have to answer to her anymore than she has to answer to you.'

Marjorie sighed. 'I wish it was as easy as that. I intended to tell Grace about us in my own time and in my own way. She has led a rather more sheltered life than you or I, and she's terribly conventional, particularly about me. She has this idea that I should behave like a proper mother. However, her idea of motherhood is some kind of 1950s ideal home fantasy - all roses round the door, frilly aprons and the scent of freshly baked bread. I blame my mother for bringing Grace up to think the way she does. It was typical of her - she never baked a loaf of bread in her life, or wore a frilly apron for that matter, but she thought everybody else should.'

'But you were raised by her and you didn't turn into little Miss Sugar and Spice did you, so what went wrong?'

Marjorie shrugged her shoulders. 'Perhaps the genes jumped a generation and Grace got my share as well as her own. She even behaved well when she was a baby. Everyone warned me about how awful it would be when she was born, that I would be up half the night with her crying and how she would make such a mess, but she never did. She was the perfect baby. She never cried; she slept all night; and she never got dirty. My mother said I didn't deserve a baby like her.' She cradled the watermelon between her hands, looking pensive. 'Grace was such a beautiful child - everyone said so. She had these enormous brown eyes, too big for her face, which seemed to follow you everywhere. I know it sounds silly, but after a while, I felt her eyes were reproaching me for being an awful mother. I never seemed to be able to do anything right. I was hopeless at changing nappies; made a mess of feeding her; left her behind in a shop; and once I nearly drowned her in the bath. Grace was too small to complain of course, but my mother more than made up for her. After a while I felt as though I would never be a good enough mother and so I left.' Her eyes glistened with tears. 'I did love Grace, I truly did, but I was very young and my mother was only too willing to play the martyr and look after her. Abandoning my baby was one more thing she could add to the litany of sins I had committed.' A tear rolled down her cheek and she fumbled for a handkerchief.

Lilith dropped her watermelon skin on the ground and put her arm around Marjorie's shoulders, drawing her close.

'Your mother was just as much a victim as you were. Women are trapped in a perpetual circle of abuse. Patriarchal society denies women power outside the domestic sphere, so the only part of their life over which they have power is their children, particularly their daughters, so it's inevitable that they end up bearing the brunt of their mothers' frustration. The victim becomes the victimiser - it's a classic syndrome.' Lilith stroked Marjorie's hair as she talked. 'But you mustn't let either your mother or Grace lay a guilt trip on you. From what you told me about how you got pregnant, you were raped. You were an innocent child of sixteen. That man took advantage of your innocence, but you were the one who was branded for transgressing the laws of society although they really ought to be called the laws of men, because that's what they are. Laws made by men, for men, in order to give men power. All this liberty and justice stuff is just a heap of steaming bullshit. In a world ruled by masculine values and masculine gods, nature and women are used and abused. They are all the same thing you know - the rape of women and the rape of nature. It's no accident that nature is referred to as "she". Why can't people understand?' It was Lilith's turn to sound despairing. 'What makes it worse is that even some women seem to want to ignore the connection between gender and the environment.' She waved her hand at the other tents. 'Since the eighties, women have begun to think that the revolution is over and feminism is dead, but they're wrong. We've allowed ourselves to be bought off for the price of a few cosmetic changes.'

'Well *we* haven't and I'm sure lots of other women will come round to your way of thinking soon,' declared Marjorie, earning herself a kiss and one of Lilith's rare smiles.

She closed her eyes and rested her head against Lilith's shoulder. She felt a comfortable sense of well-being. Although she wished Lilith would relax more and not relate everything to politics, which could be a bit tiresome after a time, she loved the way that Lilith always took her side. Other people never understood about Grace, but Lilith did. Why should mothers always have to be martyrs for their children's sake?

Being with Lilith made her feel young and carefree again, almost as though she was sixteen again, in the summer when everything changed. It had been hot then too, almost as hot as Greece, but while the heat in Greece made her just want to lie still in a cool place, the English heat had made her feel restless and prickly. She wanted to run naked down the high street and dive into the fountain near the War Memorial - *anything* to wake up the stuffy town where she lived, where even the sight of a pair of bare, unstockinged legs at the end of the 1950s was tantamount to declaring that you were a prostitute. The more she thought about it, the more she was convinced that her mother, and all those other narrow-minded people in the town where she grew up, practically *drove* her into having sex because they were so obsessed with it. Not that anyone in her mother's circle ever mentioned the word 'sex' - heaven forbid. Yet they acted as though sex was some alien horde threatening to overwhelm them if they ever let down their guard.

Perhaps they were frightened because despite all their best efforts, the alien hordes of London had managed to creep up on them and were now at their doorsteps. Until the mid-1950s, their town had been a leafy, gentle place, complete with a cricket green, duck pond and old manor house. Then, one morning, they woke up to find they had become just another outer London suburb. Beyond their well-kept lawns and neatly-clipped hedges, there now lay a vast sprawling metropolis, full of people they would rather not have as neighbours. However, they continued to fight hard to keep up the pretence that they still lived in the Home Counties, and that meant keeping sex - like undesirable neighbours - at bay.

It seemed to Marjorie that her mother saw sex in everything: in council estates; in women who wore slacks in the street; in the back seats of the local cinema; and, most dangerous of all, in coffee bars. When a vigilant member of her mother's bridge group spotted Marjorie in the newly opened coffee bar in the High Street, she was branded a scarlet woman. Feeling she had nothing to lose, Marjorie set out to live up to her reputation, and celebrated her sixteenth birthday by getting drunk on cider and seducing Edward, the vicar's eighteen-year-old son.

She settled on Edward to divest her of her virginity, not because she particularly fancied him, but because her mother always held him up as an example of the kind of nice, respectable boy who could do no wrong. However, the experience did not prove as much fun as Marjorie expected. Edward's experience of girls was limited to pouring tea for them at the Young Christian meetings his mother held in their drawing room every Saturday afternoon.

Copious glasses of cider had weakened his resolve, helped by the corrupting influence of a large portion of Marjorie's chocolate birthday cake, for while he was painfully thin, Edward had a voracious appetite. Unfortunately, when called upon to perform his allotted task, both his nerves and the cider almost got the better of him except for one brief moment when his flesh became willing. However, just as it seemed he might finally succeed in reaching his objective, Edward suddenly, and due to the chocolate cake, spectacularly, threw up over the back seat of his father's new car, impregnating the upholstery with a singularly distinctive and unpleasant aroma, which their combined efforts at scrubbing failed to disperse.

In the ensuing inquisition, Marjorie, who was practised in the art of resisting parental interrogation, adopted a policy of silence. Sadly, Edward, who had hitherto led a largely blameless existence, was unfamiliar with such tactics. On being questioned as to why they had been occupying the back seat of the car - a question prefaced by a reminder as to the wages of sin - he promptly, and tearfully, confessed.

The ensuing telephone call from his father the Vicar to Marjorie's mother had for a short time at least, made Eleanor consider converting to the local Wesleyan chapel. However, as this would be to put herself and her family beyond the social pale, she opted instead for getting Marjorie out of town until the scandal died down and it was time to return to school in the autumn. An exchange trip to France provided the opportunity, and it came with the added bonus that Marjorie's extremely poor French might be improved.

When her place of exile was announced, Marjorie protested loudly as was expected of her, but she was secretly delighted. France and all things French, like Brigitte Bardot and Alain Delon, were all the rage that year. She had visions of sitting in a small cafe on the Left Bank sipping Pernod, while an impossibly handsome Frenchman gazed adoringly into her eyes and called her 'ma chérie'.

Unfortunately, Marjorie's hopes were soon dashed. Her mother selected the family to which she was going to entrust her wayward child with great care. Monsieur and Madame Rouault were as respectable, Protestant, and socially upstanding as Eleanor could have wished. Instead of living in a nineteenth century apartment, guarded by an aged concierge, in a chic district of central Paris, they lived in a large, gloomy house in an outer Parisian suburb that could have doubled for Marjorie's home area, had it not been for the road signs.

Their seventeen-year-old daughter, Marie-Hélène, also proved a disappointment. Marjorie and her friends thought all French girls had chic, Chanel No 5 and sex in their bloodstreams, but not Marie-Hélène. She proved to be a large, clumsy girl, who still played with dolls and who wore ribbons in her hair. However, the Rouault family did at least have one advantage - Monsieur Rouault thought holidays a waste of time and money and, unlike other Parisians, the family did not join the annual exodus to the country and the coast in August. So at least Marjorie could comfort herself with the thought that she was going to spend eight weeks in Paris. Anywhere else would have been unbearably provincial.

She spent the first week of her stay in her room, ignoring Marie-Hélène's pleas to come and play with her dolls, and venturing out only at mealtimes, when she stubbornly resisted Madame Rouault's attempts to engage her in French conversation. However, while appearing to ignore the Rouault household, Marjorie was, in reality, observing them. The Rouaults soon revealed themselves as creatures of habit. Marie-Hélène went upstairs no later than nine o'clock, while her parents went promptly to bed at ten every night, and slept the deep sleep of those confident that all was right with their well-ordered world. Armed with this information and a map, on the eighth night Marjorie slipped out into the warm Parisian night with the aid of a tree handily growing outside her window, and made for the centre of the city.

Her late night explorations began cautiously at first, but within a few days, she found her way to the Left Bank. It was already after midnight, and it was a long walk back to the Rouault's, but just as she decided that it was time to start back, the soaring tones of a tenor sax in mid-jazz solo made her stand and listen.

Entranced by the sound, Marjorie followed it, clambering down a flight of shaky, wrought-iron steps to a rank smelling basement area where an open door announced a late-night club. Inside, the thick, fragrant fog of French cigarettes replaced the smell of urine and mouldering rubbish, and Marjorie spent the last francs in her purse on a Pernod. For the next hour, she sat at a table at the back, eking out her drink by adding water, listening to the music and watching the other patrons. She was entranced both by the way they smoked their cigarettes with an elegant insouciance - far from the hungry, almost desperate, puffs of English smokers, and by what they wore - mainly black jeans and black tops - whether they were men or women. At last, she had found the Paris she craved.

The music was also unlike anything she had heard in England. What little English jazz she had heard was like fairground oompah music compared to the liquid sounds which swirled and swooped around her, yet when she closed her eyes, it was as though they came from some place deep inside her. She had never seen men like the musicians who were playing either - they were black. She had heard about black people, or coloureds, as her mother called them, but had never seen any before, at least not in the flesh. What surprised and intrigued her was that they were indeed coloured rather than black. She had assumed that all black people were a uniform colour, but the men on the small stage varied from a deep, almost blue-black, to a pale coffee colour with other shades in between. However, it was to the sax player her eyes were drawn. He was very tall and elegantly lean, with skin like beaten gold and seemed to be in a musical world of his own.

In a break in the music, Marjorie glanced at her watch and realised with a shock that she had to leave if she was to get back to the Rouault's before daylight. She reluctantly reached for her bag in the hope she had a couple of sous to leave as a tip, but just at that moment, the barman brought over another drink. In halting French, Marjorie attempted to explain that she had no money left to pay, but the waiter gestured that someone in the band had sent it over. Deciding to risk the wrath of the Rouaults in order to discover the identity of her mystery admirer, Marjorie waited until the band had finished playing. That was when the tenor sax player came over to her table and introduced himself.

The exact features of Erroll's face had long since faded from Marjorie's memory, but she could still remember the expression on his face when he played as though it was only a moment ago. She could remember his voice, too. He spoke with a rich, southern drawl that was as melodic as his music.

She never told him she was a sixteen-year-old schoolgirl on holiday from England, and that she was forced to shin down a tree outside her bedroom window every night to come to the club. Instead, she had pretended to be an art student, and prayed that he would not ask to see any of her paintings.

The club became her destination every night she could get away safely. She always sat at the same table, drinking Pernod and watching Erroll. In between sets he would join her and talk about jazz. Marjorie knew nothing about music, but would tried to look suitably sophisticated by blowing long streams of smoke from her Gitanes cigarettes while Erroll spoke in reverent tones of people she had never heard of like Lestor Young, Coleman Hawkins and John Coltrane. He talked too, of how he planned to open his own club in New York one day. When the band finished playing for the night, they would stroll hand-in-hand beside the River Seine, exchanging velvet kisses like so many other lovers in the Parisian night.

Marjorie was blissfully happy, so much so that she became a model guest, eager to abide by the rules and go to bed early as well as replying in halting French whenever she was spoken to. Madame and Monsieur Rouault congratulated themselves on her transformation, believing it signified yet another example of Gallic superiority over Anglo-Saxon barbarity, however, their daughter, Marie-Hélène, was not so easily taken in.

Marjorie had made one small, but fatal, mistake. Because she had decided Marie-Hélène was of little interest to her, she assumed she was of little interest to Marie-Hélène. However, when, five weeks into her stay, Marjorie was presented with the evidence of her nightly time of departure and length of absence, painstakingly detailed in Marie-Hélène's neat italic script, she realised too late that she had been woefully guilty of underestimating her.

Marjorie looked up from the notebook. Opposite her at the dinner table, Marie-Hélène was squirming excitedly in her chair, an expression of triumph on her round shiny face. At the head of the table, Monsieur Rouault held his head high as though his nose was trying to avoid a faint but unpleasant odour. For a moment there was silence, then Madame Rouault pointed a long, accusatory finger at Marjorie.

'You are like a *veeperr* in the bosom of my family,' she said in heavily accented English, no doubt not wishing to be misunderstood, 'and I demand that you are immediately expelled from my house before you can defile it *furtherr*.'

Monsieur Rouault coughed dryly. 'I am afraid that is not possible, at least not immediately. Her expulsion must be delayed until her parents return from their holidays in Scotland, which is not for another week. No matter what their daughter has done, I believe we have a duty to the parents. In the meantime, I suggest that her bed is moved into Marie-Hélène's room. Perhaps there she will learn something of how a young girl of good family should behave.' He glanced down at his watch. 'Alors, now we must eat. It is already four minutes late past the hour for dinner.' With that, he rang the bell by his plate for the housekeeper to serve soup.

Placed in the custody of her denouncer until she could be taken to the Gare du Nord and placed on the boat-train home, Marjorie expected little mercy. However, to her astonishment, once they were alone, Marie-Hélène demanded to hear all the details of her liaison with Erroll. At first, she refused, but Marie-Hélène's pleas grew louder and more insistent, threatening to attract the attentions of her parents and further punishment, so Marjorie reluctantly relented.

Marie-Hélène proved an unexpectedly gratifying audience. She pressed for every last detail about every kiss, to the point where even Marjorie's colourful descriptive powers were exhausted. However, when Marjorie had finished, Marie-Hélène looked at her with pity.

'Eh bien, all you did was kiss? Rien d'autre? You did not, how you say...fuck?' She sniffed derisively, her nostrils curling. 'Ce n'est pas grand'chose.'

Marie-Helene's expressive shrug seemed to say that not only had Marjorie let Marie-Hélène down, but that she had also failed England. A gloomy silence descended.

Marjorie lay back on her bed, her hands behind her head, ignoring Madame Rouault's instructions to remove her shoes. She considered telling Marie-Hélène about Edward, but even with some judicious embroidery, she did not think what had happened with Edward would restore her reputation as a sexual adventuress.

On the other side of the room, Marie-Hélène thoughtfully brushed the golden tresses of one of the vast array of dolls that covered her bed. She fluffed up the doll's layers of lace petticoats and then carefully placed it back on the heart-shaped satin cushion that lay on her pillow.

'Bon. J'ai décidée,' said Marie-Hélène, seemingly addressing the doll.

Marjorie raised herself on one elbow. She had the impression that the dolls were Marie-Hélène's only friends. She certainly had not met any others during her stay.

Marie-Hélène straightened the doll's limbs. 'She must go and I will help.'

'Go? Go where?' asked Marjorie.

'To your *loverr*,' replied Marie-Hélène, rolling out the last part of the word on her tongue.

'What about your parents?'

The corners of Marie-Hélène's mouth turned down and she shrugged.

Marjorie sat up. She had underestimated Marie-Hélène once again.

'Il faut...we must choose your dress with care, n'est ce pas? Tonight will be a big night. It must be *purrfect*,' said Marie-Hélène.

With that, she opened the doors of the carved oak armoire that stood in the corner of her bedroom to reveal a selection of dressing up clothes that matched anything she put on her dolls. She turned back to Marjorie and with a broad smile, held out her hands: '*Voilà!*'

After much discussion and trying on, Marjorie's outfit was agreed: a pale pink, swirly satin skirt, a black and white hooped top, red ballet pumps and a black beret. After Marjorie had paraded up and down several times, and Marie-Hélène had adjusted the beret so she was satisfied that it perched at just the right angle on the side of Marjorie's head, they passed a couple of happy hours applying make up to each other's faces and sharing secrets. When the clock in the hall chimed half-past ten and it was time for Marjorie to leave, they clung tearfully to each other, swearing undying friendship. Then

Marjorie stood to attention as Marie-Hélène completed a last, approving inspection, setting her beret at an even jauntier angle.

As the door to Marjorie's bedroom had been locked, her normal escape route was no longer accessible, but yet again, Marie-Hélène proved resourceful. She led the way silently downstairs, indicating which step creaked in a way that suggested she was familiar with the art of creeping around the house at night undetected. She took Marjorie through the large kitchen to the larder which was kept locked at night by Madame Rouault. There, she produced a piece of twisted wire that she inserted into the keyhole with a practised hand. Almost immediately, there was a click and the door opened.

With every passing moment, Marjorie was gaining more respect for her roommate. She had wondered why Marie-Hélène was so plump when the meals served in the Rouault household were so parsimonious. Now she understood both the reason for Marie-Hélène's girth, and the bewilderment of the cooks that Madame Rouault fired so regularly, believing that they were dishonest and stole food.

The larder led to another small, dank room that had a seldom-used door leading into the back garden. After drawing back a large number of rusty bolts, Marie-Hélène proved her dexterity with the twisted wire once more, and after the application of both their shoulders, the door opened.

'I will wait,' whispered Marie-Hélène. 'Tap on the kitchen window and I will open the door.'

Marjorie was just about to ask her what she would do in the intervening hours, but she had the feeling that the contents of the larder would help pass the time, and that another innocent and bewildered cook would get her notice in the morning.

They kissed on both cheeks. Marie-Hélène clutched Marjorie's arm so tightly it hurt. 'Eh bien, remember, I must be told tout - *everything*,' she whispered urgently.

Feeling as though she was setting off to join the French Foreign Legion, Marjorie made her now familiar way across Paris to the club. August was nearly over, and Parisians had started to return from their annual holidays, so the club was much busier than usual, but a table was soon found for her. All the waiters now knew her as 'la copine d'Erroll', and as such, she was accorded the kind of deference not usually reserved for under-aged English schoolgirls.

Although Monsieur Rouault had confiscated her remaining francs, Marie-Hélène had loaned her some money for her fares as well as to buy a drink or two. However, it was a hot night and Marjorie was thirsty as well as nervous. She ordered her usual Pernod and added water before drinking it quickly down. She signalled to a waiter for another and drank it just as quickly but this time, she added less water. Spotting that she had arrived, Erroll sent her a drink. Soon, Marjorie had lost count of how many drinks she had had, and by the time the band finished playing their last set, she was decidedly drunk.

'Hey sweet thing,' Erroll stood beside her table, his dark eyes looked concerned. 'Are you okay? You don't look too good.'

Marjorie did not feel too good either, but she tried to smile. 'I'm fine. I just need a little fresh air, that's all.'

Erroll held out his right hand. 'We can soon fix that. Let's go for a stroll.'

Marjorie managed to climb the stairs to the street without stumbling, but when they emerged into the cool night air, she swayed and then stumbled as waves of nausea threatened to engulf her. Years later, Marjorie would describe to a friend how Erroll had swept her up in his arms and carried her to his rented room not far from the club. However, if she had told the truth, she could not remembered how they got to his room, only that they had got there and that the next thing she remembered was the sound of her own outraged cries as Erroll held her under a cold shower dressed only in her underwear. When she was able to stand unaided, he left her to dry herself while he crouched on the floor in the corner of the room and brewed some coffee over a small camping gas burner.

Her head throbbing and her hair and makeup in ruins, Marjorie wrapped herself in a towel and perched on his unmade bed as there was nowhere else to sit. It was then that she noticed that the only signs that the monastic room was occupied were an open music score, and an empty condom packet.

Erroll thrust a large bowl of very black coffee into her hands, and then stretched out on the bed beside her and lit a Gitanes. He grinned at her. 'I promise I didn't peek when I helped you undress. Usually when someone's had a little bit more to drink than is good for them, I put them under the shower fully clothed, but I thought you might not want to get your clothes wet.'

Marjorie glumly sipped the coffee even though it burned her mouth, not daring to look in his direction. She had made such a fool of herself.

When she had drained the coffee, Erroll propped himself up on one elbow and offered her his cigarette. He studied her face.

'You look much prettier without all that shit painted over your face.' He laughed. 'You almost look like a kid without it.'

Marjorie, who was attempting to look stylish as she inhaled, swallowed a lung-full of smoke and began to choke.

'Hey, I'm sorry… What did I say?' Erroll sat up and took the cigarette away. Then he began to gently massage her back, causing the towel to slip off her shoulders.

Had she sought out his lips first or had he found hers? All Marjorie could remember was that sex would forever taste of Gitanes cigarettes and bitter black coffee.

ELEVEN

The early morning streets of Paris were a misty haze of blues and greys as Marjorie left Erroll's room. She bought a hot croissant from a bakery that had just opened and ate it, sitting on a park bench, listening to the morning chorus of birds. Seeing a bus with the Roualt's destination on the front, she ran to catch it, settling down breathless but thankful in her seat.

Despite the early hour and her lack of sleep, Marjorie was bubbling over with the things to tell Marie-Hélène. When her gentle tap on the kitchen window was answered by the opening of the back door, she smiled triumphantly, ready to greet Marie-Hélène. However, her smile became a round 'oh' of surprise as she was confronted by Monsieur Rouault, white-faced with outrage, dressed in a long nightshirt, his usually brilliantined hair standing on end.

He presented a comical figure, but any amusement Marjorie felt disappeared when she saw the chaos in the kitchen. It seemed that Marie-Hélène was prone to over-eat when she was excited and the strain of waiting for her to come back proved too much. She had consumed most of the contents of the larder and been horribly sick, causing her parents to wake up and discover Marjorie's absence. Now, fearing the corruption of their daughter, the Rouaults were not prepared to delay Marjorie's banishment from their house a moment longer. Several angry phone calls to England resulted in Marjorie catching the boat train to Victoria the next day and her parents returning early from their holiday.

Her mother's fury descended like a black cloud over the Hamilton house, suffocating all but the most essential communication. With the threat of being sent away to boarding school hanging over her head like the sword of Damocles, Marjorie became the model daughter and pupil, surprising herself and her teachers by coming top of the class at the end of term. Her glowing school report seemed to satisfy everyone but her mother, who pointed out that this only proved how lazy Marjorie had been in the past.

It took months, but as Christmas approached, the first sign that perhaps her mother was softening at last came when she gave Marjorie permission to go to a party. Marjorie did not much like the girl who was giving the party. Not only was she one of the most boring people in her class, but Majorie's mother approved of her. However, Marjorie didn't care - it was a party and she had not been allowed out for months.

She rushed upstairs to try on her party dresses, determined that would enjoy herself, even if she had to be home by eleven and it was unlikely that anything stronger than fruit punch would be served. However, as Marjorie tried on one dress after another, the buttons that strained across her chest and the zips that refused to do up over her hips, finally forced her to admit what she had been trying to ignore for nearly five months. Her blossoming breasts and increasing waistline were not just due to puppy fat, and neither were her missed periods just the adolescent 'blips' she had read about in women's magazines - she was pregnant.

Marjorie sat down on her bed among her discarded party dresses. Paris seemed like a distant dream. She had even begun to convince herself that Erroll had not existed other than in her imagination, but here, growing rapidly inside her was the all-too concrete proof that he did.

She squeezed her eyes shut and clenched her fists, refusing to cry. It was all so stupid. Only girls who lived on council estates got pregnant - the kind of girls Marjorie and her friends laughed at. Now those same friends would laugh about her. Not to her face - that would be awful, but bearable - no, to her face they would be all gushing sympathy, but behind her back they would laugh at her. Soon the news would be round the whole school and then everyone would be laughing at her - the girl who went too far. Marjorie knew because it had happened to a girl in the year above her and she had been one of the one's who had laughed loudest. How could anyone be so stupid? The girl had been so ashamed she had left school and nobody had heard of her since.

Marjorie felt wretched. There was nobody she could to turn to, at least, nobody she could trust, and then she thought of her father. Robert Hamilton was a large, amiable man, whose vague, almost forgetful air belied the fact that he was the senior partner of a prosperous firm of City solicitors. When Marjorie was a child, it was to him she had run for comfort rather than her mother, and it was into his large hand she slipped hers when the three of them were out walking. As she grew older, her father had patiently mediated between her and her mother as their disagreements became louder and ever more bitter, and although he never quite sided with her, he never told her off either. However, if Marjorie had hoped that he would act as peacemaker this time, she was to be disappointed.

Before dinner that night, she put on the blue floral dress she knew her father liked. She disliked it because she thought its puff sleeves and high waist were childish, however it was now the only dress which still fitted her and its loose fit had the added the benefit of concealing her expanding waistline. After they had eaten, she cleared the table and washed up without complaint, then carefully measured out her father's evening drink of two fingers of whisky, topped it with a splash of soda, and took it to his study where she perched herself on the armrest of his large, leather armchair.

They sat quietly for a while, only the loud ticking of the grandfather clock breaking their companionable silence. Then Marjorie kissed her father on his bald spot.

'Daddy...'

'My wallet is in my briefcase Maggie, you'll have to run and get it.'

Marjorie kissed him again. 'You *are* wicked, daddy. I don't always want money you know.'

'Well, if it's those driving lessons you're after, your mother says you have to wait until you're eighteen, and for once I agree with her.'

'Daddy! Can't I be nice to you without wanting something?'

He patted her on the knee. 'I'm only teasing. You know how I love my little girl.'

He helped himself to a cigar, snipped off the end and waited for Marjorie to strike a match in a routine they had followed for as long as Marjorie could remember. After he was satisfied that it was properly alight and had inhaled deeply, she tried again.

'Daddy... something's happened and I don't know how to tell mother. I thought if you told her, she might not get quite so angry.'

'Why you two girls can't get along better, I just don't understand. You should be the best of friends.'

Marjorie slipped on to his lap and put her arms round his neck. 'But you're my best friend.'

Her father ruffled her hair, smiling. 'That's as it maybe, but it does not excuse you yelling at your mother my girl. So what is it this time?'

Marjorie twisted her hair around her finger.

'Well, it's like this...you see... I think I'm going to have a baby.'

Her father, who had the high colour of many sandy-haired people, went brick red, his eyes grew wide and he made a strangled sound as though gasping for breath. For one terrifying moment, Marjorie thought he was having a stroke. She jumped to her feet, wondering anxiously whether she should call for help as his lips were moving as though forming words, but no sound came out.

After a moment or two, her father regained his voice but it was cold and distant, as though an invisible barrier had sprung up between them. 'This is something women deal with Marjorie, go talk to your mother.'

After that, her father disappeared as a presence in Marjorie's life. He came and went as before, and sat opposite her at meals, but somehow, he was never around when she wanted to talk to him, his study door always closed. Her mother said he was busy, which Marjorie knew was untrue. Her mother also said the same of Marjorie when her friends telephoned or came to the door and soon they stopped calling.

Marjorie did not return to school after Christmas, and for the next two months, her mother kept her at home, forbidding her to leave the house except to take daily exercise walking around the garden, but only times when neighbours could not see her.

When Marjorie was seven months pregnant, and her condition was impossible to hide, even from the least observant, she was sent away to a clinic in Derbyshire. It was a home for unmarried mothers, but it masqueraded under the title of clinic because its clients were the daughters of families that demanded discretion and were prepared to pay high fees to guarantee it.

Despite the circumstance, Marjorie rather enjoyed being there. She quickly became firm friends with the two girls with whom she shared a room: Patsy, the fifteen-year-old daughter of a senior backbench Conservative MP, and Helena, who was seventeen, and the daughter of a retired Admiral and member of the House of Lords.

After lights out at night, the three of them swopped secrets and chainsmoked the cigarettes that Patsy smuggled into the clinic. Patsy was not sure who had fathered her baby but she seemed blithely unconcerned. 'There are three possible fathers and I'll know which one it is when it pops out. Eric is blond and looks like a Viking; Ron has ginger hair and is rather short, but oh so fiery and passionate; and Tony has thick, black, curly hair which gives me goosebumps just thinking about running my fingers through it and that's my problem,' she sighed dramatically. 'I just *can't* make up my mind between them, although I'm rather hoping that the baby will be ginger-haired because Ron's a Labour MP *and* a trade unionist, and my father will be absolutely *furious* if it's him,' she giggled.

Helena professed not to care what her baby looked like, and did not want to see it before it was taken away for adoption. She intended to marry the father, even though he was thirty-eight and already married. They planned to announce their engagement on her eighteenth birthday, allowing time for him to get a divorce, however a baby would complicate matters. 'Nobody who matters turns a hair about divorce these days, but it wouldn't look good to have a baby toddling down the aisle behind us on our wedding day, would it?' she appealed to Patsy and Marjorie, both of whom nodded their heads. 'Apart from anything else, Douglas says his wife would take him to the cleaners when it comes to the divorce settlement if she knew about it and as I'm young, there will be plenty of time for more children if I want them. His wife can't have any.'

Her roommates had wanted to know who the father of her baby was, but Marjorie hesitated before telling them. She had not told anyone about Erroll. Her mother had demanded to know who the father was, but despite threats to have her locked up in a mental asylum, Marjorie had refused to say.

'You can tell us,' begged Patsy, 'I mean...look at me, sleeping with three men, who am I to judge? If you tell us, we won't breathe a word to anyone. Cross our hearts and hope to die,' she said and they both crossed their hearts.

Marjorie took a deep breath. 'The father's name is Erroll, and he's an American jazz musician and he's coloured, you know, a Negro.'

Patsy and Helena stared at her, their eyes large and round. For a moment Marjorie regretted telling them. Then Patsy threw her arms in the air, 'Crazy! That beats both of us hands down. An American, a jazz musician and a Negro too. I want to know all the details. I've never slept with a coloured man.'

So Marjorie did, and then they stayed up late into the night debating what her baby would look like. Would it have its father's colouring, hers or maybe something in between? Marjorie laughed along with her newfound friends, pretending to enjoy their sophisticated banter, but after the others had finally gone to sleep, she lay awake, unable to sleep, staring into the darkness.

She knew she was not like Patsy and Helena. In their world, having an illegitmate baby seemed little more than a temporary inconvenience. However, in the world in which she had grown up, girls did not have illegitimate babies and walk away unscathed. There was a price to pay for breaking the rules and hers would surely be higher because she had slept with a black man. Even the baby inside her seemed to want to punish her. It felt like it was taking over her body, devouring her from within like a rapacious monster. Every day it grew larger, she felt she grew smaller. Soon there would be nothing left of her.

She was almost glad when her labour pains started, although as their intensity increased, it felt like the punishment she had feared and that it would last forever. It did not help that her midwife was an unsympathetic woman. When Marjorie screamed yet again, the midwife looked up from between her legs and snapped: 'Perhaps you should remember this before jumping into bed with a man again, but I doubt you will, girls these days have no shame.'

Then suddenly it was over and her baby was born. Marjorie struggled to sit up, but before she could catch a glimpse of her baby, it was whisked away.

'You may think we're being cruel,' said a cheerful Irishwoman who arrived a few minutes later and found her crying, 'but I think you'll find it's much better this way. If you don't see your baby, it's much easier to forget about it and you will you know. In a few years time you'll meet some nice man and get married and then you'll have lots of babies, just you wait and see. Now if you can walk, I'll take you to the room where you're to stay until your mother comes to collect you. The clinic won't allow you to remain in a room with girls who are still expecting. It's no good for them or for you. Now put this on.'

She helped Marjorie into a dressing gown and then led her to another wing of the clinic instead back to the room she shared with Patsy and Helena. When she saw the small, cell like room furnished with a single bed and a rail on which her clothes had been hung, Marjorie began to weep again.

The Irishwoman put her motherly arms around her and led her to the bed and sat her down. 'Now, now, it's just the effect of all those hormones, you'll soon feel better. Look, here's a bit of reading to help pass the time.' She pointed at some booklets about contraception had been left on the bed. 'Now for myself I don't hold with such things,' she said, 'but perhaps the clinic is right and you young girls should take a little more care. You wouldn't want to find yourself back here again now, would you? Oh, and if you're feeling a bid sore around...' she indicated her breasts her hands, 'that's normal, it's your milk. They'll feel a little tender for a week or so and then they'll be right as rain as though nothing has happened.' She delivered this with a cheerful smile, and then left Marjorie alone.

Marjorie was still sitting on her bed, sniffing when a little while later, she heard sounds outside her door. She went over and cautiously opened it to find Patsy and Helena outside. Fingers on their lips they pushed past her, but once the door was closed behind them, they burst into laughter.

'We'll be skinned alive if matron knew we were here,' said Patsy.

'But we had to come,' added Helena, 've seen your baby. We gave the nursery nurse ten bob and a packet of fags and she held her up.'

'She's gorgeous,' said Patsy. 'She has big brown eyes and dark hair...'

'And she has sort of pale brown skin, a bit like milky coffee,' finished Helena.

They sat down on her bed and Patsy produced some cigarettes. They all lit up.

'So,' Patsy demanded after she had inhaled deeply, 'tell us all, what was it like?'

'Like?' asked Marjorie.

'Having a baby,' said Helena. 'How did it feel? Did it hurt *terribly?*'

Marjorie puffed on her cigarette for a moment. 'No, it was ok,' she lied. 'It hardly hurt at all, but watch out for the midwife, she's a bit of a bitch. She reminded me of my headmistress.' She gave a theatrical shudder and they all laughed.

After Patsy and Helena had left, Marjorie lay alone in her room considering what they had told her about her baby. Up until then she had not thought about her baby as having a separate life from hers. In fact, she had tried very hard not to think about it at all. Yet according to Patsy and Helena, she had produced not just another human being with ten little fingers and ten little toes, but a pretty little daughter whom she would never see.

Although adoption had never been discussed, Marjorie knew that was what was expected. It was best for everyone. She had made a mistake, but adoption would correct it. What person in their right mind wanted to be saddled with a baby at seventeen? Yet even though Marjorie had told herself that she did not want a baby, now her body seemed to cry out that she did. Not just her painfully engorged breasts - every inch of her body ached to hold her baby in her arms.

The next day, Marjorie's mother arrived to take her home. She came into the room and sat down, straight-backed, in the chair beside the bed. She removed her gloves, smoothing them out on her lap, matching them finger against finger before folding them together and putting them into the large, square, black patent leather hand bag she always carried, before snapping the gilt lock shut, and all before she had even looked at Marjorie or said hello.

Marjorie sat on the bed, looking at the door, hoping against hope that her father would arrive and reassure her that she was still his little girl. Her mother read her glance. 'Your father's not coming. He has a reputation to protect, something you should have considered before you got yourself into this mess.' Her mother's words cut into Marjorie's flesh like razors.

Eleanor indicated the suitcase she had put beside the bed. 'Matron says you are well enough to leave, so I have brought you some more clothes. You're not coming home. I have enrolled you on a secretarial course in London and arranged for you to live in a hostel for young women while you attend. It's not what your father and I intended for you, but given the circumstances, I think it's best.' She stood up and placed her handbag over her arm. 'You can get dressed while I sign some papers in the office.'

Marjorie suddenly reached out and gripped her mother's arm with surprising strength. 'I want to keep my baby.'

Her mother prised her arm free. 'When you leave this place, you will never mention this unfortunate business again. Once I have signed the papers, the child will no longer be your concern. Your father and I have discussed it, and we are both of the same mind.' Her expression was implacable.

Marjorie rushed barefoot out of the door and ran wildly along the corridor, then down the stairs and along a second, long corridor, until she reached the nursery. She peered through the glass wall that allowed prospective adopters to view babies. The room contained twelve cots in three lines, identified only by numbers. An auxiliary nurse pushing a hamper full of laundry came out of the nursery leaving the door open behind her. She set off in the opposite direction down the corridor from Marjorie without noticing her. Marjorie seized her chance and went in, running from one cot to another, tears streaming down her face. The babies all looked so alike. Surely she should recognise her own baby instantly?

The door swung open to admit a nurse pushing a trolley loaded with feeding bottles. She looked startled when she saw Marjorie's distraught figure. 'Can I help you? Visitors are not normally allowed in here.'

'Which one's mine?' wailed Marjorie.

The nurse's expression softened a little. 'And who are you, dear?'

'Marjorie. I had a little girl yesterday.'

The nurse went over to a desk and picked up a clipboard. Her finger traced down a list and then she pointed at a cot and the end of a line. 'I really shouldn't tell you, but if your name's Hamilton, it's that one. She's a lovely little thing, so quiet you can almost forget she's there. Her new parents have already been in to see her. They've been waiting for a little girl. I think they're going to call her Penelope, such a pretty name.'

Marjorie stared down into the cot. Her baby seemed so small and fragile. She could not believe that anything so perfect could have come out of her body. She was almost frightened to touch it, fearing that she might hurt it. She hesitantly reached out and touched a tiny, curled hand. It opened out like a flower. In that moment, Marjorie knew she could not give her up, whatever her mother and the matron said. She felt someone at her shoulder. It was her mother. They stood looking down at the baby.

'I think we should discuss this in Matron's office,' said her mother after a few moments.

The discussion was long and difficult, but Marjorie had stood firm against both their anger and their blandishments, at one point threatening that she would get pregnant again if they did not let her keep her baby.

A week later, she returned home, defiantly holding Grace aloft like a trophy when she got out of the taxi so that all the neighbours could see. She did not care what they thought or said. She did not care what anyone said - or so she thought at the time.

TWELVE

Her defiance proved short-lived. Caring for Grace soon proved to be a nightmare from which Marjorie thought she would never wake. Not because of Grace - she was a quiet, undemanding child who rarely cried - but because of her mother. Despite the fact that her mother claimed she was far too busy to deal with a baby and that Marjorie would have to learn to cope by herself, Eleanor never left her alone for a moment. She was constantly at Marjorie's shoulder, criticising everything she did.

When, after six months of this, her mother suggested she do a secretarial course while she looked after Grace, Marjorie gratefully agreed. While she hated the idea of a being typist, and hated the idea of being away from Grace even more, she was desperate to be out of the house and away from the smell of boiling nappies and her mother's permanently pursed lips. After barely scraping through the course, she was offered a job in a local solicitor's office. Not because of her typing and shorthand speeds, which were abysmal, but because her mother sat on the Parish Council with the wife of the solicitor.

Then, just after her twenty-first birthday, when she was beginning to feel as though her life was over before she had even had a chance to live it, a miracle happened. A great-aunt, aged ninety-eight, died and left her a trust fund. It was only a small trust fund, but it offered Marjorie independence and she decided to grab it with both hands. Late one night, without telling her parents and after tearfully promising a peacefully sleeping Grace that she would come back for her as soon as possible, Marjorie crept out of the house with a suitcase and moved into a rented flat in Chelsea with three other girls.

The year was 1963. Although nobody knew it at the time, the heady days of what came to be called the Swinging Sixties were just beginning. Marjorie, who had no idea what she wanted to do with her life apart from having some long overdue fun, dived in head first.

One of her flatmates was a model, so Marjorie decided to call herself one too. She was young, slim, and pretty, and everyone said that she looked like a model so why not? Being a model opened doors - usually to parties it was true - but it sounded much more glamorous than saying you were a temp secretary, which was which she did when she found herself short of money.

As the months, and then the years, passed Marjorie continued to promise herself that soon, Grace would come and live with her, but somehow, the time never seemed right. She was convinced that modelling offers would start coming her way if only she was in the right place at the right time, but despite going to parties almost every night, none ever did. Once a photograph of her on the arm of a minor celebrity attending the opening of a nightclub appeared on the front page of a Sunday newspaper. This seemed to promise fame, but unfortunately, it brought fame of the wrong sort. The man was arrested for providing prostitutes to rich and powerful men, and Marjorie was forced to dye her hair and move flat in order to avoid the attentions of tabloid journalists who thought she was one of his so-called 'vice-girls'.

This did not help her relationship with her mother. Nor did her excuse that she had not really known the man in question and had only gone as his guest to the launch party as a favour to a friend. Even as the words came out of her mouth Marjorie realised she had only succeeded in making the situation worse.

As the years passed, her visits home grew less and less frequent. Seeing Grace made Marjorie feel guilty, and, as her mother complained that Marjorie's visits 'unsettled' Grace, she convinced herself that it was best for everyone if she stayed away. After all, Marjorie's parents could give Grace everything that she could not, like a settled home and a good school. Marjorie never seemed to know where she was going to be or what she was going to be doing from one day to the next. However, no matter how many times over the years Marjorie had tried to explain to Grace how difficult things had been when she was born, and why it had been so much better for her to stay with her grandmother, Grace never even seemed to want to try to understand. She just accused Marjorie of abandoning her because she wanted to have a good time. It was like hearing her mother's voice all over again. Anyway, what was the point of endlessly raking over the past? All that mattered was today.

Marjorie gently eased her head into a more comfortable position against Lilith's shoulder and looked up at Lilith's face. Lilith was asleep, but even when her eyes were shut, the expression on her face seemed fierce - it was the way her thick, dark eyebrows almost met in the middle. Marjorie reached up and gently traced the line of Lilith's eyebrows with a finger. When they first met, she had itched to take a pair of tweezers to them, but now she realised it was Lilith's eyebrows that gave her face the fearless expression she had come to love.

Before she met Lilith, Marjorie had never thought it was possible to love another woman. She wasn't even sure that she liked them very much. Apart from Patsy and Helena in the clinic, she had never even had many women friends, and although she had nothing against lesbians, she could not see the point of women having sex with each other. Yet the first time Lilith had kissed her on the lips, it had been the sweetest kiss Marjorie had felt for a very long time - filled with longing. It had aroused her in a way she had not thought possible, and that, combined with her loneliness, the wine they had drunk, and the wild, haunting music coming up from the square below, had made her let Lilith take charge that night in the hotel in Athens.

Marjorie yawned and closed her eyes. If she had known it was so much more relaxing being with a woman than with a man, she might have tried it long ago. She had not looked in a mirror or done any exercise in months, and at Lilith's insistence, she had discarded all her expensive creams and lotions. According to Lilith, the cosmetics industry was doubly oppressive to women. Not only did it trade on their insecurities and fuel a culture which valued them solely as commodities based on their outward appearance, but it also tested its products on animals, thereby not only abusing the rights of animals, but also obtaining the tacit collusion of women in their abuse.

Abandoning the tyranny of her daily beauty routine, which promised to de-wrinkle, smoothe, lighten, exfoliate, re-texture, polish, hydrate and regenerate her skin, had come as a unexpected relief. The claims made by all the different creams and lotions had begun to seem more like threats of what would happen to her skin if they were not applied religiously every day.

When Lilith said that she liked the way Marjorie looked, Marjorie believed her. When men said the same thing to her, particularly young men who claimed not to care that she was older than them, she had not believed them. How could they say age made no difference? It made a lot of difference to her. It was the reason why she craved their smooth, muscled young bodies.

She sailed through her menopause in her mid-forties with none of the hot flushes and loss of libido that other women suffered. In fact, she had suddenly found herself filled with a sexual energy that she had not previously felt, even when she was in her twenties. So it had seemed very cruel that, just as she felt at her most sexy, her body had decided to start looking decidedly middle-aged and unsexy. Annunzio had said her body was more beautiful than a young girl's because it was full and ripe, like a woman's body ought to be, and when she had looked into his unlined face and lustrous brown eyes, she had wanted to believe him. However, she had seen those same brown eyes follow every leggy twenty-something who walked by until she could bear it no more and had thrown him out of her flat.

After he had gone, she just had to get away from London. It should have been spring, but winter was grimly hanging on, shrouding every day in a chill, damp, greyness that reflected the way she felt. Without any definite plan in mind, Marjorie decided to head for the Greek islands where she had spent several glorious, seemingly endless, summers in the Sixties. She wanted to recapture that feeling of being young and free, of drifting from island to island, lying on warm, golden beaches all day and partying all night.

However, she had not made any allowance for the time of year, and had found herself standing outside a closed booking office on a deserted Piraeus dockside on a wet, chilly, Sunday morning in March, trying to make sense of the ferry timetable. She had blithely assumed that she would have a choice of dozens of different ferries going to dozens of different islands, but many of the ferry services did not start until Easter when the tourist season opened, while those that were operating did not sail very often. Shivering in her thin summer clothes, Marjorie ran her finger down the chart, trying to find a ferry that was leaving that morning, or even that day. She was about to give up in despair when she noticed another woman standing to one side of her, studying the board.

The woman was much better prepared than Marjorie for the weather. She was dressed in a hooded waterproof jacket, thick cotton sweater, jeans and rugged walking boots. Her luggage appeared to consist solely of a large rucksack that she carried easily on her shoulders, unlike Marjorie's bulging suitcase and rapidly disintegrating Duty Free carrier bags.

The woman shrugged her shoulders and gave Marjorie a rueful smile. 'I guess they weren't expecting us today, huh?' She was American.

'And I wasn't expecting Greece to be this cold either,' Marjorie replied clutching her arms round her body.

The American looked at Marjorie for a moment as though she was considering something. Then she smiled again. 'Well, it won't make the sun shine, but I do have something that might help warm you up. Come on.'

She led the way to a shelter with some wooden benches that at least offered some protection from the wind and the rain. She swung her rucksack off her shoulders, unfastened one of its many pockets and pulled out a bottle wrapped in a sweatshirt.

She held it up: 'Bourbon?'

Marjorie nodded and settled herself shivering on the bench. The American dug deeper into her rucksack and produced a metal mug. She poured a large measure of Bourbon and then, after glancing at Marjorie's pinched face, she added some more. She offered Marjorie the mug and then drank from the bottle before replacing the top. Marjorie gulped the Bourbon gratefully and then cradled the mug in her hands, as though it could give her warmth.

The American started to wrap the sweatshirt around the bottle again and then stopped. Instead, she draped it around Marjorie's shoulders. Marjorie smiled her thanks and tied the sleeves around her neck like a scarf.

The American sat down beside her. 'I think the gods are trying to say something to us, don't you? Like forget the fuck about leaving today?'

Marjorie laughed. The American's bluntness invigorated her. She drained the mug and handed it back. 'I think you might just be right. What shall we do instead?'

'How about doing some sightseeing in Athens? I'll grab that taxi.'

Without waiting for Marjorie's answer, the American leapt up and hailed an approaching taxi. When it looked as though it was about to drive past, she stepped in front of it, causing the driver to skid to a stop, swearing loudly. Before he could drive off, the American pulled the back door open. 'Pile in before he changes his mind,' she commanded.

Majorie needed no urging. She grabbed her case and her bags and pushed them in before clambering after them. The American got in on the other side of the taxi and put her rucksack on top of Marjorie's bags that were piled high on the seat between them. She leant forward and snapped: 'Athens,' at the driver then stretched over the bags and offered her hand to Marjorie: 'Lilith. Pleased to meet you.'

As they rode back to Athens, Lilith pointed as the sun suddenly broke through the clouds and, like a spotlight, its golden rays lit up the creamy marble columns of the Parthenon, crowning the Acropolis in the distance. 'It's just fucking amazing isn't it? Every time I see it, it makes me wonder what future civilisations will make of the buildings we're leaving behind, that's if humankind in any civilised form actually manages to survive. We seem intent on wrecking the very earth on which we live.' She turned to Marjorie, 'I tell you what, why don't we climb up there at dawn tomorrow and greet the sun?'

Dawn was not usually Marjorie's best hour unless it had been a particularly good party, but the next morning she managed to scramble yawning behind Lilith up the Acropolis, reaching the Parthenon just in time to see the first pink rays of the sun break through the clouds.

Lilith raised her arms and let out a great whoop of triumph, then turned to Marjorie. 'You know this was a temple dedicated to the goddess Athena; she was the goddess of wisdom and courage as well as of war and mathematics. The ancient Greeks named their greatest city after her. They really got women, unlike their modern counterparts.'

Rather like their climb up to the the Parthenon, Lilith seemed happy to take the lead in organising their stay including choosing their hotel, and Marjorie was happy to follow, even when Lilith suggested sharing a double room. Cost was not something she usually considered, but Lilith was right, it was both a lot cheaper and a lot more comfortable to share a room. Marjorie was also happy to agree when Lilith suggested they spend a few days sightseeing, even though it was something she usually avoided. She did not like to be reminded that everything had to grow old and eventually crumble away. However, Lilith had been to Greece before and she knew her ancient history. As they wandered around museums and archaeological sites, she brought the tumbled stones and headless statues alive with stories of wars and loves lost and won, of patricide and matricide, and of gods and goddesses whose human impulses caused chaos in the ancient world, and Marjorie found herself enjoying both sightseeing and Lilith's company far more than she had expected.

Marjorie also enjoyed it in evenings when they went out to dinner, even though she had always thought of going out to dinner with a woman as an admission that that there was no man available, an admission to avoid except in the direst of emergencies. They could easily have found two attractive Greek men to join them for dinner, as Marjorie was well aware of the flirtatious attention they received when they were out. Lilith attracted as much attention as her, even though she insisted on wearing what, in Marjorie's opinion, were unflattering clothes. Jeans and T-shirts did not disguise her lean, graceful figure, but neither did they do much to show it off. Marjorie's suggestions that Lilith make more of herself were met with a shrug, and invitations from men to dinner were greeted the same way. Lilith said that Marjorie should go out with men if she wanted to, but she had not felt like it. Greek men could be very handsome, particularly the young ones with their arrogantly tight jeans and their strutting walk, but Marjorie was prepared to admire them at a distance. She had only to think of Annunzio to remind herself how tiresome they could be at close range.

When, after five days in Athens, Lilith suggested that they head for the islands, Marjorie agreed. Allowing Lilith to plan their days had become second nature. They decided to make an occasion of their last night in Athens, and it took even longer than usual for Marjorie to choose what to wear. During their time in the city they had eaten well, and her clothes seemed to fit a little more snugly than she remembered. By contrast, Lilith took only minutes to shower and dress, although as a concession she swopped her usual T-shirt for a white silk blouse and her thick-soled boots for a pair of pretty, thonged sandals that, despite her objections, Marjorie had bought for her.

While Marjorie tried on outfit after outfit, Lilith lounged on the bed watching. After pulling on a tight-fitting red dress that was a particular favourite of hers, Marjorie stood sideways in front of the mirror wailing that her stomach stuck out.

'A woman's stomach is meant to be rounded, that's its glory. It celebrates women's fecundity,' chided Lilith.

Marjorie pouted. 'It's all very well for you, you could probably have six children and never put on a pound, but I want to look a little less fecund.'

'Well, I think you're beautiful as you are and I don't think you need all that crap to help you either,' retorted Lilith waving her hand at the rickety dressing table sagging beneath the weight of Marjorie's bottles and jars.

'Wait until you get to my age, then you'll change your mind,' countered Marjorie.

Lilith got up from the bed and stood beside Marjorie, looking into the mirror. They were the same height when Marjorie wore high heels.

'Your face is who you are - a beautiful, mature woman who's lived a full life. Why do you want to hide it? Be proud of it and flaunt it like you flaunt your body. You look great, believe me.' She kissed Marjorie on the cheek.

They went to their now favourite taverna in the small square below their hotel. The waiter greeted them like old friends and made a great show of taking them to a table. They were the only women dining together and Marjorie was happily conscious of the interest they aroused. Several bottles of wine were sent over from other tables, but it was amusing to refuse them while ordering more for themselves. By the time they left the restaurant, they had both had a lot to drink.

They walked back to the hotel arm in arm, haughtily ignoring the efforts of men to pick them up. Lilith followed Marjorie to her room and stretched herself out on the bed while Marjorie began to undress in front of the open window. The weather had at last turned warm and the hotel did not have any air conditioning.

'You ought to turn off the lights. Everyone in the square will be able to see you,' said Lilith raising herself on one elbow.

Marjorie, who was dressed only in her bra and pants, held her arms wide and faced the window. 'I want them to,' she declared. 'I want them all to see what they can't have.'

Lilith stood up and switched the lights off so that the room was illuminated only by the lights from the square. She came and stood close behind Majorie.

'But I don't want to see you if I can have you,' she murmured softly.

THIRTEEN

DAMN her mother, thought Grace as she flicked a large red ant off her leg. She might as well be marooned on a desert island for all the modern communications the village possessed. Workmen repairing the road to the village had inadvertently severed the telephone lines and no-one seemed to know when they would be repaired. She could call neither Roger nor the airline to see if she could get an earlier flight back to London.

She had considered going to stay in a hotel near the airport until she could get a flight - anything to get out of the village and away from her mother - but that, too, had proved impossible. Savvas, the only taxi driver in the village, had gone to his second cousin's wedding in another village, and was not due back until the following day. Further exasperated enquiries had elicited from Adonis that the bus she had arrived on only came twice a week, and was not due back for another two days. However, the town on the other side of the mountains had an excellent bus service that ran twice a day, but of course, she would have to wait for Savvas to return from the wedding in order to get there.

Grace tucked her legs under her chin and huddled in the meagre shade offered by a straggling Casuarina tree, glaring resentfully at Kelly who was stretched out on her back in the sun, her skin glistening with suntan oil and perspiration, her arms and her legs spread wide so that she tanned evenly. How could anyone actually enjoy lying in the searing heat?

Despite her protestations, Kelly had insisted on lending Grace a swimsuit so that she could come to the beach. Kelly had been round-eyed with astonishment that anyone could possibly come on holiday without at least a dozen bikinis. She had offered any one of them to Grace, but all of them were like the white one Kelly now wore - little more than three tiny scraps of material held together by thongs. Although she had not shown it, Grace had been horrified at the thought of wearing any of them. Then, just when she thought she might escape back to her room, Kelly remembered that she had brought a one-piece black swimsuit with her, as Ari had warned her that Greeks could be a little conservative. After much persuasion, Grace had agreed to borrow it.

However, as she pulled the swimsuit on, Grace realised that Kelly's concept of conservative differed from hers. Black it may have been, but it was cut low at the front, even lower at the back, high at the thighs and was held together at the sides by laces which revealed what little flesh there was left to reveal, particularly when stretched over Grace's larger frame. Grace had spent the morning on the beach constantly tugging the swimming costume to make sure that it afforded her even a small amount of modesty.

Luckily, the village beach was nearly deserted, so her discomfort had been evident to nobody but herself. A hundred yards away, a young couple had erected a beach umbrella and were watching their small three children paddling in the shallows from its shelter. At the other end of the beach, two adolescent Greek girls had like Grace, retreated into the shade of the trees that fringed the beach and were engrossed in paperback novels.

Unable to bear the heat any longer, Grace got to her feet and sprinted down to the sea. She plunged in and swam a vigorous crawl for about fifty yards, then turned over and floated on her back. The figures on the beach seemed a long way away, and she was tempted to stay there, suspended between earth and sky, in a kind of emotionless limbo, but she could already feel her nose and her cheeks beginning to burn. She turned back onto her stomach and swum a lazy breaststroke back to the beach, where she shook the ants off her towel and sat down. She could feel the salt from the water almost instantaneously drying to a prickly crust on her skin and began to apply some of the suntan lotion Kelly had given her.

Grace was not an advocate of rampant development, but from what she had seen, a hotel would be a good idea in a place like this. It had taken only one unwary workman's spade to cut the village off from the rest of the world. A hotel would mean more telephone lines, a better road, and probably a better life for everyone in the village as it would provide employment. The women in the camp only came here for a few weeks in the summer, so what did they know - or care - about what happened to a place like this in the winter when all the tourists were gone? They were only concerned with keeping things the way *they* wanted, rather like the middle class Londoners who bought a weekend home in a pretty country village and then campaigned against the building of affordable houses for the children of the people who cleaned their cottages and mowed their lawns.

As for her mother, thought Grace growing angry, she only adopted causes because they were fashionable, not because she really cared. She had never made an honest commitment to anything or anyone in her life. She had not given a second's thought to the effect coming to Greece might have on Grace's job or on her relationship with Roger. In Grace's experience, once women were past thirty, good relationships became an increasingly endangered species, so she thought her priority should be preserving hers, not terrapins. If her mother *really* cared about her, she would be trying to help, not doing her best to cause her to break up with Roger.

Grace applied some suntan lotion to her legs. When she got back to London, she would suggest to Roger that they go away on holiday. It was not something she had suggested before because she had never had time for holidays and Roger was the same, but if they spent time together in some romantic hideaway, perhaps they could resolve their problems. However, she would have to find some way of avoiding telling him what her mother had been doing in Greece as it was bound to cause yet another awful argument. She hated the idea of lying to Roger, but she could see no other option. *Damn* her mother, why did she always manage to cause so many problems?

The sun had now reached its zenith and Grace felt as though she was sitting in an oven. Beads of sweat trickled down her face and body. She glanced idly at the blockbuster novel that Kelly had lent her, but the athletic couplings of its heroine left her unmoved. She tried to use the book like a fan, but it had even less effect.

Kelly rolled over onto her stomach and propped her head up on her elbows. 'You have a lovely figure, Grace. I don't know why you hide it away. If I don't work out every day, I would get fat and Ari hates fat women. He says that was one of the problems with his first wife. She was slim when he met her, but the moment they were married she let herself go. He says Greek women are like that. They think that once they've got a husband, they've got him for life, so they get lazy, although if she'd had a son, it would probably have been different. You know how men are about their sons, especially Greek men. But I think there was a problem there too, although Ari won't talk about it.'

'That probably means he has the problem,' said Grace dryly.

Kelly looked shocked. She sat up and put on her sunglasses. 'Oh no, not Ari. He prides himself on his...well, you know, and we have a wonderful sex life. It's just that...' Kelly hesitated and began drawing patterns in the sand with her finger.

Grace sensed that Kelly wanted a confidante, but right at that moment, she did not want it to be her, she already had enough problems of her own. Then she looked at Kelly's bowed head, with its absurdly teased beehive hairdo, secured by little girl pink glittery pins, and she felt churlish. Kelly had been kind to her that morning when she had needed to talk, the least she could do was to return the favour.

Kelly looked up. 'Although Ari keeps complaining about how primitive the village it, I think it has really affected him - made him feel more, well, more *Greek* somehow. He keeps talking about his family and his roots and how important they are, and I have a feeling that it's leading up to him wanting me to have a baby. He's been married twice and is forty-six, but hasn't had any children, and this is a small village where people talk about such things.'

'You shouldn't worry about what people say Kelly. The only important thing is: do *you* want to have a baby?'

'Yes...of course I do, if it would make Ari happy, it's not that...' Kelly began tracing patterns in the sand again.

'Then what is it?'

'It's just that...well, pregnant women look so awfully *fat*. I'm afraid that Ari will leave me.' Kelly's chin quivered.

Grace suppressed an urge to smile. 'Unfortunately, you do have to put on a little bit of weight in order to have a baby, but I'm sure Ari won't mind. From what little I know of him, he will probably parade you around and show you off. It would be proof of his potency wouldn't it?'

'Do you really think so?' Relief lit Kelly's face, but vanished almost immediately. She looked down again. 'Can I tell you something I've never told anyone else?'

Grace wanted to say no. She shied away from knowing other people's intimate secrets. Usually, they were better kept secret. She steeled herself to listen.

'You see, I'm not sure I can have a baby,' Kelly continued in a low voice. 'I had an abortion when I was seventeen and there were some problems. The doctors told me that I might have trouble conceiving again.'

'Oh,' said Grace faintly. She really was hopeless at this sort of conversation.

'Abortions are no big deal any more, they happen all the time,' Kelly continued. 'Lots of my friends have had them, and some more than once, but Ari is Greek and they have funny ideas about that sort of thing. I daren't tell him.' She took off her sunglasses and looked appealingly at Grace. 'What shall do? I'm not sure I can have a baby and if I can't, he might leave me, and if I can, and I get fat, he'll probably leave me anyway. It's just not fair.'

'If Ari left you for either of those two reasons, he isn't worth having in the first place,' said Grace.

Kelly's baby blue eyes grew round and saucer-like. 'But you don't understand,' her voice wavered. 'If Ari left me I would have nothing, *be* nothing. He's always telling me so, and he's right. I'll be thirty in two years time, who will want me then?'

Grace was irritated. 'It sounds like you're the one who ought to be doing the leaving. How can you love someone who tells you that you are nothing without him? You can be anything you set your mind to, and take it from me, life most certainly doesn't end at thirty.'

'But I'm not like you. You're so strong and independent. The only important thing I've ever done is to become Ari's wife.'

Grace's irritation evaporated. Kelly looked like a small, wounded animal.

'Ari hasn't said he's going to leave you has he? Nor do you know that you can't have children, or that Ari definitely wants a child. So why get yourself into a state about something that may never happen?'

Kelly considered this for a few moments and then brightened up. 'You're right. It's so good us being friends isn't it? We can talk about men and things.'

Grace indicated an agreement she did not really feel and then stood up and began to towel the sand off her skin.

'You're not going already are you?' Kelly pleaded. 'I wanted to hear all about your boyfriend.'

The description of Roger as her boyfriend made Grace smile as she slipped her dress over her head. She doubted whether he had ever behaved like a boy, even when he was one. 'I'm afraid I really must go and see whether the telephone lines have been repaired,' she said as her head emerged. 'I've got some important calls to make.'

'Why don't you come over to our villa for drinks around eight this evening?'

'I'm not sure. It's a bit difficult, my mother...'

'Of course,' Kelly was instantly sympathetic. She began rubbing more suntan lotion onto her arms. 'Drop round anytime, you know where we are.'

Grace left the beach and walked slowly into the village which had already slipped into its usual afternoon torpor. She was intent on a cold drink at Adonis's before toiling up to her room. She peered into the dark interior. There were several tables occupied by groups of men who were deep in animated conversation. She sat down outside. She needed time to think about how to handle her mother, but, instead, she found herself thinking about Kelly.

It was hard to believe that a woman could be so completely dependent on a man. She could never be that way. She loved Roger, but they were separate individuals with separate lives and interests and she intended their lives to carry on that way once they were married.

She looked around for Adonis. She had been waiting at least five minutes to be served. The sound of the conversation inside was getting louder, and began to sound more like an argument, although she found it difficult to tell when people spoke Greek. It was a language that depended much more on emphasis for meaning than English, and people often sounded angry when they were just having an ordinary conversation. She was just about to get up and leave when Adonis at last appeared. He looked unhappy.

'I very sorry. Village business. They talk,' he waved his hand at the interior of the kafenion. 'Village President want hotel but some say no.'

Grace was suddenly curious. 'Do you want a hotel?'

Adonis shrugged. 'Maybe yes, maybe no. My family, we have small land near beach so make money, but hotel means new rooms and big restaurant, so maybe lose money if people go there and not here. It is difficult.'

'And the other people in the village, what do they think?'

'Some people say good, some say bad. Hotel means more people come to the village, but maybe they stay in hotel and not come to village. Village President he say yes because he has much land near beach, and this Ari from Australia, he is cousin of President and say he make much money. But he is only President for two more weeks and then...' Adonis's brow furrowed as he tried to find the word in English. 'We have... we choose new President.'

'An election. You vote for a new President,' prompted Grace.

Adonis nodded.

'And your President, is he like a Mayor?' asked Grace.

Adonis looked puzzled.

'A Mayor...the head of the village?' she tried again.

Adonis nodded again. 'He is very important man, and now, because of hotel there will be big fight. Yanni he say no hotel so he want to be President so he can stop it. You want beer?'

Grace nodded absentmindedly as she digested the news of Yanni's opposition to the hotel. She had not expected him to agree with her mother and the other women. Suddenly realising that she had ordered a beer, she turned to call Adonis back, but he had already disappeared. When she turned round, she saw Ari walking towards her.

'The beautiful Grace again. How lucky, twice in one day.' He pulled a chair close to hers and sat down before she could object. 'I came to see how the meeting was going, not that I have anything to worry about. I think it's going to be plain sailing. My cousin Takis will make sure of that.'

'Your cousin, the village President?' asked Grace.

He gave her a mock admiring glance. 'You're learning fast. In business it's always who you know and even better, who you are related to, that matters. In this case, I have a link to the very top.'

'Not for much longer, according to what I hear.'

Ari's eyes narrowed. 'What have you heard?'

'Only that there is to be an election and not everyone wants the hotel.'

Ari relaxed back in his chair, stretching his short, powerful legs out in front of him. 'The election is a mere formality. Too many people in this village rely on Takis for their jobs. They won't dare bite the hand that feeds them, believe me.' He turned in his chair and snapped his fingers impatiently. 'Some people round here will find they won't have a job unless they buck up their ideas. Places like this will be out of business when there's a hotel offering decent service.'

Just at that moment, Adonis came out carrying Grace's beer. His smile faded when he saw Ari.

Ari pointed at Grace's beer. 'One for me, pronto!'

They sat in silence until Adonis returned with Ari's beer. Grace no longer felt thirsty. She poured half a glass, drank it quickly and then gathered her things up.

'You'll have to excuse me. I have a lot to do.'

'Nobody does a lot in the afternoon in Greece, and they certainly don't work. Relax - enjoy your beer. You should learn to be more like the Greeks.' He poured some more beer into her glass. 'Kelly is still on the beach, I take it? She does love the sun. Still, it gives us some time alone together, doesn't it? I knew from the moment I saw you, that we could do business together.'

'Business?' Grace was puzzled.

Ari chuckled. 'Oh, come now. I'm pretty sure that you've felt what's been going on between us too.'

Grace stiffened. 'I'm not quite sure where this conversation is leading, but I don't think I...'

Ari put his large paw of a hand over hers, it was damp with sweat. Just at that moment, there was a loud scraping of chairs from inside the taverna and a group of men began to come out, still talking animatedly. At their head was Yanni.

He paused almost imperceptibly as he saw Grace. He glanced from her to Ari, and his eyes flickered. Grace pulled her hand away from Ari's, but it was too late. Yanni had gone.

The expression on Ari's face told her that he had noticed her embarrassment. He grinned evilly. 'Do I have to spell it in capitals? You're a beautiful woman and I'm a married man with an appetite for an occasional meal out, if you get my drift. Kelly knew what she was taking on when she married me. It was one of my conditions. I'm a Greek man and no one woman can satisfy my appetite, although I'm always hoping to be proved wrong.' He raised a suggestive eyebrow.

Grace got to her feet. 'For Kelly's sake, I'm going to pretend this conversation hasn't happened, and in future, although this is a small village, let's just try and stay clear of each other shall we?'

As she turned to leave, Ari caught her arm. His strong fingers dug into her skin. 'So you're another plakomouna like your mother are you?'

Grace did not understand what Ari had called her, but she could tell by the look on his face that it was not very pleasant. She picked up her glass and threw the rest of her beer in his face. As she walked away, she could hear him laughing.

FOURTEEN

Ari mopped his face with a large white handkerchief as he leant sideways to catch a last glimpse of Grace as she strode up the street. She was not his usual kind of woman. For a start, he did not like Brits, they were too stuck up for their own good. However, he liked haughty women, especially beautiful ones. As far as he was concerned, when a woman said 'no' what she was really saying was that she intended to be harder to catch. He liked that, it brought out the hunter in him. Women who said no were much more arousing. The more they said no, the more aroused he became.

The Greek community in Australia still clung to a strict moral code, and raised their daughters to say no, which was why he had once preferred Greek girls to Anglos, who were only too ready to give it up. When he was younger, convincing Greek virgins that they did not want to be good girls was his favourite sport. The more convincing they needed, the more he enjoyed it. It was a risky game, but he liked the odds. Greek girls were much less likely to cause trouble afterwards than Anglos too. They were usually too scared to say anything for fear of bringing disgrace not only on themselves but on their families too. However, he had miscalculated once, and once had been enough.

Maria was a mouse of a girl, not his usual sort, and he had not expected her to need much convincing. She was only a slim little thing, but she proved surprisingly resistant to his persuasion and he had found her resistance extremely arousing. Unfortunately, she had not felt the same way about him, and had gone straight home and told her mother that he had raped her.

It had not been rape. How could it have been? She agreed to go out with him and returned his kisses. If she changed her mind at the last minute when he was as good as inside her, what was a man supposed to do? Of course, if he had known at the time that Maria was the only child of one of the most powerful families in the Greek community in Sydney he would have taken a different approach.

Her father was grooming her for marriage into another rich Greek family whose financial interests would provide the perfect bridegroom for his daughter as well as the perfect match for his own business empire. He had not intended her to marry the son of a fisherman, even if Ari had just set up his own accountancy business in a room above a Chinese takeaway.

However, George Mavropoulos was an honourable man. He could not offer damaged goods to the son of a man with whom he did business. Ari was summoned to his office and told on what terms he was to become George's son-in-law: he would be given a junior executive position in one of the Mavropoulos property companies, where his advancement would be dependent on his abilities, rather than on his relationship to the family. In her turn, Maria would get a house just down the road from her mother that would be in her name, not in Ari's, and a trust fund would be set up to ensure the future of any sons she had until they inherited the Mavropoulos estate on George's death. In no circumstances would Ari have control over the family fortune because even if George died before his grandsons were old enough to take over his business, a board of trustees appointed by George would run it until they were able.

It was an offer not to be refused, and Ari had accepted it. Not only because he knew that if he refused, George could make it impossible for him to find any clients in the close-knit Greek community, but also because Ari believed in planning long-term. Although the tightly worded legal documents he was forced to sign before the marriage ensured that he could not get outright control of the Mavropoulos millions, he was as an accountant and he prided himself on finding ways to use other people's money for his own purposes.

Added to that, to be the son-in-law of George Mavropoulos meant something in Sydney and, unlike his own father, Ari intended to be someone. He had never understood his father. Why go to all the trouble and hardship of emigrating to the other side of the world only to end up being exactly what he could have been if he had remained on the small island where he was born - a fisherman? He had never even owned his own boat.

Being the son-in-law of George Mavropoulos would open up the kind of doors Ari had only been able to dream about opening until then. If marriage to Maria was the price to pay, he would pay it. She was a plain thing, and, if his mother-in-law was anything to go by, she would soon grow fat and develop a moustache, but Greek husbands were not expected to remain faithful and her own father was the perfect example.

It was common knowledge that George Mavropoulos was always out at nightclubs with a beautiful blonde on his arm. He was even rumoured to have a long-term mistress who lived in a large house in one of the smartest Anglo suburbs of Sydney, together with a second family of two young children. George could hardly complain if Ari did the same thing. That was how Greek husbands behaved and their wives were brought up to accept it.

However, marriage had transformed Maria. Once the ring was on her finger, the little mouse who had been so shy and hesitant in the back seat of his car, became a demanding harridan who spent all her time in her mother's house complaining about his behaviour. At first, his father-in-law took his side, pouring large whiskies and raising exasperated eyebrows at Ari as the two women raged at them, but after a year and then two passed, and there were no signs of Maria producing any longed-for grandchildren, George's attitude changed. Maria accused Ari of being the cause of her childlessness, railing that he was running around with other women, wasting what was rightly hers on them. George took Ari aside and told him that other women were not a problem if he was discreet, but Maria needed a child to keep her happy and that it was his duty to get on and provide her with one.

He had tried, God knows he had tried, even though he found it increasingly difficult to get aroused as Maria lay passively under him, her modest night-dress drawn up to her waist and her now plump hairy legs held wide, waiting for him to impregnate her, her eyes full of mute accusation rather than desire. Every month her wails grew louder as she fled down the street to her mother's house when her period arrived. In time, the entire neighbourhood came to know her hormonal cycle, and with it his inability to father a child.

It had not been his fault, of that he was sure. He could satisfy any woman, just not his wife.

After three years, she had confronted him and demanded that he go for tests. They argued, which was not unusual as they argued most of the time, but this time she rushed at him and tried to claw his face, so naturally, he hit her - not hard, although she deserved a good beating, just a cuff around the head to teach her a lesson. Unfortunately, the blow caused her lip to bleed, which made it look worse than it actually was. Wearing only her nightdress and screaming that Ari had tried to kill her, she rushed bare-foot down the road to her parent's house, blood streaming down her face.

Maria stayed with her parents for nearly a week on that occasion, which proved to be the first of many separations, each longer than the last. Their marriage managed to limp on until the morning of her thirtieth birthday. When Ari woke up, he found that Maria had gone to stay with her parents yet again, but this time she had packed his suitcases too and left him a note telling him to leave as she wanted to find herself a man who could give her a child before she was too old.

It had been humiliating. If she had wanted a divorce on the grounds that he beat her, or had other women, her father would have refused her, but he would not deny his daughter a child. Nor could Ari suggest to George that it was his beloved daughter who was barren. That would have been akin to suggesting that it was the Mavropoulos genes that were at fault, something Ari dared not do given the delicacy of his business relationship with his father-in-law.

Under George's patronage, Ari had discovered that he possessed an unerring nose for property deals. He could spot a run-down area ripe for development long before anyone else, and his father-in-law was more than happy to give him a free hand both in smoothing over any planning problems at the City Council, as well as in making sure that any troublesome tenants or planning objectors were quickly, and quietly, dealt with. Ari found that he had an instinctive grasp of whether to employ monetary inducements or strong-arm tactics. His methods wavered on the edge of legality, but nothing had ever been proved, and so long as the profit margins were good and the Mavropoulos name did not get into the newspapers, George never interfered. It was all in the art of knowing how to sub-contract, so that tax and other liabilities moved down the line, while the profits came back to the top.

After a couple of years, Ari began to feel that he had repaid George with interest for marrying Maria, so why should he continue being merely an employee with a salary? Reasoning that as long as he continued to make large profits for his father-in-law, it would not matter who owned the companies to whom the work was subcontracted, Ari set up some building companies. With his help, they submitted the kind of competitive bids that allowed him to contract them to work for the Mavroupoulos organisation so that in the end, everybody made money. Ari could see no cause for complaint.

That did not prevent him from feeling anxious when his father-in-law summoned him to lunch to sort out the divorce like civilised men. Ari knew there were two things George was not a civilised man about - family honour and money.

Despite his trepidation, lunch began well enough. George was almost fatherly in his enquiries about Ari's sexual well-being, earnestly suggesting different foods as well as sexual positions that might facilitate his potency. He ended by slapping Ari on the back and roaring a little too loudly for Ari's comfort that, if he couldn't make babies, at least he could make money, and that George wanted him to go on making plenty more for him, even after the divorce.

Ari's sense of relief was palpable. He felt as if he could breathe for the first time in days and gulped down the tumbler-full of neat whisky that had been sitting untouched in front of him. It was the wrong move.

George's eyes narrowed. 'However, that does not mean you can go on making money out of me my friend. I like you. You are a man who wants to better himself and this is good. But I do not like a man who betters himself at my expense.'

Ari felt the sweat break out on his brow and his heart began to beat uncomfortably fast, but he made an effort to stay calm and look George in the eye as he spoke. 'I do not know what you are talking about. You are the last person on this earth I would cheat. You are more like a father to me than my own father. We are family.'

'We are family no longer, Aristotle, and please, do not insult my intelligence, you make things worse.' George spread his large, thick-fingered hands on the table. 'You are clever, but not clever enough, so you must pay. I will become a silent partner in both your companies and take sixty per cent of the profits they make. That is very generous considering how much money you have made out of me.' He held up a finger to silence Ari as he tried to interrupt. 'Also, you will no longer be Managing Director of the Mavropoulos Development Company. It would be too upsetting for my little Maria to have you as the boss of one of her father's companies. However, I am setting up another company which Maria will not know about, and you will do for this company what you have done for MDC.'

Ari knew he was defeated. What could he do but accept his soon to be ex-father-in-law's terms? For a brief moment he considered moving to Darwin, but George's influence reached far beyond Sydney. He could ensure that Ari never made another cent anywhere in Australia.

He stayed away from Greek women after that. The cost of sex with them was too high. They sighed and moaned about their lack of power, but their tears and silent suffering were weapons against which men had little defence. Anglo women were the opposite. They trumpeted their independence and equality, but it was merely a thin veneer. Just look at the way most of them flaunted their bodies, it was an obvious come-on to men. In his experience, most of them could be had for just the price of a dinner.

The women at the camp outside the village were no different. There was no way a woman could really prefer sex with a woman. It was not physically possible. All that not liking men crap was really just another kind of come-on. Like all the other northern European women who flocked to the Mediterranean every summer, they had come to Greece for sex. It was a well-known known fact that Mediterranean men, and particularly Greeks, were better at sex than their northern counterparts who did not know what to do with their dicks.

However, Ari was not bothered about having sex with any of the women from the camp, far from it, he would not touch any of them with the proverbial barge pole. His problem was that they were a load of interfering busybodies who might upset his plans for the hotel. All it took was for a few hysterical agitators to start loudmouthing about the environment and saving whales or some other dumb animal, and things could snowball. He had seen it happen in Australia. Millions of dollars worth of development held up by a few butterflies on a bit of wasteland.

He did not intend to take any chances with his plans for the hotel. The development was much too important. Not only was it his chance to prove that he could do something on his own without George Mavropoulos, but he intended to prove to his father that he was wrong.

Ari emigrated to Australia with his parents when he was six. He was their only son and they believed that there was no future for him in the village. His father, Vassilis, had heard that Australia was the land of opportunity, but there had been little opportunity for a fisherman who might be able to forecast a change in the weather just from the direction of the wind, but who had little schooling and could neither speak nor write English. All Vassilis could find was a series of menial jobs cleaning up in factories and restaurants. He never made much money and sometimes no money at all. Ari's mother was forced to take in sewing in order that they survive.

Ari hated it. He hated the endless scrimping and making do, the dismal rented rooms in which they lived, the way his parents had to be nice to everyone because they were so dependent on other people for work and for food, but most of all, he hated his father's constant criticism of Australia. According to his father, everything was better back in the village in Greece: fruit grew bigger and juicier, vegetables tasted fresher, the Feta was saltier, the wine more powerful, and the bread tasted like bread. The litany of comparisons was constant, and always in favour of the village. When he married Maria, his parents were delighted. Not only was she a good Greek girl from a good, rich, Greek family, but his father's enquiries established that the Mavroupoulos family were distantly related to a family from his village. Ari could not have done better and Vassilis could not have been prouder.

Summoning the courage to tell his parents that he was going to be divorced took a long time. When he finally did, his mother screamed and ran from the room, tearing at her clothes.

Ari had turned to his father and reached out his hands, palm up. 'You see what I mean? Women are so emotional. They do not understand things as we men understand them. So, I'm going to divorce Maria, but I give you my word, I will soon marry again and this time to a girl who will give you many grandchildren.'

His father had looked at him for a long moment and then he turned away and sat down at the table, his back to Ari. When he spoke, his voice was flat. 'Do as you choose, but for myself, I will never leave this house again. My shame is too great.'

'Dad – *pateras* – please... Look, this is not as bad as it seems. George Mavropoulos has offered me a good business deal, so good I can afford to build you a house in the village. Wouldn't you like that? You are always telling me how much better things are in the village than in Australia. You and ma could retire there. I will buy you first class tickets and...' His father raised his hand bringing Ari's flow of promises to an abrupt halt.

'Enough.' His father spoke without turning to look at Ari. 'You think I could go back to the village now? Our family's shame will arrive before us. You have made it so that I can never return and I must die in exile.'

Ari opened his mouth to protest, but before any sound could emerge, his father's hand formed a sign pointing to the door. 'Go. I know you are my son and that I gave life to you, but for now I wish to forget that I did.'

His relationship with his parents had never been the same again, especially since he married Kelly, an Anglo. However, although he had not realised it at the time, the seed of an idea that was now taking the form of the hotel was sewn on that day. Before that, Ari had never wanted to return to Greece. He was an Australian and Australia was his country. Greece was just a faded childhood memory. However, his anger at his father's shame fired him with the desire to go back and destroy the myth of the village where everything was so perfect, and to show that the Koulouris family had made good. Returning with a beautiful, blonde, Australian wife on his arm made it even better. He wanted the villagers to know that the son of Vassilis Koulouris, a poor fisherman, had taken the daughter of George Mavropoulos as his wife, but had found her wanting. The hotel development would be final proof that he was now a somebody, and his father could return with his head held high.

Ari had even seen the perfect plot of land on which to build a splendid modern villa where his mother and father could retire. It was near the top of the village with a view of the harbour as well as the surrounding countryside. There was a tumbledown, one-storey traditional house on the site, but as far as he could see, there was only an elderly woman living there, so she would not be too difficult to deal with.

Ari sat back in his chair and clasped his hands across his chest. He had plans, real plans, and no women, no matter who they were, young or old, were going to get in his way.

FIFTEEN

'Roger?' Grace's voice echoed down the line. The reply was a series of mechanical chirps and crackles. She spoke louder.
'Roger, can you hear me?'
There was a distant harrumph and then the line crackled again.
'Sawbridge speaking.' Roger's voice was businesslike.
Grace felt a flood of relief. She had not expected the telephone line to be repaired yet, but she had decided to give it another try.
'Roger, it's me, Grace. I'm afraid the line's not very good.'
'Grace. Where are you?'
'Still in Greece, I'm afraid. Things here are a bit more complicated than I expected. How are you?' She tried to keep her voice light.
'By things, I assume you mean that mother of yours. What, or is it whom, has she got herself involved with this time, some randy young Greek? I just can't understand why you had to go haring off like that, it's about time she learned to sort herself out...'
'Roger, *please*,' Grace interrupted, 'I didn't call to argue about my mother. I just want to talk.'
'Talk? Talk about what? Expensive long distance calls are not the way to talk about anything. If you'd been prepared to have a rational discussion when all this began, there would have been no need for you to slip away like a thief in the night. It was quite a shock coming home to that note of yours.'
Grace hesitated. She had called because she needed to hear the familiar sound of his voice, telling her that he missed her so that she could say she missed him too, but that moment seemed to have passed.
'Yes, I know. I'm sorry about the note. I shouldn't have left like that, but I thought my mother was in trouble and needed me. *Please* Roger, can we not talk about it now, I just wanted to make sure that you were managing all right. I made sure there was plenty of food in the fridge.'

There was a moment's silence then he cleared his throat. 'Actually, I only caught your call by chance as I've just dropped into the house to pick up the post. I've moved back in with mother. It seemed the best thing to do in the circumstances. She's been splendid about it of course, but it was dashed awkward trying to explain why. That mother of yours has a lot to answer for.'

Grace was just about to retort that his mother had a lot to answer for too, but she bit it back. She was the one who had left without telling him. He had every right to go and stay with his mother.

'When are you coming back?' asked Roger, a plaintive note creeping into his voice. 'We are meant to be going to two drinks parties as well as rather important a dinner this weekend. Your absence from the dinner in particular would be noticed.'

'I hardly think my absence from one dinner party on urgent family business will affect your chances of becoming an MP, Roger.'

Why should she rush back just to avoid upsetting the numbers at some tedious dinner party where she would no doubt be forced to spend the evening being charming to some pompous Party agent from the shires? There were times of late when Grace wondered whether Roger had proposed to her only because it did not look good for a prospective Conservative MP to be 'living in sin'. It was his expression, not hers, and he always laughed loudly when he said it. But she knew it made him uncomfortable in the same way that it made her feel uncomfortable when he said that she would be a good wife for an MP and help his image. What was it he had said once? 'The thing about you Grace, is that you look wonderfully exotic but at the same time you're so terribly pukka. Can't be bad for the voters can it?'

Even as the words came into her mind, Grace felt guilty. Roger had meant them as a compliment. He was a bit old-fashioned and could express himself a little clumsily at times, not the best of attributes for someone who wanted to be an MP, but it was his ambition and she had promised to give him her wholehearted support.

'I'm sorry if I sound a little short-tempered,' she said. 'It's just that things here are a bit difficult. I'm calling you from a phone box in the village square as I can't find another phone, so believe me, I have no intention of staying here a moment longer than is absolutely necessary.'

'Well, you'd better give me the number of your hotel, just in case.'

'If there was a phone where I'm staying, I would have used it to call you. I'm staying in a room. There are no hotels here.'

'No hotels, that's ridiculous,' protested Roger. 'I must have a number where I can contact you.'

'I'm sorry Roger, I must go as my money is running out. I promise I'll call you when I know what I'm doing. Bye.' Grace put the receiver down.

Her money had not run out, she still had plenty of change left, but what was the point of talking any longer? It was hopeless trying to have a conversation with Roger on the telephone about something important. While his eloquence in summing up a case in court was legendary, his telephone manner left much to be desired.

He had proposed marriage to her on the telephone, or at least on her answering machine, and it had been yet another example of how old-fashioned he was. One Monday she had come back to the office after lunch to find Libby, her secretary, giggling loudly. Libby followed her into her office and pointed wordlessly at her telephone where the message light was flashing. Grace pushed the play button.

'Grace? Oh it's that damn machine again.' There was an explosive harrumph as Roger cleared his throat, then he began again: 'Grace. This is Roger Sawbridge. I'd just like to know whether you would consider becoming my wife. Er...that's all. Just thought you'd like to know the way I was thinking.'

Grace shooed a now uncontrollably giggling Libby from her room and called him back.

'Roger, it's Grace. I got your message.'

There was another loud harrumph. 'Splendid. What do you think?'

'It would be nice if you would ask me yourself Roger.'

There was a silence.

'I thought I had.'

'What I mean is that it would be nice if you asked *me* rather than my answering machine. After all, it is a rather important question. Perhaps the most important question I may ever be asked.'

'Do you think so?'
'Yes I do Roger.'
'Well I suppose in that case...'
'Yes?'
'Are you sure? I thought you might like some time to think about it. I mean, there's no need for us to rush into anything. I just wanted to run it by you, find out the lay of the land and all that.'
'Roger! *Yes* I do want some time to think about it, but first I want you to propose to me and not to my answerphone.'
'Well of course, if that's the way you feel...' Roger sounded hurt.
Grace tried to control her temper. The situation was getting out of hand. 'Roger, *dearest*, I do think it's rather the done thing for you to ask me in person.'
'We can't take it as read?'
'No!'
'Well in that case...' He cleared his throat again. 'Grace, will you do me the honour of accepting my hand in marriage?'
It was not the most romantic of proposals, but Grace believed that the affection and respect they had for each other would deepen into something far longer lasting than the great romantic passion that Yanni had described. His kind of love flared brightly, but almost as soon burnt itself out. She was rather glad that she had not felt that kind of love. It sounded unpredictable, even dangerous. She and Roger might not burn for each other's bodies, but there was much more to life than sex.
Grace put the rest of her change back into her purse and stepped out of the telephone box into the square. It was nearly five thirty and the light had begun to soften. A sleepy looking teenage boy clattered the blinds open on the tiny general store just up the high street. Yawning, he undid the padlock on the ice-cream freezer that stood on the pavement outside and reached inside for a multi-coloured lollipop. He stripped off the wrapping and dropped it on the ground, then, licking contendedly, he sat down on the doorstep to await his first customer of the evening.
Grace stood watching him. Speaking to Roger had made her realise that, even though he could not say it, he needed her. Suddenly resolute, she put her purse back into her bag and walked

away from the phone box. She would call the airline office first thing tomorrow morning and get the next available flight to London. She would also get them to book a taxi to come to the village and pick her up tomorrow. Even if she was forced to wait a couple of days for a flight at a hotel near the airport, she did not intend to spend a moment longer than necessary in the village.

Grace was so deep in thought as she started to walk, that she did not see the motorbike coming round the corner into the square. It skidded to a halt, almost on its side, but its rider skilfully managed to get a foot down, righting the bike before it could hit the ground.

'Signomi, lipame...' the rider said, hurriedly switching off the engine. It was Yanni. 'Please, I am very sorry. Most people, they hear motor...' he looked at her enquiringly.

'I'm sorry. I was thinking. I didn't hear a thing...' Grace suddenly realised that her legs were trembling from shock at her near miss.

'These must be very deep thoughts. Come.' Yanni gently took her arm and guided her over to the seats outside the small taverna in the square.

A waiter immediately appeared from inside.

'Would you like a drink?' asked Yanni.

Grace shook her head. 'No, really, I'm alright.'

The waiter went away.

Aware of Yanni's anxious eyes on her, Grace summoned up a weak smile. 'I'll be alright, really. It's just been one of those days.'

'So, tell me.'

'I really don't want to talk about it.' Grace avoided his eyes.

'Perhaps this Ari has upset you? You threw your beer at him, no?'

Grace was startled. 'How did you know about that?'

'This is small village. A beetle he goes...' Yanni made a hopping motion with his fingers, '...everybody know.' He grinned.

Grace could not help smiling back.

'But this Ari, he is not a nice man,' Yanni grew serious. 'I do not like him. He makes much trouble in the village. He thinks only about himself and money. This hotel, maybe it make money for the village, but I think it also makes much trouble.'

'But surely a hotel would bring jobs as well as tourists and money? Change doesn't always have to be bad,' said Grace.

'Have you been to Mykonos or Thira, the place you call Santorini?'

Grace shook her head.

'In these places they have many tourists and much money, but when tourists go, there is nothing. Tourists are easy money, so the young men, they do not fish or look after the fields, and soon they are fit only to be waiters. They live only for the summer and the tourists, especially the women tourists. It is not good for Greeks. Life should be more than these things.'

Yanni stared into the distance for a few moments as though he could see the future. Then he looked at Grace and gave her another boyish grin.

'Ela...come, I show you something.' He stood up and held out his hand.

Without thinking, Grace obeyed him. He led her back to his motorbike and kicked it into life and indicated the pillion seat.

Grace shook her head.

'Please. I want to show you something.'

Grace gesticulated at her skirt. Yanni shrugged his shoulders and mimed that she should pull it up. Grace looked around. Nobody appeared to be watching so she gathered her skirt around her knees and awkwardly climbed on behind Yanni, trying to tuck her skirt under her thighs. Yanni indicated where she should rest her feet and with a sudden forward motion, started the bike.

Grace tried to sit erect and away from Yanni, but it was impossible on the speeding bike. As he leaned sideways to go round a corner she found herself thrust forward against his body, her face against his back and her arms clasped tightly round his waist.

As the bike gathered speed, she clung to him, not daring to open her eyes, at first only aware of her terror and of the wind catching at her skirt and whipping her hair around her face. However, after a little while, she also became uncomfortably aware of how intimately her body pressed against Yanni's, her thighs locked to his body, her breasts pressed against his back. They were both wearing clothes, but she felt naked. If she could feel the contours of his body through his T-shirt and her thin blouse, then he must be able to feel hers.

It was a long time since she had held a man apart from Roger, and Yanni's body felt very different to his. Roger had begun to put on weight lately and if she had gripped him around his stomach, she would have felt rather a lot of spare flesh. Yanni felt tautly muscular, and with her cheek pressed in the hollow of his shoulder blades, Grace was also conscious of the scent of his body which was made even more potent by being infused with the heady perfume of wild herbs from the surrounding countryside.

She forced herself to open her eyes and relax her hold slightly. She lifted her head, allowing the wind to cool her burning cheeks. The road they were following was little more than an unmade track and dangerously rutted and potholed, but Yanni handled the bike smoothly, his body counterbalancing its motions as he manoeuvred from side to side at a speed that would have been dangerous in other than expert hands. Because she had had her eyes closed, Grace had not been aware that they had been steadily climbing uphill. Now, as she cautiously looked to her left, she could see the sea down below, the coastline scalloped by several small bays.

Yanni pointed at one of them. 'See, that is the where the women stay,' he called over his shoulder.

Grace looked in the direction of his finger and saw a ramshackle collection of about a dozen tents pitched around a clearing in one of the bays. Brightly coloured clothes fluttered like bunting in the breeze from lines suspended between the tents. The next moment she was forced to once more grab Yanni tightly around his chest as they went over the crest of the hill and he veered off the track. The bike began to bounce dangerously across rocky ground.

Grace closed her eyes again. If they crashed, her insurance would not cover her for riding on a motor bike without a helmet or protective clothing. Roger would no doubt insist on sueing, although Yanni was unlikely to be insured. Despite having to cling to Yanni as the bike swerved perilously to avoid a large hole, Grace could not help smiling as she imagined what Roger's face would look like if he found out what she had been up to.

The bike skidded to a halt at the bottom of a rocky outcrop and Yanni switched off the engine. Grace hurriedly let go of him and pulled her skirt down before dismounting.

'So what was it you wanted to show me?' she asked, running her fingers through her hair in a fruitless effort to tidy it.

'Ela.' Yanni held out his hand.

Grace ignored it, keeping hers firmly at her side. He shrugged and began to leap nimbly from rock to rock. Grace followed, scrambling awkwardly, using her hands. Yanni stood waiting, an amused expression on his face. With a determined effort, she caught up with him, and stood dusting her hands on her skirt.

Yanni touched her arm, staying her hands. 'Look,' he said simply.

They were standing at the head of a bay. Below lay a crescent of glittering white sand shelving gently down to a lapis lazuli blue sea. Unlike the rocky, barren terrain that surrounded the village, the land beyond the beach was green and verdant, and dotted with tall cypress trees pointing gracefully to the sky. It was like a hidden valley.

Grace turned to him, her eyes wide with wonder. 'It's beautiful.'

He gave a satisfied nod and then began to climb down to the beach. Grace stood looking for a few moments more, not wanting to let the view out of her sight, then she followed him. When she reached the beach, her feet sank into the soft sand. She reached down and picked up a handful. It sparkled like diamonds as it ran through her fingers.

'It is marble, like the rocks.' Yanni picked up a rock and showed it to her.

It was white marble streaked with copper red and emerald green minerals. Grace was entranced but Yanni tossed it away and took off his worn espadrilles, stuffing them into his back pockets. Then he rolled his jeans up to his knees, revealing tanned legs. Grace kicked off her sandals. The sand under her feet was warm from the sun.

She spotted the pure white feathery skeleton of a tiny starfish, and crouched down to pick it up. Then she saw another, larger one, and picked that up too, and then another and another. There were hundreds of them, scattered across the beach like snowflakes.

She looked up to Yanni to ask where they had come from, but he was walking purposefully towards a large clump of ten-foot high reeds that fringed the beach. She picked up her sandals and followed him. As she reached him, he put his finger to his lips, indicating that she should be silent, then parted the reeds. Beyond was a large dark pool.

There was a scuttling sound and the plop of several objects entering the water. At first Grace could not see what was causing the sounds, and then she saw a hump moving rapidly across the surface of the water preceded by a smaller object which appeared to have two eyes, then she spotted several others. There was a movement just beside her feet and she looked down to see a terrapin scuttling through the reeds into the water.

She turned to Yanni, smiling. 'What an idyllic place.'

Yanni waved his arm. 'This is where Ari wants to build his hotel.'

Grace looked around. 'Isn't there some way a hotel could be built here but keep the pool and the surrounding area preserved for the terrapins? It's a very large beach.'

'It is not just a pool. This water comes from a spring. Tourists like to have many showers and baths and they will use all the water from the spring. There will not be enough for the terrapins and for the valley as well as the tourists.'

'Surely the developers will think of that and pipe water from somewhere else?'

Yanni shrugged. 'We are Greek. There is water here. Why pay more money to bring it from elsewhere?'

Grace looked uncertain. 'I suppose you're right. But I would have thought that with some compromise and careful planning...'

Yanni gave her a pitying look. 'Is this how you live your life, with this compromise?'

'No, of course not. Well, not all the time perhaps, but sometimes you have to...' Grace protested, but found herself forced to look away from the intensity of his gaze.

Yanni studied her face for a few moments more. Then he touched her lightly on the shoulder. 'Come. I show you something else.'

Without waiting to see whether she would follow him, he began to make his way through the tall undergrowth surrounding the pool. Grace pulled on her sandals and followed him.

About twenty yards from the beach there was a small olive grove. The trees were gnarled and twisted, but their silvery green foliage was young and fresh. It looked as though some ancient hand had planted them in a circle, and their branches had stretched out to meet, forming a shady canopy beneath which wild flowers grew in a lush carpet. Yanni was perched on a mound of lichen-covered stones in the centre of the circle. He seemed to be listening to something far away.

Grace stood at the edge of the grove watching him. She felt as though she was intruding on something private.

Yanni eventually turned his head and looked at her. 'Do you know the story of Orpheus?'

'Bits of it, yes. Although it's an awfully long time since I learnt about it at school,' confessed Grace.

'Ela, ela. Come,' Yanni gestured her over.

Feeling a little bemused, Grace perched on a rock next to him.

'Orpheus was the son of the King of Thrace and the Muse Calliope,' Yanni began, his voice low but clear. 'The god, Apollo, give him a lyre and the muses, they teach him how to play and sing so that it is like magic. Even the trees and the rocks they follow him to hear him play. Then, one day, he met Eurydice, and she was so beautiful that he fall in love with her and she with him. But another man, Aristaeus, he wants her too, and he try to force her, so she run away, but as she run, she step on a snake and it bite her and she die.'

Yanni lowered his head as though reliving the moment. All around them, the grove was silent. When he spoke again, his voice was charged with emotion. 'But Orpheus, his love is so great that he decide he must follow her even to death. So he play his lyre and Charon the ferryman take him across the River Styx where he play and sing for Hades, the god of the underworld, who like his music so much, that he say Orpheus can take Eurydice back to the upper world. But he also say that Orpheus must never look back to see if Eurydice follow him. So, Orpheus play the most beautiful music he ever play so that Eurydice hear and know the way back to the sun and Eurydice hear, and she follows. But Orpheus, he love her too much and must see her, so he turn and look...'

Yanni looked over his shoulder as though he thought he would see the ill-fated Eurydice behind him, '...and so he lose Eurydice forever.' Yanni lowered his head and was silent.

In the stillness, Grace could hear a bird singing high up in the branches of one of the ancient olives. She looked up, trying to see it, but all she could see were the leaves rustling as a soft breeze blew like a sigh through the grove. It was easy to understand why the ancient Greeks imagined their countryside to be alive with gods. She looked at Yanni's dark profile. At that moment, he seemed to belong more to the mythical world he had conjured up than to the world of blue jeans and motor bikes.

'His heart broken, Orpheus has only his music left, so he decide to serve Apollo, the god who give him the gift of music, but another god, Dionysus, is jealous and he want Orpheus to serve him too. Orpheus say no, so Dionysus, he get angry and he order the Maenads...'

Yanni looked up at Grace, a small smile playing around his lips. 'Do you understand the Maenads? They are *very* bad women. They drink too much and are not very nice to men. These Maenads, they kill Orpheus and then they tear him apart.' He demonstrated graphically with his hands. 'Then they throw him into the sea. But his body is carried by the waves to this very island and his head is buried with his lyre here,' he indicated where they were sitting, 'and because of this, the nightingales in this place sing sweeter than anywhere else in the world.'

As though to demonstrate, the invisible bird began to sing again.

'Is that a nightingale?' asked Grace in a hushed voice.

'No. You must come at night to hear them.' He looked into her eyes. 'If you want, I bring you.'

To her irritation, Grace felt her cheeks grow hot. She jumped up and walked to the edge of the grove.

'That story about Orpheus must earn you some big tips from the other women tourists you bring here. I bet they just lap it up...' Her voice was harsh.

Yanni sprang up and came towards her, his eyes dark with anger. For a moment, Grace was frightened and then he shook his head slowly, as though in pity.

'*You* are the only woman I bring here.'

SIXTEEN

'I see a terrible disaster ahead.'
Hecate's doleful lament silenced the women sitting round the fire. It had become a ritual to gather at the end of the day and share a bottle of wine or some beer and talk. Most of them were sitting well back from the fire as it was a balmy night. Only Hecate did not seem to feel the heat of the flames and sat close to the fire. She did not even seem bothered by the green pine logs someone had foolishly put on the fire that spat molten resin and emitted eye-watering smoke. All she could see were the Tarot cards spread out in front of her in an arc on the ground.

As she looked up at the circle of now expectant faces, her face was illuminated by the flickering flames. 'I have consulted the cards and they counsel against precipitate action, so, too does my spirit guide, the goddess Demeter. All the signs portend misfortune. We must follow the path of enlightenment, not the tainted path of politics. We take that path at our peril.'

She lapsed into silence, gazing sightlessly into the heart of the fire, leaving the women to look nervously at each other.

'How can you be so sure?' someone asked.

Hecate picked two cards and held them up. They depicted a hanged man and death.

There was a sharp intake of breath, including from some of the women gathered around Lilith in a small group away from the main body of the camp. Lilith's eyes narrowed. When she first came to the camp, she had been happy to play along with Hecate's superstitious games as they seemed harmless enough. They had also helped to take her mind off the mess she had left behind in Chicago.

Lilith had been part of a collective printing a women's magazine, but increasingly, women were not buying feminist literature anymore, at least not the kind she wanted to publish. Sisterhood appeared to have been abandoned. Instead of articles about low pay for women migrant workers, women wanted articles about whether a feminist could wear lipstick and high heels and have cosmetic surgery, or whether it was politically correct for a lesbian to want a baby.

As if the endless arguments about what they should be printing were not enough, a developer bought the block of buildings in which the collective had its offices. Everybody else in the buildings - most of them so-called 'alternative' businesses like theirs - quickly sold out. By the time Lilith and her co-workers finally agreed to sell – she was outvoted by eleven to one – they were no longer in a position to play hardball with the developer. They had to accept less than the other businesses as the developers outflanked them by getting the city sanitation department to declare the building unfit for use. This last was especially galling as Lilith had been trying for years to get the sanitation department to take action against the old landlord as the place was a slum, but nobody had listened to her.

The collective found a new office and started a new magazine, but Lilith's heart was no longer in it and she decided to get as far away from Chicago as she could. When she read an article about the women's camp, it sounded like the perfect antidote - a remote Greek island with unspoilt beaches and hopefully, lots of sun, sand and sex. Yet here she was, not only involved in yet another battle against a developer, but also fighting to convince women that they were not going to stop the bulldozers by sitting round in circles chanting to a goddess.

She had gathered a small group of like-minded women around her. However, now that Hecate had publicly declared herself against any direct action, she could see by their expressions that even some of them were beginning to waver. Realising she had no choice but to confront Hecate or lose the support she had, Lilith reached for the plastic bottle of local red wine that they had been passing round the circle and drank deeply. She grimaced as the rough metallic-tasting liquid coursed down her throat, but the second mouthful didn't seem to taste quite as bad. She handed the bottle back to Marjorie.

'Bullshit!' she declared loudly.

Faces that had been looking at Hecate turned towards her.

'I thought we had agreed that no-one would use patriarchal terms of abuse,' ventured a small voice. It was Psyche. She was sitting with Juno's arm draped protectively around her shoulders.

'The lesbian thought police strike again. Heaven, or should it be the goddess, preserve us,' said Sîan drily. She lay stretched out on the ground, her head cradled in her arms, looking up at the stars.

Her remark provoked a chorus of angry exclamations from the other side of the circle and Juno scrambled menacingly to her feet. Sîan seemed unconcerned, but Marjorie spoke quietly to Lilith.

'I think you'd better do something, Lilith darling, we don't want another fight like the other night.'

Lilith stood up. 'Let's all try and keep our cool, okay? Maybe some of us are guilty of speaking out of turn, but quite frankly, I think we're in danger of getting bogged down in a load of mystical mud.'

A ripple of interest ran around the circle. Women who had been lounging half-asleep on the ground sat up expectantly. The camp had been bristling with the tension between Lilith and Hecate for weeks.

Hecate's close group of followers waited for her to react to Lilith's denunciation, but she remained impassive. Only her hands, twisting the large crystal pendant that hung around her neck, betrayed any emotion.

Hecate had dreamed of coming to Greece ever since she was a little girl, when she had been enchanted by tales of Greek gods and goddesses, but life had not provided her with the opportunity until now. She had nursed her semi-invalid mother for nearly thirty years, working as an assistant librarian to supplement their income. Paying for home help was too expensive and, as she had only been able to work part-time for the last five years of her mother's life, every penny had counted. Sometimes she had lived on lentil soup for weeks in order to keep the house heated and pay the bills.

The funny thing was, when her mother died, she discovered that although not rich, they had been a lot wealthier than she ever imagined. Her mother had squirreled quite large amounts of money away into several savings accounts. According to the solicitor who handled her mother's estate, her mother was of the generation that saved for a rainy day, but it seemed to Hecate - or Lorna as she was known then - that the last thirty years had been one long rainy day. Hecate transferred all her mother's savings into her own bank account then sold her mother's house, even though the solicitor advised her that if she was prepared to wait, she would get far more for it as property prices were rising.

Thirty years of caring for her mother had taught Hecate how to wait, but she was prepared to wait no longer. Years of study into the occult, late into the night after her mother was asleep, had convinced her that she had been living in only one of her many lifetimes. Now, she felt as though she was a butterfly, emerging from the tightly wrapped chrysalis that had been called Lorna. To celebrate her rebirth, she gave herself the name Hecate: goddess of the moon and of magic and witchcraft; who could see everything, whether in the past, present and future; and who was a virgin untouched by man or god, as indeed, Hecate, at the age of fifty, still was. Finding out about the women's camp had been like a sign from her namesake.

Although she had never been further than Brighton - the place that had introduced her to the Tarot and the study of the goddess - Hecate applied for her first passport two years ago, packed her bags and found her way to Greece and to the island. Most of the women only came to the camp during the summer, but she, along with a few other hardy souls, lived there all the year round. Although cold and wet, Hecate preferred the winter months. It was then that she could really recharge her spiritual batteries and commune with the goddess.

It had never been her intention, but, within a short time of arriving, Hecate found that the other women in the camp started to look to her for guidance and leadership. What began as Tarot readings led to her being looked up to as a spiritual authority on the ways of the goddess. In order to fulfil the trust the women put in her powers, Hecate began to follow a strict routine of fasting and meditation.

Soon, she found she needed to eat very little, and as her appetite lessened, her powers grew, and she began to realise that she could see auras around people. Sometimes the aura was very faint and wavery, and sometimes it glowed. It also changed colour according to the type of energy the person gave off. From the moment Lilith arrived, Hecate knew there would be trouble. Her aura was very powerful and radiated intense energy.

Now Hecate let her hands drop into her lap and gazed levelly across at Lilith. She did not intend to be drawn into a fight with the American as there was no need. She knew the time would come when she would be proved right. The cards had fortold it.

Lilith stared back. She was not going to let some witch outmanoeuvre her. After a moment or two, she realised that Hecate was not going to say anything, and feeling vaguely disquieted, she scrambled to her feet.

'I'm not trying to dispute that it's important for women to get in touch with their inner spirituality. I'm all for it. It's essential that we get back to understanding matriarchal values. For far too long, patriarchy and its gods have taught that Mother Earth and her resources exist only to be exploited. Animals, like women, have been relegated either to serve, or to be served up, for the benefit of men. As women, we understand the interconnectedness between the earth and ourselves more than men, and as sisters and true feminists, we understand that all oppressions come from the same root. We cannot fight one without fighting them all,' she finished passionately.

Sîan held her arm up, as though she were at school. 'Could I enquire what this has to do with your suggestion that we reclaim the taverna in the village square?'

Lilith turned and glared at her, but Sîan coolly returned her gaze.

'For those of you who need this explained in words of one syllable,' Lilith continued, her voice heavy with sarcasm. 'In villages like this, our Greek sisters are virtually excluded from public life. They dare not go into the tavernas and bars, particularly at night, unless they are with their families. To do so, would cause them to be branded as prostitutes. Even Westernised women like us feel uncomfortable in some places. Look what happened to Ullie and Jo the other night. They were enjoying a quiet drink in the taverna in the square and Andreas the policeman asked them to leave because they were holding hands.'

The two women Grace had seen while having breakfast on her first morning in the village nodded vigorously. They were sitting entwined round each other, touching and probing each other's body like grooming animals. They continued to touch even while they talked.

'He said there was some law...' began Ulrika.

'...to do with kissing in public,' finished Jo.

'I replied that laws should ban people hating each other...' Ulrika turned and kissed Jo on the lips.

'...not ban people loving each other,' Jo added before turning her attention back to kissing Ulrika.

'The twins are at it again,' joked someone.

'I thought incest was illegal,' someone else piped up.

Laughter greeted this, and people relaxed and began to talk.

Realising that she was losing their interest, Lilith held up her hands for silence. Then she pointed at Hecate. 'The point I am trying to make is that bulldozers will not be stopped by Tarot cards and crystals.' She looked slowly around the circle of women. 'Sisters, we have a choice. We can sit here and hold hands and hope for divine intervention, or take the struggle to the root of the problem. I am suggesting that we occupy the taverna in the square because it is owned by the Mayor. All village business is decided during men-only sessions in there, and that includes deals to build the hotel. We must demonstrate that they can't intimidate us, and that women have the right to go where they want. If we don't, then what is all this about?' She waved her arm at the surrounding tents.

There was silence, apart from the crackle of wood burning and the snap of a can of beer being opened. Lilith sank down next to Marjorie and reached for the bottle of wine.

It was Hecate's turn to speak, but she poked the fire with a stick, causing a shower of sparks to flare upwards, before looking around. Her face was pale in the moonlight.

'It is not for me to say what we should do,' she said slowly. 'I am merely an instrument through which the goddess allows her will to be known. It is up to each of you to choose your own way. Remember, we all agreed. The woman's way is that we are all one and all equal.' She lifted her head and looked directly at Lilith so that nobody could mistake the meaning of her next words. 'No one woman can dictate to the others.'

Juno nodded vigorously. 'Hecate's right, we agreed. We act collectively or not at all. We should take a vote.'

'Could we have a secret ballot?' ventured Psyche.

'Perhaps we should have a vote on that too,' said another voice.

There was a ripple of laughter at this.

'Well *I* vote we should all go along tomorrow night and have a kiss-in and drive all those great hairy Greek men wild,' said Sîan, generating even louder laughter.

'Sex is all you ever think about. Some of us are trying to rise above it and discover our spirituality,' accused Juno.

'So that's what all those strange noises were coming from your tent the other night - you and Psyche were practising non-sexual levitation,' countered Sîan.

Juno scrambled to her feet again. 'You're a *slut*. You have sex with everyone, even men. You're not one of us.'

Sîan got to her feet too. 'Whom I choose to have sex with is my affair, but at least I limit myself to sex between consenting adults and don't prey on poor confused little girls who don't know what they want - men or women.'

The two women faced each other across the fire, the flickering light illuminating their angry features. With her arms crossed, and massive legs planted apart, Juno looked dangerous, but Sîan stood her ground, even though she gave away at least four stone in weight.

Hecate stood up and stepped between them. 'The cards were right. We are already turning one against the other.'

'I agree with Hecate,' said Lilith. 'Let's try and remember who we're fighting here, shall we?'

Juno glared balefully at Sîan for a moment then returned to Psyche's side.

There was an uncomfortable silence. Only Ulrika and Jo seemed unconcerned. Before the argument had started, they had moved outside the circle to the sand dunes that separated the camp from the beach. They had removed their T-shirts and were using them as pillows as they lay, bare-breasted, gazing up at the stars. Ulrika had rolled a large joint, and they passed it back and forth, pausing only to almost absentmindedly caress each other's breasts.

Now Jo raised her head and waved the joint. 'Hey, come on everybody, chill out. Anyone want to join us? Ulrika got a parcel today and its good stuff.' As if to emphasise her point, she took a long draw and sank back onto the sand.

Sîan pulled off her t-shirt exposing her naked breasts. 'I don't know about anybody else, but I think this meeting's well and truly over,' she declared.

Trailing her sarong behind her, she walked across the circle and stepped over Juno's outstretched legs. She accepted the proffered joint, and inhaled deeply, before kissing Jo on the lips and Ulrika on her right breast.

As other women began to undress and join them, Marjorie stood up and unbuttoned her blouse. 'Aren't you coming?' she asked Lilith.

Lilith shook her head. 'There are more important things to think about. We've got to plan a campaign.'

Marjorie let her skirt drop onto the ground and kicked it away. 'Why can't we just enjoy ourselves for once? I thought we were meant to be on holiday,' she said as she headed for the dunes.

Lilith found herself standing alone with Hecate. Perhaps it was her imagination playing tricks on her, or perhaps it was too much Greek wine, but there were times when Hecate really did not seem quite of this world. She had an inner stillness about her that made Lilith, who liked to be on the move all the time feel uncomfortable, just as now, as she felt Hecate's wide-set orange-tawny eyes watching her for the second time that evening.

'Sometimes it's easier to fight battles against the whole world than to confront the demons inside yourself, and you can't run away from them, no matter how far you travel. Believe me, I know.'

'Please don't waste your spiritual claptrap on me, Hecate,' Lilith was curt. 'The last thing women need is yet another quasi religion telling them how they should feel. I know what *I* feel.'

'Do you? I wonder,' said Hecate.

Lilith was just about to reply when Hecate's hand on her arm silenced her. 'Why don't you join Marjorie,' Hecate said gently. 'I think she's waiting for you.' With that, she melted away into the darkness leaving Lilith looking at the space where she had stood.

Lilith turned back to the light of the fire. She must not let a woman with weird eyes get to her.

'Lilith darling, do join us.' It was Marjorie plaintive voice.

Lilith reluctantly pulled her T-shirt over her head. Marjorie's childlike ability to live for the pleasure of the moment had been attractive when they had first met, but it was getting less so. First thing tomorrow morning, she would call a meeting to plan a campaign of direct action. She walked slowly over to the dunes and stood looking down at the semi-naked bodies lying entwined around each other.

Sîan had just rolled another joint. She held it up. 'Peace pipe?'

Lilith took it and sat down beside her. 'Yeah, why not?'

Sîan lay back on the sand and put her arms behind her head. 'I'm with you on the taverna, and so are a lot of the others. Although sometimes when I look into Hecate's eyes, I have to remind myself that she's just a Tarot reader from Croydon, and her stormtrooper lieutenant Eva Braun von Juno is enough to put the frighteners on anybody.'

For the first time that evening, Lilith smiled.

Sîan reached for the joint and took a long draw. 'I'll be seeing nymphs and satyrs behind every rock soon. Maybe I've had just a little bit too much of the funny stick.' She laughed.

Marjorie started to laugh too. 'I haven't had this much fun since the Sixties.' She put her hand over her mouth. 'Did I really just say that? I'm giving my age away.'

Sîan rolled over onto her stomach. 'We might be having fun, but it looks like Eva Braun and Tinkerbell are having an argument.'

They all looked in the same direction. Psyche was struggling to free herself from Juno's embrace.

'I'm *going*! I don't care what you say. I want to have some fun too.'

She marched past them onto the beach where she stripped and ran into the sea, her body white against its blackness.

Juno stood on top of the dunes. 'Psyche! Come back. It's too dangerous.' She watched helplessly, as Psyche swam away from the shore. *'Please...'*

'Eva Braun can't swim. Do you remember her rebirthing?' asked Sîan, 'it was nearly the death of her.' She began to laugh.

'She's right though.' Lilith sat up, suddenly alert. 'It's stupid to go swimming so soon after eating and drinking. The water will be cold and there are some strong currents out there.'

They all sat up and strained their eyes, trying to see Psyche. After a moment or two, her head appeared above the surface, her face towards the shore. She was swimming back. She stood up in the shallows, her breasts gleaming palely in the moonlight.

She waved. 'Juno! See I'm...'

Her voice was drowned out by the roar of four motorbikes that suddenly appeared over the dunes, further along the beach. They sped along the beach and came to a stop in front of Psyche. She put her arms across her breasts and shrank down into the water.

The men kept revving their engines as they yelled at her in Greek, gesticulating that she should come out.

'Oh my god, what shall we do?' gasped one of the women.

'The only thing we can do,' said Lilith as she rose to her feet. 'Come on, there's more of us than there are of them. Grab a stick, a rock, anything you can.'

She reached down and picked up a piece of driftwood. The other women did the same.

'Shouldn't we put on some clothes?' asked someone.

'No, let's give them the surprise of their lives,' replied Lilith. 'They want naked women, so let's give them naked women.'

She looked across at Juno who had armed herself with a large stick. Juno swiftly unbuttoned her shirt, revealing vast pendulous breasts.

Lilith looking round to check that everyone was carrying something. 'Keep together, and when I say go, make as much noise as you can. Okay?'

She held her piece of wood like a rapier in front of her. *'Charge*!' she yelled, and with a wild, banshee like scream, she ran towards the motorbikes.

Juno leapt after her, yelling loudly, and the others followed, their shouts and screams gaining strength as they went. Despite her size,

Juno was surprisingly fleet of foot. Within a few yards, she overtook Lilith.

The motor cyclists attempted to wheel around to face them, yelling wild directions at each other. Two of the bikes collided and another spun out from underneath its rider as he revved the engine too much. As he tried to right it and get back onto the seat, Juno brought her stick down on his shoulder with a satisfying thump and he cried out in pain. As he clutched his shoulder, she grabbed his hair and wrestled him to the ground. One of the other riders, who had regained control of his bike, drove straight at her, but she sidestepped and managed to thump him on the kidneys as he went past. Then, forgetting her fear of water, she waded into the sea where she gathered a shivering and near hysterical Psyche into her arms.

The rest of the battle did not last long. Lilith bloodied the nose of one of the other riders before he escaped. The fourth, who had driven straight at the women, hoping to force them to scatter, had to run a gauntlet of sticks and fists before he finally roared off along the beach, swerving from side to side only to crash into a sand dune when Hecate suddenly loomed up in front him, whirling a stick over her head. He left his bike, wheels still spinning and ran off.

The women stood looking at each other panting. Lilith started to grin. 'We won!' she yelled triumphantly, and brandishing her stick, she executed a high-kicking victory dance.

The other women joined in, hugging and kissing each other.

Lilith was still dancing when Juno came across, one arm around a wan-looking Psyche. She held out her other hand to Lilith.

'Sisters?'

Lilith stopped dancing. For a moment she stared at the proffered hand and then grasped it. 'The taverna?' she asked.

Juno smiled grimly. 'The bastards won't know what's hit them.'

SEVENTEEN

The crash of cooking pots slammed down onto a hard surface made Grace wince. Not for the first time that evening, she wished she had followed her better instincts and gone back to her room. Instead, her guilt at her jibe about him taking tips from women had allowed Yanni to persuade her to come to his taverna. She wanted Yanni to think well of her, but another crash made it abundantly clear that his mother, Anthoula, did not.

Under the cover of sipping her wine, Grace glanced surreptitiously into the kitchen, only to meet Anthoula's angry glare yet again. Arms akimbo, she had been waiting at the door of the taverna when they returned from the beach. She was only a tiny woman, barely five foot high, and her black widow's weeds made her seem even tinier, but her voice would not have shamed a regimental sergeant major. To Grace's ears, Yanni appeared to stand accused of what sounded like a vast catalogue of heinous crimes against humanity, even before he had dismounted from his motor bike. She tried to make her excuses and leave, but Yanni insisted she stay and eat, claiming that the argument had nothing to do with her. However, his mother's looks and gestures said otherwise.

Grace offered Anthoula a friendly smile, but that only resulted in her starting to chop aubergines and tomatoes with terrifying ferocity. Grace looked away, not wanting to see bloody fingers flying everywhere. Yanni was carrying crates in from outside and loading beer bottles into the fridge near her table. She watched him, enjoying the muscularity of his movements. She had not thought he was aware of her gaze, but suddenly he caught her eye and once again, she felt an uncharacteristic blush on her cheeks. To cover her embarrassment, she indicated the bottle of wine he had insisted on opening for her, despite her protestations that she was not much of a drinker.

'Won't you join me in a glass of wine?'

Yanni glanced in the direction of the kitchen where Anthoula had stopped chopping and was watching them, a large knife in her hand. 'I am sorry, but I must help my mother in the kitchen, we have much food to make. Maybe later?' He started to walk away.

'Yanni.'

He stopped and turned back, an eyebrow raised interrogatively.

Grace ran her finger round the rim of her glass. 'Are you sure I'm not the reason why your mother is so angry?'

He shrugged. 'Why should she be angry with you? I have told her there is nothing between us. You are my friend, that is all.'

'Of course,' agreed Grace quickly. 'It was just the way she...'

'People in the village talk. They see us ride on my bike and they think there is something more. I do not care what people think, but my mother...' He shrugged again, this time holding his hands up as though in supplication. 'In Greece, people do not think a man and a woman can be friends.'

A Volkswagen camper van full of German tourists arrived just at that moment, demanding his attention. Grace was grateful for the diversion. She felt in constant danger of making a fool of herself around Yanni. She poured herself another glass of wine. He had made it quite clear that he was not in the least bit attracted to her, and that he thought of her as a friend, nothing else. How could she have been so stupid as to think otherwise? She was acting like a silly adolescent girl. She was engaged to be married and, even if she hadn't been, holiday flings were her mother's style, not hers.

She watched as Yanni welcomed the German tourists. By their greetings, they had obviously been to the village before. There were eight of them and they looked impossibly tanned and healthy. A statuesque red-headed woman of about forty appeared to be the mother of at least four of the children, judging from their close resemblance to her, including two nubile girls of about fifteen and sixteen. The woman and her two daughters now gazed flirtatiously up at Yanni, who clearly enjoying their attention. The mother touched Yanni's arm every time she selected something from the menu, and, when Yanni bent down to look at something she was pointing at, his dark head almost met her shining red hair putting him within inches of her jutting breasts.

Grace waited for the man she assumed to be the red-head's husband to show his disapproval, but he seemed to be egging her on. As Yanni walked away, they leaned across the table to talk to each other, their laughter and glances in Yanni's direction making it quite clear they were talking about him. To Grace's irritation, when Yanni returned with their drinks, despite refusing to join her, he accepted their offer of a glass of wine, then pulled up a chair and sat down between the mother and her elder daughter. He seemed happy to remain sandwiched between the two women - one arm caressed by the mother, the other by the long tresses of the daughter - until a sharp command from the kitchen brought him reluctantly to his feet.

To Grace's surprise, the elder daughter followed him into the kitchen where she hugged a now smiling, Anthoula. Looking completely at home, the girl picked up a teacloth, tied it around her slim waist and began to slice vegetables. Even though the kitchen was barely large enough to accommodate two, Anthoula did not seem to mind this intrusion, nor that it caused Yanni to have constantly to squeeze past the daughter in order to get around.

The taverna was now becoming busier and it was some time before Yanni came over to Grace's table with plate of savoury pastries.

'You try, yes?' he asked.

Grace ignored the food and indicated the other table. 'You accepted a drink from *her*.'

Yanni looked at her with an amused expression in his eyes. 'I am sorry,' he said gravely,'but they come every year. It is good business, I must accept.'

It had not looked much like business to Grace, but she swallowed the temptation to say so. She had already made enough of a fool of herself.

'I'm not very hungry. Perhaps I ought to be going.'

Yannia picked up a small filo pastry and offered it to Grace. 'My mother made these especially for you...as my friend.'

Grace looked across to where Anthoula was now standing behind the counter watching her, her eyes hostile.

'Well, that's very kind, but I don't think...'

He held out the pastry. Reluctantly, Grace went to take it from his hand but he held it, indicating she should open her mouth. Embarrassed, she complied and he fed her. She swallowed quickly.

'That was very nice, thank you. And thank your mother too.'

Yanni looked satisfied. 'Eat more. I will come back later and then I will have a drink and we will talk. Yes?'

There was a burst of laughter from the table where the German tourists were sitting. Grace looked across. The mother and her two daughters were all looking in her direction.

She shook her head. 'I'm sorry. I really must go. Perhaps we can have that drink another time.' She opened her purse. 'Can I have my bill please?'

Yanni waved his hand. 'There is no bill.'

'Oh but I must insist...' Grace awkwardly held out some drachma notes.

Yanni's features darkened. 'It is of no importance,' he said, ignoring the proffered money.

'Please. I really can't let you...'

Grace knew it would be more dignified to accept and walk away, but why should she bow to his stubborn pride? She had just as much right, if not more, to insist on paying. She thrust the notes at him again, but as she did, there was a sudden commotion on the terrace outside. Yanni went to the door. Grace hesitated for a moment or two and then, reluctantly stuffing her money back into her purse, she followed him. Whatever was happening outside might give her the chance to slip quietly away and save her from further embarrassment.

She couldn't see what was causing the disruption, but, above the noise of over excited Greek voices, she could hear what sounded like a choir. Assuming it was some sort of religious procession, she pushed her way through the people clustered round the door. The procession had just turned the corner and was about fifty yards from the taverna. Grace reasoned that if she hurried, she could keep in front of it and get back to the quiet of her room. She had no appetitie for crowds.

She started to walk away quickly, but as she did, for the first time she heard the singing clearly. It bore no resemblance to Greek religious music. A rich contralto voice sang, then the chorus was taken up with great, if not always tuneful, gusto by other voices. Grace paused, trying to catch the words. They were distinctly un-Greek. The words of the chorus sounded something like: 'sisters are doing it for themselves'. She turned back, curious to know what was happening.

Walking down the road behind her, their arms linked, were about twenty or thirty women from the camp. They were led by Lilith and Marjorie, and three other women Grace recognised from the rebirthing ceremony. One was the woman who had introduced herself as Sîan, the other two were the large shaven-headed woman and her small skinny friend, who Grace had mistakenly thought was trying to commit suicide.

As the women drew level with the taverna, a table-full of young Greek men stood up and began to laugh at them, making what, even without translation, were clearly obscene gestures. A middle-aged Greek woman remonstrated with them but they ignored her, and their comments grew louder and more raucous. Grace had seen enough and she turned to go, but it was too late. Before she could get away, Marjorie caught sight of her and breaking rank, seized her by the arm and pulled her into line next to Sîan.

Just as she did, a woman shouted: 'Hey! That's one of the men on the motor bikes.'

The women surged towards the terrace, her mother's grip taking Grace along as they took up their song again. It was led by the powerful contralto which Grace now realised issued from the ample chest of the shaven-headed woman whom she had heard called Juno.

The women stood face to face with the catcalling men, both sides trying to drown each other out. However, Grace was not looking at the faces in front of her. She was searching for Yanni, hoping he would not see her with the women. At first, she could not see him as there was now quite a crowd on the terrace, but then she spotted him standing at the back. Their eyes met for an instant, and then he was gone. All she could see was a row of mocking faces.

Before she could even think about what she was doing, the line wheeled around with almost military precision, and Grace found herself being marching marched down the road towards the village square with the rest of the women.

'So you've decided to join the sisterhood then?' whispered Sîan, under the cover of the singing.

'Not exactly,' hissed Grace. 'What on earth is going on?'

'We're taking direct action,' said Marjorie, hearing her question. 'They tried to invade us, but we saw them off. Now we're going to give them a dose of their own medicine.'

Grace looked from one to the other, bewildered. 'Direct action? Invasion?'

'Ever heard of the Furies?' asked Sîan.

'Something in ancient Greece?' replied Grace, searching her memory for long forgotten school lessons for the second time that day.

'Crones with snakes for hair, dog-like heads, bats' wings for arms and coal black bodies. They carried brass-studded scourges and hounded their victims relentlessly before tearing them limb from limb, and causing them to die in terrible torment,' said Sîan with relish. 'They were the ultimate diesel dykes. They would have gone down a treat in S & M clubs, although I think the uniform needs a bit of an update. The snake, dog and bat wing bits are a tad too retro for me, but the death's head rings on Juno's knuckles will more than make up for the brass-studded scourges.' She laughed. 'You should have seen her tearing down the beach tonight, her bare breasts flying in the wind. She looked ready to tear these guys on motorbikes to bits, they looked scared shitless!'

'We *all* did our bit,' said Marjorie peevishly.

'Yeah. I noticed you have a pretty effective right hook, Gaia,' laughed Sîan.

Grace stared at her mother. 'What on earth have you been up to now? What motorbikes?'

Marjorie giggled. 'It was such fun! Some of the boys from the village decided to try to scare us, but we turned the tables on them. I hit one of the boys with a stick and then punched him on the nose,' she clenched her fist to demonstrate. 'He just stood there, looking ready to burst into tears surrounded by all these naked women!'

'You were naked...' Grace's voice started to rise but she was forced to stop speaking by Lilith calling for silence.

'Quiet, *quiet*...'

The singing stopped. They were standing in front of the taverna at the corner of the village square. Inside men were sitting at tables playing tavli and talking.

Lilith turned to face them. 'Now you all know what you must do.'

The women nodded vigorously.

'Remember, if anyone gets into trouble, we're all behind you, all you have to do is holler. Just make sure nobody gets separated from the rest of us. Are you ready?'

There was a low murmur of assent.

Lilith turned and held up her arm. 'Forward!' she urged and led the way inside the taverna.

Grace pulled back but Sîan grabbed her arm. 'Come on. This will be fun and you have to admit, there isn't much else in the way of nightlife round here.' She smiled encouragingly.

'But I don't know what we're meant to be doing,' protested Grace weakly.

'Just follow me,' said Sîan pulling her.

EIGHTEEN

With almost military precision and to the openmouthed astonishment of the men already there, the women marched in silently in and occupied every empty chair in the place, including those at tables where men were sitting. Sîan pulled Grace down onto a chair at a table close beside the door, and she sat there, looking around, wondering what she was doing.

She recognised some of the woman from the rebirthing ceremony, but others she had not seen before. It was her first real chance to study them and they were a much more disparate group than she expected. She could distinguish a variety of different European accents, as well as American and Australian. For the most part, their appearance would not have excited attention anywhere, although some of the younger women wore large amounts of pierced jewellery, not just in their ears, but also in their noses, and several wore rings through their lips and eyebrows.

Lilith and Marjorie, together with Juno and Psyche, had occupied the table at the centre of the room and the four of them were now looking around as though they were prepared to take on all-comers. Juno in particular looked as though she would like to challenge the men to arm wrestle, her sleeveless T-shirt revealing broad shoulders and muscular arms. As it was, she confined herself to the visual equivalent of arm wrestling - engaging the hostile stares of the men until they looked away.

'We're not such a bunch of freaks after all, are we?'

Grace jumped at Sîan's enquiry. It was almost as though Sîan had been reading her mind.

'I wasn't thinking anything of the sort. It's just that...'

'We're not your usual sort of people?' Sîan raised an enquiring eyebrow. 'Don't worry. You're not the first person to think what you're thinking and you won't be the last. You're not the least like your mother, are you?'

'I sincerely hope not,' retorted Grace.

'Tell me to mind my own business if you want, but do I sense that you and Gaia are not the best of friends?'

'Marjorie,' said Grace with some asperity, 'is not the easiest of women to have as a mother.'

'Is anybody?' asked Sîan. 'I have this terrible fear that it's hormonal, and that when I get around to having children, I'll become just like my mother, doomed forever to complain at, and be complained about, by my daughters. It's the double whammy that nature has in store for all women. Our inescapable fate - like death. However, when I have children, I'm going to try and cheat old Mother Nature by producing only boys.'

She grinned at Grace, and Grace found she could not help smiling back.

'I daren't say it too loud around here, as I suspect I might get burned at the stake as a heretic,' Sîan continued in a voice that suggested she would not go to the stake without a struggle. 'But I suspect some women are just as anxious as their mothers to hang on to the psychological umbilical cord which binds them together. It relieves them of taking responsibility for their lives, because they can always blame their mothers for what goes wrong.' She waved her hand. 'Look at this lot in here. With a few notable exceptions, until Lilith came along, they were all engaged in a search for some kind of mystical mother as if they hadn't had enough with their own. It's as though they are intent on hauling themselves hand over hand along some cosmic umbilical cord until they can disappear back into the womb so to speak, and in doing so, avoid having to deal with reality. They claim there was some golden age when women and mothers reigned supreme and everyone was happy, which seems a contradiction in terms to me. According to legend, the so-called Great Earth Mother was as likely to eat her children as to nurture them, but they seem to conveniently forget that side of her character.'

'So what are you doing here?' Grace looked puzzled. 'I mean, if you don't believe all this goddess nonsense and you're not a lesb...' She stopped. 'What I mean to say is, if you want to have children...what are you here for?'

Sîan laughed. 'Sorry to disappoint you, but I'm here for the women too, although my fantasies about orgies of writhing brown flesh have so far been unfortunately thwarted. Still, a girl can dream.' She looked directly into Grace's eyes when she said this.

Grace felt her cheeks grow hot.

Sîan laughed. 'Don't look so worried Grace. You're a very foxy lady but I'm not going to leap on you. At least...not unless you want me to,' she added in a throaty voice.

'It's not that I don't think you're ... well, you're very nice but...'

Grace was saved from further embarrassment by raucous laughter outside the taverna. A group of about a dozen young men, some of whom had been at Yanni's taverna earlier, had gathered around the doorway. One of them yelled for the waiter, and Nondas, a plump, balding man, who had been conspicuously absent since the arrival of the women, appeared from the kitchen. He put some bottles of beer onto a tray and, keeping his head down, took it outside to serve the men. When he came back, Juno tried to attract his attention, but he ignored her and disappeared back behind the bar.

There was an angry mutter from the women. Juno got up and walked to the bar. She thumped on the counter.

'We were here first. We *demand* to be served.'

There was no response from behind the plastic strip curtain that covered the door into the kitchen.

Juno stood for a moment or two, her hands on her hips. Then she strode behind the counter and opened the fridge. Loading her arms up with bottles of beer, she distributed them among the tables before returning for some more.

Psyche looked nervously at the bottle Juno had put in front of her. 'Do you think we ought to? Surely it's stealing?'

Lilith snapped the top off and drank some of hers. 'Bullshit. We're going to pay, *if* the man isn't too frightened to take our money.' She raised her voice as she said this and was rewarded by a twitch of the curtain. She raised her bottle. 'Here's to us.'

Her toast was greeted by a rousing cheer.

Grace left her beer untouched. 'How long are you planning to remain in the taverna?' she asked Sîan.

'As long as it takes. Some of these women are veterans of Reclaim the Night and Clause 28 demos, so reclaiming a taverna should be a doddle for them.' Sîan nodded towards the door. 'I think I spy reinforcements.'

A small, but imperious looking man, stood in the doorway. It was Takis the Mayor. He had the confident air of a man accustomed to crisply starched clothes, and to having his commands obeyed. Behind him was the local policeman, his cap pulled down onto his forehead and his eyes shaded by mirrored aviator sunglasses, even though it was now nearly half past ten at night. The women went quiet.

Lilith looked around. 'We're doing nothing wrong. This is a public bar. They're just trying to intimidate us, but we won't be intimidated, will we?'

There was an answering chorus of 'nos'.

The Mayor walked slowly into the taverna. The policeman followed, one hand on the shiny brown leather gun holster on his hip as though he was expecting an ambush. Two men got up and offered their seats to them, and then made a hasty exit. Nondas appeared as if by magic, and delivered a bottle of metaxa and two glasses to the Mayor's table. Then he went back and this time stood behind his bar as though waiting for something to happen.

Lilith snapped her fingers at him. 'Four more beers,' she ordered curtly.

Nondas glanced uncertainly at the Mayor who shrugged his shoulders, seemingly indicating he should comply. He placed the beers on a tray, and then made a great play of counting the number of bottles already on the tables before making out a bill that he presented to Lilith as he served the beers. He stood waiting for her to pay, one eye on the policeman for security.

Lilith pulled some notes out of her back pocket and slapped them down on the table. Nondas counted them several times before returning to the bar, where he stood polishing and repolishing the counter, the sweat glistening on his bald patch.

The policeman at last took his hand away from his holster and picked up his glass. Grace gulped a mouthful of beer. Her mouth had gone dry. The women were acting as though they were at some sort of party. Surely they had made their point and it was time to leave? Her heart sank as she intercepted a glance from Lilith to

Ulrika and Jo. They immediately put their arms around each other and in full view of the Mayor and the policeman, began a long, slow passionate kiss.

'I think the touch paper has just been lit,' murmured Sîan.

The Mayor glanced at his watch as though timing them and then stood up. He smoothed back his hair, hitched up his trousers, and then walked across to their table. Clicking his heels in a military fashion, he gave a self-conscious little cough and then spoke in English.

'It is an offence against Greek law to behave in this way in public. If you do not stop, I must ask for the policeman to arrest you.' The Mayor inclined his head, and with another click of his heels returned to his table where he sat down and carefully crossed his legs, trying not to ruin the crease in his trousers.

Ulrika and Jo drew apart. The Mayor gave a little satisfied nod to the policeman and lifted his glass to his mouth, but it was only a momentary pause. Ulrika had only stopped long enough to turn round and this time, reposition herself astride Jo's lap. She then made a great play of putting a hand inside Jo's T-shirt and caressing her breasts before they began to kiss again, their bodies moving up and down in unison. There was a loud whooping noise and a barrage of whistled encouragement from the other women.

The Mayor looked as though a rather unpleasant smell had dared to waft under his nose. He uncrossed his legs and brushed his trousers, removing imaginary specks of dust, then walked across to Jo and Ulrika's table and once again clicked his heels while coughing discreetly. Jo and Ulrika ignored him. He coughed again, this time a little more loudly.

'Madames, I have warned you the first time. This time I must ask the policeman to arrest you. You are an offence to public morals.'

Ulrika and Jo continued to kiss.

The Mayor beckoned to the policeman who pulled his cap even lower down on his forehead and loosened his gun in his holster before marching across the room. He stood beside the Mayor, one hand on his gun. There were some encouraging shouts from the doorway, and the policeman looked grateful, but the Mayor held up his hand to silence them. He then turned to the policeman who, after patting his gun once more as though for reassurance, tapped Ulrika on the shoulder. She continued to kiss Jo. The policeman placed a hand on her shoulder and pulled. Ulrika clung to Jo. Frustrated, he grabbed her by both arms and pulled even harder, but his efforts only succeeded in pulling both of them as well as the chair along the floor. Defeated, he let go.

The women who had been drumming their feet on the floor and yelling protests, now laughed derisively and applauded.

There was an angry exchange in Greek between the two men. From the Mayor's gestures it appeared he was demanding the immediate arrest of the two women, but the policeman's even more expressive gestures seemed to indicate that he had a bad back and had no intention of lifting them both together and carrying them to jail. Although he was the smaller man, the Mayor appeared to swell up and tower over the hapless policeman. After another series of shrugs and gestures which appeared to be addressed more to an uncaring and heartless world than to anyone in particular, the policeman removed his hat and placed it upside down on a table and then placed his sunglasses carefully inside.

Despite the gun strapped to his hip, without his reflective sunglasses the policeman no longer looked menacing. His hatband had left a shiny red indentation around his forehead, while a few straggling hairs combed across his bald pate revealed why he had kept his hat so tightly on his head. He blinked nervously as he approached Ulrika and Jo once more, dark patches of sweat spreading visibly under the armpits of his blue shirt. However, before his outstretched hands could touch the women, they stopped kissing.

Relief etched on his features, he turned back to the Mayor, his upheld palms indicating he could do no more. As he reached for his hat, the Mayor made an apoplectic noise and pointed a quivering finger at Juno and Psyche who were now locked together in another kiss. The policeman's shoulders sagged, but mindful of his duty, he took a deep breath and prepared to arrest them. However, before he could make a move, Lilith and Marjorie began to kiss, and then two women at the next table put their arms around each other, followed by another two. Within moments, the taverna was full of kissing women.

The Mayor's face turned unhealthily red and he waved his arm wildly. 'You are *all* arrested,' he yelled angrily.

The policeman looked ready to burst into tears. He seemed unable to decide whom to arrest first and stood making strange jerking movements as though he had lost control of his limbs.

Grace began to laugh. She had almost forgotten what it felt like. It surged up from somewhere deep inside her, forcing its way out and making her sides ache so much that she was forced to clasp her arms around her middle. The absurdity of the situation threatened to overwhelm her. Not only was she trapped in the middle of nowhere with a bunch of madwomen who appeared to be running some kind of coven, her mother was making love, or a pretty good approximation of it, to a woman in the middle of a room full of people.

She could have gone on laughing for a long time, but a sudden loud retort, followed by a shower of glass and sparks as the ceiling light exploded, turned her laughter into a gasp as the taverna was plunged into darkness and screams and shouts erupted followed by the sound of glass shattering and furniture being upturned. Fearing for her mother's safety, Grace started across the taverna in an attempt to reach her, but Sîan grabbed her hand, pulled her towards the door.

'Let's get out of here before it turns nasty,' said Sîan as she pushed their way through a crowd of people trying to get in to see what had happened.

'What about the others?' asked Grace as they stumbled onto the street.

'They'll be alright, don't worry. Aside from Lilith who can handle herself anywhere, there are some tough old war horses of Greenham Common and other battles in there. They won't let anyone come to any harm. Pity the poor men. They're not used to women like us.'

'But it's my mother I'm worried about,' said Grace pulling herself free of Sîan's grip and turning to go back inside.

Sîan put a hand on her arm. 'Grace, I don't think you know your mother very well, although from what I've seen, she knows you all *too* well. She's got you dancing around on the end of her stick.'

Grace shook her hand away. 'You don't understand. She *needs* me.'

'Listen to yourself will you Grace?' pleaded Sîan impatiently. 'For a moment in there when you started laughing, I thought you were beginning to loosen up. Your mother's not the problem, *you* are.'

'Well, if that's how you feel...'

'If I told you the way I feel about you right now Grace, you'd probably run a mile. But I'll settle for being just good friends if you agree to finish this bottle of Metaxa with me,' Sîan held out the bottle.

Grace looked aghast. 'You took the Mayor's brandy?'

'It seemed such a shame to waste it. Isn't there some rule about the spoils of war?' laughed Sîan. 'Truce?'

Grace hesitated for a moment or two, and then smiled.

Sîan linked her hand through Grace's arm. 'I think this may be the beginning of a beautiful friendship,' she announced, as they walked off down the street.

NINETEEN

'Did you know that the Milky Way was formed when milk from the goddess Hera's breast spurted across the heavens?' asked Sîan, waving her arm at a sky encrusted with glittering pin points of light.

Grace looked up. It was probably the effect of the half bottle of Greek brandy she had drunk, but she had never seen so many stars so large, or so bright. It would be so much more romantic to believe that they were droplets of milk from the swollen breasts of some ancient goddess, rather than chunks of lifeless rock resulting from some explosion. Her mother always complained that she was far too literal-minded and lacked imagination, even when she was a child. She replaced the nearly empty bottle of brandy in the sand castle she and Sîan had built, and eased into a cross-legged position. A few feet away, the sea gently lapped the shore. She looked down. Sîan was lying on her back and appeared to be trying to count the stars.

'You seem very knowledgeable about Greek mythology.'

Sîan stopped counting and turned her head. 'It's weird what sticks in your memory from school despite a misspent youth. I went to an old-fashioned all-girls school that I hated, particularly as they taught classics. I loathed Latin, but our teacher lightened Greek lessons with tales from Greek mythology. It really got my attention when I discovered that far from being about a boring load of old dead people, it was all about sex and violence.' She laughed. 'Zeus was quite a character, he had it away left, right and centre with any young nymph he could lay his hands on. I could really identify with someone who wanted sex so much he would do anything, including turning himself into a swan, to get it.'

'So you didn't identify with the goddesses?'

Sîan rolled onto her side and propped herself up on one elbow. 'Only with Artemis, the virgin huntress. She preferred wearing masculine clothes and hated anything to do with family life, which I could identify with. According to legend, she and her handmaidens were bathing naked, after hunting in the hills of Arcadia with their hounds, when they discovered that they were being spied upon by this guy called Actaeon. So Artemis set her hunting hounds on him and they tore him to pieces. Really gory stuff don't you think? Mind you, I've always had my own theory that Artemis and her handmaidens were up to more than just a little naked bathing, and that Acteaon was the first old man in a dirty raincoat at a peep show. The idea of seeing two women making love to each other is a universal male fantasy, if not to say obsession, I'm sure you've noticed.'

'Not really,' said Grace faintly.

Sîan sat up. 'Not that its any of my business, and please tell me to butt out if I get too personal, but are you married or cohabiting or anything?'

'I'm engaged.'

'Now that's a very old-fashioned word. I wasn't sure that people used the term anymore, or perhaps it's just the kind of circles *I* move in.'

'We live together too,' Grace added, not wishing to appear too antiquated.

'So why have you got engaged? Why not just tie the knot if that's what you really want to do?' asked Sîan.

'Well, because...' Grace stopped. What *was* the point of being engaged?

'You're not wearing a ring.'

Grace automatically checked her hand. Roger had given her a ring. He said it was a family heirloom. It was a large emerald surrounded by diamonds and pearls. She did not like it, but did not want to hurt his feelings, so she rarely wore it, telling him it was much too valuable to risk losing.

'Roger gave me one, but I don't really like to wear it...'

Sîan looked interested. 'So, tell me about this Roger. I love the idea of settling down with someone, but I know myself too well. I just can't resist a pretty face and the idea of only having sex with one person for the rest of my life terrifies me. Every time I have great sex with someone, I think this is it, this is the right person. But then I get to thinking - suppose I meet someone else with whom I can have even *better* sex...' She laughed and shrugged her shoulders.

'But you've obviously got the sex thing sorted with Roger. I envy you.'

Grace picked up a handful of sand and let the grains trickle through her fingers. Great sex was not one of the main reasons she decided to marry Roger, it wasn't even one of the minor ones. She'd had other relationships before Roger; one started at university and lasted until she was twenty-three, the other, when she was in her late twenties, lasted nearly two years. She assumed both would end in marriage, and although there had been no great quarrels or betrayals, they just slowly, but surely, petered out. She was sad at both of them ending, but could not claim to have been devastated. She had remained friends with both men and gone to their weddings. One of them had even asked her to be the godmother to his first child. It had all been very civilised. After that, she had been quite happy being single. She had her lovely little house in Putney and her work as an editor, which she loved. Roger had slipped into her her life almost without her even noticing. No great declarations of love or sexual fireworks - he was just *there*.

'It's not really about sex with Roger,' she began. 'It's just that Roger makes me feel safe. He sort of *rescued* me. I have a good job and a good life, but I've always felt that I don't belong anywhere, not even in my own family - like an outsider, looking in. But Roger knows where he belongs and he's such a *solid* sort of person that being with him makes me feel as though I belong somewhere at last.' Even as she said the words, Grace realised that she had never admitted her feelings about being an outsider to anyone before, not even Roger. 'I know it doesn't sound much like love, but then again, is there some barometer or gauge that can tell us that if we feel this much we're in love,' she held her arms out wide, 'and if we only feel this much, we aren't?' She held her thumb and forefinger a little apart. 'How do you *know*?'

She reached for the brandy and drank a couple of mouthfuls. 'Anyway, it seems to me that too many people use love as an excuse to hurt other people,' her voice was harsh. 'And as for sex,' she added angrily, picking up a pebble and hurling it at the sea, 'sex isn't everything in a relationship.'

Sîan looked sympathetic. 'Hey, tell me about it! I'm the world's number one sucker when it comes to mistaking sex for love. You'd think I'd learn as I get older, but I still go rushing in, my hormones working overtime. I keep on telling myself roll on the menopause because that's it, but now they have HRT...' She laughed.

Despite herself, Grace smiled. 'The menopause never stopped my mother. I don't think anything will.'

'She's quite a character your mother. A true free spirit,' said Sîan approvingly. 'My mother was the "sex strictly for procreation only" type, bless her heart. It wasn't really her fault, too much Irish Catholicism at an early age. But she would have as much run off with another woman as eat meat on a Friday. I bet growing up and learning about sex was a lot easier with Gaia around.'

'Believe me, you wouldn't say that if she was your mother,' said Grace with feeling. 'She told me the facts of life almost before I could read. When I look back, I think it was part of the war she was fighting with my grandmother about how I should be brought up. She was never around very much, but when she was, she tried to undo everything my grandmother had done. All Marjorie ever talked about was sex and having fun, and all my grandmother talked about was duty and responsibility. I was merely the little piggy-in-the-middle, a pawn in the battles they fought with each other. Sometimes I wondered whether either of them *really* cared about me...' her throat suddenly constricted making it painful to speak and she stopped.

'I'm sure they both cared about you in their own way,' said Sîan.

'They had a very strange way of showing it if they did,' said Grace. 'My grandfather was different though.' Her expression softened. 'I sometimes think he felt as out of place as I did. When I was small, we created our own private world that we told no-one about, especially my grandmother. To other people my grandfather was a rather dry, if not to say staid, lawyer, but he used to make up the most wonderful stories to tell me. In all of them, the heroine was a little girl called Grace who had the most uncontrollable head of curly hair which was always getting her into the most terrible trouble, but she always escaped, usually by using magic. He should have been a writer of childrens' books. When I think about it, perhaps that's why I became an editor. I want to discover someone like my grandfather whose talent would otherwise be wasted.'

She was silent for a moment or two. Sîan waited. 'Once my grandfather died, my grandmother insisted on sending me away to an all-girls boarding school. Of course my mother disapproved and to get her own back, she kidnapped me and took me to live with her in a squat.'

'Kidnapped you?' Sîan laughed. 'How can your own mother kidnap you?'

'My grandmother was so determined that my mother should have no influence over me, that she forced my grandfather to go to court and have my mother declared an unfit parent, and they became my legal guardians. It wasn't a hard case to win. At the time my mother had just spent a year wandering round India on the hippy trail and when she returned to England, she lived in a squat. She turned up at the court hearing with two hippy friends. They were barefoot and draped with bells and beads, and they passed a joint around. Well, I'm not sure it was *actually* a joint, but it certainly smelled strange. Anyway, when asked if she had a lawyer, my mother stood up and said she needed no defence because I had issued from her womb and she did not recognise the court as it was a bourgeois institution created for the protection of property, or some such rubbish. The judge nearly had a heart attack and promptly granted my grandmother's wish.'

Sîan started to laugh and then stopped. 'I'm sorry. It can't have been very funny for you, but I can just imagine your mother. Did anyone bother to ask you what you wanted to do?'

Grace shook her head. 'But it was probably just as well. I hated my mother for being so embarrassing and yet, at the same time, I would have done anything to be with her.'

'That's the problem with mothers: you love them and hate them and often both at the same time,' said Sîan.

Grace hugged her knees. 'The court ruled that my mother could have supervised access, and she was given permission to visit me at my boarding school and take me out on my fifteenth birthday. One of the teachers came along as a chaperone, but my mother had it all planned. Her friends were waiting outside the hotel where we went for tea, and when we came out, she bundled me into this old Volkswagen camper van before the teacher could do anything. It was awful. My mother was living with about twelve or fourteen other people in a squat in a large old country house in the middle of some fields. It was during her so-called, radical politics phase. Her then boyfriend was some kind of anarchist, or maybe he was a Trotskyist. I was never sure and I don't think my mother was either, but she pretended she did. She's very good at pretending.'

'They claimed that it was some kind of commune and removed all the inner doors so that nobody could have any privacy, because privacy was bourgeois. There weren't even any doors on the bathrooms or toilets, and people walked in and out and talked to each other while sitting on the loo.' Grace shuddered and hugged her knees closer. 'I found it excruciatingly embarrassing. I'd been brought up in a house where doors were always closed and no-one even *mentioned* the existence of a toilet. I used to try to wait until late at night to go to the loo when everyone was asleep, but because there was no electricity that meant stumbling over bodies in the dark and sometimes the bodies weren't sleeping. Between fear and embarrassment, I soon developed a bad case of constipation.

'I can't begin to tell you how wretched and humiliated I felt. When I first arrived they built a large bonfire in the garden and my mother forced me to throw my school uniform into the flames. Watching it burn was about the only time I felt warm all the time I was there. It was February and the house was freezing. My mother lived and slept in a fur coat and everybody slept together fully clothed in order to avoid freezing to death, rather than for sex. I don't think anyone did much washing and the place was squalid and stank. I just wanted to curl up in a corner and die, but there was worse to come.' Grace looked at Sîan. 'Have you any idea what my mother gave me for a fifteenth birthday present?'

Sîan shook her head.

'She made hash cookies to serve as a birthday cake, and there was some disgusting home brewed rhubarb wine to drink. Then, after she had insisted everyone sing happy birthday, despite their protests that it was a bourgeois tradition, she handed me this little package. I unwrapped it in front of the whole squat and there it was - this round, rubber thing, a *diaphragm*. I didn't even realise what it was at first and held it up so that everyone could see. They all cheered. I wanted the earth to open up and swallow me whole.'

Grace paused. Sîan was making a strange noise but her face was turned away so Grace couldn't see her expression but her shoulders were shaking. 'Sîan?'

Sîan gulped. 'I'm sorry Grace, really I am. But the thought of you holding up that diaphragm...' This time she couldn't control her laughter.

Grace stared at her for a moment and then started to laugh too. For several minutes the two women lay on the ground whooping with laughter.

'Oh god,' gasped Grace at last, sitting up and trying to catch her breath. 'I think I've had too much to drink. Is there any brandy left?'

Sîan wiped her eyes and handed her the bottle. 'Just between us - did you make use of your birthday present?'

Grace choked and brandy ran down her chin. 'Good heavens, *no*! Although there was a very sweet boy who was about a year older than me in the squat. He had long blond hair and curly eyelashes that made him look very girlish. We exchanged a few long, mournful looks, but we didn't get any further. I was far too cold and constipated, and I suspect he was about as keen on sex as I was at the time. However, he was the reason I was found. It turned out that his father was a Lord or something like that, and he owned the mansion in which we were squatting. He arrived early one morning with the police to evict the squat only to find that it was his son who had let them use the house. One of the policemen recognised me from my photograph that had been circulated as I had been declared a missing person. Despite my mother's protests, they took me away.'

'So all's well that ends well,' said Sîan.

'That would have been nice,' said Grace, 'but in my relief at being rescued, I forgot about the diaphragm, and when I got back to school they found it in my pocket. Nobody bothered to ask me whether I had used it. There was a dreadful fuss about kidnapping and under-age sex and the police raided the house once again and my mother was lucky not to get a prison sentence for kidnapping and pimping a minor.'

'Where was your father in all this?' asked Sîan looking curious. 'You've never mentioned him.'

Grace looked down. 'I don't know who my father is. I'm not sure anyone does, apart from my mother.'

'And you've never asked her?'

'For a woman whose sex life has been the talk of London at various times, my mother can be very secretive when she wants to be,' said Grace. 'On the occasions I raise the subject, she always accuses me of only wanting a father because I don't love her enough. My mother is very adept at making other people feel they are in the wrong when it's really her fault.'

'I'm sorry,' Sîan's words were heartfelt. 'I was lucky. My father is marvellous. He has always encouraged me to be the person that I want to be. He's one of those rare people who can love unconditionally. He is the perfect balance to my mother.'

Grace began drawing patterns in the sand with her finger. 'Sîan...do you mind if I ask you a personal question?'

'Fire away. It takes a lot to embarrass me,' Sîan replied cheerfully.

'You don't seem like a...like the other women. You seem so... well, *normal*. So why don't you like men?'

Sîan snorted with laughter. 'You mean why don't I wear dungarees and shave my head instead of my legs?' She stroked her smooth tanned legs. 'You really shouldn't believe everything you read in the tabloids Grace. And anyway, who said I didn't like men?'

Grace looked up, startled. 'But when we were in the taverna I thought you said...'

'That I was here for the women? I did and I am. But when I use the term lover, I mean in the generic sense - as in both men and women.' Sîan sighed theatrically. 'My problem is that I just can't make up my mind which I prefer. Every time I tell myself I'm ready to give up women and settle for men, I look across a room and see a woman, and notice the curve of her hips, or the outline of a lacy bra against a thin blouse, or the way she moistens her lips with her tongue, and it makes me realise I can't. So then I decide to give up men, but that never seems to last very long either. There's something about the scent of certain men - I guess its all that testosterone -

combined with the feel of their muscles and the roughness of the hair on their body against my skin, that could almost make me decide to go straight, until I remember the scent of a woman's body.' She laughed. 'I guess I just like sex too much, be it with men or women. However, the one thing I've learned not to do is to mix the two. It's rather like drinking grape and grain together - you end up with the mother and father of a hangover. That's why I'm here. I decided I needed a complete rest from men.' She looked wistful. 'I also thought that the one woman who could help me to make up my mind between men and woman once and for all would be here, but I was mistaken.'

'I can't imagine what it would be like to make love to a woman. How can it be satisfying without...well, without a man?' asked Grace hesitantly.

'Don't you mean without a prick? Believe me Grace, if just having a prick guaranteed sexual satisfaction, this world would be a much happier place. Don't get me wrong, I *adore* pricks. In the right pair of hands and in exactly the right place and the right time, they can light me up like a Christmas tree. But there are an awful lot of big pricks out there who wouldn't know good sex if it jumped up and grabbed them by the short and curlies. Anyway, if God had wanted sex to be merely man penetrates woman in bed with lights out once a week, he wouldn't have invented dildos and vibrators. Or perhaps,' said Sîan thoughtfully, stretching out full length on the ground again, 'dildos and vibrators prove that Hecate is right: God really is a woman!'

Grace started to giggle violently. The fit lasted several minutes, her whole body shaking. When it subsided, she wiped her eyes. 'Oh dear, I think I must be awfully drunk. I'm not normally like this.'

'Perhaps you should be,' said Sîan rolling over onto her stomach and propping herself up on her elbows. 'I'm still curious about you and your mother. Why have you come here? It's her life. Let her get on with it.'

'I wish I could, but she's always getting herself into trouble and calling on me to help her. She was the one who asked me to come here. I couldn't let her down.'

'But she's not in trouble. She's just trying to stop the building of an ugly hotel complex. What's wrong with that? Have you seen the beautiful beach where they are planning to put it?'

'It's not the hotel that bothers me. I've seen where they plan to build it and I agree with her about that at least.'

'So what *don't* you agree with her about?' asked Sîan.

Grace was silent. 'It's Lilith,' she said finally. 'Please don't get me wrong,' she begged, 'it's not that I'm prejudiced against lesbians or anyone else for that matter. I just think its wrong for my mother. She's always liked men. In fact she likes men far too much.'

Sîan rolled over and sat up facing Grace. 'Listen to yourself,' she said in an exasperated voice. 'I could shake you! Are you saying that women aren't allowed sex lives after fifty, or have choices about whom or how many people they have sex with?'

Grace shook her head. 'No, but...'

'Look, if it's any comfort to you, I suspect Marjorie is just experimenting a little. It often happens with women of her age and generation. They are post-children, post-menopausal, and often post-marriage too. Their husbands may have run off with a younger woman, or died, or it may be that their marriage has just plain run its course. Whatever has happened, when you spend the first fifty or so years of your life constantly caring for the needs of others, waking up to find you're no longer needed can be a great shock. Some women feel adrift, but others feel liberated and they discover a newfound sexual freedom.'

Grace looked thoughtful. 'I agree with a lot of what you say, but in my mother's case it doesn't really apply. She has always experimented with her sexual freedom and has never bothered with conventional relationships.'

Sîan laughed. 'Okay, so you've got me on that one. But, if that's the case, why does it bother you so much? You sound like a mother worrying about her wayward daughter rather than the other way round. Loosen up a bit, Grace.'

Sîan scrambled to her feet and unzipped her shorts.

'What on earth are you doing?' asked Grace as Sîan pulled her cotton sweater over her head revealing that she was bra-less.

Sîan pushed her hair out of her eyes. 'I'm going for a swim.'

She set off down the beach, stepping out of her knickers as she walked. Without pausing, she dived into the sea, emerging moments later, swimming a strong crawl. After about twenty yards she turned over onto her back and just floated.

'It's absolutely glorious,' she called. 'Aren't you going to join me?'

Grace stood up and looked around. The night was still. Not even the whisper of a breeze ruffled the surface of the sea. The village was over the next headland, but it could have been a hundred miles away. There were no signs of human habitation in the low hills that sloped down to the small bay.

Above her, the great glowing orb that was the moon seemed so near she felt she could distinguish every tiny boulder and indentation on its surface. She slowly turned around, wanting to see every star, no matter how small or how far.

The splash of a body cleaving through water made her start. Sîan had dived under the water again. She surfaced several yards away, shaking drops of what looked like molten silver from her hair. Grace unbuttoned her blouse and then her skirt, folding them carefully and placing them on the ground beside her shoes. She walked self-consciously down to the water's edge in her underwear. Sîan was floating on her back about ten yards away.

Grace turned her back to the sea and quickly removed her bra and knickers. Then, taking a deep breath, she plunged into the water.

TWENTY

'*Malakes!*' snarled Ari and stomped over to the edge of the terrace of his large, salmon pink villa and gazed out to sea, his jaw working angrily. Then he whirled round and strode back to loom menacingly over the Mayor, who was sitting drinking a glass of brandy to steady his nerves, having come to report what had happened in the taverna. 'I just can't believe that you let those dykes get away with it, Taki. If I'd been there, I would have let them have what for.' He held his clenched fist in the Mayor's face causing the Mayor to flinch. 'Women are always demanding equal treatment so let's give it to them. There's only one way to show who's the boss.'

The Mayor held his hand in the shape of a gun and mimed a trigger being pulled. 'The gun it went off and the lights went out, pouf! There was too much noise, too many people. I tried to hold one woman but she bit me.' He rolled back his shirt sleeve to show a small circle of livid teeth marks. 'Yiorgos the policeman, he take one woman to his car, but when he put her inside, the other women they take her out and then they smash his lights.' He demonstrated the women smashing the headlights. 'It was very bad, very bad.' He shook his head sorrowfully.

'How could you allow yourselves to be humiliated by a few women?' Ari demanded. 'What were the other men doing? They are a bunch of malakes. The village will be the laughing stock of the island. Our honour is at stake. We cannot let them get away with it.'

The Mayor shrugged his shoulders and held out his hands, palm upwards. 'What is there to do? We cannot arrest them all. They are tourists, women, we must be careful.'

'But they aren't respectable women,' stormed Ari. 'Think of the hotel. People won't come here on holiday if they think they will be surrounded by a load of bull dykes. And think of yourself.' He put his hand on the Mayor's shoulder and bent down to speak in his ear. 'It's the election next week. Do you think people will vote for you, if you cannot control a few women and allow them to damage police cars?'

'But my wife, she says we must leave them alone. She says it is better we have these women. The other tourist women come here and run after our sons and put wrong ideas into their heads, these women do not care for our sons. And my wife does not want a hotel. She says it will bring only bad things to the village and that the old ways are better.' The Mayor looked doleful.

Ari snapped his fingers at Kelly and pointed at the Mayor's empty brandy glass. She leapt up from her chair to fetch the bottle and refilled his glass. Ari pulled a chair over and sat down so that he was knee to knee with the Mayor.

'What has your wife to say in this? What does she know about hotels? She is only a woman and should stick to the business of children and cooking. Look what happens when women involve themselves in politics - they get hysterical and scream and shout. They do not understand how to argue and reason like men. Only women could think that a turtle is more important than a man.'

The Mayor nodded agreement. 'You are right of course, but my wife...' He held up his hands.

'You are my cousin, Taki. Would I advise you wrongly?' asked Ari.

The Mayor shook his head.

'Tell your wife that the hotel will mean that you will become very rich. All women like money. Only poor men have trouble with their wives. I want you to repeat that to every man in the village, and tell them that if they vote for you, you will make sure the hotel is built so that everyone will make money.' Ari pushed his chair back and crossed his arms. 'I will make it happen because I know the right people in Athens, but I will only do it if you are the village President. I like to keep things in the family. It's much better that way don't you think?'

The Mayor nodded. 'I can say this to everyone, but what about the foreign women?'

'First *we* - and by that I mean you Taki - have to make sure that there are no objections to the hotel among people in the village. The promise of money should clinch it. The foreign women are different. If we let them stay around any longer they might get the attention of international organisations and then the press, and governments do not like that, particularly when they want grants from Europe. So we must encourage them to leave.'

The Mayor looked puzzled. 'Encourage?'

'Incidents like tonight can get into the newspapers. We must think of a way of getting them to leave as quietly and as quickly as possible,' said Ari thoughtfully.

Kelly perched on the arm of Ari's chair and put her arm around his shoulder. 'I could talk to my friend Grace. She might have some ideas.'

'Friend!' snorted Ari. 'Is that what you call her. I should be careful if I were you and watch my back, that bitch is one of them.'

Kelly pulled her arm away. 'Ari! That's a terrible to thing to say. Grace is engaged to be married.'

'That's what *she* claims. Why would any decent woman be on holiday by herself, you tell me that? I know what she's after,' declared Ari.

Kelly leapt up. 'You're wrong! She came to find her mother because she thought she was in trouble.'

'And we all know what kind of trouble her mother is in, don't we?' sneered Ari.

Kelly faced him, her eyes flashing. 'I *like* Grace, she's my friend and I think you're being horrible about the women. Why shouldn't they camp where they want to, and I like turtles too. You could build your hotel anywhere.'

For a moment, Ari was taken aback by Kelly's defiance, then he laughed indulgently and exchanged glances with the Mayor. 'See what I mean? It's catching. First your wife and now mine. We've got to get rid of those women.' He gave Kelly a sharp slap on the bottom. 'Fill the President's glass and then run along upstairs and paint your nails. Taki and I have got some business to discuss.'

Kelly stared at him for a moment or two and then turned on her stiletto heels. 'Pour your bloody drinks yourself,' she retorted and marched inside, her high heels clacking on the tiled floor.

Ari watched her go, his eyes narrowing. Kelly had never stood up to him before and, once the Mayor had gone, he intended to make sure she would never stand up to him again. He did not like losing face in front of his cousin. It would be all over the village within hours. It was one thing to complain about your wife if she was Greek, everyone understood that, but if he was seen to be unable to control Kelly, he would become a figure of ridicule.

He reached over and poured some more brandy into his cousin's glass, smiling with an indulgence he did not feel. 'Women!' He topped up his own glass. 'They need regular beating to let them know who's master. It keeps them faithful, like a good hunting dog, eh my friend?'

The Mayor nodded, smiling.

'But times are changing and not all for the better. You can't open a newspaper these days in Australia without reading about some Sheila screaming rape or sexual harassment. I put it down to them not getting enough, which isn't surprising since the ones who yell loudest are usually real dags. Now you take my Kelly, when you look like her, believe me, you don't have to go around yelling rape to get attention. But catch her on the wrong day of the month and even she can be like a witch. It's in their hormones.' Ari drained his glass. 'My friend, I tell you, unless you nip things in the bud with those women right now, your women will start behaving the same way.'

The Mayor smiled his agreement and drank some more brandy. He did not know what hormones were - something Australian women had perhaps? All he knew was that every day was the wrong day of the month with his wife, and she had become much worse since their only son had married a German girl and gone to live in Hamburg. The way his wife berated him with it every day, anyone would think it was his fault. Perhaps she had guessed that although he missed his son, he was secretly glad that the poor boy had got away, even though it meant that now his wife could only complain at him.

Her complaints had grown louder since he had mentioned the building of the hotel. She was convinced that thousands of blond-haired, blue-eyed, German and Swedish women would descend on the village, marry every available Greek man and have affairs with the ones who were already married. The Mayor sipped his brandy thoughtfully. Ari might be right. Perhaps if he could convince his wife that he would make a lot of money from the building of the hotel, she would be quiet. She was forever pointing out that neither he, nor their family, had profited from him being Mayor of the village. According to her, what was the point of him having control over where houses and roads could be built, or where water pipes could run, if he did not make money out of it? People were laughing at him behind his back because he did not make use of his position.

The Mayor lit a cigarette and, closing his eyes for a moment or two, enjoying the feeling of the smoke filling his lungs. His doctor had ordered him to stop, but as long as his wife didn't find out he was still smoking he would be alright. As he exhaled, he wondered about Ari. Could he trust him? To come too firmly down on one side when there was an election approaching could be dangerous. Yet Ari seemed to have a lot of money and he knew the right people. Even in Greece, people had heard of George Mavropoulos. On the other hand, Ari was an accountant, which was almost as bad as being a lawyer. Neither could be trusted. They always seemed to make money even when their clients were losing theirs. He would have to be very careful.

'Endaxi, so you have a plan for these women?' he asked.

Ari had been thinking hard. He needed to find a way that would get the women out of their camp before they caused any real damage, but he did not want anyone to know it was his idea. Then, if things went wrong, although his cousin would probably lose the election, at least he would not be implicated. After a decent interval that would leave things clear for him to approach the new Mayor and offer him a deal - money always talked.

Ari was not really being disloyal. Naturally enough, he would like his cousin to win since he was family, but business was business, and, after the debacle in the taverna, Takis no longer had much chance of winning anyway.

'Far be it from me to suggest how you should run your village, but if I were you, I think I would ask myself where do these women get their water? Supposing the public water fountains suddenly had a problem?' He held out his hands, palms upward.

The Mayor nodded thoughtfully.

'And supposing the rubbish dump behind the village became too full,' continued Ari, 'would it not be healthier to start another dump away from the village, perhaps near the beach? First of course, you would have to dig a large hole, which would cause much dust, then, when the rubbish is put in the hole, it would cause many flies. Who would want to camp in such a place?'

The Mayor took another cigarette from his case and lit up, his eyes gleaming with hope. 'You think this would work?'

'Trust me,' said Ari firmly. 'I've had years of experience in getting people out of their homes in Sydney. The law says that I cannot go round and tell them to leave, but if things happen that make them want to leave, things that of course have nothing to do with me, that perhaps make them feel unsafe...' he held out his hands, 'am I to blame?' He leant forward. 'Perhaps if some of the young men were to go to the camp one night when the women are asleep and maybe give them a fright...'

'A fright? What is this fright?' the Mayor asked anxiously.

Ari tapped the side of his nose. 'That is not for you or me to say, but you know what young men are. Perhaps if someone told them that the women think that the young men of the village are scared after what happened in the taverna tonight, who knows what they might do?'

'Scared? Greek men are not scared of women,' declared the Mayor, puffing up his chest. 'Tonight was just unfortunate.'

Ari sat back and watched him. He knew his cousin. He would have a few brandies in the kafenion and repeat what Ari had said, particularly the part about the women thinking the men were scared. It would be around the village in no time at all.

The Mayor regretfully drained his glass and put it on the table, then struggled slightly unsteadily to his feet. 'My friend, I must go. We will talk again?'

Ari nodded and stood up. He held out his hand and the Mayor clasped it warmly and pulled him into a hug.

'We men, we must stay together, yes?' the Mayor slapped Ari on the back as they walked together to the edge of the terrace.

Upstairs, Kelly slipped inside from the balcony where she had been sitting in the dark listening, and hurriedly undressed. She wanted Ari to think she was asleep when he came to bed, not that it had ever stopped him from disturbing her.

She had not meant to overhear their conversation, but she had been so angry with Ari when she went upstairs, that she had taken her exercise mat and some weights out onto the balcony, intending to have a brisk work-out before going to bed. Hard exercise always helped her to control her stress levels. Ari had given her a Stairmaster for her last birthday and she often used it three or four times a day. She had brought a suitcase full of exercise equipment to Greece, incurring Ari's wrath when he was forced to pay a large amount for excess luggage at the airport.

Kelly opened a drawer and pulled out a pair of cotton pyjamas that were at the bottom of the layers of black and red, silk and satin lace-trimmed nightwear bought for her by Ari. She usually saved them as comfort wear for when Ari was away. He called them passion killers and hated her wearing them, but tonight she didn't care what he thought. She intended to kill any thoughts of passion on his part. She put them on and got into bed, lying with her back to the door and breathing deeply as though she were asleep, although her mind was racing.

She didn't know what had caused her to be so defiant earlier. She had never defied Ari in that way before, and when she got upstairs, she found that her hands were trembling. Since they arrived in Greece, she had been trying hard to make allowances for his bad behaviour, as she knew he was nervous about coming back, even though he would not admit it to her. Before they came, she could almost have wept for him as he was so desperate to make a good impression in the village from which his father had emigrated as a poor man so many years ago. Ari would not have thanked her for her tears, but knowing that appearances were important for a man in his position, and that a wife should reflect her husband's achievements, she had tried especially hard to do her part by making sure she always looked good. However, until tonight, she had never questioned just *how* Ari had achieved what he had achieved.

Staring wide-eyed into the darkness, Kelly remembered how, when they first met, he took her on a tour of a run-down area of Sydney. He had boasted how it would be transformed into a vast shopping mall, and a year later, it had been. She had attended the opening ceremony feeling so very proud of Ari who was now her husband. At the time, she had not given a thought to the people living in the houses that were bulldozed to make way for the multi-storey car park. The houses were little more than slums, or at least that was what Ari called them, and she had been filled with admiration that he was getting rid of them. Surely no-one actually wanted to live in them? However now, when she thought back, she remembered an evening news broadcast showing an elderly woman weeping as she was forced to leave the house where she was born and had raised her own family, and people waving banners and sitting on the ground in an attempt to stop the bulldozers. Ari said they were outside political agitators and she believed him. Now she was not so sure.

The bedroom door open and Kelly closed her eyes, breathing even more deeply. She heard Ari dropping his clothes on the floor and felt him getting into bed. His hands reached for her and she tried not to react. He gave a grunt of dissatisfaction as he made contact with her pyjamas and then moved closer, pressing his body against hers. She could smell the whisky on his breath. His right hand reached down inside her pyjama trousers, but she kept her thighs tightly together, despite the roughness of his probing fingers. His hand moved round behind her and she clenched her muscles even more tightly. Her hours spent on the Stairmaster had made her buttocks and thighs rock hard. Usually, this would have been enough to dissuade him, but Ari was not about to be dissuaded tonight.

His breathing became faster, as he grew more aroused by her refusal. He pulled down her pyjama trousers, and without any warning, entered her roughly from behind. Kelly gave a cry of pain and tried to push him away, but he held tightly to her hips, his fingers digging into her flesh.

It did not take him long to climax, and with a satisfied grunt, he rolled over onto his back and began to snore loudly, leaving Kelly to lie wide-eyed in the dark, tears trickling down her face onto the pillow.

TWENTY-ONE

'I've decided to stay for at least a week. Can you let Bartle and Duncan know?' asked Grace as she gazed out from the phone booth in the village square. It was nearly twelve o'clock, and the usual morning bustle of people was subsiding as mid-day approached. She found it hard to believe that she had arrived in Greece only three days ago, so much had happened in that time. Her secretary's voice on the telephone seemed as though it was from another world, rather than just from London.

'I can see the tops of their heads in their office,' replied Libby, 'do you want me to put you through?'

'Would you mind awfully if I leave it to you to make my excuses, Libby?'

'It'll be my pleasure. You're way overdue a holiday. You let those two take advantage of your good nature far too much in my opinion.' Although younger, Libby was motherly in her attitude towards Grace. 'How's it going?' she asked eagerly. 'You must be having a good time if you want to stay longer. Is your hotel comfortable?'

Grace wondered what would Libby think if she told her that she had swum naked in the moonlight and slept on a beach last night? At least she had the excuse that she had been drunk. However, that morning she had been quite sober when she ran down the beach naked and plunged into the sea with Sîan, so she could not blame Greek brandy for filling her with a sense of freedom as her body surged through the limpid blue water, or for making her skin tingle, as though charged with electricity. Her sense of being had been so intense, it was almost as though she had been someone else all her life.

After basking naked on the beach and allowing the warm sun to dry their bodies, Sîan had gone back to the camp, while she strolled back to village in her crumpled clothes, her hair stiff with salt and her skin encrusted with sand. For what seemed like the first time in her life, Grace had felt unconcerned as to what people might think of her appearance. Without going back to her room to clean up, she sat on Adonis's small vine-shaded terrace and ordered a large bowl of yoghurt and honey, which he served with a plate of ripe cherries. She wolfed them down, her fingers and lips stained wine-red by the time she had finished.

Adonis came out to offer her coffee. Smiling broadly, he indicated the empty bowl and the large pile of cherry stones. 'You are hungry, yes? This is good. It says you are happy.'

And he had been right. She was happy. It had taken a fourteen-year-old boy to name the sensation she had been feeling since she had opened her eyes on the beach and seen the perfection of the blue sky above her. It was at that moment she had decided to stay - at least until the mayoral election.

Before calling Libby, she called Roger at his office. Fortunately, he was in court so she left a message with his secretary to say that she would not be back for a few more days. She knew it was wrong - both feeling happy that she did not have to speak to him and leaving a message with his secretary - but she knew Roger would have cross-examined her, and, right at that moment, her reasons for staying would not have stood up to his relentless logic.

No, Libby was about the only person she could cope with that morning, even though, having asked Grace where she was staying, she had not waited for an answer, and had chattered on about some awful hotel where she had once stayed in Morocco.

'...anyway, we decided in safety in numbers and it ended up with six of us staying in the one room, it was a scream! We had to barricade the doors and the windows to keep the Moroccan waiters out, but we managed to barricade the entire mosquito population of North Africa in! It was a choice between being bitten to death by the little monsters in our room, or being bitten to death by the little monsters outside! We opted for the lesser of the two evils even though nobody had remembered to bring mosquito repellent. But by the end of the holiday, we had discovered a sure way to repel Moroccan waiters. One look at us, covered in lumps and scratching every possible part of our bodies, sent them running! They thought we had some form of awful communicable disease!' Libby giggled.

'I hope you're watching out for creatures that bite during the night, human or otherwise.'

'I'm just enjoying a quiet rest,' lied Grace, conscious that even a hint of what was happening would ensure it being broadcast on the office grapevine.

'Can I give this number to the Burgess twins if they ask?' enquired Libby.

Grace had phoned Libby and asked her to call back on the payphone number.

'No, I'm afraid this is a public payphone, the place I'm staying is a little basic. I'll check in with you again in a few days.'

'Wow, that sounds absolutely idyllic - a place with no phone. What's the night-life like? I went to Corfu once. It was amazing. There was this disco and it had...'

'I have to go now,' said Grace firmly. She was not sure if she could take another of Libby's holiday anecdotes.

'Well, you have a really wonderful holiday, Miss Hamilton,' urged Libby, 'and I'll hold the fort. But remember, watch out for those Greek waiters, there was this one in Corfu who...'

Grace had put the receiver down. She hadn't mean to be unkind, and she would apologise the next time she spoke to Libby. It was just that she could take no more of Libby's amorous holiday adventures.

Grace yawned. She suddenly felt tired and grubby, and her head ached. She needed a shower and a couple of hours sleep in a proper bed. The route back to her room now seemed as familiar as that between her house and Putney High Street, only here she was wished a friendly 'kalimera' or 'yassou' by everyone she passed. She paused at the bottom of the steps that led to her room as this last part always left her breathless.

'Hello.'

The voice was such a tiny whisper that at first Grace thought she had imagined it. Then she looked up and saw Kelly huddled in the corner of the small stone landing outside her front door. She remained there, unmoving, waiting for Grace to climb the steps.

'Kel...' began Grace as she reached the top, but Kelly reached up and grabbed her wrist.

'Don't say anything until we're inside,' she whispered fiercely, 'I don't want anyone to know I'm here.'

Grace opened the door and Kelly almost crawled inside before standing up. She was not wearing her usual acid-bright, body-hugging clothes. She wore jeans and an oversized black T-shirt which swamped her slim frame. Her hair was covered with a silk scarf and her face was almost obscured by large, Jackie Onassis-style sunglasses. However, if the intention had been to render her inconspicuous, the effect was exactly the opposite.

'I need to talk to you,' she declared clutching Grace's arm so tightly it hurt.

Grace's heart sank. All she wanted to do was sleep.

'Couldn't it wait?' she asked sinking wearily onto her bed. 'I'm exhausted.'

'I've been waiting for you since six o'clock this morning,' said Kelly stubbornly.

'You've been sitting out there? Since six o'clock this morning?'

Kelly nodded and removed her sunglasses. She was not wearing any makeup and her eyes were rimmed with red, rather than eyeliner. She had been awake most of the night, lying on the edge of the bed, her back to Ari. She had not wanted to fall asleep and inadvertently roll over to his side of the bed, as he would have taken this as a signal she wanted more sex. The whisky ensured that he slept heavily, but she had still slipped out of bed as soon as it was light.

Ari had often been rough with her when having sex, but never like last night. When they met, he told her that it was his first wife's lack of interest in sex that had caused their marriage to fail, and that any woman who took him on would have to understand that he had a high sex drive which he needed to satisfy, if not with her, then with other women. However, it was not just because of this that she always said yes to him, even when she frankly did not feel like having sex, it was because she loved him, but now she was no longer sure.

Kelly's eyes glistened with tears and Grace felt ashamed of herself for wanting to get rid of her. She patted the bed.

'You'd better sit down and tell me what's happened.'

Kelly sat down and pulled off her scarf, twisting it between her fingers.

She took a deep breath and then the words tumbled out like a hurt cry.

'I don't think I'm in love with Ari any more.'

'That's quite a big leap to make, are you sure? You don't normally just fall out of love with someone.' Grace could not understand how anyone could be in love with Ari in the first place, but she knew this was not what Kelly wanted to hear.

'Why not? You fall in love with people, why can't you fall out of love with them?' Kelly's voice was tremulous.

'That's true, but perhaps it means you weren't in love with them in the first place,' Grace said lamely. In her advanced state of weariness, she was finding this discussion of the metaphysics of love difficult.

'But that makes it even worse,' wailed Kelly. 'It means I've wasted all these years on someone I don't love.'

'Don't say that, don't even think that,' Grace tried to offer some comfort even though she felt little herself. 'I'm sure you loved Ari. But sometimes the person you think you love is not necessarily the person you love, because you love them for reasons that are to do with you rather than with them and then you change and...' She trailed off lamely as she realised Kelly was gazing at her with a bewildered expression in her eyes. 'So,' she began again, trying to get back onto firmer ground, 'has something happened between you and Ari? Perhaps a bad quarrel?'

Kelly looked away. She couldn't tell Grace what Ari had done to her, she could never tell anyone. She felt disgusted with herself and was sure that other people would feel the same way.

She shook her head. 'Not really. Although I did yell at him.'

'You must have had a reason,' encouraged Grace.

Kelly recounted the conversation between Ari and the Mayor in a low voice. 'I wish I hadn't listened,' she finished. 'It's my own fault really. If I hadn't heard him say those things about getting rid of the women everything would have been alright.' She looked on the verge of tears again.

Grace took Kelly by the shoulders. 'Listen to me. Ari's behaviour is absolutely nothing to do with you. What you have to do now is decide what *you* want to do.'

Kelly's face crumpled. 'But I don't know,' she sobbed. 'All I ever wanted was to be married to Ari.' She fumbled for a tissue and wiped her eyes, then looked beseechingly up at Grace. 'Perhaps he was only trying to talk big in front of the Mayor, men are like that, but they don't really mean it, it's just their way. Underneath it all he's really very kind and he loves me, I know he loves me.' She started to cry again and buried her wet face into Grace's shoulder.

Grace put her arms around Kelly's heaving shoulders and began to rock her soothingly backwards and forwards. Looking down at Kelly's blond head, she saw that her dark roots needed attention. It made her seem even more vulnerable, yet Grace felt powerless to help her as so many of her own certainties had been undermined too.

Had this place induced - or perhaps seduced was the better word – her into the same state of madness as her mother and all the other women? Before coming here, nothing would have made her believe that her mother could really love another woman, but now she was no longer sure. Grace had also started to think about her own life in a way she had never allowed herself to do before. Last night she had told Sîan things that she had kept private since she was a child. Admittedly, she had been under the influence of a large amount of strong Greek brandy, but like opening Pandora's box, now she had let them out, she couldn't put them back in. They were flying around and around in her head, demanding answers, especially about her father.

All her life she had wanted to know what he looked like and whether she was like him. However, what he had looked like was no longer as important as knowing whether her mother loved him. Was she the result of love, or merely random coupling?

She knew that Roger would say it didn't matter. That if you started asking awkward questions about love, you were likely to get answers that were even more awkward. You might even end up wishing you had not posed the questions in the first place. Roger's golden rule was never to ask a question unless you already knew the answer, but life was not like a court of law. When it came to love, the guilty and the innocent could be one and the same person.

Kelly gave one last, huge sniff and then sat up, wiping her eyes. 'I don't think I can face Ari yet. Can I spend the day with you?'

Grace hesitated. She had promised herself some time off, not only from her job, but also from her mother's problems, but she could not ignore Kelly's revelations. Given the mood the women had been in last night, any actions by Ari and his supporters in the village would be vigorously resisted. People might get hurt - her mother and Sîan among them.

She stood up. 'Make yourself comfortable while I take a shower and change, then we'll go to the camp. I think they ought to be told what's being planned.'

Kelly looked nervous. 'You mean go to the camp where the women are? But Ari says...'

Grace dropped her blouse onto the floor. 'Don't worry,' she called over her shoulder as she turned on the shower. 'I promise you, they're just like you and me - perfectly ordinary women.'

TWENTY-TWO

'You're only doing it because of this foreign woman. You want to impress her, make her think you are a big man in the village, everyone knows. Riding around on the back of your motorbike, holding you here,' Yanni's mother demonstrated. 'She is shameless this woman, like all these tourists.' She spat the word out. 'Their men are geldings so they come here and take ours, flaunting their bodies like...like whores.'

Anthoula stood in front of Yanni, her hands on her hips. She was barely taller than him when he was sitting down, but her temper was a match for any man. Yanni's father had been a big man for a Greek, but many a time Anthoula had chased him out of the house, beating him over the head with her broom if he stayed out too late playing cards in the kafenion.

Like so many men in the village, in order to make a living, during the long winter months her husband served in the merchant navy, sailing on ocean-going ships from the port at Piraeus. During the summer, he fished and worked in their fields. Anthoula always feared that he would drown in some winter storm on the high seas far away, but when death came, it was on a calm summer's afternoon, just as he had set out to sea in his small fishing boat. A large motor boat, driven by a seventeen-year-old boy, smashed into him. The boy was a Swedish tourist and he was very drunk.

Yanni was fifteen that summer. He had ambitions to go to university and then to travel for a few years around Europe, avoiding military conscription for as long as he could. His father's death put an end to all his hopes and plans.

The Swedish boy's father offered Anthoula compensation to avoid his son going to prison, but wild with grief, she refused it, screaming that blood money could not pay for her husband's life. She wanted a life for a life. Eventually, the village priest convinced her to accept it, pointing out that now she had to support both Yanni and his younger sister, Eleni. The money remained in the middle of the table where the priest put it for nearly six months, while Anthoula sat silently, refusing to see anyone or to leave the house, her hands folded in her lap, staring at it as though it had caused her husband's death.

While Anthoula mourned, Yanni took his responsibilities as the new head of the family seriously. He left school and became a waiter in one of the tavernas in the village. He did not earn much, but together with the fruit and vegetables he harvested from the small patch of land the family owned, it made sure there was food on the table. When the taverna closed for the winter, he began working for a local fishermen, then he was offered a full-time job on one of the large, deep-sea trawlers that occasionally docked in the harbour to take on supplies. It would mean him being away from home for many weeks at a time, but it was much better pay, so Yanni accepted.

When he told his mother, it was as if she was awakening from a deep sleep. She seized him by the arm, bundled him into his room, and locked the door. He climbed out of the window and rushed back into the house, but his mother had disappeared. He and his sister frantically searched the village and the seashore for several hours before returning home. There, surrounded by friends and neighbours, they waited, fearing the worse, but, just as Eleni was being assured yet again by a gloomily well-meaning neighbour, that if Anthoula had chosen to end her life, it was probably for the best as a woman's life was over once her husband was dead, Anthoula walked in the door.

Yanni and Eleni were pushed aside as the villagers crowded round her, noisily demanding to know where she had been and declaring they had never believed she would take her own life, even if others did. Anthoula held her hands up and loudly demanded silence.

'I do not know why anyone would think that I would kill myself. I had some business to do. I have bought the taverna at the road that leads out of the village, the one owned by old Michaelos who died last year. My son will run it.'

There was silence for a moment as her news was digested, then a voice said: 'But this is good news at last. We must have another glass of brandy, this time to celebrate.'

There was a general chorus of agreement and hands reached for the glasses that had already been filled many times from Anthoula's meagre supply of alcohol. However, Anthoula held the front door open and stood back as though waiting for people to pass.

'I thank you for your support, but I am sure you are all eager to get back to your business as I am to mine.'

As she closed the door firmly behind the last of them, Anthoula dusted her hands. 'Hypocrites, every one of them,' she announced to Yanni and Eleni. 'They sat in my kitchen, drinking to my death and then they want me to believe that they are happy I am alive. Did you see the bitter taste in their mouths when I said I had bought Michaelos's taverna? They are small-minded people who have never wished me good fortune because I am not only an outsider, but I from Crete.'

Yanni and Eleni tried to convince her that their neighbours meant her well, but the belief that nobody in the village believed she would make a success of the taverna had driven Anthoula into working to the point of exhaustion. Yanni worked alongside her, his ambitions to go to university and to travel only a distant memory. Eleni helped out at weekends, but although his mother thought education wasted on a girl, the price of running the taverna had been Yanni's insistence that his sister stay at school.

When, at eighteen, Eleni announced she wanted to go to business school in Athens, he also supported her against their mother. Anthoula had alternated between angry weeping and bitter silences, refusing to accept that Eleni would not instantly become a prostitute the moment she arrived in Athens. However, Yannis could be as stubborn as his mother, and Eleni went.

She did not return after she finished her studies, and he did not blame her. What was there for her in the village? He did not want to watch her becoming like their mother. It was different for him. He had thought he wanted to escape, but now he knew he could never leave the island.

At just what point this dawned on him, Yanni could not recall, just that it was true. The first few years of running the taverna had been very hard. His mother had taken out a high-interest loan to help buy the taverna because the compensation had not proved enough. To repay both the loan and pay for Eleni's studies in Athen, there were times when he was forced to work eighteen or twenty hours a day, seven days a week, and he wanted to walk away. Get on a boat. Go anywhere.

Perhaps because he had so little time for any life outside the taverna, he learned to value the rare, quiet moments when he was able to just sit and look. During these moments, he began to see the familiar landscape that he had explored as a boy, differently. It was as if he had never really seen its beauty and luminosity. Slowly but surely, he began to feel as rooted in the landscape as the ancient olive trees which, despite the bruising storms of winter, and the fierce, hot wind that blew up from the Sahara in the summer, not only survived but flourished in the poor, stony soil of the island.

Trying to make sense of his feelings, he had begun to write, and unbidden by him, the words had shaped themselves into poetry. A few had even been published by a small press in Athens. However, Yanni had kept their publication secret from his mother. To her, poetry belonged to another world, and she would worry that he would want to follow his poetry to the mainland. Proud that she had been able to set her son up in business, the only thing that now mattered to Anthoula was to find him a wife - good Greek girl who would bear her grandsons. Eleni was happily married to an Athenian and had a son, but that was not the same thing. Daughters married into someone else's family.

Yanni wanted to get married too. He wanted a wife who would share his thoughts as well work alongside him, and he wanted children who would bear his name and ensure his roots ran even deeper into the soil he loved. However it seemed impossible to make his mother understand that her criteria for a good wife - that she was clean, a good cook, had strong arms and stout, child-bearing hips, and most of all, would honour her mother-in-law - were not the same as his.

Every once in a while, he would come home to find a young woman looking suspiciously over-dressed having coffee with his mother. He was always polite, but, the moment the young woman left, the arguments would begin.

His mother constantly accused him of wanting to run away with a foreigner and it was true, when he was younger, he had often gone to the rooms of attractive tourists, although he had never deceived himself into thinking that any love was involved. Sex was the payment in a simple transaction. He had physical needs and they wanted a holiday adventure. He had no time for love, and neither had the girls, although some of them would come to the taverna afterwards and sit, gazing mournfully at him, thinking themselves to be in love but how could they love him? They knew nothing about him. Eventually, even the sex became empty and meaningless. He could not remember one girl from another. Their round-eyed, smooth-skinned faces began to blur into one, so he stopped going to their rooms.

Then, two years ago, when he was staying with his sister in Athens during the winter, he thought he had found the woman he was seeking. Her name was Eleftheria and she was a student of politics and philosophy. She was the first woman to see him as more than a brief sexual adventure, or as suitable husband material because he would one day own a taverna. She seemed to see into his soul and understand things about him that even he did not understand.

It was to Eleftheria he had shown his first attempts at poetry and she not only encouraged him, but, through her contacts, got his poetry published. For three months, from December to February, they barely spent a moment apart. They talked and made love, and made love and talked. As winter neared its end, the time came for him to return to the island and Eleftheria begged him to stay in Athens. When he said he had to go, she yelled that he was crazy to want to return to a small backward village, that he needed the intellectual stimulation of Athens. He had tried hard to make her understand. He held her in his arms as he described what it was like in his village in the first weeks after the chill winter winds had abated. How the hesitant spring sunshine began to warm the earth and how he could almost feel the ground coming alive again through the soles of his feet, stirring his blood, making him walk faster, breathe deeper. He had described too, what it felt like to wake up one morning to find the fields suddenly covered with a rich, fragrant carpet of wild flowers and herbs, signalling that winter was finally vanquished. Then he had begged her with tears in his eyes to understand that he could not feel the earth coming alive under the pavements of Athens, and that he could not smell wild lavender and cyclamen, only the traffic fumes which threatened to choke him.

He asked her to marry him and come with him, but she said she could not, for just as the fumes of Athens choked him, she would be choked to death by life in a small village. Some of the things he hated about Athens were the very same things that gave her the freedom to be herself. In a small village, she would only be his wife.

So he had come back alone, and had remained that way ever since. He was no longer sure what he was looking for in a woman. He thought he had found everything he wanted in Eleftheria, but he was wrong, and he did not want to be wrong again.

Grace was the first woman to interest him in a long time. He had noticed her because she was beautiful, but it was not this alone that had interested him. What intrigued him was that unlike other beautiful women, Grace seemed unaware of the effect she had on other people and she did not seek the attention of men - quite the opposite. At first, he had thought her arrogant, but he had changed his mind. Now he would very much like to get to know the person behind the barriers Grace put up against the world. However, no matter what his mother claimed, it was not because of Grace that he had spoken to the village secretary that morning and declared himself a candidate for Mayor. He had no wish to be Mayor, but if nobody else in the village was prepared to take a public stand against Takis and his Australian cousin, he felt he must.

Yanni was not against the Australian because he was an outsider, but because he saw greed in Ari's eyes, and greed was infectious. Since Ari arrived, Yanni had watched it spread around the village like a plague. Now, the only thing men talked about as they played Tavli in the kafenion, or repaired their fishing nets, or paused for a drink of water as they worked in the fields, was the promise of the easy money they would earn from the building of the hotel.

The Australian had let it be known that he knew people in Brussels, people who might be convinced to send large grants the way of the village if he just dropped an encouraging word in their ear. Now everyone claimed to know someone who knew someone who had made a fortune out of European grant money. Dealing with bureaucrats was like playing Tavli, they said, you employ any and every method to win – even cheating was acceptable so long as your opponent understood the rules, because everyone knew beaurocrats cheated.

Yanni knew that the living yielded by the land and sea was hard, barely more than enough to get by and sometimes even less than that, but while most people earned very little, at least they had pride in what they did. People in the village did not seem to understand that, if they lost their connection with the sea and the land, they would lose not only an essential part of themselves, but also their pride, and a man was nothing if he did not have pride.

Yanni neither expected, nor wanted, to win the election. He just wanted to show people that they had a choice.

'Mama,' he said gently taking his mother's hands. 'I am not doing this for any foreign woman. I am doing this for you and the village. You have told me yourself, there are many people in the village who do not want this hotel, but they dare not speak up because Takis has the power to make life difficult for them. But if no-one speaks up, life will be difficult for everyone.'

'But if you stand against him, it will be worse for us,' his mother protested. 'Everyone will think you are on the side of these foreign women who come here and try to tell us what to do. People will talk.'

'Let them,' retorted Yanni. 'People always talk. It is their nature. But I do not care what they say, if it is not true. These women may be foreigners, but sometimes it takes a stranger to show us what we have. People in the village work so hard they do not have time to look up and see what is around them. The Australian is a foreigner too. His parents may be Greek, but he is not a Greek because he sees only with his eyes and not with his soul.'

'So you are saying you do not like this English woman?' demanded his mother.

Yanni let her hands go. 'She has nothing to do with this. She is just a friend, nothing more.'

'She wants to be more than a friend. I watched her yesterday, sitting there.' Anthoula jerked her head at the table that Grace had occupied the evening before. 'She is after you, this woman. She pretends she is not, but I know, I am your mother.'

'Mama, please. There is nothing between us. Grace is a nice girl, but she is engaged.'

'Pah!' his mother's lips curled contemptuously, 'since when does that matter for these women? They are shameless. A respectable woman would not be here alone.'

Yanni stood up. 'Mama! Enough! We have work to do.'

He picked up a crate of empty beer bottles and carried it outside, then began to move the large stack of crates that he had put on one side of the terrace to the opposite corner. There was no need to move them, but he suddenly needed some hard physical work. It was nearly two o'clock in the afternoon, and most people had already retreated to the cool of their houses. Within minutes his T-shirt was soaking with sweat and he stripped it off. He could feel his mother's eyes gazing disapprovingly at him from inside the taverna where she was sitting beside an open window to catch the breeze, her hands busy shelling broad-beans, but he ignored her. He knew her too well. Once she got an idea in her head she would not let it go.

His muscles bulging with the effort, he heaved the last of the crates onto the top of the pile, then turned on the hosepipe and held it over his head, closing his eyes as the chill water gushed over him, cooling his sweating body. The more he thought about it, the more he was convinced that his mother was wrong. Grace was not after him. She had behaved very strangely yesterday and last night he had seen her marching off down the road with the women from the camp. Her mother had a girlfriend, so why not her, too?

Yanni turned the hose onto the terrace. Dark rivulets of water ran down onto the dusty road, seeking the sanctuary of ruts and potholes to turn into muddy, miniature lakes. On the other side of the road, the sea looked lifeless and dull in the heat, its surface untouched by even the hint of a ripple.

He turned off the hosepipe. Inside his mother was now clattering loudly around in the kitchen. He knew he should be helping her prepare food for that evening, but he could not face either her questions or what he hated most - her long-suffering silence. He lit a cigarette and sat down on the terrace steps.

Staring out to sea, he did not at first see the two figures walking towards him until one of them called out.

'Yassou, Yanni.'

He automatically raised his arm in reply, only then recognising them. The speaker was the blond woman who was the Australian's wife. Her companion was Grace.

As they drew level with him, he greeted her. 'Yassou.'

Only a slight inclination of her head showed that she had heard. Behind her sunglasses, her eyes were invisible. The two women walked on.

Yanni watched them until they disappeared round a bend in the road, then he dropped his cigarette on the step and stubbed it out. He would have to be careful. Not only was Grace working with the women from the camp, but she was also friends with the Australian. She was a very dangerous woman.

TWENTY-THREE

'Please slow down, Grace honey! I thought I was fit, but you could win the Olympic 100 metres,' pleaded Kelly, panting as she raced to keep up with Grace's long stride.

Grace reluctantly slowed to Kelly's pace. She wanted to put as much distance between herself and Yanni as possible. She had seen him long before he spotted them. He had been standing barefoot on the terrace gazing out to sea, his faded jeans rolled up over his calves, water glistening on his bare chest, and damp hair curling untidily around his face. There was something elemental about his beauty that attracted and repelled her in equal measure.

As though she could read Grace's thoughts, Kelly spoke. 'Yanni's very attractive, don't you think? If I was going to cheat on my husband, he would definitely be the one I'd go for. Back in Sydney, my girlfriends have affairs all the time. They say it's payback time for all the times their husbands cheat on them, but even if I wanted to I couldn't, Ari would kill me if he found out.'

Grace was beginning to regret suggesting they walk to the women's camp, but neither could she face staying cooped up in her room with Kelly a moment longer. All Kelly wanted to do was to pick over her relationship with Ari and each time she did, she discovered something new that had been wrong. Grace had instinctively disliked Ari from the moment she met him, and found it almost impossible to understand how Kelly could have lived with him for so long without seeing his faults. However, at least Kelly had been so absorbed with her own misfortunes that she had not noticed the look Yanni had given Grace as they walked past. It had only been a flash and then his face had been impassive, but it had made the colour rise to her cheeks.

Just as she thought she could not bear to hear Ari's name mentioned one more time, Grace spotted Sîan in the distance walking towards them. Filled with relief she waved wildly, even though she could see that the figure walking beside Sîan was Lilith. Sîan took off her straw hat and waved back.

Kelly grabbed Grace's arm, her eyes large and round. 'Are they...you know?'

Grace nodded and uncurled Kelly's fingers. They had left red marks on her skin. 'Don't worry. They won't jump on you or anything.'

'Oh.' Kelly sounded almost disappointed. She applied some lip salve and checked her face in her compact mirror then put her sunglasses back on. She nodded at the approaching figures. 'They're really quite attractive aren't they, for...you know. Ari says...'

An exasperated glance from Grace quelled her next words.

As she approached, Sîan smiled. 'Hey, great minds think alike!' She kissed Grace on the cheek. 'Hope you're not feeling too hung over after last night. Lilith and I seem to be the only ones not overdosing on headache pills today. They had quite a victory party when they got back to the camp.' She held out her hand to Kelly. 'Hi, I'm Sîan.'

With a slightly apprehensive glance at Grace, Kelly shook hands.

'This is Kelly,' Grace introduced her to Sîan and then indicated Lilith, 'and this is Lilith.'

Lilith nodded at Kelly, her eyes concealed behind her Ray Bans.

'I gather we left before the real fun began last night,' said Sîan. 'That dickhead of a policeman tried to arrest your mother. She hit him over the head with a bottle and then Juno sat on him. It took four men to pull her off.'

Grace blanched as she had visions of her mother spending time in a Greek prison for grievous bodily harm. 'Was the policeman hurt?' she asked anxiously.

Sîan shook her head, laughing. 'No. The bottle was plastic and full of water. I think it was just his pride that was injured. I'm told the funniest sight was the Mayor doing a runner. He couldn't get out of there fast enough. So much for Greek machismo.'

'But they intend to get even, so you've got to be careful,' Kelly's warning voice interrupted their laughter.

Sîan and Lilith looked at her.

'They're making plans, the Mayor and my husband...'

'Kelly is Ari's wife,' explained Grace.

Lilith looked at Kelly and her eyes narrowed. 'His *wife*!' She almost spat the word out.

Kelly shrank back a little behind Grace.

'She wants to help,' said Grace.

'How do we know?' demanded Lilith. 'Maybe her husband has sent her to spy on us.'

'I think we should at least listen to what Kelly has to say. If she's with Grace, she's okay by me,' said Sîan, earning herself a hostile glare from Lilith.

'Oh for heavens sake, stop being so paranoid,' Grace said impatiently, 'we're not fighting World War Three.'

A loud sniff from Kelly interrupted the argument. Everyone turned to look at her. She was scrabbling in her bag for a tissue.

'I don't know what to do...I don't think I love him any more...' Her chin began to tremble.

Sîan put a motherly arm around her shoulders. 'Come on. The camp isn't far. Let's go and get a cool drink, I think we can all do with one.' Sîan led Kelly off, talking to her as if she was a small child.

Lilith began to walk slowly after them and Grace matched her pace. Up ahead, Kelly seemed to have recovered quickly and was happily chatting away with Sîan, her earlier reservations forgotten.

The heat seemed to be growing more oppressive and the numerous flying insects buzzing around her face began to prey on Grace's nerves. She flailed wildly at a particularly bothersome fly.

'You must be wearing some sort of man-made substance like perfume which they like,' said Lilith disparagingly. The insects did not seem to bother her.

'I don't wear perfume, at least not in this heat,' retorted Grace waving her hand in front of her face.

'Then it's probably some cream you've put on your skin or your deodorant. It's Nature's way of saying don't use harmful chemicals to suppress your natural bodily functions.'

Grace couldn't trust herself to speak. She dabbed her forehead with a tissue already sodden with perspiration and wished Sîan would slow down. Just at that moment Sîan glanced over her shoulder and gave her an encouraging smile. It suddenly dawned on Grace that Sîan was walking ahead for a purpose: she wanted Grace and Lilith to have some time together.

What was it Sîan had said on the beach last night? That she and Lilith were alike, particularly in the way they both took life too seriously. Grace had been stung by this. She wasn't in the least bit like Lilith. However, Sîan was right about one thing - ignoring Lilith was not going to help her relationship with her mother. Marjorie took a perverse delight in provoking her. The more she disapproved of something, the more likely her mother was to do it. Perhaps if she showed that she did not mind Lilith, her mother would get bored of trying to be outrageous by pretending she was a lesbian.

Grace looked sideways at Lilith. 'I agree with you about the beach.'

'Beach?'

'The beach where they want to build the hotel,' explained Grace. 'I took a... a walk down there yesterday. It's beautiful. According to my guidebook, it's the site of some ancient monument, so that's another argument for it being preserved even without the terrapins, although they're very sweet,' she added, not wanting to appear unconcerned about their fate.

'We are not trying to save the terrapins because they're sweet,' snapped Lilith. 'That's the same crap argument as saying we must save the rainforests because they're useful to us. We must save them because they are an integral part of the ecosystem, not because they are beautiful, useful or goddam sweet. The moment we fall into the patriarchal trap of judging worth on the basis of usefulness or pleasure we become just like men - believing that the earth and everything on it is here to serve us.'

Grace stopped in her tracks. 'Look, I'm trying very hard to be polite to you, but every time I try to make some sort of friendly gesture, you greet it with outright hostility or a lecture on politics.'

Lilith carried on walking for a moment or two and then she stopped. She turned around and retraced her steps. 'I know you think I'm some sort of feminist extremist who has brainwashed your mother, but there are reasons why I come on so strong sometimes.'

Grace crossed her arms defensively. 'And they are?'

Lilith pointed to a large fig tree in the middle of a field, its gnarled branches spreading outwards to provide a cool circle of shade. 'Why don't we take a break?'

They scrambled over the low stone wall and walked across the field. The ground beneath the tree was hard, but at least they were out of the sun. Grace leaned back against the trunk and closed her eyes for a moment. She could feel the beginning of a headache. Lilith sat cross-legged beside her and opened the small rucksack she had slung over her shoulders. She produced a bottle of water and offered it to Grace.

'It's advisable never to go far in this heat without taking some water along with you.'

Grace drank gratefully and handed the bottle back. Lilith drank a few mouthfuls and then splashed some over her face. They sat in silence for a few minutes. The air around them seemed to vibrate with the insistent throbbing of cicadas.

'Gaia said you wouldn't approve of me. She says you never approve of any of her lovers.' Lilith's voice was accusing.

'That's not true,' Grace protested. 'I have approved of some of the men she's gone out with. For instance...' She tried hard to recall one of her mother's many boyfriends whom she had liked, but failed.

'Tell me something Grace, are you angry because your mother is having a relationship with a woman or because that woman is me?' asked Lilith. 'Too many so-called good liberals are happy to mouth fashionably chic sentiments about accepting lesbianism. But when someone near them, like their mother - who, as we all know, is meant to be a sexless being - comes out, then they are brought face to face with lesbianism being not just about gender politics, but about sex between women. Most liberals are apt to get hostile at this. It's similar to the "some of my best friends are black, but we all like to keep to our own neighbourhoods" syndrome.'

'I don't mouth liberal sentiments,' said Grace angrily.

'No, I don't suppose you do. Gaia tells me you're engaged to a proto-fascist, who is a Tory parliamentary candidate.'

'Roger is not a fascist,' said Grace heatedly. 'He may be conservative with a small 'c' but there's no harm in that. My mother has made her feelings about him quite clear. She seems determined to stop us getting married, *not* that it has anything to do with her. Tell me, why is it fine for her to disapprove of my relationship without giving any consideration to *my* feelings, but heaven forbid that I should suggest that there's anything wrong with the choices she makes? Has she told you what a wonderful mother she was? After the novelty of having a baby wore off, she dumped me with my grandparents so she could go off and have a good time in London. She treated me like a doll. When it rained she came home and played house with me, dressing me up in pretty clothes and pretending she loved me, but immediately the sun started to shine, she was gone, eager to find another bright shiny toy to amuse her. My mother has a very low boredom threshold, so I should take care if I were you.'

Grace waited for Lilith to react angrily to this, but she didn't. Instead, she looked thoughtful and pulled at a tuft of dry grass before looking up.

'That brings me to my second question. Are you angry with your mother because I'm young enough to be her daughter? Your mother abandoned you once. Do you feel she is doing it again by giving me the affection you feel should be yours?'

Grace stared at Lilith. '*Me*? Jealous of *you*?' she said furiously. 'I've never heard anything so ridiculous.'

'Are you sure?' asked Lilith, but this time her voice was almost kind. 'I love your mother, but that doesn't make me blind to her faults. Why do you come every time she calls? Aren't you trying to prove you love her in the hope that she'll love you back?'

Lilith's steady gaze made Grace look away.

'It's not unusual you know, for a daughter to feel she has to earn her mother's love if her mother is absent either physically or emotionally, and it seems to me that you have spent your whole life trying to please Gaia, while she has spent her whole life trying to please herself. You see, it's that very same selfish quality which attracted me. Gaia may seem outwardly disorganised and even scatty, but inside there's a steely core of determination. She plays at being weak in order to get people, especially you, to do exactly what she wants. There's a theory that we choose our partners in the subconscious hope that they will solve our problems and that we will find in them something we lacked or were denied in our childhood, but that's an awful burden to put on each other, don't you think?'

Lilith did not appear to want an answer. When she spoke again, it was almost to herself, her eyes fixed on some spot in the distance. 'My mother was absent in a different way to yours. She was always physically present in the house. She never went anywhere. I used to think that the term housewife, as in "married to the house", was especially invented for her. However, while she was physically solid, emotionally she was like the invisible woman. The only person who mattered - matters - in her life is my father. She invested her entire self in him, to the point where it seemed she had nothing left for anyone else. My brother and I came along, but although she went through the motions of caring for us, we lived in a world that revolved around the maxim: "wait until your father comes home". It isn't my father's fault. He is a kind man who is embarrassed by the depths of her devotion, and he tried to do his best with us. When he saw I had problems with my mother, he sent me to analysis, three times a week. I was only ten at the time, but hey, that's how good, liberal, middle-class American-Jewish parents show their love. So you see, maybe I am as guilty as you.' Lilith looked at Grace at last. 'Perhaps I'm seeking something from your mother I didn't receive from my own.'

For a sympathetic moment their eyes met.

'Did analysis help?' asked Grace.

Lilith gave a humourless bark of laughter. 'I fell in love with my analyst. Everyone said it was quite normal, even though she was a woman, and that I would grow out of it. I didn't. I left home at seventeen, gave up analysis and moved in with my former analyst. We were together for five years.'

'Have you ever loved a man?' asked Grace.

'No.' Lilith's reply was emphatic.

'But I thought...' began Grace and stopped. She wasn't sure any longer what she thought.

'That lesbians are women who have failed relationships with men? It makes it easier to accept, doesn't it? In this male-centred world, people cannot conceive of women whose lives do not in some way relate to men. It scares them. They talk about the natural order of things, and yet loving women is the most natural thing in the world to me.'

Grace scrambled to her feet and started to dust herself down. 'I've listened to you Lilith, and I've tried to understand. I accept what you say about it being natural for you, but I just can't accept that it's natural for my mother. I think that it's just another game she's playing.'

Lilith stayed sitting on the ground, looking up at her. 'I wasn't aware that I either asked for, or need, your understanding or acceptance, Grace. And as for Gaia, I rather think that what she does is up to her, don't you?'

TWENTY-FOUR

Grace flailed savagely at the cloud of tiny midges circling her head. How dare Lilith claim that she was jealous of her? She glanced round as she reached a bend in the road. She could still see Lilith in the distance, a small dark figure, sitting in the middle of the field. She looked so self-contained, so sure of herself. Grace strode on angrily.

It was typical American psychobabble. Nobody could feel straightforward emotions, like wanting to protect their mother, anymore. There had to be some unconscious psychological agenda instead. Lilith had spoken with her for two minutes, and then felt qualified to make an instant diagnosis of her problems. How could Lilith possibly understand her relationship with her mother? There were far too many third-rate Freudians like Lilith around, offering emotional placebos that allowed people to shed their responsibilities, it was unhealthy.

Grace stopped and dabbed vainly at her face and neck with a now disintegrating ball of tissue. Since leaving Lilith, the road had meandered along a valley between rocky hills that acted as a sticky heat trap. She felt hot and exhausted, but standing still for any length of time attracted not only midges, but also a variety of fierce insects whose buzz may have been worse than their bite, but Grace did not intend to wait long enough to find out. She dropped the remnants of the tissue into her handbag and started to walk as briskly as she dared in the heat.

After another, relentlessly hot, mile, Grace reached a fork in the road where she hesitated, unsure of the way. Her indecision was solved by the murderous intentions of an enormous black bee, whirring like a miniature kamikaze pilot at full throttle, which panicked her into taking the left fork, thrashing blindly with her bag in attempt to ward it off. After about ten yards, she slowed down and looked around, but the only witness to her humiliation was a large white goat, standing on its hind legs as it stretched to reach a few choice leaves on the lower branches of a tree. It munched placidly, watching her with round, golden eyes.

Feeling foolish, Grace took a deep breath and then set off again. After another hundred yards or so, she turned a bend and ahead lay the shimmering turquoise expanse of the sea. Whispering ten-foot high grasses grew on either side of what was now little more than a narrow track. After another hundred yards it ended, and Grace emerged onto a wide curving beach. To her left was the rocky promontory over which she had scrambled to witness the rebirthing ceremony. It had only been yesterday morning, yet Grace felt as though she had lived a whole lifetime since then.

Shading her eyes from the glare, she surveyed the beach to her right. The figure of a bronzed, naked woman rose up from behind one of the sand dunes that fringed the beach and walked down to the water's edge. She was joined by a second naked woman. Holding hands they walked into the sea until it came up to their waists and then they turned to each other and began to kiss passionately.

Grace looked away. She did not want to intrude on anyone's privacy, but her instincts told her that the camp could not be far away from where the naked women had been sunbathing. She took off her sandals and, holding them in one hand and her handbag in the other, she set off across the beach, averting her eyes from the two women. As she neared the dunes, she could hear voices and then some music blared out.

'Do we have to listen to this tape again?' a voice asked wearily.

It was answered by a loud chorus of yesses.

'If I have to listen to k.d. lang wingeing on about her bloody Chateleine one more time, I think I'll slit my wrists,' it was the first voice again. 'Hasn't anyone got something a bit more lively, like Madonna?'

'I think k.d. is the goddess's gift to women,' said another voice. 'She makes me go weak at the knees.'

'That doesn't take a lot with you,' retorted someone else.

This caused laughter as well as protests that sounded as though they might end in argument. Grace turned to walk away. Perhaps this was not a good time to make her presence known. However, as she did, a head popped up.

'Hey, we've got a peeping Jane!'

Before she could get away, Grace found herself surrounded by about half a dozen naked women.

Grace blushed. 'Look, I'm awfully sorry...I didn't mean to intrude...'

'Why are you creeping about spying on us?' demanded one of the women aggressively.

'I wasn't creeping about,' replied Grace defensively. 'I was just taking a walk.'

'Aren't you a little bit overdressed for a walk on the beach?' asked another of the women suspiciously.

'That's my daughter you're talking about, and she's always overdressed.'

The women stood back to let Marjorie through. She wore a large floppy patchwork quilt hat, sunglasses and nothing else.

'*Mother*!' exclaimed Grace.

'Oh for heaven's sake, don't be so prudish Grace. We're all women and we've got nothing to hide. Calypso is right,' Marjorie indicated the woman who spoke last, 'you're the one who looks inappropriately dressed, and quite frankly, ridiculous.'

'Me? Ridiculous? Have you taken a look in the mirror lately?' demanded Grace. 'You're the middle-aged woman who's running round naked, worshipping god knows what, and chasing after a woman young enough to be your daughter.'

They glared at each other.

'I think that the rest of us should perhaps make ourselves scarce,' said Calypso, backing away.

The others followed her, hastily gathering up their towels and bottles of sun tan lotion, making their way to the tents that were pitched on some flat ground about a hundred yards away. Grace had not been able to see the camp before, as it was screened from the road by the tall grasses and, on the seaward side, by the dunes.

She waited until the last of the women were out of earshot before speaking. 'I think it's about time we had a long talk, don't you mother?'

'If you insist,' replied Marjorie pettishly, 'although it never bodes well when you get that tone in your voice. It has that same "this will hurt me more than it will hurt you" tone of righteous indignation that my mother always used.'

'If you will behave like an adolescent on a hormonal rampage, what can you expect?'

'One minute you accuse me of being middle-aged, the next adolescent. Couldn't you at least try to be a little more consistent?'

'Mother! Stop it! This discussion is about you, not me.'

Her mother's eyebrows arched. 'Is it?'

Grace took a deep breath and tried to swallow her anger.

'I'm sorry. It's a long walk from the village and I feel extremely hot and sticky. Is there somewhere cooler we can talk like civilised beings?'

'And I suppose you'd like me to put some clothes on too?'

Grace could not trust herself to answer.

Marjorie stretched up and kissed her rather damply on the cheek.

'Give me credit for one thing, dear, you are my daughter and I can read your face like a book.'

She gathered up a length of gaily coloured cloth from the ground and wound it around her body, tying it over her breasts. She then picked up a battered paperback, giving Grace a glimpse of the title - it was an ancient Jackie Collins novel - before tucking it under her arm and setting off across the dunes to the camp site. She waved her free arm at the tents.

'I'm afraid this isn't exactly Butlins. We don't have many facilities as you'll see. The tent Lilith and I share is a bit basic, but we manage. A lot of the time we sleep on the ground outside, although when we need a bit of privacy, we go down to the beach. But it can get a bit crowded down there on hot nights,' she laughed. 'I do hope you're going to stay around long enough to see Lilith. She went for a walk to the village earlier, but she should be back soon.'

'I know. We met,' said Grace curtly.

Her mother studied her face for a moment or two.

'I see.'

They walked on in silence, Marjorie leading the way. There were tents of all shapes and sizes and colours. Some were little more than a piece of canvas slung over a rope tied between two trees, just large enough for one person to crawl inside, others were brightly coloured, custom-made edifices, large enough to allow people to walk around inside. The campsite had an air of permanence. Many of the women had cleared the stony ground around their tents and built low walls to create tiny gardens. Few plants grew in the hard ground, but, taking their cue from the village, they had recycled empty containers into pots and filled them with geraniums and anything else that would grow. Other people had given up the fight against the arid, salt-laden earth, and had used seashells and multicoloured pebbles to created fantastic mosaics instead of flowerbeds.

A large clearing with a circle of white stones, enclosing the remains of a bonfire, marked the centre of the camp. Hecate was sitting near it on a large cushion, shaded from the sun by a striped awning held up by some lengths of bamboo. The shelter looked in imminent danger of collapsing, but Hecate appeared unconcerned. Dressed in a white cheesecloth shirt and multi-coloured leggings, she was studying the Tarot cards that she had laid out in triangular pattern on the ground. She looked up and smiled as Grace and her mother walked past. Grace was once again struck by the youthfulness of her face beneath her grey and white streaked hair that was piled haphazardly on top of her head and secured with what looked like knitting needles.

'Is this your daughter, Gaia?' she asked. 'I noticed the resemblance the other night on the beach. It's quite remarkable.'

'I had Grace when I was very young, of course,' said Marjorie.

Grace held out her hand. 'How do you do,' she said awkwardly. Somehow, Hecate demanded a formal greeting.

Hecate took her hand, but instead of shaking it, she held it in hers and looked searchingly into Grace's face for a moment or two before letting go. Then she looked at Marjorie.

'You're very lucky to have a daughter. I would have liked to have one. The bond between mother and daughter is powerful as well as sacred. It is the conduit for the sharing and the passing on of the mysteries that only women can understand. To be a mother of a daughter is to be blessed by the goddess.'

Marjorie nodded vigorously. 'I quite agree.'

Grace raised a disbelieving eyebrow at her but she ignored it.

Hecate indicated the cards. 'Would you like me to give you a reading Grace? I think you would find it very interesting. Most people think it is merely a silly fortune telling game, but it can be a way to greater self-knowledge. Too many people look to other people for answers to their questions, but the answers may be inside them all the time if only they would seek them, and we all have questions we need answering don't you think? Some of us more than others.'

Grace felt disconcerted. It was all nonsense. Hecate's words could apply to anyone. Yet under Hecate's clear-eyed gaze it was easy to believe that perhaps she did know something about how she was feeling, but how could she?

'No thank you. It's very kind of you to offer, but my mother and I have something urgent to discuss, don't we mother?' She looked hard at Marjorie.

'If you say so dear.'

Grace grabbed her mother's arm and led her away.

'The problem with answers is that they sometimes raise only new questions, so be careful what you ask Grace,' Hecate called after them.

Grace hurried her mother along. 'That woman is a bit odd if you ask me.'

'Luckily nobody's asking you,' said Marjorie shortly. 'You shouldn't dismiss everything you can't understand as being wrong. You're too fond of seeking only logical, mundane explanations for everything. You were like it even as a child. I remember once when I tried to tell you about the fairies who lived at the bottom of the garden, you became very solemn and lectured me on why there were no such things as fairies or elves. You were only about four or five at the time. I think that was the only time I could have spanked you. It's quite natural for a child to be naughty, but a child who doesn't believe in fairies and make believe is not natural at all. You were never naughty. I sometimes wondered how you could be my child.'

Grace turned her face away at this. She did not want her mother to see the tears that suddenly clouded her vision. When she was a small child, her grandmother told her that only well-behaved little children were loved, so she had prayed every night for God to make her good so her mother would want her back. By day she became the perfect child. Never running, always walking; reading quietly in a corner; never playing loud games or getting her clothes dirty. Now here was her mother saying how she had wished she had been a naughty child. Even then she and her mother were at cross purposes.

It was not her grandmother's fault. It could not have been easy for her to raise a small child. Eleanor was not born in the days when people were aware of child psychology and worried about the effect their words might have on the impressionable mind of a small child. Eleanor had wanted a peaceful life, not a boisterous, demanding child. Luckily she'd had Grace - always eager to please and desperate to earn love.

Whatever it was that gave other people like her mother the confidence to expect love as their due was not granted to Grace. She had been taught that she was expected to earn everything in life, including love.

'Here we are,' Marjorie stopped in front of the small tent she shared with Lilith, 'home sweet home.'

There was a mat and some cushions in front of the tent. She indicated to Grace to sit while she crawled inside. Grace plumped up the cushions and settled herself down, undoing the top buttons of her dress. As an afterthought, she unbuttoned her cuffs and began to roll up her sleeves.

Marjorie stuck her head out of the tent.

'I can lend you some more suitable clothes if you want. I'm sure I can find you a couple of T-shirts and some shorts. You'd be a lot more comfortable.'

'I'm perfectly comfortable as I am, thank you mother,' Grace replied, rolling her sleeves back down and rebuttoning them.

Marjorie crawled back out of the tent and stood up. She removed her sarong and slipped a loose, tie-died cotton shift over her head that Grace could not help but envy for its coolness, then slipped a large array of bangles onto her wrists, and looped several rows of beads around her neck. After clipping on a pair of large dangling earrings, she reached inside the entrance of the tent and pulled out a box of fruit. Making herself comfortable on some cushions, she peered into the box and, after a moment or two of deliberation, selected a pomegranate. She cut it into quarters and offered a piece to Grace. Grace shook her head and reached for a large apricot.

Marjorie sucked some pomegranate seeds from one of the quarters, smearing red juice around her lips as she did so. 'Did you know that eating a pomegranate is tantamount to performing oral sex?' she enquired.

Grace nearly choked on the apricot she was eating. 'Do you always have to be quite so, so...I don't know, coarse?' she demanded, after her fit of coughing had passed.

Marjorie raised an amused eyebrow. 'My mother, the blessed Eleanor, raised you well, didn't she? That's just the kind of expression she always used, particularly to describe things I liked and she didn't, which was just about everything.' She scooped some more pomegranate seeds onto her fingers. 'The amusing thing about pomegranates is that they are bisexual. The ancient Greeks believed that their seeds were like semen, and that any woman who tasted them was no longer a virgin, but to lesbians, they mean female power. The red of the flesh is menstrual blood, while the seeds are like female ova, and if you lick the fruit, it feels like the clitoris to the tongue.'

Marjorie demonstrated. 'I think the analogy is rather apt, don't you? It's both sweet and bitter at the same time, rather like sex, and speaking about the bitterness of sex, how is Roger taking your absence? I can't imagine him being too happy about you being away. Men like him are creatures of habit. They like the world to remain exactly the same, day after day, year after tedious year. Everything and everyone in their place.'

Grace searched for a tissue on which to wipe her sticky hands. Her mother was right for once, but she had no intention of letting her know it. She found a tissue at last. 'Can we leave Roger out of this please?' she demanded as she carefully wiped her fingers. 'He is not the issue here. *You* are. After all, you're the one who summoned me to Greece.'

'Not to discuss my relationship with Lilith though,' said Marjorie quickly.

'But what did you expect me to say when I found out about her. How wonderful for you mother, I think Lilith will make the perfect husband?'

'That's one of the big differences between you and me Grace - I always expect the best of people and you always expect the worst.'

'That's not true...'

'Isn't it?'

Grace was silent, disconcerted by what her mother's words. Was she right yet again? Had she come expecting to find something wrong and therefore found it?

Someone in a nearby tent switched on some music. It was the same song that had earlier raised such heated emotions. Grace listened. The singer's voice was beautiful but hauntingly mournful.

'Mother...' Grace's voice was gentler. 'If you are really sure and it makes you happy, then I will try to accept that you have become a lesbian and be happy for you.'

'I'd much prefer you to be happy for yourself, Grace, and I haven't just *become* a lesbian. Lilith says that all women are lesbians but most of them don't know it or haven't discovered it yet. A lesbian is a woman who loves herself, and some women never learn to love themselves because society - masculine society - teaches them to hate themselves.' She patted Grace on the knee. 'I only wish that you would learn to love or even like yourself a little Grace.'

'I've never heard such a load of rubbish,' protested Grace. 'You can love yourself without having to go to bed with a woman. You've been brainwashed by Lilith.'

'I can't see that's any worse than being brainwashed by a man, and anyway, I haven't been brainwashed. For the first time in my life, I'm learning to think for myself, free from the patriarchal propaganda our male-centred society pumps out. You see, I think that *you* are the issue, not Roger or me. Although you probably can't see it, we're very much alike in some ways,' Marjorie placed her hand on Grace's arm as Grace began to shake her head. 'And by that I mean we can both be stubborn. I'm stubborn about not admitting to my mistakes, and as you know, I've made rather a lot of them in my life. You're stubborn in your loyalty to people, even when they don't deserve your loyalty like me and even though you don't believe it, in some things I know you better than you do yourself, Grace. Once you marry Roger, you'll stick loyally with him to the bitter end because unlike me, you won't run away from your mistakes. Back in London, every time I've tried to talk to you about it the shutters have come down over your eyes. That's why I wanted you to come here. I don't want to see you waste your life, Grace, and I thought that if you did, you might see things differently.'

Grace felt anger constricting her chest again. She scrambled to her feet. 'For once you're right mother. I *do* see things differently. It's far too late for you to play the role of the caring mother. There was a time when I was a child when I needed you to be exactly that - a caring mother - but you were nowhere to be found. From now on, I'm not going to come running every time you want me, and if you intend to continue this ridiculous relationship with Lilith then I wash my hands of you.'

'Are you asking me to choose between you and Lilith?' Marjorie looked up at Grace. 'Because if you are, think carefully about it. I may not make the choice that you want.'

'If you mean you won't choose me, there's nothing new in that. You got rid of me once before when you decided I was too much trouble, so let's save us both a lot of pain by making it final this time,' retorted Grace and, without giving Marjorie time to reply, she stalked off.

TWENTY-FIVE

Grace lifted her head cautiously and looked at the door. A scuffling noise, like that of a small animal trying to get in, had disturbed her. She had been lying on her bed for hours, drifting listlessly between wakefulness and sleep. Her body was sticky with heat, but the doors and windows were shut. She did not want to see anyone.

As she watched, a piece of paper appeared under the door. She held her breath, hoping the messenger would go away. There was the sound of footsteps retreating and then silence. She waited a moment or two longer just to be sure, and then padded across the floor. The one-line message was from her mother. It read:

'We must talk. Love M.'

Grace tore it into tiny pieces, scattering them on the floor like confetti as she walked back to the bed. She lay down again and stared at the ceiling. The citrus-coloured fingers of sunlight probing through the shutters had lengthened as they moved across the walls, indicating that it was now late afternoon.

Twice before that day, someone - her mother or maybe an emissary sent by her mother - had knocked on her door. She had ignored them. During the long hot walk back from the women's camp the day before, she resolved that she would have nothing more to do with her mother. Marjorie had chosen a life with Lilith, so from now on she was Lilith's responsibility. How dare her mother try to interfere in her relationship with Roger? She had tried to cloak her interference under the guise of caring about Grace, but that was nonsense. Her mother knew little enough about her life let alone Roger's, so how could she be so sure they were wrong for each other?

Grace considered the ceiling again. She was beginning to think that she knew every lump and crack in its uneven surface in intimate detail, but lying there in the suffocating heat was punishing no-one but herself. She sat up and swung her legs over the side of the bed. Her room was a mess. She had started to pack her suitcase after getting back from the camp, intending to get as far away as possible from her mother. However, as though the fates were conspiring with her mother to keep her in the village, when she trudged down to the telephone box in the square to call the airline office, the recorded message said that the office was closed for the day and would not be reopening until Monday morning - two full days away. She had returned to her room, swept her suitcase onto the floor, thrown herself onto the bed and then wept in frustration and not a little anger: not only at her mother, but also at herself.

She began to pick up her clothes, shaking the creases out as best she could before folding them neatly and packing them into her case, keeping out only what she would need for another two days. After a shower, she felt a little better and went out onto the balcony to let her hair dry in the warm breeze. It was early evening and the cicadas had stilled their throbbing rasp. As the shadows softened, flights of swifts and swallows took the place of the wheeling, harsh-voiced sea gulls, effortlessly cutting through the translucent evening air after their insect prey.

Grace leant forward in her chair and rested her arms on the balcony rail. Directly below was the courtyard of a house that the neighbourhood cats had turned into a gladiatorial arena for their bloody fights and equally fierce bouts of yowling sex. In between fighting and sex, they draped themselves over the numerous stone figurines that the house-proud owner had placed around the courtyard, providing nymphs and driads with comical fur caps. Every so often, a woman emerged from the backdoor of the house and tried to chase them away. She brandished a broomstick as she chased them, her voice high-pitched with despair at the futility of her efforts, for as soon as she went back inside, the cats slunk back, yellow-eyed with defiance.

The fragrance of cooking wafting from a nearby house made Grace's mouth water. She glanced at her watch. It was nearly six o'clock in the evening. She had only ventured out of her room once since the day before, and then only to the bakery to buy a loaf of bread. This and some large, ripe, tomatoes bought from a pick-up truck in the street, were all she had eaten in over a day.

She did not want to go to a taverna because she did not want to risk meeting anyone, whether from the women's camp, and most especially she did not want to meet Kelly and Ari. Twisting her hair into a topknot, she slipped on a dress, and armed with her guide book and its list of Greek phrases, she set off for the tiny village shop which she had noticed on her way to the bakery.

Inside it was an Aladdin's cave of a place, stacked to the rafters with everything from baby food to a wet suit. Half an hour of pointing and tasting later, she emerged triumphant onto the street laden with a carrier bag containing feta cheese, olives, yoghurt, garlic-laden sausages and a litre of local red wine. Tucked under her arm was a brown paper parcel containing a pair of espadrilles and a man's red cotton shirt, and on her head she wore a straw hat.

Perhaps it had been the genial grey-haired shopkeeper, who had introduced himself in broken English as Polychronos, and who had pressed samples of different cheeses and olives on her with such pride and generosity, that had made her buy the last three items. His wide smile had only faltered when she said she was staying for only another two days. He had looked sad and wished that she would take only good memories of his village home with her, causing her to feel churlish. She certainly could not spend another two days in her room, so the least she could do was to try to enjoy herself. This left her with the problem of what to wear as the clothes she had brought with her were unsuitable for either the beach or the countryside. Polychronos had shown her some rather garishly printed t-shirts but then she had spotted the red shirt hanging from a rafter and he had hooked it down. The bright blue espadrilles would be much better for walking than her strappy sandals, and Polychronos had suggested the straw hat, insisting she try it on as he held up a mirror. He had been right. Its wide-brim suited her perfectly and would also protect her face from further ravages by the sun. They had parted the best of friends, and as she walked back to her room, Grace had found herself smiling for the first time in what seemed a very long while.

When she got back to her room, she ate hungrily. The wine was strong and a little harsh at first, but after a few mouthfuls she no longer noticed, and after several large glasses she slept deeply. The next morning, she woke early, feeling refreshed despite the wine.

Rolling the sleeves of her newly acquired shirt up and knotting it at her waist over a linen skirt, she set out for a walk, wearing the espadrilles and carrying her straw hat in her hand.

It was still quite cool, and dew sparkled in hollows where the sun's rays had not yet penetrated. Grace headed south from the village, in the opposite direction to the women's camp. At first she walked as briskly as she did in London, hardly noticing her surroundings, until a small dun-coloured bird shot up into the air a foot or so away from where she was walking, loudly shrilling its alarm. Startled into curiosity, she crept forward and pulled aside a large tuft of grass, revealing a nest containing four tiny speckled eggs. As she bent over, marvelling at their delicacy, loud shrieks made her look up. Four or five gulls were circling and swooping above her, their beaks wide and sharply menacing. Hastily patting the grass back into place she retreated, allowing the anxious parent bird to settle back onto its fragile charges.

Looking around, Grace became suddenly aware that, at that early hour, the countryside was alive in a way she had not noticed during her hot afternoon walks. A shepherd and his dog urged a herd of unco-operative sheep across a far distant hilltop. Their figures so tiny they were barely discernible, but the musical sound of sheep bells carried faintly on the morning breeze. Closer at hand, rainbow-hued dragonflies jet-propelled themselves from plant to plant, while butterflies of every colour and size pursued a more graceful search for nectar. The sandy banks of a dried up riverbed revealed a colony of birds, whose brilliant metallic blue, yellow and scarlet plumage shouted their presence, unlike the bird she had disturbed earlier.

Grace followed the riverbed down to the sea, where she perched on a rock, enjoying the antics of some birds whose puffed up little bodies seemed too fat for their long, spindly legs, as they waded around on the seashore, bobbing up and down like comically obsequious royal courtiers.

Deciding to explore still further, she scrambled over the rocks at the edge of the sea and found herself in a small cove. The sun was warm on her back and she took off her espadrilles and paddled in the shallows. The water felt invigorating, and, after checking there was nobody around, she quickly stripped off and dived into the crystalline blue depths of the sea. After a while, she swam lazily back to the shore, where she basked naked on a large flat rock, feeling the sun evaporate the moisture from her skin, its warmth like a balm to her emotions.

For the rest of the morning she swam and lay in the sun. Only when the sun was reaching its zenith did she walk slowly back to the village. After showering, she settled down to do some work, determined to make up for lost time. She hardly noticed the time passing, and when she finally looked up, it was evening. Taking the remnants of her shopping expedition out onto the balcony, she ate large chunks of bread and cheese accompanied by olives, washing them down with the rest of the wine, as she watched the sun set in a crimson surge that stained the sea blood red.

As the sky darkened, Grace went back inside her room and found her handbag, then set out to go the phone box. She felt guilty. She hadn't thought about Roger all day. She should have called him that morning to explain about the delay in getting a flight. She would not tell him about her mother and Lilith, she reasoned as she walked down into the village, at least not until she was sure it was more than just a casual fling. She could well imagine Roger's reaction to the news that his mother-in-law to be was a lesbian, and the thought made her smile, even though she knew it shouldn't. A black clad old woman, walking in the opposite direction gave her an answering smile and wished her 'kalispera'.

She might even suggest that they come to Greece on their honeymoon, thought Grace. Although she had not liked the place when she arrived, she was beginning to understand why people came to Greece. There was something about the light and the stark beauty of its landscape that had opened her eyes even though she had not wanted to look. She could not quite explain how, even to herself. They did not have to come to this particular island, in fact, it would probably be a good idea if they didn't, but there were many others from which they could choose, as well as the mainland. She was sure Roger would enjoy it as he was bound to have had a classical education at the public school he had attended. If nothing else, he could spend the time lecturing her on classical Greek history and there was nothing more that he enjoyed than giving a good lecture.

Perhaps if they could agree on a honeymoon, they could also agree on a date for their wedding. They had got engaged but had never discussed exactly when they would get married, other than reaching a vague understanding that it would be next year. She was sure that if they set a date, and one as soon as possible, her anxiety and indecision would disappear. It was not as if they needed the time to get to know each other, they had been living together for nearly two years. Neither did they need the time to save up to buy a house, or anything else. Between them, they had everything that anyone could need.

Filled with a new resolve, Grace reached the telephone box only to find that there was someone using it and, by the look of the large pile of coins on the shelf beside him, he was going to be a long time. She wandered down to the harbour to wait.

As she walked, she noticed signs of the mayoral election everywhere. Posters featuring the smiling face of the little moustachioed man she had seen the night the women had reclaimed the taverna, were plastered onto every flat surface. However, a graffiti artist, or maybe artists, had been hard at work on many of the posters, adding lines to suggest he was a puppet, dancing in the hands of an unseen puppeteer, and on other posters transforming him into a pig at a trough. The graffiti made Grace smile and she wondered whether the women from the camp had had anything to do with it - not that she cared what they did any more.

It was now dark and most of the fishing boats had already put out to sea. Only a few remained, bobbing gently at their moorings. Grace sat down on some stone steps and gazed up at the sky. The stars seemed brighter than ever, and, remembering Sîan's story about the goddess Hera, she smiled again.

A light flaring briefly on one of the moored boats made her realise she was not alone. The glowing tip of a cigarette betrayed someone's presence. A figure stood up, leapt agilely from the boat to the quay and walked towards her. Grace shrank back into the shadows, hoping that whoever it was would carry on past her.

'You are always alone.'

The softly spoken words made her jump. She turned towards the speaker. The pale moonlight illuminated one side of Yanni's face, leaving the other in darkness.

'You walk alone, stay alone in your room and you eat alone. Always, you are alone.'

'I like being by myself,' retorted Grace. 'Anyway, how do you know so much about what I do?'

Yanni shrugged. 'This is a small village. Everyone sees everything. We Greeks like to be together. It is difficult for us to understand why a woman would want to be by herself unless she is a widow. You do not wear black, so people talk. Some people thought you are with the other women, now they say this is not so, but you are also not with a man.' He shrugged again.

'I suppose I should feel flattered that people take such an interest in my life,' said Grace, but her attempt at irony was lost.

Yanni looked puzzled. 'What is this...flattered?'

'It...it's like pleased, but it also means false, not true,' ventured Grace.

Yanni stiffened. 'You think I am false? The other time, when I took you on my motor bike, I think then that you believe I am being false. That I chase after tourist women.'

Grace realised she had hurt his pride and shook her head vehemently. 'No, I didn't mean it like that... What I meant was that I was surprised that anyone should take any interest in me.'

'You are very beautiful and I think you are a good person, so why should I not think you interesting?'

'Do you really think I'm beautiful?' The words came out before Grace could stop them. She was glad it was dark. Her cheeks were hot.

'This man of yours, he does not tell you you are beautiful?'

Grace wanted to say that Roger did, but it would be a lie. He had never complimented her, even when they first met. Roger was not much given to compliments. He said the givers of compliments were not to be trusted as they usually disguised an ulterior motive; something he spent his time exposing in court.

'No. But we've been together a long time...'

'Then he is a foolish man.' Yanni touched her shoulder. 'Look up at the stars.'

Grace did as she was commanded.

'They are beautiful are they not?' asked Yanni.

She nodded.

'And next year or even in a thousand years when you look up at them they will be equally, if not more, beautiful.' He looked at her. 'A man who does not see what is in front of him deserves to be blind.'

Once again Grace was glad of the protection the dark afforded her.

Yanni dropped his cigarette and ground it out with his foot. 'There is a special festival tonight, up in the mountains. The music will be good. You will come?' Without waiting for an answer, he walked over to where his motor bike stood.

Grace hesitated for a moment or two and then followed him. 'What about your mother and the restaurant, doesn't she need your help?'

'There are only one or two people. My mother will close soon. There is no problem.'

'But it's getting late,' said Grace lamely.

Yanni laughed. 'We Greeks begin to enjoy ourselves when you English go to bed.' He held out his leather jacket, which had been lying on the motor bike. 'You will need this. It is cool up in the mountains.'

Grace slipped her arms into the sleeves as he held it for her. Then he stood in front of her, hooked the zip into place and pulled it up. As he did so, he could not avoid touching her, and their eyes met. For a second, Grace thought he was going to kiss her, but instead he turned away and pulled on a jumper. Grace felt a surge of disappointment, which swiftly turned to embarrassment. Had she betrayed her thoughts with her eyes?

But Yanni was already astride his motorbike. If he had noticed, he gave no sign.

'Ela!' he bade her, holding out his hand.

Grace stared at his outstretched hand. It was only inches away, yet she had a feeling that if she took it she was in danger of crossing into unknown territory. All thoughts of her phone call to Roger forgotten, she reached out and felt his strong, brown fingers closing round hers.

TWENTY-SIX

Her hair whipping around her face, Grace moulded herself against Yanni's body, mirroring the movements of his body with hers as he leant to the left and then to the right, his knee sometimes almost touching the ground as the bike rounded a particularly sharp curve on the mountain road. She soon understood why he had suggested she wore his jacket. The night air grew noticeably colder the higher they climbed. However, his body protected her from the full force of the wind and she felt warm and safe, despite the speed of the bike and the sheer drop down rocky mountainsides, which she glimpsed when she opened her eyes.

After about forty minutes, she felt the bike begin to slow and the tension go out of Yanni's body. She loosened her grip and cautiously sat up a bit higher so that she could see over his shoulder. Ahead was a brightly lit village, its streets festooned with gaudy lanterns, and alive with people. Yanni slowed the bike down to a walking pace as they entered the village, expertly weaving his way through the throng of people. After the wild ride through the silent darkness, it was like being in Piccadilly Circus on a Saturday night.

Soon it became impossible to ride the bike anymore, and Yanni parked it in a narrow alleyway. Then he took her hand and led her deeper into the crowds. Everyone seemed to be trying to get to the same place, and Grace gripped his hand tightly in case she lost him.

The village had the air of a gigantic street party. Everyone was eating or drinking, whether walking in the street, or in the packed tavernas where harassed waiters dodged in and out with perilously loaded trays, as people plucked at them, yelling still more orders. Some of the tavernas were cooking whole sheep on spits out in the street, and the air was redolent with the aroma of roasting meat and herbs and another, more pungent, smell that Grace could not quite place.

There were now so many people that Yanni had to force his way through physically, but nobody seemed to mind being pushed aside.

Everyone was in a party mood. With one last shove they emerged into a square. Its sides were packed with people, but the centre was empty, apart from a group of horses and their riders.

The horses looked magnificent, their ornate harnesses and saddles decorated with brightly coloured braid and tassels. They pranced and whinnied with protest as their riders pulled at their reins to hold them back. Grace now realised that the smell she had not been able to identify earlier was the pungent aroma of horsesweat mingled with dung.

The crowd around the square was as excitable and restless as the horses, and Yanni put his arm around Grace and protectively drew her closer. 'It is an old tradition. They have horse races here every year. These are the winners and now there will be prizes,' he explained.

As he spoke, a man wearing a dinner jacket and a bow tie walked into the centre of the square and self-importantly banged the microphone he was carrying. There was a loud screech of feedback and the crowd covered its ears and yelled in cheerful complaint. For a few confused minutes, the man in the dinner jacket tried to quiet the crowd and at the same time get the microphone to work. Eventually, he succeeded at both and pulled out a sheaf of papers. Loudly clearing his throat, he began his speech, but the crowd did not stay quiet for long. A few drunken voices at the back began to heckle him and soon everyone was talking. The man began to shout into the microphone, trying to outdo the noise, but he only succeeded in causing another screech of feedback. It was too much for one of the horses, which attempted to bolt into the crowd.

There were shouts of alarm and Yanni pushed Grace behind him, putting his body between her and the horse. She found herself staring mesmerised over Yanni's shoulder into the bulging eyes of several hundred-weight of rearing, whinnying horseflesh. For a few, terrifying moments, the battle between rider and mount seemed unequal, but lashing with his whip and digging his heels into the horse's sweating flanks, the rider reined in his mount and it pranced backwards on its hind legs, the danger over.

Grace suddenly realised that she was clutching Yanni tightly and she released her grip. All around them, the crowd was nervously laughing and joking, urging on the man in the bow tie who, all thoughts of speeches gone, was now nervously attaching rosettes to the harnesses of the horses, jumping to one side if any of them moved. Without any ceremony, he pressed a silver cup into the hand of the winner, who brandished it with a triumphant yell, causing his mount to rear again. In his haste to get out of the way of the flailing ironclad hooves, the dinner-jacketed man slipped in some dung and sprawled on the ground, causing renewed laughter.

The prize-giving over, the crowd began to drift away and the horses trotted obediently off up the street. Waiters dashed out from the tavernas bordering the square, laying claim to their territory by swiftly arranging rows of chairs and tables which were no sooner in place than they were occupied by eager diners.

Yanni turned to Grace. 'It is too busy here. We go elsewhere for a drink?'

Grace nodded, only too glad to get away from the crowds. They left the main street and walked down a side road with high stone walls on either side. It was much quieter. The light and noise from the village was behind them, while the way ahead seemed dark and deserted, but then Grace heard the sound of music. It was nothing like the music she had heard in the village, or the cheerful, repetitive bouzouki rhythms of the Greek music she had heard elsewhere. It was wild and haunting, its rhythms more suggestive of Asia than Europe.

Lights strung from branches up ahead revealed its source. A makeshift taverna had been erected in a clearing among some trees. A group of musicians sat to one side, intent on the piercing melodies their fingers produced from the strings of their instruments. Sparks flew from a large barbecue where an enormous man, dressed in a blood-smeared apron, his face darkened by smoke, turned over slabs of meat. Every so often, he wiped the sweat off his face and bald pate with his hand, leaving livid streaks of charcoal and blood, like tribal markings. Behind him, stood large wooden chests filled with ice and piled high with bottles of beer and wine.

Yanni and Grace sat at one of the rickety tables and a boy, barely more than ten years old, rushed over to take their order. Yanni asked for beer for them both. As they waited, Grace looked curiously around. Most of the people at the other tables were like those in the village, clearly dressed in their Sunday best to match the occasion. However, over at the far side of the clearing were men and women, their features dark even by Greek standards, their clothes either black, or in bold, bright colours. Their children were barefoot and wild-eyed and rushed around screaming, while their babies sat naked on the dusty ground. As Grace grew accustomed to the light, she could make out the dark forms of horses tethered to the trees behind them. She leaned across to Yanni.

'Who are those people over there?' she nodded at the far group.

'Gypsies. Bad people,' Yanni replied in a low voice.

'Why do you say they are bad?' asked Grace.

'Because they steal. But they have the best horses.'

'Surely not all gypsies steal. They're like the rest of us. Some are good and some are bad,' Grace protested.

'All Greek gypsies are bad,' said Yanni in a voice that invited no argument.

Grace sipped her beer. The music had changed to an undulating melody. Suddenly, a woman of about seventeen or eighteen got up and began to dance, her arms swaying sinuously above her head, her hands almost floating as they twisted and turned, each seeming to perform a dance by itself. Then she slowly began to gyrate her hips. A young man ran forward and joined her. He went down on one knee in front of her, holding his arms wide, his body swaying from side to side in time with hers. She moved closer to him, her eyes locked to his, dancing only for him. The insistent rhythm of the music was charged with a voluptuous, almost hypnotic eroticism that rose to a climactic ending. For a moment, the couple stared into each other's eyes, then the spell was broken, and they walked quietly back to their separate tables, almost as though they had been performing an old-fashioned waltz.

The music changed, and one of the gypsy men walked to the centre of the clearing. He stood still for a few moments, his eyes closed. Then, almost in slow motion, he began to dance, dipping down to touch the floor and then leaping, as though trying to fly, his arms spread wide like wings.

Grace began to feel like a trespasser in a world that was separated from hers by more than just a few hundred geographic miles. The audience had become still, but the man seemed to be dancing not for them, but for himself. His eyes remained closed, yet the expression on his face changed as though he was communing with something deep inside himself, something that dared him to leap ever higher, as though he could break the pedestrian laws of gravity.

Grace was so intent on watching that she did not realise that Yanni had left her side until she saw him standing beside the gypsy, his eyes closed and his arms spread wide, like a bird preparing for flight. Then he, too, began to dance as though lost to the present.

At first, like they circled each other like eagles wheeling on high. Then the music began to pick up pace and the men in the audience sat forward on their seats, their eyes gleaming, urging them both on, as if it was a gladiatorial contest, with their prowess measured by the fierceness of their leaps, the thrust of their arms and the deftness of their swoops to the ground.

The music became faster and faster, and Yanni and the gypsy moved in ever more dizzying circles. The men in the audience were now on the edge of their seats, yelling and clapping, and then suddenly, with a dying wail of music, it was over. The two men stood still, their breath coming in hoarse gasps, sweat glistening on their faces and darkening their shirts.

Grace found that she, too, had been on the edge of her seat, her body tense with excitement. She sat back and tried to compose herself, hastily rubbing the palms of her hands, which were damp with sweat, on her skirt as Yanni walked back to the table. He stood for a moment looking down at her, but she got the impression he did not see her at first. Then his eyes cleared, as though he was waking from a trance, and Grace found herself caught in his gaze. Although unable to look away, she was aware of everything around her - of the intense heat and noise and the acute odour of horses mingling with that of cooked meat and human sweat.

'Ela,' Yanni commanded roughly at last. 'Now we go.' And, with that, he turned and walked away.

TWENTY-SEVEN

'I'm not your daughter Gaia, so please don't pull the little girl lost stunt on me, it won't work,' snapped Lilith, tossing clothes out of the tent behind her onto the dusty ground. The clothes formed a growing mound at Marjorie's feet but she ignored them.

'I'll stop behaving like a little girl if you will stop treating me like one and lecturing me all the time,' she retorted. 'I've been a woman much longer than you, so don't keep telling me what a woman is meant to feel and think. *I* know.'

Clutching the book she had been looking for, Lilith crawled out of the tent and settled cross-legged on the ground.

'Age does not necessarily beget wisdom. If it did, then Ronald Reagan was one of our greatest ever Presidents,' she said testily.

'I knew it!' Marjorie's voice was triumphant in its accusation. 'You think I'm old, don't you?'

'I never said anything of the sort,' replied Lilith. 'You introduced the subject. The age difference between us has never been an issue with me. I think you're a beautiful, mature, woman. How many times do I have to say it?'

'Mature! I told you so,' Marjorie declared, she picked up and armful of clothes and tossed them back inside the tent. 'That's just another way of saying I'm old.'

'Look Gaia, if you want me to tell you that you still look twenty-one, then you picked the wrong woman. You do not look twenty-one or even thirty-one. But why do you want to look young? Why can't you just be who you are? I thought we'd talked this through when we first met and we agreed that you would throw away all those stupid anti-ageing creams.'

'I think you want me to look old so that no-one else will find me attractive. Look at me,' Marjorie plucked at her hips. 'I've put on at least twenty pounds since I met you and I haven't got crows' feet round my eyes, I've got ostrich feet!'

'That's because you spend too much time sunbathing.'

'What else am I meant to do around here? There's nowhere to go, not even a proper shop.'

'There are plenty of books to read, some of which might even help you understand yourself better, that's if you could tear yourself away from those trashy sexist novels you keep trying to hide from me,' said Lilith through gritted teeth. 'And if you need something to do, you can help with the hotel campaign.'

'I thought you already had an enthusiastic little helpmate. I'd hate to think I might be getting in the way.'

Lilith angrily tossed her book aside. 'So this little tantrum is all about Kelly.'

Marjorie began taking washing from the line that hung between their tent and a tree. She folded it with exaggerated care.

'I never mentioned Kelly, but since *you* brought the subject up, you seem to be spending an awful lot of time with someone whom you described as an airhead and the worst kind of unreconstructed female when she first arrived.' Marjorie folded a T-shirt up into a tiny square.

Lilith got to her feet. 'You're being absolutely ridiculous. I was wrong in my judgement of her and I've admitted it. Kelly has been very brave in agreeing to go back to her husband so that she can get us inside information on his plans.'

Marjorie reached for a towel pegged to the line, but her arms were full of washing. Lilith tried to help her, but Marjorie ignored her and, in her efforts, dropped some clean clothes on the ground. Lilith reached down to gather them up.

'That doesn't mean you have to spend hours huddled inside a tent with her,' accused Marjorie.

Lilith straightened up. 'We were working on the leaflet we intend to distribute in the village. Kelly has been learning Greek so that she can surprise that prick of a husband of hers, and between her, the dictionary and the little bit of Greek I learned at school, it took us a long time to write. We then had to master the intricacies of the laptop she managed to steal from Ari for the afternoon, so that she could take it back and use his printer to run off our leaflets. And she did it all at considerable risk to herself I might add.'

'So Kelly's the heroine of the hour. However, I don't suppose that curvaceous little twenty-something butt of hers has anything to do with you suddenly elevating her to Joan of Arc status?' said Marjorie, dropping the rest of the washing she was holding into the dust.

Lilith snatched it up. 'Grace was right about you refusing to grow up,' she said angrily. 'You're behaving just like a child, craving attention all the time, and jealous of anyone else I spend time with.'

'I am *not* jealous, and don't you bring Grace into this. My relationship with my daughter has absolutely nothing to do with you.'

'Yes it has. You've changed since she arrived. We were fine until she came along. I warned you that something like this would happen.'

'She's my daughter and if I want her here, there's nothing you can do about it. You're always telling me what I should or should not feel.' Marjorie's voice rose. 'How can you understand what its like to be a mother, you're a ...' She clapped her hand over her mouth, her eyes stricken.

'Go on. Say it,' urged Lilith throwing the washing back onto the ground. 'I'm a dyke. So tell me, what does that make you?'

They stood, staring at each other.

'Do I detect just a tiny frisson of bad feeling in the air this fine morning?' Sîan's cheerful voice was a welcome interruption.

She ducked beneath the washing line and stood beside them. Kelly followed her, holding a sheaf of leaflets in her hands.

Sîan looked questioningly from Marjorie to Lilith. As usual, her heart gave a little lurch when she saw Lilith. The way Lilith's black eyebrows formed almost a single straight line above her grey eyes when she was angry was so sexy. Sîan fantasised about kissing her fierce eyes and tracing the outline of her high cheekbones with her fingertips. However, it was a hopeless daydream, doomed to disappointment. Lilith had never given her a second glance.

She had first seen Lilith more than two years ago, when she had come over from Chicago to speak at a women's studies conference in London. Women's studies bored Sîan, but conferences were a happy cruising ground for new women, especially those from out-of-town.

They also made a change from London's clubs and bars, that could be stale at times. The same old faces seemed to turn up in every place.

For once Sîan had paid attention at the conference. Lilith delivered a paper entitled: "Sister Nature - the Greening of Feminist Thought", in which she argued that the only true feminism was ecofeminism. Her paper had not been well received by all the women in the audience, particularly her remarks about what she called the sentimentalisation of animals by women who used them as emotional props. Her argument, that it was akin to the exploitation of animals for food, provoked a lot of comment. When someone demanded to know what she meant, as an example, Lilith described what she called the English lesbian cat culture.

Given the nature of Lilith's audience, Sîan had thought this a rather unwise example, and she was proved right by the heated argument that followed. Eventually Lilith had been bundled from the room for her own protection, even though she had protested loudly that she could look after herself.

For a while after that, Sîan had religiously checked the names of speakers at any upcoming women's conferences in the hope that Lilith might come back to London. She had long since given up hope of seeing her again when Lilith had arrived at the camp with Marjorie at the camp earlier that summer. Sîan had been there a week and having found the camp an unfulfilling hunting ground, had already booked her return flight to London. However, once Lilith appeared, she cancelled her flight and settled down, prepared to wait for the moment she would get Lilith alone and hopefully, seduce her.

However, the moment had never come. Marjorie and Lilith seemed to be in love. Neither of them moved far from the other's side, leaving Sîan no chance to exchange more than the occasional and inconsequential word with Lilith. What made it worse was that she liked Marjorie. She thought her amusing, and admired the way she had chosen to lead her own life, refusing to conform to the social pressures that a woman of her age and background would have been under.

Sadly, Sîan's admiration for Marjorie had not stopped her lusting after Lilith, so she had remained in the camp in the hope that the sensual effect of the heat and being surrounded by brown, naked bodies might make Lilith feel in need of additional sexual stimuli. They certainly had that affect on her. However, as the weeks passed, she became increasingly frustrated. Neither the heat nor nakedness appeared to affect Lilith. Short of openly propositioning her, Sîan did not know what to do.

When Grace turned up, she had felt a flicker of interest. In many ways, Grace and Lilith were alike. Both were tall, dark and slender, and both had an equally glacial reserve, although Grace's began to break down the night they got drunk together. Sîan had been sorely tempted to try to seduce Grace on the beach, but, while she might have succeeded, she knew Grace would have woken up hating herself as well as Sîan, and Sîan liked her too much for that. Added to that, when she sobered up the next day, she had realised that part of the reason for wanting Grace was because it was a way of getting at Lilith through Marjorie.

In the past, she would have gone right ahead, but she did not want Lilith to think badly of her - a sure sign that she was in love, Sîan thought ruefully. However, from the heated words she had just overheard, it looked as though Grace was causing problems between Lilith and Marjorie without any help from her.

Sîan raised an interrogatory eyebrow at the two angry women. 'I hope you two haven't started playing that insidious little game known as "definitions of dykeness", so beloved of women when two or more of them gather in the same place to navel gaze?'

She turned to Kelly who looked wide-eyed with bewilderment. 'For those less accustomed to the ways of women, or perhaps I should say "wimmin", perhaps I should explain. This is a game where you try to define how many times a woman has to have sex with another woman before she is defined as a dyke, and what level of dykeness - if any - applies to a woman who now has sex with women but has had sex with men in the past,' she began. 'This causes a dilemma for some women, but they resolve it by claiming that they only had sex with men because society told them to and they really didn't enjoy it, so it doesn't count. Mind you, there are a whole lot of women who just don't *do* sex, at least not with another person - male or female. Heresy though it may be, but there are times when I wish I had been born a man and could spend my time having sex rather than endlessly talking about it in the way women, gay *or* straight, do.'

Kelly started to giggle at this and Marjorie visibly relaxed. Only Lilith still looked angry.

Marjorie tenderly cupped her hands around Lilith's face. 'I'm sorry Lilith darling. I've been behaving like a silly old woman. Will you forgive me?'

Lilith kissed her gently on the tip of her nose and put her arms around her.

Sîan felt angry with herself. Once again she had stupidly said the wrong thing in front of Lilith. Why couldn't she learn to keep quiet, instead of letting her big mouth run away with her?

She swallowed hard and tried to smile. 'Hey, you two, that's enough, we've got work to do. There are terrapins out there that need saving, so let's discuss the next phase of our campaign.'

Marjorie and Lilith reluctantly let go of each other. Marjorie brushed her hair back with her hands. 'I think a nice cup of camomile tea would calm us all down. I'll just see if we have any gas left.' She busied herself inside the flap of the tent, bringing out a kettle and a small camping stove. Lilith gathered up the washing that had fallen on the ground.

Kelly held out the large sheaf of paper she was holding in her arms like an offering to Lilith. 'I've printed all the leaflets you asked for. I had to get up at three o'clock this morning to do them as Ari was making phone calls to Australia until after twelve. The time difference makes it awkward for him to do business. Luckily he's a heavy sleeper, especially after he's been drinking.' Kelly looked down. 'I've been rather encouraging him to drink. It means he gets too tired for sex, at least at night, but it means I have to get up early in the morning or else he wants it then.'

She looked at Lilith and then, if Sîan wasn't mistaken, she blushed. Lilith didn't seem to notice, she just continued folding the washing. Sîan gave Kelly an encouraging smile. 'You deserve a medal for courage beyond the call of duty.'

Kelly smiled gratefully back. 'I'm not sure if I can do any more leaflets. Ari is bound to notice that some of his paper is missing, and then he might guess. Everybody in the village is talking about who is responsible for the leaflets and Ari and the Mayor are getting really angry. They've already had a row with Yanni about them.'

'Don't you think it's time we had a talk with Yanni?' asked Sîan looking at Lilith. 'He's declared himself a candidate for Mayor and he's against the hotel. Shouldn't we join forces with him?'

Lilith dropped the washing inside the tent.

'We don't need a man to help us win our battle.'

Marjorie looked up from where she was squatting beside the stove. 'But Yanni's sensitive. He's not like the other men in the village, he writes poetry.'

Lilith snorted. 'Poetry! I bet it wasn't poetry he was after when he roared off last night with your daughter perched on the back of his motor bike. He's just like all men - led by his cock.'

Marjorie sat back onto her heels. She looked startled. 'Grace? He went off with Grace? Are you sure?'

Lilith crossed her arms. 'I'm sure I'm sure. In fact, I'm sure that it was her I saw the other day on the back of his motor bike too. I think your daughter is not quite the little miss goody-two-shoes you claim.'

Marjorie busied herself making tea.

'Lilith, I know my daughter,' she said firmly, 'and one thing I can promise you, is that Grace is the last woman on earth to have sex with a Greek waiter.'

TWENTY-EIGHT

Grace moistened her lips. They tasted of salt. The sun was warm on her face and her throat felt uncomfortably dry. She opened her eyes. High above, two seagulls were just specks of white as they spiralled effortlessly upwards in the translucent morning air.

She tried to move but couldn't. An arm lay heavy across her body, whilst her left leg was trapped by another. Grace twisted her head to look at Yanni. He was still sleeping. His face partially veiled by his unruly hair.

Yanni's arm was muscular and burnt dark by the sun and the sea. Black hair curled aggressively down his forearm, but the curve of his shoulder was smooth with a deep coppery sheen. She could feel the calluses on the palm of the hand that cupped her right breast. It was accustomed to hard work, but it was not a labourer's hand. The fingers were long and slender, and the nails were surprisingly well kept. However, either he or someone else had been careless once. An old but still angry scar ran in an arc from the base of the index finger down to the wrist, and then round to the fleshy part of his thumb where the skin was puckered, as though whoever had stitched the wound had pulled the stitches too tight.

Even when he was younger and slimmer, Roger's body could never have matched the naked vigour of the body that weighed hers down, thought Grace, and its vigour seemed to infect her. She could feel every tiny grain of sand and every blade of silvery-green sea grass that pressed against her skin.

She turned her head. About a yard away, a small silver lizard darted through a clump of sea lavender, stopping every few moments to raise its head, as though trying to scent danger. Its objective was a flat rock where it splayed itself out to warm its cold-blooded, reptilian body.

Grace closed her eyes and breathed in the smoky scent of the sea lavender's purple flowers, reliving the wild ride through the mountains that had brought them to this place. Yanni had brought his motorbike to skidding stop, throwing them both onto deep, soft sand where they had sex. Making love did not describe what had happened between them that first time. Yanni had been like a man satisfying his hunger, and like a man desperate for food, she felt that any body would have done, not just hers, but it had not been one-sided. They had both taken what they wanted from the other. There had been no emotion, not even guilt on her side at first, only physical need. Her betrayal of Roger had happened later in the night, when she and Yanni had really made love. Not just once but several times.

'You are crying.'

The words were spoken so softly, Grace almost didn't hear them. She had not realised Yanni was awake. She roughly brushed away the tear that had rolled down her cheek without her knowing.

'No I'm not. My eyes are watering, the sun is too bright.'

Yanni rolled over onto his back then sat up, looking down at her. He pushed the hair back out of his eyes. Grace wondered how she had not noticed the scar on his hand before.

'I think you are crying for your boyfriend. You are sorry for what we did last night.'

Grace suddenly felt very naked. She sat up and hugged her arms around her knees, covering her breasts.

'No, I'm not...at least not perhaps in the way you are thinking.'

'In what other way is there to think? A woman is to be married, but she sleeps with a man who is not her boyfriend. This same woman says she is happy with her boyfriend, so tell me, why does she make love with another man?'

'Because...oh because it just happened. I was drunk. It was romantic on the beach... Who cares?' Grace replied angrily. 'It's over. Done with. It will be just another one of those silly little holiday romances and you can add me to the long list of tourists you've no doubt slept with.'

Yanni sprang to his feet and stood with his back to her, pulling on his jeans. He zipped them up and then turned to face her, the muscles in his jaw still clenched.

'What is it you tourists want? You come here on holiday and say the water is not hot enough. When we say we will build a hotel so you can have hot water you say no, we do not want a hotel.' He gestured at his face. 'You make the eyes at Greek men and want to sleep with us, but when we make love with you, you do not like us. Tell me, what is it you want?' He held out his hands.

Grace hugged her knees tightly and stared at the sea shimmering on the horizon.

'I thought I had what I wanted,' she said slowly, 'but now...' She shrugged.

Yanni dropped onto his knees beside her. He reached out a hand and stroked her hair, which had formed into thick ringlets.

'I make love with you last night because I like you, *very* much. I could make love with many tourists, but I do not,' he said proudly. 'For me, it has to come from here,' he put his other hand on his heart. 'You understand?'

Grace nodded.

He looked at her steadily for a moment or two, and then took her face between his hands and kissed her tenderly on the lips.

'Endaxi,' he said standing up. 'Now we must go back. It is late.'

Grace dressed quickly and climbed onto the back of his bike. He stopped and let her off before they reached the village in order to avoid anyone seeing them arrive back together. He brushed her forehead with his lips and then roared off. Grace walked slowly after him, pausing to splash her face with water from an ancient Turkish drinking fountain beside the road. She felt exhausted, numb, as though she had used up every emotion she had to feel. As she reached the village, she quickened her pace, threading her way through the mid-morning bustle of people, looking neither to left nor right.

She was longing for a cup of coffee, but decided against stopping at Adonis's kafenion for breakfast. Above all else, she wanted a shower. Adonis saw her and darted out into the street, calling after her, but she just turned and waved. She would go back later and have an early lunch.

It was nearly mid-day, and the last part of the climb up to her room, which she had begun to pride herself on managing quite effortlessly, felt like the north face of the Eiger today. She paused for breath and looked up. There was a man sitting on the steps leading to her room, his face obscured by the newspaper he was reading. Whoever it was, he looked incongruous in a dark business suit.

As she approached, Grace could see that the newspaper was *The Daily Telegraph*. She felt sick. She looked at her visitor's shoes. Dust had dulled their usually burnished appearance, but they were unmistakably Roger's.

'Roger?' Her voice was little croaky, but at least it worked.

There was a loud 'harrumph', and the newspaper was lowered.

Roger did not look happy.

His was the kind of English complexion that did not adapt well to a hot climate and his round and normally good-natured face looked very flushed. Carefully folding his newspaper, he stood up. Grace could not help noticing that the buttons across the front of his waistcoat were looking a lot more strained than the last time she had seen him. His mother had no doubt been feeding him on the stodgy puddings he so loved. Every time they went over for Sunday lunch - winter or summer - there was always treacle pudding or spotted dick swamped in custard for dessert. His mother always gave him a serving that could feed six men while at the same time delivering her weekly homily about the way to a man's heart being through his stomach and how thin Roger was looking - a pointed reference to Grace's failure to cook calorie-laden puddings. Grace had long-ago given up trying to defend herself by pointing out that she was not so much depriving Roger, as looking after his blood pressure.

'Roger,' Grace repeated, almost as though to convince herself it really was him, 'how nice to see you.'

She lifted her face and waited for a kiss. She received a perfunctory touch of lips to her cheek.

She stepped back. 'I wasn't expecting you.'

'So it appears. Have you any idea how long it has taken me to get here? I virtually had to cause an international incident at the airport to rent a car, and I'm convinced they rented me the smallest and most uncomfortable wreck they possessed just to get even. Damn foreigners! They couldn't - or wouldn't more likely - provide me with a map, so I've driven twice round the island looking for this place and then, when I finally arrive, I spend an hour trying to find the hotel where you are staying only to discover that they have no such things as hotels. How can a civilised place not have a hotel? Eventually some young boy rescued me and brought me up here, but that was an awfully long time ago.'

It dawned on Grace why Adonis had been waving so energetically at her. 'I'm sorry. I always go for a walk in the morning but this time I went a little bit further than I intended.' She indicated her clothes. 'That's why I look a bit worse for wear. If I'd known you were coming, I would have met you at the airport.'

Her voice sounded quite normal. There was not a tremor or a break in it. She had never lied so blatantly before and she felt shocked that she could do it so easily and so convincingly.

'Well, I would have called if you had left me a number where I could reach you,' Roger sounded injured. 'I had to ring your office to get any information at all. That silly girl who works for you was very cagey. She intimated that if you had not told me where you were, it was because you didn't want me to know. I pointed out to her in no uncertain terms that as my fiancée, you have no secrets from me.'

Grace swallowed her urge to smile at the thought of what Libby had probably said to Roger. She owed Libby a very expensive lunch when she got back.

'Libby was just being a little overprotective. I told her that I didn't want anyone to know where I was. You know what people are like at the office, they would be trying to send me faxes and calling me half the night. After I left that message with your secretary I tried to call you a couple of times to let you know where I was, but the telephone lines from here are dreadful.'

Lying became easier the more you did it.

'It was rather a last minute decision to come,' explained Roger. 'Knowing what your mother is like, I was worried sick that she had got you into some sort of trouble, so, when two of my cases were adjourned for the normal time-wasting social workers' reports, I thought I would pop across in case you needed my help. I've been having visions of you and your mother being dragged off to some Greek jail.'

'I assure you Roger, neither my mother nor I are in that sort of trouble. If you'd like to come up to my room I'll explain.'

Roger picked up his suitcase and walked up the steps behind Grace, mopping his face with his handkerchief.

'I don't know how people can live in heat like this. That damn car of mine doesn't even have air-conditioning. I'm thinking of suing the hire company for compensation when I get back to London.'

'I'm afraid my room isn't air-conditioned either, unless you count this,' said Grace walking across and throwing open the balcony doors.

'Doesn't that let in a lot of flies?' Roger heaved his suitcase onto the bed and sat down beside it, still mopping his face. He surveyed the room with displeasure. 'Is this all you have?'

'There's a bathroom through there, but I hope you don't mind if I use the shower first, I feel really sticky after my walk.'

Without waiting for a reply, Grace went into the bathroom and closed the door behind her. She sat down on the edge of the toilet and leant forward, her head down, trying to still her racing heart. After a minute, she got up and undressed. Standing under the shower she soaped her body with great care, then soaped herself all over again. Just as she was rinsing the last of the soap away, the water became a trickle and then stopped.

She rubbed herself down and then put on Roger's bathrobe and opened the door. Roger was still sitting disconsolately on the bed.

'If you take your suit off and change into something lighter, you'll feel much more comfortable,' Grace suggested. She went over to check whether there was any bottled water in the fridge in order to make a cup of coffee.

Roger stood up and began to undo his tie. 'What I need now is a bath to get rid of some of this damn dust.'

Grace turned, bottle in her hand. 'I'm sorry Roger, but the water has just been cut off. It happens about once a day, I'm afraid. Water shortages.'

Roger ripped his tie from around his neck.

'Damn and blast foreigners!'

TWENTY-NINE

Yanni lowered a bucket into the large water butt he kept in the courtyard for when the water supply was cut off, and then poured the water over himself. It was icy cold but he welcomed the shock, he needed to clear his head. He rubbed his face. He badly needed a shave, but it would have to wait until later. He doused himself again and then padded back inside the house, rubbing himself vigorously with a towel and leaving a trail of wet footprints on the floor. His mother would be angry if she knew he had washed himself down in the courtyard rather than heaving buckets of water up to the bathroom.

He could hear her voice in his ears: 'What would the neighbours say? That my son is the son of a Cretan woman who washes himself like some wild mountain man in the back yard with no shame for his nakedness.'

Yanni smiled affectionately as he pulled on the clean jeans and T-shirt his mother had laid out like a silent reprimand on the bed that had clearly not been slept in. Having sat up and waited for him last night, his mother would have gone down to the taverna extra early that morning. By the time he got there, she would have scrubbed the floor and the tables, washed everything it was possible to wash, and prepared all the food for the day, so that he would have no work left to do. It was her way of punishing him when he stayed out all night.

There were times when he wished he had been born a woman. Although his sister, Eleni, had many problems, a daughter did not have so many obligations to her mother, and she could at least escape without her mother threatening to kill herself. As much as he loved his mother, at times it was difficult to cope with her belief that she lived and died through him, and that her life had no purpose other than to conceive and raise a son. It was a heavy debt to repay.

As he rode his motor bike back down to the taverna, Yanni steeled himself for the coming confrontation with his mother. It would not happen immediately. She would pick her moment carefully, storing up her anger until it was sharply honed. He would tell her that he had met some people at the gypsy races who could help him with his campaign to be Mayor, and that he had drunk with them until late and been too tired to return until the morning. She would be angry, but she would understand. After virulently opposing his decision to stand for Mayor, his mother was now fiercely determined that he should win. Like her decision to buy the taverna, she wanted to show the village that her family could succeed.

He left his motor bike in the shade of a fig tree that grew beside the taverna and paused to light a cigarette. He wanted to delay seeing his mother until the last possible moment. As he lingered, he heard his mother's voice through the open window. The voice that replied made him drop his cigarette and bound up the taverna steps.

'Eleni!'

'Yanni!'

His sister rushed to him and they held each other tightly, rocking from side to side. Eventually Yanni drew back and, taking her hands in his, looked her up and down.

Eleni had inherited their mother's tiny stature, but she had the kind of energy and expansive personality that more than made up for her lack in inches. Her thick wiry hair, which she had inherited from their father and so bemoaned in her teens, was now cut into a very sophisticated style, like her clothes. She looked the successful business-woman that she had become.

'What are you doing here? I didn't expect to see you until the winter. Is anything wrong?'

'Aren't you pleased to see your little sister?' teased Eleni.

'Of course I am,' protested Yanni, leading her to a table where they sat down opposite each other, still holding hands. 'Now tell me, is everything alright?'

'I'm fine. Giorgos is fine. The children are fine. Everything in Athens is fine, although much too hot. You are like mama, you worry too much.'

Their mother came and stood beside the table. 'You see, Eleni is a good daughter. She flies all the way from Athens this morning and still comes to help me in the taverna. She has not even unpacked her suitcase.'

Eleni let go of Yanni and took both her mother's hands. 'Mama, you are not being fair. Yanni works very hard and he is entitled to a night off now and then. He is a man and he needs time to himself. I'm sure he would like a cup of your coffee and I would like one too. No-one in Athens can make coffee as good as yours.'

Mollified, Anthoula went off to the kitchen. Eleni waited until she was gone and then turned back to Yanni. This time she spoke in English.

'Mama called me. She says you are standing for Mayor to try to stop the building of some hotel.'

Yanni nodded.

'She also says you are in love with an English girl.'

'Is that why you've come? To tell me I must find myself a good Greek girl?'

Eleni shook her head, smiling. She put her hand over Yanni's. 'I would be the last person to tell you that, but are you in love with this girl?'

Yanni shrugged. 'I do not know. All I know is that I think of her all the time and I want her, I want her very much...'

'We cannot help who we fall in love with,' said Eleni gently. 'But if you are thinking of marrying her, think carefully. Could she live in your world or you in hers? What do you really want out of your life, Yanni? When you can answer that, find a woman who wants to share it with you because she wants the same thing.'

'And what about mama?' asked Yanni.

Eleni laughed. 'Mama will live whatever she says. She is a strong woman. No woman will ever be good enough for you in her eyes. You could come home with the goddess Aphrodite on your arm and you know what she would say? She is too beautiful for her own good. A beautiful woman does not make a good wife because she will spend too much time looking in the mirror, and what about all the men who will chase after her? She is bound to be unfaithful. And if that is not enough - how can you marry a goddess? She has her head in the clouds. She'll be too proud to clean your house and prepare you fasolatha for lunch the way you like it. And what would become of the children, half god, half human?'

They both began to laugh loudly.

Anthoula came out of the kitchen carrying a tray and set it down on the table. She put small cups of coffee and glasses of water in front of Yanni and Eleni and a plate of tiny pastries between them.

She smiled at their laughter. 'When families are together they are happy. That is how families should always be, together.'

Eleni raised an eyebrow at Yanni but said nothing.

'Mama, you have not made coffee for yourself,' said Yanni.

Anthoula shook her head. 'I am getting old. Coffee is not good for old people. Their hearts are not so strong...' She put her hand to her chest.

'Mama, your heart is stronger than that of an ox. You will outlive us all and see your grandchildren grow up to have grandchildren of their own,' said Eleni, gently pulling her mother down on the chair next to hers.

'Grandchildren,' Anthoula held up the palms of her hands in a hopeless gesture, 'how I would like to see my grandchildren. But two of them live in Athens and the others may grow up in a cold country far away without knowing their grandmother.'

'Mama!' chided Yanni sharply, 'I have no plans to marry and leave the village. This is my home.'

His mother shrugged. 'So, she will live here but she will not be like a good Greek wife. Foreign girls do not respect old people, they do not care if you live or die. She will put me away in a home as they do to old people in England. They do not understand the pain of motherhood, the tears we must cry.' She put her head in her hands and began to rock backwards and forwards.

Eleni put an arm around her shoulder. 'Mama, *please*. Yanni has said nothing about marrying this English girl. You must stop upsetting yourself about something that may never happen. It is not good for you.'

Anthoula peeped through her fingers. 'Then ask him why he spent last night with this woman if he does not love her.'

'Mama! Yanni has a right to some privacy. He can see whom he wants to in the evenings, he is not a little boy,' protested Eleni.

'It's alright,' Yanni put his hand over hers and stilled her. He looked at his mother. 'If you want to know, I met some people up at the races who might be able to help me with my campaign. We talked until very late and drank a lot - you know how men are when they discuss politics - so I thought it best I should not ride my motor bike back in the dark. You are always telling me I should not ride it when I have been drinking.'

His mother looked satisfied and began to nibble on a pastry. Eleni grasped the change of subject.

'Tell me all about your campaign, Yanni. That's why I have come back. Mama told me you needed help.'

Yanni shrugged. 'It's okay. There was no need for you to come.'

'No need! If my big brother is going to be Mayor, I want to be here to see it happen. Now what are the main points of your manifesto? Who is organising your campaign meetings and canvassing for you? Where are your posters and leaflets?'

Yanni looked sheepish.

'You mean you haven't done anything?'

He held up his hands. 'This isn't Athens. It's only a small village. Everyone knows I am standing for Mayor. They will vote for me if they think it's right.'

Eleni looked incredulous. 'If I didn't know you better I'd say you were a fool. How can you expect people to know what is right unless you tell them? You are a romantic if you think people somehow magically know what is best for them. People are stupid, not least some of the people in this village. The only thing they care about is money, so if Takis and this Australian mama has told me about say they will get money if the hotel is built, they will vote for the hotel.'

Anthoula nodded approvingly as Eleni spoke. Yanni looked stubborn.

'You are wrong. There are people like me who care about the village and about our island. You have spent too long in Athens. Not everyone cares about money.'

'Yanni,' Eleni's tone was gentler. 'I'm not saying people in the village are bad, but they live hard lives. Sometimes it is difficult for them to think beyond whether they will be able to put food on the table, pay for their daughter's wedding or buy a new engine for their fishing boat. You must convince them to think beyond these things, to think not only of their children, but of their children's children. People understand these things if you explain it to them and you must if you are going to win.'

Yanni still looked unconvinced. 'Takis has been a good Mayor in some ways. People will believe him if he says a hotel will bring prosperity. The Australian has spread talk of European grants and you know what people are like, they think Europe is a fat cow and that all you have to do is pull its udders and you will get an endless stream of milk and honey. Everyone can tell a story about someone they know who knows someone who has become a rich man through a European subsidy.'

Eleni nodded. 'People talk that way in Athens too, but you must run a negative campaign like the politicians. You must tell people that Takis is the puppet of an outsider who comes from the other side of the world with his foreign ways and tries to tell men who have lived here for generations how they should run their lives. You must also ask them whether they want bureaucrats from Brussels coming here with their regulations about what size lobsters they can catch, and how much wine they can grow, and telling them that the way they make their Feta is unhygienic and not fit for human consumption. If you are to be a politician you must think like one.'

Yanni waved a dismissive hand. 'I am a poet not a politician. I prefer to write of the beauty of our island than to talk of European subsidies.'

Eleni reached across and took his hand in hers. 'There will be no beauty left to write about if you do not take action. I will run your campaign for you. I will knock on doors, write your speeches, anything you want, but only if you are prepared to make a fight of it.'

'He will,' said Anthoula proudly. 'The men in our family have always known how to fight. We fought the Germans and before them the Turks, with our bare hands when it was necessary. And we must not forget,' she added darkly, 'it's the Germans who control this Europe, whatever the French think, and I spit on their money.' She made a spitting motion.

Eleni smiled. 'It seems you have no choice in the matter, Yanni. Your war-like women-folk have declared hostilities on your behalf. All you have to do is to lead us into battle.'

'Unfortunately that is the problem,' said Yanni gloomily. 'Too many women have already interfered.'

'Women?' Eleni looked puzzled.

'The women from the camp outside the village - they are lesbians. They have been stirring up trouble and campaigning against the hotel. Takis and the Australian are saying that I am just their dupe.'

'It's Yanni's own fault, he would not listen to me, oh no. I am just his mother so what do I know about these things?' Anthoula raised her hands. 'I have told him, if he runs around with one of these women, people will talk and it will bring shame on our family. The whole village is laughing at him.'

'No-one is laughing at me,' Yanni protested angrily. 'Grace is not one of those women. Her mother has fallen into bad company and Grace has come to take her back to England. She is a good daughter.'

His mother made a snorting noise. 'Like mother, like daughter. Bad blood runs in the family.'

Eleni looked thoughtful. 'The women are a problem, but we must find a way of turning them to our advantage. Have you talked to them?'

Yanni shook his head.

'Then I will go and talk to them. If they want what we want, then we must work together, it is only sensible. You men, you are all afraid of women despite your macho posturing, and women who don't need you frighten you most of all,' she laughed.

'You must not go to the camp. I forbid it,' declared Anthoula. 'The family name, it will be...' she made a spitting motion again.

Eleni put a hand over her mother's. 'Mama, if Yanni becomes Mayor, what will people think of our family then? Think how proud it would have made papa. His son, Mayor of the village where he was born, surely we should do anything to help Yanni win, for papa's sake?'

Anthoula looked up at the old photograph of her husband that hung on the wall and crossed herself.

'He would be proud, you are right,' she said, tears in her eyes. 'We will fight and we will win.'

THIRTY

Grace stared sightlessly at the typescript pages in front of her on the table. She had read a whole chapter but could not remember anything of what she had read. That afternoon, guilt had driven her to try and do some work, just as it had driven her to make love to Roger. The results had been equally unsatisfactory.

She looked across at the bed. Roger was still asleep. Almost without her noticing, his hair had turned from fair to grey, but in sleep at least, it still curled boyishly over his forehead. He was lying on his back, his hands resting on his stomach, its dome shape confirming her earlier suspicions that the nursery food he so loved eating had done its worst. She went over and gently pulled the sheet that had become twisted around his knees, up to his chin.

Roger was tired and hot and had not wanted to make love. He was a strictly nocturnal creature when it came to sex, and it was only her repeated cajoling that eventually made him agree. Maybe she should have cajoled him more in the past. However, their increasingly infrequent sleepy couplings suited her too. At the end of a long day, a friendly cuddle was often the most either of them wanted.

She should also have waited to explain about her mother and Lilith until dinner when she could have done it over a glass of wine that might have made him more receptive, but it had all tumbled out. She had only just managed to stop herself telling him about Yanni. The compulsion to confess had been almost overwhelming. It would have been so much easier just to get it out into the open and then to beg his forgiveness. What was it her grandmother always used to say? Confession was good for the soul.

Instead, she had made love to him, telling him how much she missed him and how glad she was that he had come to Greece and had made it so much worse by lying to him, not just with words but with her body too. His body had not wanted her, at least not at first. He was surprised, if not shocked, when she started to arouse him - it was not something she had done before. He tried to push her hand away, saying that he was too tired after the journey, but she persisted and his body had begun to respond. He had lain beneath her, allowing her to do all the work until he came in a quick spasm that seemed more like pain than pleasure. Then he had fallen asleep, even while she knelt panting astride him.

Gently disengaging herself from his sleeping body, Grace prayed that the water was back on. For once, the gods heard her, and she stood under the shower for a long time. That morning, although she wanted to keep the fragrance of Yanni's body clinging to her skin as long as possible, she had scrubbed her body hard, not wanting Roger to guess that she had slept with another man. After making love to Roger, it was not Roger she wanted to scrub away, but her disgust with herself.

Grace gathered the sheets of paper together and made a tidy pile. It was no use trying to work. From the length of the shadows on her balcony, she knew it must be late afternoon. Soon Roger would be awake and wanting to eat, which presented another problem. Her last words to Yanni were that she would go to his taverna that night. She could not possibly go there with Roger, but what would Yanni think if she did not turn up? She sat with her head in her hands, questions swirling around in her mind, making her feel dizzy.

The knock at the door made her jump. She looked across at Roger. He turned over, but did not wake. There was a second, much louder knock. Grace leapt out of her chair and ran across the room.

Her mother stood outside, her fist raised to thump the door again. 'Oh, so you've decided to answer the door at last, have you?'

Grace put her finger to her lips and stepped outside, pulling the door shut behind her.

'Can you please keep your voice down,' she begged in a low voice.

A knowing expression spread across Marjorie's face. 'So that's what you've been up to since you disappeared from view. I've been wondering why you haven't been answering the door. I would have left you in peace if I'd known. A bit of hot sweaty sex in the afternoon, or any time of the day for that matter, is just what you need.'

Grace motioned that they should walk down the steps. When they reached the bottom, she turned to her mother.

'I have not been holed up in my room having sex, sweaty or any other kind. I've been ignoring the notes you've been sticking under my door because I needed some time alone to think.'

Her mother studied Grace's face, her eyes bright with curiosity. 'So who's upstairs in your bed asleep? And don't tell me your room's a mess and you don't want me to see it. There's one thing I can always recognise and that's guilt, and your face is a picture of it.'

Grace looked down. 'Roger.'

'Roger!' Marjorie shrieked with laughter. 'Then I take what I said back. Sex is most definitely *not* the reason you've been avoiding me. When on earth did he arrive?'

'This morning. I wasn't expecting him. A couple of his cases were postponed, so he thought it would be a chance for us to spend some time together.'

'More likely he wanted to know what I was up to and whether I was corrupting his darling fiancée,' retorted Marjorie, her tongue lingering sarcastically over the word fiancée.

'Mother, *please*. Things are difficult enough without you two starting your usual arguments,' said Grace miserably.

Marjorie looked up at Grace's face again. 'There is something going on, isn't there?'

Grace looked away. Her throat felt as if it was in some sort of vice. She swallowed.

'I slept with Yanni last night.'

Marjorie put a hand on her arm. 'I *knew* something had happened. Do you want to tell me about it?' her voice was gentle.

Grace nodded.

Marjorie slipped her hand through Grace's arm. 'Let's walk down to the beach. I like this time of the day best, it's so calm and the sun has lost the worst of its heat.'

They strolled silently through the village. Grace was aware of her mother's questioning looks, but for once she seemed to sense Grace's mood and remained silent. When they reached the village beach, they made for a small patch of prickly grass in the shade of a

Casuarina tree. Marjorie placed her shawl on the ground and they sat down.

Grace hugged her knees to her chin and gazed at the sea. Her mother was right. This was a beautiful time of the day. The late-afternoon sun cast its soft, golden light over the landscape, making everything glow.

Her mother made an explosive little sound. 'Well, are you going to tell me, or do I have to drag it out of you?'

Grace was silent for a moment more. Then she turned to look at her mother.

'I've been so stupid.'

'*Good!*'

'Good? How can it possibly be good for me? I feel so... so... wretched.'

Marjorie put a hand on Grace's arm. 'My darling, if you felt otherwise I would be worried. No, what I meant by good was that sometimes we can learn more by the mistakes that we make than by our successes. It really worries me the way you strive for perfection in yourself and in others. It's one thing to aim for perfection in your work, but to do so in your emotional life is so unforgiving. Emotions are unpredictable, and if you try to control them too tightly, either they become twisted and contorted and apt to break loose in the most inappropriate ways, or you bury them so deep they die for lack of use. I know you think I live too much by my emotions, but I think you live too little by yours. If passion, or love, or just plain animal lust drove you to lose control of yours last night with Yanni, I think it was a good thing. You need to be reminded how strong and how important emotions can be, as well as how enjoyable.'

Marjorie studied Grace's face, trying to interpret her expression, but Grace turned her face away. 'It was enjoyable, wasn't it?' she asked.

Grace nodded, a dull red blush creeping across her cheeks.

Marjorie patted her hand. 'Now I know what your next question is going to be and the answer is no, you mustn't tell Roger. I can see it in your eyes. You think you've sinned and now you must seek forgiveness from the person against whom you've transgressed. But take it from me, an old and practised sinner, Roger will not thank you for telling him and will probably never forgive you. Not because you've slept with another man, but because you told him. Like the good lawyer he is, he will immediately start digging into your past record to try to find other offences to take into consideration. The only person you should be seeking forgiveness from is yourself. You're a hard taskmaster, but it's about time you stopped punishing yourself and learned to accept that you, too, can be prey to human emotions like desire. As for Roger, leave him in blissful innocence if you want to marry him.'

There was silence.

'You *do* still want to marry him, don't you?' asked Marjorie.

Grace was bemused by her mother's attitude. 'You've always hated Roger. I thought you would be the one encouraging me to leave him rather than giving me advice on how to keep him.'

'My darling Grace, while I may know a lot about affairs, I'm hardly the world's greatest expert on marriage. I've never made it a secret that I thought Roger was wrong for you, but you thought he was right for you, so only you can make the decision as to whether that has changed. But I'll tell you one thing. Although I never thought I'd hear myself say it, there is something to be said for having the security of knowing that there will be a warm body in the bed beside you every night, and the same face across the table from you at breakfast every morning.'

Grace scrutinised her mother. Beneath her suntan, her face was drawn.

'Is there?' she asked bleakly. 'I'm not really sure about that any more.' A tear trickled down her face.

Marjorie reached out with both arms and encircled Grace, gently rocking her while she sobbed.

'I'm all right, really I am,' sniffed Grace pushing her mother's arms away and searching blindly for a handkerchief.

Marjorie pulled a thick wad of paper napkins out of her pocket. As tissues and toilet paper were expensive in the village shop, she emptied napkin containers every time she went into a taverna.

Grace gratefully took one and blew her nose then dried her eyes. 'I'd better be getting back. Roger will be awake soon.'

'He's a big boy now, Grace. He can wake up without you being there beside him. Anyway, before you go back, you must make sure that you know what you're going to do. If you go up there all tearful and with red-rimmed eyes, he'll know there's something wrong and you'll find yourself subjected to third degree questioning and then you're bound to confess.'

'But I don't *know* what I want to do,' said Grace despairingly.

'Well, in that case tell him you need some more time by yourself.'

'But I can't. He's come all this way to find me. He's never done anything like this before. I can't tell him I don't want to see him and that he has to go back to England.'

'Why not? You didn't ask him to come. It will do him good if just for once you don't fall in with his plans. Stop playing the martyr, Grace, it's really very unbecoming. Women who play the martyr all the time get these horrible little wrinkles around their lips from that long-suffering expression they wear.'

'That's one lot of wrinkles you won't have to worry about getting, isn't it, mother? You never put anyone else's needs before yours,' retorted Grace.

'That's my Grace, back to her old fighting self again.' Marjorie patted Grace's hand. 'Now I'll tell you what I'll do. On my way back to the camp, I will pop into Yanni's taverna and warn him about Roger's arrival. And don't worry,' she said quickly catching the alarmed expression on Grace's face, 'I'll be discreet. In return, I want you to come to the camp tomorrow. The campaign against the hotel is really hotting up and we need your help. Lilith is doing her best, but she can be a little heavy-handed at times. We need someone like you who's a little more diplomatic with words. Anyway, I would have thought you would want to support Yanni now that you and he...' Marjorie raised a quizzical eyebrow.

Grace couldn't help smiling. 'Mother, you're incorrigible.'

Marjorie scrambled to her feet. 'It's one of my better traits. Now, as it's getting cooler, I'd better be heading back to the camp. I've promised myself a brisk walk at least once every day. I've allowed having a good time to go to my hips and I'm determined to lose a few pounds. I may not be able to do much about getting older, but I can at least try to stop myself getting fatter.'

Grace stood up and shook the sand out of her mother's shawl, before handing it back. 'Thank you.'

Marjorie draped it around her shoulders. 'Thank you for what? For being a mother? Haven't you heard - it's meant to be a thankless task.'

And with a gay little wave over her shoulder, she strode determinedly off.

THIRTY-ONE

'That couple over there seem to think they know us. I don't recognise them unless he's someone I've prosecuted. He looks the criminal type. They always favour loud prints and flashy jewellery - and that's only the men.' Roger laughed at his own joke and sipped his wine. He grimaced. 'If I had my way, I'd make it a criminal offence to serve this as wine. Are you sure this is the best they can do?'

'Roger, we're in Greece, not in your club with its gourmet wine cellars. They tend to drink their wine young here,' replied Grace in a low voice.

Roger had already sent three bottles of wine back after declaring them disgusting and she could not bear further embarrassment. Adonis had seemed quite impressed, but some of the other Greeks in the kafenion had not looked very happy.

'This isn't young. It was stillborn,' he declared, holding up the glass to inspect the colour of the wine, but he drank some more. 'You know, the girl he's with is really quite pretty, if you like showy blondes. Criminal types tend to go for that sort of thing.' He prodded experimentally at the chunks of meat on his plate. 'Are you sure this is lamb? After that paint stripper masquerading as wine, I don't want to take any chances. You know what my stomach is like. I have to be very careful. I wouldn't like to be at the mercy of the medical system in a place like this.'

'The lamb here is much fresher than anything you could buy in a butcher's in London, and it won't be pumped full of hormones and other unhealthy things either,' said Grace with as much patience as she could muster.

Roger stabbed a piece of meat with his fork and suspiciously lifted it to his mouth. He closed his eyes and popped it in, then began to chew, slowly at first and then with more enthusiasm. He opened his eyes and stabbed another piece with his fork.

'You're right. This is really quite edible.'

As Roger tucked into his meal, Grace took the opportunity to look surreptitiously over her shoulder at the couple Roger had described. They could only be Ari and Kelly. Much to her surprise, Kelly was playing kittenishly with the gold medallion draped around Ari's thick neck.

Before Grace could look away, Kelly caught her eye and mouthed 'hello'. Ari caught the exchange and beckoned Grace to come over. Grace shook her head with as polite a smile as she could manage.

'So you do know them?' asked Roger, catching the exchange.

'They're an Australian couple on holiday here. We've chatted a couple of times.'

Roger snorted. 'Australian! That explains it.'

'Please don't start on about colonials, Roger. They're really very nice people, or at least she is.'

'I'll reserve judgement on that till I meet them, which I think is about to happen. They're heading in our direction.'

Grace's heart sank. She pushed her untouched dinner away.

'I was beginning to think you'd disappeared off the face of the earth Grace. I haven't seen you in days, but Kelly here tells me you and she have been spending nearly all day, every day, spread-eagled on the beach, and I must say, you're looking good on it.' Ari grinned suggestively at Grace.

'It's been such fun, hasn't it Grace?' asked Kelly anxiously. She put her hand on Ari's arm. 'I keep telling Ari how nice it is for me to have a girlfriend to gossip with while he's busy making deals and whatever else it is he does all day.'

Ari looked at Roger. 'And they complain they have a hard time! Us men don't have time to slack off and sit in the sun, do we? We have to work so that these pretty little ladies can go to the hairdresser whenever they want to.'

Roger looked rather oddly at Grace. She tried to keep her face expressionless.

'Ari, Kelly, this is my fiancé Roger Sawbridge. He arrived today.'

Ari reached out a large paw and pumped Roger's hand. 'Well, this is a surprise and a pleasure. We didn't think we'd get to meet you.' He turned to Kelly. 'You didn't tell me Rog was here when you got back from the beach this avo.'

Grace saw Roger's eyebrow arch menacingly as Ari shortened his name to Rog. She also sensed Kelly's trepidation at Ari's question.

'Roger sprung a big surprise on me by arriving today. I didn't know he was coming,' Grace interjected quickly. 'So Kelly couldn't have known because I didn't know myself when we met at the beach.'

Kelly flashed a grateful smile at her rescuer. Grace smiled faintly back. Had it taken so short a time for her to become so practised at deception?

Ari dragged a chair over from the next table and sat down next to Roger. He hooked another chair over with his foot and indicated that Kelly should sit, oblivious to the disapproval emanating from Roger.

'She's quite a character, this soon to be mother-in-law of yours, isn't she? I haven't as yet had the pleasure, if that's quite the right word, of meeting her, but I've heard all about her little escapades. Running around with a girl half her age; dancing naked on the beach; beating up the Mayor and the village policeman; causing riots. And I thought Greek mother-in-laws were a problem!' Ari slapped Roger on the back and roared with laughter.

Grace held her breath. She had told Roger some things about her mother and the women's camp, but there were others she had omitted, like their habit of running round naked, and the story about the night they reclaimed the taverna. She waited for him to get angry, but Roger's features remained rigid.

'People often get a bit carried away when they're on holiday. It's a combination of too much sun and cheap wine. It goes to their heads,' she explained lamely.

'Their heads are not the only part of their anatomy which is affected,' guffawed Ari. 'According to what I've heard they're at it like turbo-charged...'

'How do you like Greece so far, Mr Sawbridge?' interrupted Kelly with a dazzling smile.

It was Grace's turn to feel grateful to Kelly.

'If it wasn't for the heat, the parlous state of the roads, and the lack of the basic necessities of civilised life, like water, it would be quite a nice place. What it needs is a few decent hotels,' replied Roger.

'I knew it,' roared Ari slapping his thigh, 'a man after my own heart. This place needs to be dragged kicking and screaming into the twentieth century.'

Roger looked slightly taken aback at finding himself in agreement with Ari, but he managed to nod his head.

Ari leant forward, his eyes narrowing. 'Well now. You look like a man who has an eye for a good investment, so perhaps we can talk business. There's some prime real estate just on the edge of the village that's crying out to have a hotel built on it. If you want, I can take you to have a gander at it tomorrow. Anyone coming in on the deal at this stage is set to make a killing.' He broke off to lean back in his chair and snap his fingers at Adonis. 'Four large brandies. Pronto!'

Roger made a half-hearted attempt to demur, but Ari waved his objections aside. 'The wheels of commerce need to be oiled. I never trust a man who won't drink with me. It's the Greek way.'

When Adonis arrived with the drinks, Ari raised his glass, 'To making money.'

Roger drank to the toast with more enthusiasm than Grace thought necessary. She barely touched the glass to her lips and then replaced it on the table. Kelly did the same.

Grace reached across and put a hand on Roger's arm. 'Roger dear, it's late, we ought to be going. You've had a long day.'

'Always the little women trying to keep us in check, eh Roger?' asked Ari. 'Lose weight, don't drink too much, don't stay up too late. They take over from our mothers. What is it they say? Take a good gander at a girl's mother before you marry her, as women always turn into their mothers, so be warned.'

Roger patted Grace's hand. 'That's one thing I don't have to worry about,' he said jovially. 'Grace could never be like her mother, chasing after young boys and the like. I sometimes wonder how Marjorie could have produced such a sensible daughter. This latest escapade of hers is only one in a long line of irresponsible acts primarily aimed to discomfort me. A man in my position has to be careful.'

Grace pulled her hand away. 'I don't think my mother spends much time thinking about your career Roger, at least not in the way you think she does, and she certainly wouldn't try to hurt you on purpose. She's just very impulsive and sometimes she gets over-enthusiastic about the causes she supports.'

'Impulsive! Is that what you call it? And just what cause is she supporting by sleeping with just about anything in trousers, or should I now be saying skirts? It's not HRT she needs but bromide. That mother of yours is quite frankly over-sexed. She ought to know better at her age.'

'Why is it that if a middle-aged man takes up with a girl half his age nobody bats an eyelid and some people even smile indulgently? Yet if an older woman takes up with a younger man...' Grace let the words hang in the air.

'Well, it's just not the same for a woman is it?' blustered Roger shifting uneasily in his seat.

He couldn't quite pin it down, but there was definitely something different about Grace. Perhaps as the old maxim said, absence really did make the heart grow fonder, as he had missed her more than he would have thought possible. He had thought it would be fun being a bachelor again, spending time at his club and seeing some of his old cronies with whom he had lost touch since he had met Grace. However, whether his memory was at fault, or the club had changed, he had not enjoyed himself at all. The place seemed full of lonely men finding comfort in bad food and too much wine.

He had also been invited to a dinner party by a colleague from chambers and had gone along in the hope this would cheer him up. However, everyone else had been in couples, which had only made him feel worse. In his bachelor days, a single woman had always been invited to make up numbers, but as he was now considered part of an established couple, it was not considered appropriate.

The evening had only succeeded in making Grace's absence even more painful, particularly as feeling a little left out of the banter between the other couples, he spent most of his time remembering the first time they met. It had been at a very similar dinner party and he could recall almost every single detail. Being a single man of a certain age, he was accustomed to being invited to dinner parties where attempts were made to match him with a friend of the hostess or a friend of a friend of the hostess. Usually, his intended match was a middle-aged divorcee or widow who, after a glass of two of wine, became dangerously brittle with anger or sadness. As being an entertaining companion was the price of dinner, he prided himself on always having a fund of amusing little anecdotes to help the conversation along and to avoid any embarrassing silences. However, the evening Grace was his intended match, he had been rendered almost completely inarticulate by her beauty and quiet poise, managing only to offer a few inane and stuttered comments on the weather and its effect on the England v Australia cricket match. It had not been a promising start.

However, as he was leaving, he asked the evening's hostess for Grace's telephone number, and two weeks later, aided by a stiff whisky and soda, he got up the courage to call and ask her out to the theatre. He was pretty sure that he wanted to marry her from the first moment he saw her, but he had waited until he felt they had been seeing each other for the right amount of time, before asking her. He was so convinced that she would laugh in his face and say no, he hadn't even proposed properly. Instead, he left what he hoped would sound like an offhand, almost jokey message on her answering machine. That way, he reasoned, if she said no, neither of them would be embarrassed and they could at least continue as friends.

He had been astounded when she agreed, so much so that later that day, for the first time in his life, he lost the thread of his argument in court and was forced to hand the case over to a junior brief, pleading a bad case of indigestion. Luckily, the judge hearing the case was well-known for being frequently laid-low by dyspepsia, so no harm was done. His disbelief at his good luck was matched by just about everyone who knew him. When news of his engagement to Grace got out, he was slapped on the back and declared a lucky old dog so many times that his shoulders were in danger of being dislocated, and he could see the envy in the eyes of the younger men in his chambers as they imagined his sex life.

Yet sex did not have a lot to do with his relationship with Grace. Not that their sex life wasn't perfectly satisfactory, it was. However, it was a known fact that sex just wasn't important to some women and since Grace was perfect in every other way, he wasn't complaining. That afternoon had been the first time she had taken the initiative in their love-making and it had frankly taken him by surprise.

Both this and a number of other things he had noticed since his arrival, had given him the unsettling feeling that she was somehow slipping away from him. He knew whom to blame - it was Grace's mother, Marjorie. She had always been against their marriage and had done everything she could to persuade Grace to change her mind. Knowing this, when Grace left a message saying she was going to stay on the island for a little longer, he had immediately asked his secretary to book him on the next flight to Greece. It had been very inconvenient as he had a heavy caseload, but he dared not stay in London and risk losing her.

The instant he saw her returning from the beach that morning, he knew he had made the right decision. She looked even more beautiful than usual. Her skin was deeply tanned and her hair was wild and loose, blowing round her face in a way he had never seen before. It suited her. Looking at her across the table now, he wondered whether he could persuade her to repeat her earlier performance. He had not been in the mood for sex when he arrived, as he had been feeling far too hot and tired. However, he was feeling much better now he had eaten.

He faked a yawn. 'You're right my dear, it is late.' He stood up and held out his hand to Ari. 'Perhaps we can talk about this scheme of yours tomorrow.'

Ari pumped his hand. 'Let's meet back here in the morning when the girls have gone to the beach. I'll bring you some facts and figures.'

Kelly gave Grace another conspiratorial smile. 'I'll see you at the harbour about ten. Perhaps we could walk to the far beach tomorrow.'

Grace nodded and caught up with Roger, who was standing at the counter trying to count out drachma notes to pay the bill. She took the money from his hand and gave Adonis the right amount.

'Kalinichta Adonis, efharisto.'

'You seem to have made yourself at home,' said Roger when they were outside. 'I never knew you spoke Greek.'

'I've learnt just a few words. It seems only polite to try, even if you make mistakes.'

'I had classical languages drummed into me at school, but the language they speak here sounds Greek to me.' Roger laughed loudly at his joke.

Grace was silent.

'That Australian chap wasn't as bad as I expected,' he continued as they walked slowly back up the hill. 'He's got a point about building a hotel. It would be the making of the place.'

'I rather like it the way it is,' said Grace.

Roger looked at her. There was something about the tone of her voice that suggested a change in the subject might be diplomatic. He put his arm around her shoulder.

'I'm glad I came. I enjoyed this afternoon, but I was a bit tired. Now I've had a sleep and something to eat, I'm feeling a bit friskier. Could we try it again?'

Roger felt Grace's body stiffen. She pulled away from him.

'I'm sorry Roger, but this time it's me who's feeling tired.'

THIRTY-TWO

'HALT! Who goes there?' A figure dressed in a grubby T-shirt and combat trousers leapt out from behind some tall reeds and stood in the road in front of Grace. 'Who are you and what are you doing here?' demanded the woman, her arms held wide, barring the way.

Grace glared angrily at the woman whose straggly, multicoloured hair looked as though it could do with a wash. She was in no mood to play games this morning. She had already had enough with Roger.

He had woken up like a dewy-eyed honeymooner wanting to make love. Even in the early days of their relationship, Roger's morning routine had never included sex. He claimed that it took the edge off his performance in court, so he practised abstinence, like a boxer before a big fight. However, this morning, he had even nibbled her ears, which was completely - and disconcertingly - out of character. She had pulled away from him and lied that her period was starting. This would normally guarantee Roger taking a wide berth around her for a few days, as he did not like to be reminded of the natural functions of the female body, but once again, he had reacted completely out of character. He had fussed around, insisting she remain in bed while he made her coffee and then swallow some paracetamol that he produced from the enormous first-aid kit, big enough to supply a hospital in a war zone, that he had brought with him. Only when he was satisfied that she was comfortably propped up in bed, with something to read within easy reach, did he leave to meet Ari.

Grace had waited ten minutes. Then, feeling absurdly like a criminal, she dressed and crept down the stairs outside her room, alert for any sight of Roger. She had made her way out of the village by taking a tortuous route through narrow back alleys, avoiding the square and the main street.

Already angry with herself, her bad humour had not improved as she walked the long, dusty road to the women's camp, and now she had no intention of obeying the commands of a woman with a ring through her nose. Grace tried to walk past, but the woman leapt in front of her again. Grace sidestepped again, but once more the woman anticipated her move and blocked her progress.

'This is a public road,' snapped Grace. 'I can go where I damn well choose.'

'This is the domain of the goddess. Nobody can enter without stating their business,' replied the woman stubbornly.

'Oh for heaven's sake, I'm going to see my mother, Marjorie Hamilton.'

The woman crossed her arms. 'We do not recognise the labels of patriarchal servitude in the domain of the goddess.'

Grace fought an overpowering desire to grab the woman by the shoulders and shake her hard.

'She calls herself Gaia,' she said through clenched teeth.

The woman reluctantly stood aside and Grace stalked past her.

'You won't find Gaia in the camp,' the woman called after her. 'They've had to move to the dunes. And if I were you, I'd go over the rocks...'

Grace ignored her. She had no intention of scrambling over the rocks. She just wanted to get to the women's camp as soon as possible. She had no clear idea in her mind why she wanted to go there, just that she wanted to get away from Roger.

Grace slowed down. There was a very odd smell in the air. She had noticed it before but it was now becoming overpowering. As she turned the corner in the road, she stepped in something unpleasantly soft and squashy. It was a large and very rotten aubergine. Bluebottles were feasting upon it, and they rose up in a buzzing cloud and swarmed around her. Feeling queasy, Grace looked around for a stone to scrape the mess off her shoe. It was then that she spotted the source of the stench and the flies - a huge pile of rotting rubbish. It was about twenty yards away where the track turned into the beach, but even at that distance, she could see that it was shimmering with flies as well as carrion crows and seagulls, fighting noisily over the putrefied entrails of some large animal.

Grace almost gagged. She stumbled off the road and ran across the field. She didn't stop until she had reached the top of the rocky outcrop, where she gulped in the fresh, salty air. As the stench cleared from her nostrils, she looked down at the beach. The women were gathered among the dunes. Grace made her way towards them. As she approached, she could hear angry voices.

Juno was pointing at Kelly. 'If you're looking for the Trojan horse, you need look no further,' she declared. 'All that simpering about how badly her husband treats her was just a ruse to get into the camp so she could spy for him.'

Some of women murmured their agreement.

Lilith put a protective arm around Kelly, but it was Marjorie who sprang bristling to her defence. 'Don't be ridiculous. We can't blame Kelly for her husband. Isn't it bad enough that the poor girl is married to him? Anyway, a few flies won't hurt us.'

It was Psyche's turn to protest. 'A few flies! I've used enough fly spray in our tent to wipe out the ozone layer for the next million years. It's all right for you on your side of the camp, you can't *smell* the rubbish. It's disgusting.'

The two opposing groups of women began to shout at each other again, and Grace took the opportunity to approach Sîan who was not taking any part in the argument.

'What's going on?'

Sîan turned and gave her a welcoming smile. 'Sometime yesterday, somebody dumped a load of rotting food and other rubbish near the camp. We woke up to a plague of flies. Everyone has been blaming everyone else for not keeping better watch. We agreed that there should always be at least two women in the camp at any one time to keep an eye on things, but yesterday Hecate had half the women dancing though the countryside playing handmaidens and communing with goddesses, while Lilith sent the other half to the village to tear down the Mayor's elections posters and distribute leaflets. Everyone was so busy, nobody saw it happening. Now we've agreed on a rota for guard duty, but expressions like horses bolting and stable doors come to mind.' She looked curiously at Grace. 'Talking about being busy, where have you been for the last few days? I know I can be a bit of a big mouth, so if I opened it too much on the beach the other night, tell me.'

'I just needed some time to myself,' Grace began, but further explanation was prevented by a loud voice.

'STOP, please! This is getting us nowhere.' The speaker's English was accented, but nearly perfect.

A diminutive figure, dressed in a canary yellow linen dress and matching highheeled sandals, who Grace had not noticed before, pushed her way into the space between the two groups of women and held up her hands for silence. The noise gradually died down.

'We are all agreed that we want the same thing: that is, to prevent the hotel being built on the beach in the next bay, yes? What we seem unable to agree upon is how to achieve it.'

'I don't remember seeing her before. Who is she?' asked Grace in a low voice.

'Yanni's sister, Eleni. It seems she lives in Athens but has come back to help his campaign,' replied Sîan.

'But what is she doing here?'

'She marched into the camp first thing this morning and went from tent to tent asking all the women to come to this meeting. She's extraordinary. She seems utterly unfazed by anything, even Juno. She wants us to help with Yanni's campaign. That's what started the argument.'

'If I can get someone to come with a tractor and remove the rubbish, will you agree to help me?' asked Eleni.

'Why should we help a man win power?' someone demanded.

The question was rewarded by a loud chorus of agreement.

'Because if my brother gets elected, he will stop the hotel. Isn't that what you all want?' asked Eleni impatiently.

Hecate stepped forward. Up until this point, she had not been taking any part in the argument. She looked imperiously around, silencing all murmurs. 'I agree with Gaia. I do not think Kelly is to blame for what has happened. We should accept her as one of us if that is what she wants. '

She looked at Kelly who, still a little tearful, nodded gratefully.

Hecate then turned to Eleni. 'As for myself, and I think I speak for many of the women here,' she swept an arm around to emphasise her point. 'What we want is to be free from all unwelcome intruders who taint the sanctuary of the goddess and prevent us from setting out on our journey to meet the eternal matrix within each of us.'

At this, she clutched the large teardrop shaped crystal that she always wore around her neck. Even though her hair was wild about her face and she was dressed in a shapeless baggy shift of indeterminate colour, she still managed to look like the reincarnation of an ancient priestess.

Eleni looked up at her. Hecate stood a full head taller and with her mane of hair she dwarfed Eleni's petite figure but Eleni refused to be daunted. She was accustomed to dealing with people who were both powerful and difficult. Many obstacles had been placed in the way of her rise up the company ladder, but she had overcome them all to become the company's first woman chief executive officer. However, whilst most of the obstacles to her advancement had been men, experience had taught her that women were often the real problem.

From her mother, to her female co-workers, to the wives of her male colleagues - they all watched her like hawks, waiting to swoop if they could find one tiny fault in her as a wife or a mother, anything that would allow them to say: 'I told you so'. She had always thought that if they would only stop trying to find fault in each other and looked instead to the men in their lives - especially their sons - the world would be an easier place for all women. However, as Hecate's clear, wide-eyed gaze met hers, for once Eleni could detect no malice or hidden purpose.

Satisfied that no opposition would come from this quarter, she turned her attention to Lilith. Here was a woman she understood almost too well. Even though they had barely spoken more than a few words to each other, Eleni had immediately recognised that she and Lilith were very alike, and because of that, she knew Lilith would not give ground easily. However, if she could win Lilith over, Eleni was convinced that most of the other women would follow her. She looked her squarely in the eye.

'My request is two-fold: that we come to some agreement on the wording of the leaflets you've been printing, and that you won't stage any more demonstrations in the village. That way, if you will not help my brother, at least you will not hinder his campaign. In return for this, he will make sure that the rubbish is removed and see if it is possible to install a stand-pipe for water nearer to the camp site. Do we have a deal?' she asked.

'Let me get this straight. You want us to tone down our leaflets and to forget direct action? In other words, forget our principles in the cause of your brother's political ambitions?' demanded Lilith.

'No. What I am asking is that you use language that is more acceptable in a small Greek village,' Eleni explained patiently, trying to keep irritation out of her voice. 'I think that a lot of the women in the village, and even some of the men, do not want the hotel, but because of the way you present the case against it, they do not dare support you or anyone else that they think you support, like my brother.' Eleni held up her hands as Lilith began to protest. 'I am not saying you are wrong, but we are a conservative society and there are many things it is difficult for us to accept.' She turned to the other women. 'To put it another way: supposing a group of Greeks came and camped outside one of *your* villages and tried to interfere in local politics, what would you think? When the Americans brought Cruise missiles to your villages in England, you did not accept their word that the missiles were necessary for world peace, you made up your own minds, and then demonstrated until they left. Believe me, you are like Cruise missiles to some of the people in the village - alien and destructive to their way of life.'

At this there was a murmur of agreement.

'That sounds reasonable enough,' said Lilith grudgingly.

'And as to direct action,' continued Eleni, 'I have some ideas for a few little surprises we might spring on the opposition, which seems only fair considering the dirty tricks campaign they've launched against you. Perhaps we could combine forces?'

Lilith considered this for a moment or two. 'Ok. But let's meet back here this evening when its cooler and the flies aren't so active.'

Eleni smiled and inclined her head. 'Thank you. In the meantime, I'll see what Yanni can do about getting the the rubbish moved.'

The women began to drift away talking. Hecate tossed her head defiantly.

'No good will come of it, I warn you,' she declared, but she had already lost her audience. She turned and walked away, her disciples following behind in a dispirited single file.

Marjorie caught sight of Grace for the first time. She came over and kissed her on the cheek. 'I'm so glad you've come. I was worried you might change your mind. Kelly told me about dinner last night in Adonis's kafenion, didn't you, dear?' Marjorie turned to look for Kelly, but she and Lilith were walking away.

'Lilith...?' Marjorie called uncertainly after them, but they continued walking, so deep in conversation with each other that their heads almost touched.

'Marjorie!' Eleni came up and placed a small, exquisitely manicured hand on Marjorie's arm. 'Thank you so much. I couldn't have managed without your help.'

Marjorie indicated Grace. 'This is my daughter, Grace.'

Eleni held out her hand. Her touch was light but firm. 'I am pleased to meet you,' she said looking searchingly into Grace's eyes, 'I have heard a lot about you. I hope you will come to our taverna soon. It would be nice to talk further with you.' She turned back to Marjorie, 'I must go now, thank you again for your help. I will come back this evening so we can make plans. This Lilith, she is a strong woman, I can tell. She will be good to have on my side. The election is in three days so we do not have much time.' She walked to a car parked in the shade of a tree on the far side of the camp and drove away.

Sîan began to undress. 'Time for a swim I think. Are you two coming?'

'I'd like to talk to Grace first, so why don't you go ahead and Grace and I will join you in a little while,' replied Marjorie, taking Grace's hand.

Sîan ran naked down the beach and plunged into the sea, striking out into the bay.

Grace turned to her mother. 'How do you know Eleni?'

'She was in the taverna when I went to see Yanni. We talked about the situation and I suggested she come to the camp and meet the women.'

'What else did you talk to her about?' demanded Grace.

'Nothing!' protested Marjorie. 'However I did manage to get a moment alone with Yanni and I told him about Roger. He seemed heartbroken, the poor love.'

'Mother, you're exaggerating again. I can't imagine Yanni being anything of the sort.'

'That's where you're wrong. A man does not have to say something in order for you to know what he feels. I could see it in his eyes, and Yanni has exceedingly beautiful ones, with eyelashes to die for. Combined with that beautiful body of his, I quite understand why you've fallen for him.'

'*Mother*!' declared Grace, embarrassed.

'My dear, we're both grown women. If we can't discuss men and sex now, when can we? But then, you never did like discussing sex, did you? Remember that time in the squat when we sprang you from your school? You were so scandalised when...'

'Mother, *please*,' begged Grace. 'Can we stick to the present and to Yanni?'

'If you insist,' said Marjorie archly. 'He said he'd meet you in that old ruined windmill just outside the village at four o'clock this afternoon.'

'But I can't... Not while Roger is here...'

Her mother looked up at her. 'So, you'd have sex with Yanni if Roger was back in England but not while he's here?'

Grace felt her cheeks colouring again. 'I'm not sure what I want to do.'

Marjorie started to undress. 'Well, I know what I want to do and that's cool down. Are you going to join me?'

Grace shook her head. All she could think about was Yanni.

Marjorie twisted her hair into an untidy knot on top of her head and tied a brightly coloured scarf around it. 'Well I'm not going to suggest you do anything. Whatever I say, and whatever happens, you'll blame me. However, if I were you, I know what I'd do.'

She kissed Grace on the cheek, then, at a stately pace, walked down to the sea where she waded carefully into the shallows and then sank into the water until it covered her shoulders. She began to swim a leisurely breaststroke, holding her turbanned head up high.

THIRTY-THREE

The face reflected in the mirror above the washbasin was not hers. Grace knew what her face looked like. She had looked at it every day for nearly thirty-six years, but when she glanced up after brushing her teeth that morning, she had been shocked. The eyes were familiar, but little else. Her skin was deeply bronzed, and, as a result, her face seemed thinner, more defined, her cheekbones accentuated, her mouth wider and her lips fuller.

She studied her face again. Did familiarity breed blindness? Did she only see what she expected to see, an image of herself fixed in her mind at some point in the past, rather than what was actually there?

The mirror was cracked and its silvering was coming off in places, so maybe it was distorting her features so that they looked out of proportion and the image she was looking at was just an illusion, however her hair was no illusion. She didn't need to see the unruly mess framing her face in the mirror to know that the sun and the sea had wreaked havoc with it and the crazy rides through the countryside on the back of Yanni's motorbike hadn't helped either.

And that's just what she was - crazy. The face that looked back at her in the mirror was the face of a mad woman. What else could explain her behaviour during the last few days?

Everyone could be allowed one mistake - one wild, drunken moment when they yield to temptation and behave badly. Her moment happened the night she and Yanni went to the gypsy horse races in the mountains. If she had been in her right mind, she would have run away, back into the reality of Roger's secure arms and stayed there. Instead, like some mad woman, she had gone back to Yanni not just once, but again and again.

In the sweltering heat of the afternoons, they met in the ruined windmill just outside the village where they made desperate, sweating love among the rubble. Afterwards, Grace felt scorched, as though she had flown too close to the sun. Yet she kept returning for more, unable to resist the temptation to fly higher and higher, all the time knowing that she was tempting the fates to send her crashing to the ground.

She looked at herself in the mirror again. The changes in her were not just physical. Her need for Yanni went beyond that. It was not just his body she wanted, but the intensity of his emotions. Sometimes they frightened her - not because they were dangerous - but because she feared that if she lost them, she would also lose the new landscape that they had opened up for her, full of luminous colour and sound and feeling, unlike anything she had ever experienced before.

There was an urgent knock on the bathroom door.

'Are you going to be much longer in there, Grace?'

She splashed some water on her face, and taking a towel, opened the door.

Roger rushed past her. 'Sorry, emergency again.'

Grace only just managed to step into the bedroom before he banged the door shut.

She went out onto the balcony. It was morning in the village. A little boy protested shrilly and dragged his satchel in the dust, fighting against the inevitability of school as his older brother pulled him along, a long-suffering expression on his face. Grace counted the six sets of enormous long johns hanging on the washing line of a large white house down below. It was the same as every morning apart from Sundays. Grace was idly contemplating whether there was one very dirty man living in the house, or the poor woman was washing clothes for six, equally large men, when Roger emerged red-faced onto the balcony.

'Whew! Nearly didn't make it that time.' He was holding a medicine bottle and a teaspoon. 'That stuff they gave me in Boots doesn't seem to be having much effect, so I thought I might try some of this. My mother used to swear by it for diarrhoea and gyppy tummy. You can't beat some of the old remedies.'

He poured himself two teaspoons of milky white liquid.

Grace watched him. 'Do you think you ought to take two lots of different medicine? I'm sure it won't do your stomach any good.'

'I don't think there is anything left in my stomach after what I've just been through in that bathroom. It's all that damned olive oil they pour over everything here.'

'Olive oil is very good for you. The Mediterranean diet is very healthy.'

'Not for me it isn't. When I get back, I never want to look at another tomato for the rest of my life,' declared Roger.

'It's your own fault. I did warn you about eating and drinking too much, then sitting in the sun. There won't be anything left of your liver if you keep drinking Metaxa with Ari.'

'Ari's not such a bad chap. I don't know what you've got against him,' said Roger peevishly. 'He might be Australian but he's got all the right ideas. I've told him they should just send the police in mob-handed and get rid of those women. They're a damned nuisance.'

'That damned nuisance includes my mother as well as people I consider my friends.'

Roger looked hard at her. 'I think you've been spending a little too much time with your mother lately. She's a bad influence. She and those... those *women* are a menace to society.'

Before Grace could reply, Roger clutched his stomach and bent nearly double.

'Damn tomatoes,' he muttered as he fled to the bathroom.

Grace turned her back to the room and looked down at the village, trying to control her irritation with Roger and to ignore the sounds coming from the bathroom.

She was trying not to feel too upset at not seeing Yanni at the windmill as usual that afternoon. Tomorrow was election day, and Eleni had organised a lunch in the taverna to make a last bid to woo the votes of some of the people in the village whom she considered important to Yanni's campaign, so he had to be there.

According to Yanni, Eleni was angry with him because she thought he was not putting enough effort into his campaign. She was determined that Yanni should be elected, not just in order to stop the hotel, but also in order to tackle other problems faced by the village. She had prepared a list of other issues she wanted him to talk about at lunch, which included the threat faced by local fishermen who were being ruined by the large factory ships that were depleting fish stocks, and European Union hygiene regulations which threatened to close down the local cheese factory. Yanni had promised he would read her notes as well as write his speech for the meeting, which was going to take place in the village square at eleven that night, so he did not have time to come to the windmill. Neither would Grace see him that night after Roger had fallen asleep. The meeting in the square was the last meeting of the campaign, and was unlikely to finish before the early hours of the morning when voting began.

In her heart, Grace knew that Eleni was right. The election should not just be about the hotel. The village needed a Mayor who was prepared to work hard to help all the inhabitants, not merely his family and a few cronies, but the idea of a day without seeing Yanni filled her with despair, which was not helped by the sounds of Roger's loud bowel movements. However, when the bathroom door finally opened and Roger emerged grey-faced, his shoulders sagging, Grace felt a sudden stab of guilt. She guided him to the bed, where he slumped down.

'Why don't you lie down for a while?' she urged gently. 'I'll go to the shop and get some more bottled water. You should drink as much as possible or else you'll get dehydrated. I'll get some fresh bread from the bakery too. A little dry bread and some yoghurt might help.'

Roger groaned. 'I couldn't touch a thing, and even if I could, I can't think of anything worse than bread and water and that disgusting stuff you and the Greeks eat.'

Grace sat down beside him and began to massage the nape of his neck with her hand. It normally soothed him.

He winced and pulled away. 'Ouch! That hurts.'

Grace located the source of his pain. The back of his neck between his hairline and his collar was red and peeling where he had been sitting with his back to the sun.

'You poor dear. You really have been in the wars haven't you?' she said sympathetically.

Roger nodded sorrowfully.

Grace got up and fetched a tub of her moisturising cream, then she soaked one of the T-shirts Roger used as vests in some cold water and wrung it out. She gently massaged the cream into the back of his neck and then made him lie down, placing the folded damp T-shirt across his forehead.

Roger sighed gratefully and closed his eyes. 'That feels much better.'

Grace leant down and kissed him tenderly on the cheek. He smelt of Imperial Leather soap and baby powder. She stood looking at him. He could be so infuriatingly pompous and at other times so endearingly helpless. She brushed a loose strand of hair off his face.

Roger caught her hand in his and held it to his lips. 'Stay with me please,' he murmured.

Grace's heart missed a beat.

'Stay with you? Why would I leave you?' she demanded, guilt lending a rough edge to her voice.

Roger looked momentarily startled at her vehemence. Then he patted the bed beside him. 'I meant sit down for a while. I'm sure we've got enough water in the fridge. You can go to the store later on.'

Grace sat down and leaned back against the headboard. Roger reached over and took her hand like a child needing reassurance that she was really there. Within a few minutes his breathing became deeper and his grip on her hand relaxed.

Grace sat quietly until she was sure he was asleep, then she carefully got off the bed and got dressed.

The sound of a motorbike wending its way up through the houses made her rush out onto the balcony and grip the rail, waiting for it to come into sight, willing it to be Yanni. When it emerged onto the narrow track below she felt dizzy with disappointment. The rider was a middle-aged man with his wife sitting side-saddle behind him, clutching a basketful of groceries.

Grace closed her eyes. She had to survive a whole day without Yanni. It yawned, terrifyingly empty, before her.

THIRTY-FOUR

Ari's eyes narrowed. The crowd had listened politely enough to the Mayor's speech, but the applause greeting Yanni's was both loud and enthusiastic. People had even leapt to their feet and cheered. What was worse, some of the enthusiasm had come from people Ari thought supported his cousin, or so they had assured him yesterday when he plied them with expensive malt whisky at considerable cost to his own pocket.

The atmosphere in the crowded village square was more like that of a fiesta than a political meeting. Fairy lights strung from the trees gaily illuminated the crowd and the tavernas and kafenions were doing good business. From his vantage point behind the Mayor on the makeshift platform erected for the night, Ari carefully noted the people who returned his gaze and those who avoided it. He never forgot or forgave people who double-crossed him, but he was also conscious that he should not make himself too conspicuous. There had been a lot of muttering about his role in the election. People were saying that the Mayor was in the pocket of a rich foreigner. Ari looked across to the other side of the platform. Also standing in the shadows to render herself less conspicuous was Yanni's sister, Eleni. To his annoyance, she looked serenely confident.

He hated her type of woman - all sharply tailored suits and high heels that clicked self-importantly when they walked. They thought they could outwit men, but when they couldn't, they wept crocodile tears and cried discrimination. Sydney was full of them, but this one was cleverer than most. She knew exactly when to walk two paces behind a man and when to put herself forward. Ari was sure that she was responsible for the note of realism that had suddenly appeared in Yanni's campaign. He also had a suspicion that she was responsible for the change in the behaviour of the women in the camp. Their strident demonstrations had been resented by most of the villagers and had greatly helped his cousin's campaign, but they had suddenly gone very quiet and, when they did come into the village, they acted like maiden aunts. He was convinced the women were behind the Mayor's campaign posters being ripped down or defaced every time they were pasted up, but he couldn't prove it. Whoever was doing it did it late at night, and the raids were so well-planned that nobody had been caught. The Mayor's campaign had cost him a lot more than he intended, and paying some of the boys in the village to mount a counter campaign to rip down Yanni's posters as soon as they went up, had made it even more expensive. However, he was now in so deep financially that he could not afford to let Yanni win. The hotel had to be built. It was not only the money. It was also a question of losing face, not just in the village, but also back in Sydney.

Originally, he had intended the hotel to be his project and his alone, but he had soon realised that he needed the kind of money and influence that only his ex father-in-law, George Mavroupoulous could provide, so he had been forced to swallowed his pride and offer him a stake. He had sold the project to his ex father-in-law by convincing him that it would be the first step in building a Mavroupoulous construction empire in Europe. George had loved the idea, particularly when Ari assured him that he had the whole village, including the Mayor, in his pocket. However, he had omitted to mention that there was going to be an election and that the fate of the hotel depended on its outcome.

Given his past history with his ex father-in-law - especially all that fuss about him trying to swindle him out of money - life in Sydney would be very awkward if he failed to deliver what he promised. George had a very vindictive streak in his nature.

Ari looked across at Eleni again, only to find that she was watching him. Her gaze was cool, but Ari was sure there was the suggestion of a triumphant smile on her lips. Someone in the crowd yelled a question at Yanni and she stood on tiptoe and whispered into his ear. Yanni turned confidently back to the audience and began his answer while Eleni stepped back into the shadows. As she did, the headlights of a car trying to negotiate its way through the crowd briefly illuminated the crowd pressing close to the front of the stage and Ari spotted Grace looking up at Yanni. Eleni saw her at the same time, and from the look on Eleni's face, Ari could see she was not pleased. Ari smiled. Anything that disturbed Eleni's confident composure made him happy.

Yanni and the Mayor shook hands, signalling the end of the speeches. Ari kept to the back of the stage as the Mayor began shaking hands and clapping backs. He was more interested in what was happening in the opposing camp, where Yanni was standing with his head bowed close to his sister's so that he could hear what she was saying above the noise of the square. He had not seen Grace who had moved to the side of the stage as the atmosphere in the square grew rowdier. Even though her face was in shadow, Ari could sense she had eyes only for Yanni. A smile crept across his lips.

Two days ago, he was returning to his villa after another long and expensive lunch with yet more people his cousin had assured him he should meet in order to clear the way for the hotel, when he had seen Grace leaving her room. She was some distance away and did not see him wave, but the way she looked around before ducking into an alleyway, instinctively made him follow her.

She led him to the ruined windmill just outside the village. Yanni's motorbike stood against the wall outside. Ari recognised it instantly, but just to be sure, he waited a few minutes before creeping up to the building and peering through a gap in the wall. He had not been able to see the faces belonging to the two bodies writhing around on the floor - he had not needed to - but he watched for a long enough to confirm that Grace had a very good body.

His secret had made listening to that supercilious husband of hers, endlessly pontificating about the superiority of all things British, intensely enjoyable. According to him, if Australians ever voted to get rid of the Queen as head of state, they would be down on their knees begging her to come back within a year. Normally Ari would have taken great delight in telling a Galah like Roger exactly where to get off, but instead he had nodded and smiled, all the while treasuring his secret, waiting for the right moment to use it like an exocet missile to explode Roger's pompous little world. However, now he had thought of a way he could put it to even better use.

Ari mentally rubbed his hands together. Knowledge was power, which was why he had enjoyed being an accountant. He knew altogether more about his client's affairs than their wives, their mistresses, the taxman or even their lawyers.

Across the other side of the platform, Grace had finally attracted Yanni's attention, but, even as he started to bend down to speak to her, Eleni took him firmly by the arm and led him off the platform towards a group of people who instantly surrounded him. He made an apologetic hand gesture at Grace and then turned away, laughing and joking as people pressed round him, demanding his attention.

Ari seized the opportunity to put his plan into action. Grace's face was white with misery, and she did not see him approach or register his presence until he had slipped his arm through hers.

'I think it's about time we found a quiet place to have a little chat, don't you?' he murmured in her ear.

Before she could protest, he gripped her arm and led her away from the crowded square where music, booming from one of the tavernas, made conversation impossible. He propelled her down a narrow path between the high walls of some darkened houses and then pushed her back against a wall and stood in front of her.

'That's much better, don't you think? We Greeks take our politics seriously and it can get very boisterous - no place for a woman, particularly a foreigner. Or hadn't you noticed you were unwelcome?'

'Unwelcome? Whoever said anything about me being unwelcome?' Grace tried to speak firmly. In the gloom of the alleyway, Ari's physical bulk was menacing. 'I just wanted to offer my support to Eleni and Yanni.'

'From where I was standing, it didn't look as though they wanted it.'

'Perhaps you are not quite as observant as you think,' retorted Grace, beginning to recover herself.

'Oh, I'm very observant, very observant indeed,' said Ari smiling unpleasantly. 'I see all sorts of things that nobody else does.'

'I'm quite sure that absolutely nothing you've seen could possibly be of interest to me.'

Ari's smile broadened. He was enjoying himself. He moved closer to Grace. She could smell the whisky on his breath.

'You like to give the impression that you're Miss "butter wouldn't melt in your mouth",' he mimed inverted commas in the air with his fingers, 'or anywhere else in your, if I may say so, rather delightfully shaped anatomy, don't you? But I know better.'

Grace turned away, hoping to see someone coming down the alleyway so she could make her escape, but there was nobody. She turned back. 'It's getting late, so if you have something to say, kindly say it.'

'Let's just say that I happened to be walking past a certain windmill one afternoon and there was a lot of grinding going on but it wasn't of wheat, if you get my drift.'

Grace raised her hand and for a moment, Ari though she was going to slap him, but then she let her arm drop to her side. She closed her eyes and rested her head back against the wall.

'Roger is going to be awfully upset when I tell him. He rather fancies himself as an MP doesn't he? I wonder what your English newspapers would make of his wife's little bit on the side? It would make quite a spread in one of your tabloids wouldn't it?'

Grace opened her eyes. They were dull with misery. 'Blackmail is illegal, even in Greece.'

Ari spread out his hands. 'Who said anything about blackmail? Did I mention money? All I wanted to talk to you about was your mother and those women. I'm sure someone like you could convince them that it would be sensible to move to another camp-site. There are at least two other villages on the island which claim to be Sappho's birthplace, surely they should give them the benefit of the doubt?'

Ari waited. He had Grace just where he wanted her, defenceless. It made her look even more beautiful. He remembered what she had looked like, naked on the floor of the windmill, and felt a sudden urgent hardening in his crotch. Perhaps he should suggest one more little service she could provide as the price of his silence?

'Fuck *off.*'

Ari felt a jolt. The words had been spoken with so much vehemence that he wasn't sure he had heard them at first or if they had come from Grace's lips.

'Wha...?'

This time it was Grace who brought her face close to his. She spoke in barely more than a whisper, but her voice was like a razor.

'You heard me. Stay away from me and from my mother and stay the fuck away from Roger.'

Shoving him hard in the chest with her hand, she walked towards the lights of the square.

Recovering from his surprise, Ari made after her. As he reached the end of the alleyway he stopped and yelled at her, only to have his angry expletives drowned by a chorus of whistles of approval from a group of young men as Grace walked by. She ignored them and disappeared into the crowds that were now spilling out of the square.

Impotent with rage, Ari stared after her.

One of the men who had whistled at Grace called out to him in Greek. 'Stuck up bitch that one, she's not for you my friend.'

Ari looked at the men. He recognised them. He had seen them drinking in the kafenion. They were conscripts from the local army post where they were doing their National Service. They were young - barely out of their teens - and from their manner, had already been celebrating the election for some time. He could almost smell the testosterone surging through their bodies. What if he told them about the women at the camp?

He beckoned them over. 'If you're looking for some fun with some women tonight, I think I can help you.'

The men looked at each other and grinned.

THIRTY-FIVE

Hecate sat bolt upright in her sleeping bag and tore off her sleeping mask. She had been having an unusually vivid dream in which she was journeying through a strange but beautiful landscape, drawn towards a place where she knew that she would find what she was looking for, even though she did not know what it was. She had been tantalisingly close to her destination, knowing it was just beyond her fingertips, when there was a flash of light followed by a rush of hot wind that seared her face and made the walls of her tent billow out.

At first, she thought she was still dreaming. Even now, although she was wide-awake, she still felt a dreamlike presence lingering in the air. However, after a moment or two, rather than a psychic emanation, her nose suggested the presence was a strong smell - rather like pungent incense. Hecate felt beside her sleeping bag for her watch. She never wore her watch during the say as she did not like to feel that her life was being regulated by what she considered to be artifical, man-made time. However, when she was alone at night, she found the watch's extra large illuminated dial that allowed her short-sighted eyes to read the numbers, comforting. Now it showed that it was just after four-thirty in the morning. Dawn was not far away.

As she sat contemplating whether she had experienced some sort of celestial visitation, as a result of the rituals she had performed the night before to greet the new moon, Hecate became aware that there was a lot of noise outside her tent. Whatever she had experienced, other people had experienced it too. She crawled out of her sleeping bag and put her head out through the flap of her tent. In the gloom, confused half-naked and naked women milled sleepily around. Hecate reached behind for her wrap and then scrambled to her feet, pulling it around her.

'What happened?' she demanded. It was only then, in the half-light, that she saw a plume of smoke. She pointed at it. 'Fire!'

There were loud exclamations of alarm and women rushed to their tents to grab clothes. Inside her tent, Marjorie heard the commotion. She had been woken by the explosion and instinctively reached out for Lilith, only to discover that the sleeping bag beside her was empty and had not been slept in. Lilith had not come back last night from the election meeting in the village.

Fearing the women might cause trouble, Eleni had asked them to stay away from the meeting, but despite this, Lilith and a few of the other women had gone, saying they would be careful and keep a low profile. Marjorie had refused to go. She was not only bored of politics, but if she was absolutely honest, she was also becoming bored of life in the camp.

All she wanted was to bask in the sun by day and make love under the stars at night, but Lilith was preoccupied with the campaign. She spent most days with other, like-minded women, talking politics and producing leaflets, and when she returned in the evening, she expected the tent to be tidy, the washing to be done and something ready to eat. Even after their meal, when Marjorie wanted to relax and talk, Lilith either went off to another meeting or began questioning her, to see if she had read the books about feminism that Lilith had given her to study. It was worse than being married or being back at school!

Marjorie sighed then pulled on a large T-shirt and crawled out of the tent. She stood up, her nostrils wrinkling at the acrid smell. Women were standing around unsure what to do, conjecturing as to what had happened.

'Maybe it's some kind of military exercise,' suggested someone.

'It's possible, there's an army post not far from here,' agreed another woman.

'Has anyone seen Lilith?' Marjorie asked joining them. She was beginning to feel anxious.

The women shook their heads.

Sîan came running towards them through the tents. 'We've been bombed.'

'Oh my god,' shrieked one woman whilst another started to cry hysterically.

Juno crawled out of her tent. She was dressed in mens' striped pyjamas. Her hair, which was normally stood upright in gelled spikes, lay flat and wispy, like baby's hair.

'Right, stop that stupid noise for a start,' she commanded handing the weeping woman a large white handkerchief. The woman buried her face in it and loudly blew her nose.

With a nod of satisfaction, Juno looked at Sîan. 'Has anyone been hurt?'

Sîan shook her head. 'I don't think so. I didn't dare look.'

'Has anyone seen Lilith?' repeated Marjorie, her voice beginning to rise.

'Where was it?' demanded Juno ignoring Marjorie.

Sîan pointed to the far side of the camp.

'The latrines!' exclaimed Juno and began to run in their direction.

The latrines were Juno's pride and joy. Built both at her insistence and under her command, they were a legacy of her short army career. Juno had dreamed of being in the army since she was a little girl and had enlisted as soon as she was old enough. She had intended to make the army her life, but, after five blissful years in the signals corps, she made the mistake of falling for the wrong woman. She was given the choice of resigning or facing a court martial, but her commanding officer made it clear that, should she decide to fight her case before a military court, it would end in a dishonourable discharge. Juno had accepted defeat and resigned - the army was too big an opponent to take on single-handed. However, she had sworn to herself that she would never back down from a fight again, and right at that moment, looking down at the mess that had once been the latrines, she would have single-handedly taken on those responsible, even if they proved to be the whole Greek army.

The other women gathered silently around her, staring at the black, smoking hole in the ground. At last someone spoke: 'Do you think anyone was using them?'

The women looked at each other, stricken expressions on their faces.

'No-one would have been using them, not in the middle of the night. Surely they would have just gone in the bushes nearest their tent, I do,' said Sîan uncertainly.

Marjorie pushed her way to the front of the crowd and looked down. 'I haven't seen Lilith since yesterday.'

Sîan put an arm around her.

Juno knelt down and poked a stick through the rubble with the air of someone who knew what she was looking for. 'We'd know if there had been someone in there,' she said with an authoritative air.

'How would we know?' asked a reedy voice.

Juno stood up and looked round. 'Believe *me*, we'd know,' she replied sternly.

'But where's Lilith?' asked Marjorie plaintively.

'She can't have gone far. She's probably sleeping on the beach. It was very warm last night,' said Sîan soothingly. 'Why don't we take a look?'

Juno crossed her arms. 'I think we have some clearing up to do here, and someone's got to report this to the police.'

'I hardly think the local policeman is likely to rush out here to help us after what happened to him in the taverna the other night, so I think the exploding latrines can wait until we've had a chance to get breakfast, don't you?' suggested Sîan.

'And just supposing the perpetrators are still hiding around here? They may have other bombs or even guns,' replied Juno angrily.

'Look around you,' Sîan waved her arm at the now peaceful scene. 'Do you see an army of Greek guerrillas waiting to attack?'

'Sîan's right,' declared Hecate who had just joined them. 'Someone is trying to frighten us. We must stick together and not show them that they have succeeded. Let's make a large pot of strong tea and then discuss what to do next. We're not going to let them frighten us away are we?' She looked around but few of the women met her gaze.

'We'll join you when we've found Lilith,' said Sîan and guided Marjorie towards the beach.

Juno stood gazing mournfully down at the remains of the latrines for a few moments more, and then followed the rest of the women back to the tents.

As the last of the women were out of earshot, Ari breathed a sigh of relief. Crouched in his hiding place behind a large rock, his cramped limbs were aching. He stretched out his legs as he considered his next move, scratching vigorously at the various insect bites that had been inflicted on him while he was hiding.

The plan had been to get away before the bomb exploded, but it had not worked out that way. Although drunk, the soldiers he recruited were younger and more agile than him. They got away quickly, leaving him to stumble around in the dark and twist his ankle, which was looking purple and swollen. When he finally caught up with them, he would have a thing or two to say about them abandoning him. He always thought the rules of war dictated that soldiers returned for an injured comrade. He would also have some choice words to say about the size of the bomb.

When they made their plans in the kafenion last night, he had been quite specific about only wanting a little bang. Nothing too dangerous he told them, just enough to give the women a fright. However, whether they weren't as expert with explosives as they claimed to be, or they had had too much to drink, the resulting explosion had nearly killed him. His eardrums were still throbbing, and to add insult to injury, he and his clothes stunk. Whatever it was the women kept in their outhouse, it smelled as though it was well past its sell-by date.

Ari clambered stiffly to his feet and gingerly tested his ankle. He could walk, but only just, and it was a long way back to the village. The dangerous part was to get past the camp without being seen, as it was now alive with women. He began to limp as fast as he dared, crouching low and following the line of the sand dunes which divided the camp from the main beach, in the hope that they would provide him with cover until he got to the safety of the rocks. However, even though it was still cool, the effort made him sweat, and he had to stop to rest his foot and mop his face more often than he liked. Only the angry voices from the camp kept him going.

Forced to stop yet again to catch his by now rasping breath, Ari rested his hands on his thighs. The rocks seemed to be receding into the distance rather than coming any closer. The sun was now just above the opalescent horizon, and he could see the surrounding countryside. As he tried to steady his breathing, the memory of a day on this beach with his father, before they emigrated to Australia, came back to him.

He could almost feel his father's large, calloused hand enclosing his tiny one as they had walked along the shore. He could remember looking up at his father's face and not being able to see it as the sun was in his eyes, but he could still recall the sound of his voice as they walked. His father led him to a cave in the rocks where he had played as a boy that nobody else knew about. Inside it was dark and gloomy and smelled of fish, and Ari had cried because it had frightened him. His father had been angry with him as boys were not meant to cry, but his anger had quickly evaporated and he had walked back to the village, proudly carrying Ari on his shoulders.

With his breath back to normal, Ari set off again. If he could reach that cave, he could hide there and rest his ankle, before making the long journey back to the village. As he neared the rocks, he searched for the entrance, praying that he could remember where it was. As he looked up at the cliff face, for one awful moment he wondered whether his father's cave had been a dream, but then he saw the large rock, marbled emerald green and red, like dried blood, and beside it a bush covered with tiny yellow star-shaped flowers that concealed the cave entrance. Gritting his teeth against the pain from his ankle, Ari scrambled up the cliff.

It took only a few minutes to reach the bush but it seemed much longer than that. Wiping the sweat that was streaming into his eyes away with a filthy hand, Ari pulled the bush aside. Stepping forward, his foot did not find the solid ground it expected as the entrance to the cave had eroded through the years, and he fell head first, rolling over a couple of times before he was stopped by something that was soft and yielding. It let out a loud and indignant squeal matched by his yell of fright.

'What the fuck's going on?' demanded an American voice.

Ari pushed himself away from his soft landing and sat up, his back against the rough cave wall.

'I could ask you the same thing,' he snapped as fear turned to anger and his eyes adjusted to the light coming from a large fissure in the roof of the cave that he did not remember from his childhood visit.

Like a pointing finger, a shaft of dusty sunlight illuminated a naked Lilith.

Just then, the body that had softened his fall turned over and propped itself up on one elbow. It was Kelly. She too, was naked, her honey blond hair cascading around her shoulders like a golden waterfall in the sunlight. All she needed was a tail to look like a mermaid sitting among the fronds of seaweed that carpeted the cave floor.

Ari stared at her, slack-jawed.

Lilith put two arms proprietorially around Kelly, drawing her back so that her head rested between Lilith's small high breasts.

Kelly gazed at him, her eyes round and blue. 'Ari, I'm sorry...'

'There's no need to apologise to that bastard, Kelly. You've just given him what he deserves,' said Lilith fiercely. 'Remember what he did to his ex-wife and all the other women who've had the misfortune to meet him. It's only fitting that he should learn the truth this way.' She stroked Kelly's breasts.

'You...you...' Ari tried to make a strange noise that could have been a grunt or a groan, but it was strangled at birth.

'Be careful what you call me,' warned Lilith. 'There are names for men like you.' She smiled thinly. 'How does it feel to know that you couldn't give your wife the kind of sexual satisfaction a woman can?'

Ari made another guttural, animal-like sound.

Kelly got to her feet and began picking up their clothes.

Lilith yawned and stretched her arms. 'I think we should leave your ex-husband to spend some time in quiet contemplation, don't you Kelly?'

She stepped naked over Ari's outstretched legs, and climbed up to the entrance of the cave, pausing only to see if Kelly was following her. Kelly hesitated as though frightened that Ari might grab her, then, clutching their clothes, she also stepped quickly over him and followed Lilith.

As the bush swung back to conceal the cave entrance, she thought she heard the sound of hoarse crying, but glancing back, she realised that it was just a seagull that had been disturbed on its nest among the rocks.

Lilith was already down on the beach and and as Kelly watched, she ran towards the sea and plunged in, swimming with long, powerful strokes. Kelly scrambled down the rocks after her, dropping their clothes as she raced across the sand to join Lilith in the waves. Behind them, Ari crawled out of the cave and half fell, half slid down onto the beach, before stumbling off in the direction of the village like a blind man.

On the far side of the beach, partially concealed by a large dune, two figures watched.

'So the goddess Artemis has finally torn Actaeon to bits,' Sîan murmured almost to herself.

Marjorie looked at Sîan, misery etched on her features. 'Artemis?'

Sîan shrugged. 'It's a long story about a man who spies on women and gets his just rewards. Only this time I'm not sure who was Actaeon - the dreadful Ari or me.'

Marjorie started at her uncomprehendingly for a moment and then gestured at Lilith and Kelly who were clinging together kissing in the surf.

'Did you know?'

Sîan shook her head. 'Not for sure. But I had a feeling...'

'I didn't,' said Marjorie, her voice trembling. 'I thought women were different - that they wouldn't betray someone who loves them.'

Sîan smiled ruefully. 'Whatever gave you that idea?'

THIRTY-SIX

Roger harrumphed loudly as he shook his four-day-old copy of *The Daily Mail* out. He was not in a good mood. He had risen early that morning and driven to a town on the other side of the island in the hope of buying an English newspaper, as he considered a day that began without a newspaper not to have begun at all. Unfortunately, the result of his three-hour round trip had been an elderly copy of the *Mail*, a newspaper he considered fit only for women. There had been no *Daily Telegraph* or *Times*, but at least he had a newspaper. He harrumphed again and ostentatiously turned to the editorial.

Adonis stopped speaking and looked nervously at Grace.

'Don't worry, carry on,' she urged. 'I'm listening.'

Glancing nervously at Roger, Adonis continued. He had rushed to greet them when they had arrived for lunch, grinning broadly as he announced the news that Yanni was to be the new Mayor and the hotel was not going to be built, at least not on the beach. As far as Grace was able to make out from his excited speech, there was now talk of a smaller hotel being built in the village, where everyone could share its benefits, as tourists would spend their drachmas in the kafenions and tavernas, as well as in the hotel. Polychronos the shopkeeper was already making plans to extend his shop and sell souvenirs.

'Is good news is it not?' he finished.

Grace smiled wanly. She should have been elated at Yanni's triumph, but she had hardly slept for two nights. When she had returned to her room after the election meeting, she had sat for a long time watching Roger gently snoring. She had been really shaken up by Ari's attempt at blackmail. This was not so much because she had been frightened - although she had been at first - but because of the realisation that if she was angry enough, as she had been at Ari, she would be capable of striking someone. It was not a side of herself she recognised.

She knew that she had to make a decision. If anyone was going to tell Roger about the affair, it should be her, she at least owed him that much. However, if she was going to tell him, she had to decide whether she wanted to stay with him. She had a feeling that he might be noble and forgive her if she agreed to stay with him, but she did not want to be seduced by nobility into doing something she would later regret.

She cared deeply about Roger, of that she was sure, but was caring enough? Why couldn't they just continue as they were - jogging along gently, comfortable with each other, was that really *such* a bad way to live?

However, the answer to the question filled her with despair. If she stayed, she betrayed herself, but if she left, she betrayed Roger.

The day after the election, Roger was still not feeling well, so she had seized on his frailty to put off making the choice between the two betrayals. Perhaps she was trying to salve her conscience, but she stayed in their room looking after him, trying to coax him to eat and drink. He was pathetically grateful, and kept telling her how wonderful she was, repeating that he could not live without her, until her nerves were jangling, and she wanted to scream at him that of course he could, he was a grown man not a child.

After barely a few hours of restless sleep, she had woken that morning, knowing that if she spent one more hour in the room alone with him, she would tell him she was leaving. Luckily, after ten hours of uninterrupted sleep, Roger was feeling much better and he had cheerfully driven off to search for a newspaper, giving her a chance to regain a sense of equilibrium.

Adonis returned to their table with their lunch: Greek salad for her and large plate of lamb chops and chips, with a side plate of stuffed aubergines, for Roger, whose appetite had clearly returned. The smell of the lamb chops made him put his newspaper down and order a bottle of red wine. Grace demurred, saying it would not be good for his stomach, but he insisted, and, after a while, she was glad that he had. The wine began to mellow him, and he became the amusing companion she remembered from the early days of their relationship, telling her funny stories about his more villainous clients and the vicissitudes of the legal system, that made her laugh and almost forget her dilemma. For a while, the terrace seemed like a small oasis of dappled green light.

Then Grace saw Roger's eyelids beginning to droop, and she counted some notes out of her purse. She waved them at Adonis who was sitting behind the counter looking bored. 'I think its time we went home. Poor Adonis is longing for his siesta.'

As they walked slowly back to their room, she put her arm through Roger's. He patted her hand. 'I think this place has done you a world of good, Grace. You look a different woman from the one who left England. Perhaps we should come to Greece next year on our honeymoon, would you like that?'

Grace looked away to hide the tears that had sprung to her eyes. She knew there was only one possible answer to her question. As much as she cared about Roger, she could not marry him. She had crossed over a line that had become a chasm, and Roger was on the other side. There was no going back.

'I've just remembered. I promised to go over and see Kelly this afternoon, do you mind?'

She was being a miserable coward not telling him and she knew it, but Grace reasoned with herself that now was not the right time. Roger had drunk nearly a bottle of strong Greek wine and was still feeling the effects of his upset stomach.

'Girl talk again I suppose? Off you run. I'm going to get an hour's shut-eye. That wine has done for me just as you said it would. I should listen to you more carefully, Grace. You always know what's best for me.'

She kissed him on the cheek and watched him walk off. As he reached the top of the street, he turned as though to reassure himself she was still there. She gave him a little wave that he returned before disappearing round the corner. Grace waited for a moment or two longer and then set off for Yanni's taverna.

She was not sure if she would find him there, but she did not know where else to look. However, even before she reached the taverna, the noise and number of vehicles parked outside told her that this was where she would find him.

Inside it was crowded with friends and well-wishers. It looked like celebrations had been going on for many hours. Grace hovered uncertainly in the doorway, craning her neck to spot Yanni in the mass of people. Someone tried to press a glass of wine into her hand but she waved it away. She felt completely out of place. A voice at her side made her look down.

'Grace! What a surprise.'

Eleni was smiling, but Grace did not get the impression that she was a welcome surprise.

'I was just passing by, so I thought I would come in and offer my congratulations.' She could lie with a smile equally well.

'This is not a good moment. There are many important people here that Yanni must see.' Eleni took Grace's elbow to guide her out of the door. 'Perhaps tomorrow?'

Grace hesitated. She could hardly ignore Eleni. Then she caught sight of Yanni and waved. He started towards her, but his progress across the room was very slow, as everyone wanted to talk to him.

He looked different. He was dressed in a sober black suit, white shirt and tie, and his hair had been cut short and slicked back. It no longer curled around his neck in the way Grace loved. She looked around the room. Most of the other men were dressed in similar black suits. Grace felt a sudden hollow feeling in the pit of her stomach. Yanni belonged to them now, not to her. He was no longer Yanni the poet and the dancer, but Yanni the Mayor. She watched as he bent his ear to everyone who demanded it, nodding gravely as they talked, then offering a few words and a handshake before moving on to the next supplicant with the ease of a practised politician.

When at last he reached them, Grace found her welcoming smile frozen on her face.

'I was just explaining to Grace that now is not a good time to talk, you are too busy,' said Eleni who had remained at her side like a jailer.

'Eleni is right,' agreed Yanni avoiding meeting Grace's eyes. 'But you are welcome to join us. We are celebrating.'

'Please... I need to talk to you,' pleaded Grace, no longer caring what Eleni thought.

Yanni looked directly at her this time. The expression in his eyes was sad. 'Come,' he indicated, 'we go outside. Would you like a drink?'

Grace shook her head, not trusting her voice.

'Yanni...your friends. They are waiting,' said Eleni reprovingly.

'I will be only a few minutes. You entertain them, you won the election,' Yanni retorted sharply.

Grace waited for Eleni to argue, but instead, she put a hand on Grace's arm, a look almost of pity in her eyes. 'Please, don't keep him too long. We are grateful for the help your mother and all the women gave us, but Yanni has a hard job to do now, and he will need all his energy to do it. It is difficult for an outsider to understand village politics.' With that she turned and was swallowed up by the crowd.

Yanni led Grace to a table at the far end of the terrace. He pulled out two chairs and they sat, facing each other.

'Now,' he said, 'what is it you want to talk about?'

Grace swallowed hard, fighting to regain her composure. 'Congratulations on winning the election.'

He bowed his head solemnly. 'Thank you.'

'Orpheus can now rest in peace in the olive grove and the nightingales will sing sweetly over his head.' Grace tried to make her voice sound light, but the accompanying smile died before it reached her lips.

A look, almost of pain, crossed Yanni's face. 'You remember.'

'How could I forget?'

Grace's voice cracked. She looked away, tears clouding her vision. Across the road from the terrace was a small, pebbly beach and beyond that the sea. She could not remember it looking more beautiful than at that moment.

'Yanni...would you read some of your poetry to me?'

It was not what she had intended to ask, but it was what she needed to know. If he would share with her the intimacy of his poetry, then the man she had seen dance like a gypsy - the man who had thought he could fly - was still inside the sober suit and tie.

He looked at her oddly. 'I write in Greek... It is impossible...'

'But you speak good English. Surely you could translate just a few lines?' urged Grace.

Yanni shook his head. 'The words, yes, maybe, but poetry is more than words. It comes from here,' he touched his heart. 'These things are difficult to say, so I say them in my writing. I do not think I could say them in English.'

Grace felt hope slipping through her fingers.

'There is something wrong?' Yanni leant forward. 'I feel it in the square two nights ago but I could not speak, you understand?'

She nodded, although she did not.

He reached out and took her right hand. 'Tell me.'

'I'm not going to marry Roger.'

He looked at her hand rather than at her. 'This is a big thing. Are you sure?'

Grace nodded.

'So what will you do when you go back to England?'

Grace snatched her hand away from his. 'I'm leaving Roger because I'm in love with you. I want to stay here. Live with you...'

Yanni ran a hand through his hair and looked away, misery etched across his features. 'You know nothing about me and I know nothing about you.' He looked back at her, holding his hands out towards her as though trying to grasp something. 'We cannot understand each other's thoughts, each other's dreams. How can we be in love?'

Grace felt as though someone had kicked her in the stomach.

'But you said that you could fall in love with someone with just one look, and, in that look, see everything you needed to know. You said it standing right here,' she said, gesticulating helplessly.

He took both her hands in his, gripping them tightly as she tried to pull away.

'But I did not say I had fallen in love with *you* this way.'

Grace felt a tear escape, but she could not wipe it away because Yanni would not let her hands go.

Yanni looked up into her eyes. His expression was gentle.

'I think you are in love with this place, not me. Maybe me a little too,' he smiled ruefully, 'but only because I am a part of this place. I have watched you change since you first arrived, all... how do you say? Stuck up? Every day your face has grown softer, like a woman in love, but it is the sun that has kissed it like this, not me. Look at your hair,' he released one of her hands and touched her hair. 'Now it is so beautiful because you have allowed it to escape, to be itself.'

He closed his eyes and was silent for a moment or two. Grace found herself looking at the scar on his hand. It looked even more violent than usual.

Yanni looked at her again. 'I cannot say that I do not love you. I would not go with you in the way I do if I did not care for you, very much. But it is not the way you want me to love you. I think perhaps like you, I was looking for an escape and I saw it in you.' He looked thoughtful. 'Perhaps we each gave the other the courage to escape, to do something we could not do without the other. Once I had dreams. Great dreams...'

His voice trailed off, and for a moment, his face nakedly revealed the battle he was having with his emotions, then he won. 'But now I am Mayor and my life is here, in this village. It is hard for me to explain these things to you because you are English, but here there is a saying that Greeks have their heads in the cloud and their feet on the ground. For a while, with you, my head was in the clouds, but from now on, my feet must be on the ground. When I marry it must be with a girl whose world is here, in this village. You could not be like that. If you became my wife, you must become like a Greek woman.' He shook his head. 'I do not think you are ready for this. You would not want me to set you free only to put you in a cage again.'

Yanni released her hands and they sat, unable to look at each other.

A man came out from the taverna and called to Yanni in Greek. Yanni waved him away.

'Go,' said Grace in a muffled voice.

'I cannot leave you like this,' he protested.

Grace looked up at him, her eyes glittering with tears. 'How else did you mean to leave me?'

He stood up.

'I am sorry, Grace. Signome. *Please*, forgive me.'

THIRTY-SEVEN

'I was beginning to wonder if you'd run off with one of those strapping Greek fishermen,' Roger looked up with a smile as Grace came through the door. 'I've been looking everywhere for you. After I had a siesta, I went in search of that Australian chap and his wife but their place looked deserted, so I went back to the kafenion. That young lad in there seems to know everything. According to him, Ari has packed his bags and left. Just like that, no goodbyes, nothing! He didn't even stay around to hear the results of the election. I obviously had him pegged right from the start.'

His tone was jovial, but there were anxious questions in his eyes. Grace avoided them. Since leaving Yanni, she had been walking aimlessly for hours. She couldn't remember what she had been thinking, or even if she had been thinking at all. She just felt numb.

Roger held up his glass. 'Would you like a gin and tonic?'

Grace glanced at the duty free bottle on the table. It was almost empty. Roger had drunk nearly half a bottle. She nodded and went into the bathroom, closing the door behind her. She had to face him, but not yet. She went over to the basin and splashed her face with cold water.

'And Ari's not the only one who's packed his bags.' Roger called through the door louder than was necessary. 'According to Adonis, there's been some sort of trouble up at the women's camp and a lot of them have gone too. Savvas the taxi driver has been making a fortune, ferrying women to the airport all day.'

Grace dried her face and then began to tug a comb through the tangles in her hair. It hurt, but she wanted it to.

'I've been thinking, Grace. Now that everything is sorting itself out here, why don't we take the hire car and tour the island for a few days before returning to London? It would be a splendid opportunity for us to spend some time together, away from the demands of your mother.'

There was silence. Grace knew he was waiting for her to spring to her mother's defence, but when she remained silent, he continued.

'I thought it would also give us time to talk. I know you haven't been happy lately...'

In the mirror, Grace saw her face blur as her eyes filled with tears. She put a hand across her mouth, trying to stifle her sobs, her body shaking with their force.

Roger knocked on the door and then tried the handle. 'Grace...? Are you all right?'

She gulped for air. 'I'll be out in a minute.'

She splashed some more water on her face and then shakily applied some lipstick. When she opened the door, Roger was standing beside it. He handed her a gin and tonic. She took it and walked onto the balcony where she stood looking down at the village. The setting sun was a perfect orb of molten gold in a sea of blood red orange. Yanni was right. She had fallen in love with this place. She felt Roger coming to stand beside her.

'We could set a date for our nuptials if it would help, it would give us something to plan for, and although we haven't discussed it before, perhaps we should think about starting a family soon. Neither of us is getting any younger, and since there is every possibility I'll be selected by a constituency before the next election, the timing would seem perfect. Once we know where my constituency is, we can buy a large house there - room for children to grow and all that. You could have a study and work from home if you want, as I wouldn't think you'd want to carry on going to an office, not with children to look after. Although of course there's always the possibility of a nanny,' he added quickly. 'I know some women think differently these days.'

Grace toyed with her glass. The village had even affected Roger. He looked relaxed, and his skin was beginning to get a healthy glow, although his choice of a pale pink shirt did not really complement his complexion. He had been thinking about their relationship too, something she suspected he rarely did. She tried to picture herself in a large house, perhaps in the country or at least somewhere leafy, with one or two children - a boy and a girl. It would also be possible to continue working as an editor from home. She certainly wouldn't miss the daily commute in crowded tube trains. If she married Roger, she could have everything she had always thought she wanted.

She drank a large mouthful of gin and tonic. 'Roger...'

He looked expectantly at her, but she kept her gaze fixed on the horizon.

'Roger, there's something I must tell you and I'm afraid it will affect your plans for us.'

'Only in the best possible way, I hope.' His voice was jocular but Grace could sense his body tensing.

'I wish I didn't have to tell you Roger, but I must,' she said slowly.

Roger swirled the ice around in his drink, watching it as though he could read a secret in the bottom of his glass.

'Nobody *has* to tell anybody anything Grace, particularly if it will help the case for the prosecution. The urge to confess is not always a good thing. The innocent can get hurt as well as the guilty.'

Grace looked at him. Had he guessed? His tone had been bantering, but the healthy glow had gone from his skin.

'Roger, I care about you a great deal, but I'm not sure I want to marry you.'

'The imprecision of your terminology leaves your statement open to at least two interpretations.' For the first time Roger's voice had an edge. 'Are you saying you *don't* want to marry me, or are you saying there is still a possibility that you will?'

'Please don't come the trial lawyer with me, Roger, this is difficult enough as it is,' begged Grace.

'Difficult for you!' Roger snorted. 'Your mother is behind this, isn't she? She's never wanted us to marry and she's been doing her damned best to wreck our relationship. It's bad enough that her own head is filled with a load of nonsense about women, without her filling your head with nonsense too,' he said angrily.

'This has nothing to do with my mother and everything to do with us,' said Grace gently. 'You and I are two people who have got into the habit of living with each other. We like each other, are *incredibly* fond of each other, but I want something more than that.'

'But that's just what I was saying,' he said defensively. 'If we get married as soon as possible and you have a baby, I'm sure things will improve.'

'So you think that if I spend more time looking after you as well as a child, I will feel more fulfilled?'

'Why not? I thought you wanted a family. You always said that you wanted to give a child what you never had.'

'This is not about children, or my job, or whether I should be at home more. It's about love.'

'You've met somebody else, haven't you?'

Grace did not reply.

He looked at her, comprehension dawning. 'You're leaving me for someone else. I knew it!' He slammed his fist down on the rail. 'I could sense there was something different about you when I arrived. Who is it? Good *god*! It's not another woman, is it?'

Grace looked away. 'No it's not, but I thought you said there were some things best left unsaid?'

Roger grabbed her arm, forcing her to look at him. 'I'm not a fool. I can see myself in the mirror. You're a very good looking woman and your work gives you plenty of opportunity to meet men. Don't you think it has crossed my mind before now that you might just occasionally sleep with one of them? I decided long ago that I could deal with that happening so long as you were discreet. That sort of thing doesn't necessarily have to ruin a marriage if it's handled properly.'

Grace stared at him in shock. 'You think I could have casual affairs? I thought you knew me better. But even more than that,' she added, ' I thought I knew *you* better.'

'Well if it isn't someone you work with, who is it?' he demanded roughly.

'Does it matter? He's not important. I'm not leaving you for him.'

'Well, at least it's a man. You've left me that much dignity.'

'It's Yanni.'

'Yanni? The boy who runs the taverna?'

'Yes.'

'Good *god*, Grace! What are you thinking about? Have you no self-respect? Running around like some kind of Shirley Valentine, having affairs with Greek waiters!'

'It wasn't like that. Yanni isn't like that,' said Grace stubbornly.

'Isn't like what?' He laughed, but it was mirthless. 'He's just waiting until you leave and then he'll be chasing after the next available woman who comes to town. All men are like that, given half a chance.'

'You spend too much time with criminals and liars and cheats. Not everyone is like them,' Grace retorted.

'And on that faint hope, you're going to break our engagement?' asked Roger caustically.

'I make no excuses for what happened between Yanni and me. It was wrong, and I'm very sorry that I've hurt you. However, what happened is nothing to do with my decision to break our engagement. It's my fault. I've changed, and now I can see that our relationship was going nowhere, but before I couldn't see it, or perhaps I just didn't want to see it. It was so much easier to blame my mother for what was happening between us.' Grace smiled sadly. 'I know it won't be any consolation, but you and my mother are for once in agreement. She told me I shouldn't say anything about Yanni. She even encouraged me to stay with you.'

Roger's features sagged. 'But we can come to some agreement. I don't want to lose you Grace. I'll do anything you want. If you want children, we can have them and nannies too. If you want to continue working, and don't want children, I'll be happy with that as well. I don't care so long as I have you,' he begged miserably.

'That wouldn't work, you know it wouldn't. A relationship isn't about what just one person wants. We would end up hating each other, and I don't want that. I care far too much about you.' Grace gently wiped a tear from his cheek.

He pushed her hand away and stumbled back into the room. She heard him pulling his suitcase out from under the bed.

'What are you doing?' She demanded from the doorway.

'I'm going to drive to the main town and stay in a hotel until I can get a plane back to London.'

Grace went over and closed the suitcase lid. 'You can't drive tonight, Roger. You've had too much to drink. If you must go, go tomorrow. I'm going to the camp to see my mother and to find out what's going on. I think its best if I stay there tonight, but I'll be back in the morning. We can talk again then.'

She tried to put her arms around him, but his body stayed rigid in her embrace. She stepped back.

'I'm sorry Roger, I truly am. I wish you'd believe me when I say I care about you, because I do and I always will.'

THIRTY-EIGHT

'Who needs PMT twice a month?' Sîan thumped hard on her suitcase and then sat back on her heels and glared at it. It had stubbornly rejected all her attempts to close it. 'I've had it with women. From now on, its men only for me. They're such simple creatures. Their hormones only ever tell them to do two things: fuck or fight.'

Marjorie knelt down beside her and opened the case. She removed the clothes that Sîan had angrily stuffed inside, folding them neatly before replacing them, and snapped the case shut. Sîan smiled ruefully and then tipped the contents of her wash bag onto a towel on the ground outside her tent and began shaking containers to see if there anything left inside.

Marjorie perched herself on the suitcase and watched. 'I don't think you should give up on women just because of Lilith,' she said after a moment or two. 'You fell for the wrong one, that's all.'

'We both did,' retorted Sîan. 'Hasn't it put you off?'

'Lilith was a first for me, at least when it comes to women, so I can't really make any comparisons. But I've had plenty of practice with men and that hasn't put me off. I certainly don't regret Lilith, even though I think I shall probably go back to men, *if* I can find the right one.'

Sîan threw an empty bottle of suntan lotion to one side. 'But why are the right ones always unobtainable? I fancied Lilith the first moment I saw her, but she only seems to like straight women whom she can turn. So in her own way, she's after the unobtainable too.' With an exclamation of frustration, she threw all the contents of her wash bag to one side and then settled down, cross-legged, in front of Marjorie. 'There have been times when I've felt like dancing naked in front of her, shouting: have me, I'm available, but apart from the fact she was with you, available clearly isn't attractive to her. Now she's with Kelly, it makes me wonder if she gets some sort of power kick out of taking women away from men?'

'I don't know what it is, but Lilith certainly has something. She convinced me that when she looked at me, she saw a beautiful woman. Not just outside, but the me inside,' Marjorie put her hand on her heart, 'the person that you rarely allow the world to see, especially men. It was a powerful aphrodisiac at a point when I was feeling very low. Getting men never used to be a problem for me. When I was younger, there always seemed to be so many handsome, sexy men around. So why settle down with one when tomorrow, you might meet the love of your life? But he never came along and suddenly I found that there weren't so many men who were interested in me...' Marjorie's voice trailed off.

Sîan wordlessly stretched out a hand. Marjorie gratefully clasped it and they sat in silence.

'Mother?' The bewildered question floated to them on the warm night air.

Marjorie stood up and waved. 'Grace? We're over here.'

Grace stumbled towards them, picking her way through the remnants of the camp.

'What on earth has been going on?' she asked as she finally reached Sîan's tent. 'The place looks even more like a bomb site than normal.'

Sîan and Marjorie looked at each other and began to laugh, but Marjorie stopped when she saw the look on Grace's face.

'I'm sorry, but let's just say that for once, we really do have an excuse.'

Grace looked at Sîan. 'Why are you packing?'

'The summer's over, at least for me. A lot of the women left today and more are leaving tomorrow although Hecate and some of her followers are staying. She claims that she read the cards wrong, and that while the hanged man and death can fortell disaster, they can also mean the death of the old life and the rebirth of the soul. So she and the turtles will have peace and she can get on with worshipping the goddess or whatever it is she intends to get up to,' Sîan laughed.

Grace looked at Marjorie. 'Are you and Lilith leaving too?'

'Lilith's already left,' she paused, 'with Kelly.'

'With *Kelly*...?' Grace was stunned.

Sîan patted the ground beside her. 'Pull up a pew, there's a story you ought to hear.' She pointed to the tent. 'Marjorie, if you reach inside, there should be the remains of a bottle of Metaxa somewhere in there. I suggest we have a wake.'

Grace hesitated. She wanted to talk to Sîan, especially if she was leaving in the morning, but she needed to speak to Marjorie first.

'Sîan, I'm sorry. I don't mean to be rude, but I really need to speak to my mother.'

Sîan scrambled to her feet and gave Grace a hug. 'You don't have to apologise. I understand. Why don't you two take the bottle with you? I think I've consumed more than is good for me during these last few months. It's time to sober up and get back to reality. You will keep in touch when you get back, won't you?'

Grace hugged her back. 'I promise, and thank you.'

'Thank you for what?' asked Sîan.

'For being a friend.'

Marjorie linked her arm through Grace's as they walked away. 'I never thought I'd say this about you, but you're full of surprises Grace.'

'Surprises?'

'You and Sîan.'

'She's one of the few good things that have come out of all this.'

There was a catch in Grace's voice as she spoke. Marjorie gave her a searching look, but asked her no more questions until they got to the beach. It was deserted and they sat in companionable silence for a while, then Grace looked at her mother.

'Why is everyone leaving?'

'Some of the men from the village blew up our loos on election night. We think that dreadful man Ari was behind it.'

'Blew them up? Was anyone hurt? What did the police say?'

Marjorie shrugged. 'We didn't bother to report it. Why bother? The local police are not exactly fond of us. Anyway, it was only a small bomb, probably more of a large firework, and although it made a big mess, no-one was injured.'

'Ari is a bastard. It's a pity he didn't get blown up too,' said Grace.

'Well, he got his comeuppance of a sort. He stumbled on Lilith and Kelly making love.'

Grace started to laugh. 'Kelly? Making love with Lilith?' But a look at her mother's crumpled face told her it was not a joke. She put a comforting hand on her mother's arm. 'I'm sorry, really I am. I had no idea.'

'I thought you would have been happy. It isn't as though you approved of Lilith,' Marjorie said tremulously.

Grace moved closer and put her arm around her mother's shoulders.

'I can't deny I wasn't shocked about Lilith at first, but my real problem was that I just didn't like her very much. I hope she will be a lot kinder to Kelly than she has been to you. When I first met her I thought Kelly was a tough little man-eater, but she is really very vulnerable.'

'Lilith likes people who are dependent on her, so perhaps it will work out,' said Marjorie pulling out a handful of paper table napkins and loudly blowing her nose. 'Anyway, you know me. I'm a survivor when it comes to broken love affairs. I've always refused to have regrets. Harping on about the past and what might have been never does anyone any good.' She blew her nose again. 'What was it you wanted to talk to me about?'

'I've decided to leave Roger. I told him so this afternoon.'

Marjorie was open-mouthed. 'I never thought you'd do it.'

'Aren't you going to tell me "I told you so"?' asked Grace.

It was Marjorie's turn to put her arm around Grace's shoulder. 'Even though it's nice to be right for once in my life, I wish it were otherwise, Grace. There's no way I would wish unhappiness on you, surely you know that? I love you. Perhaps I'm never been much of a mother to you, but I can only love you in the way I know how, and I'm truly sorry if that hasn't been good enough for you.'

'I've never said that,' protested Grace.

'But I've seen it in the expression on your face. It used to be disappointment when you were a little girl, but then it slowly but surely turned into disapproval, and I can't blame you. As mothers go, I haven't exactly been a model figure. I thought you were going to marry Roger just to get back at me. I haven't provided you with a father, so you were going to marry one instead.'

Grace took a deep breath. 'What was my father like?' Once the question was out, it seemed so simple. Why had she waited so many years to ask it?

Marjorie looked down and took Grace's hands in hers. Without looking up, she spoke in a low, hesitant voice.

'It was a long time ago, Grace, and I hardly knew him. I can't even remember what he looked like, although in a strange sort of way I can remember his smile and the way he sounded...it was beautiful.'

'You mean his voice?'

'Not just his voice, but the music he made. When he played or when he spoke, it was as if he was caressing you. I used to love watching him play. He had beautiful hands too, long, slim, fingers, like yours.' She traced the shape of Grace's fingers with one of her own. Then she held up her own hand and smiled at Grace. 'See? These are the Hamilton fingers, square and practical. You inherited your father's hands.'

'He was a musician? In an orchestra?' There was so much Grace needed to know.

'He was a jazz musician, a saxophonist. He played with a band in a club in Paris. Your grandmother sent me to France to learn French because she wanted to turn me into a proper young lady, but I'm afraid she didn't succeed,' Marjorie chuckled.

'So I'm half French?' asked Grace.

'Erroll was from New Orleans.'

'Erroll...' Grace said her father's name for the first time in her life.

'He was black.'

'Black?'

'Black is such a dull word for the colour of his skin. It was more like gold. I thought he was the most beautiful man I had ever seen.'

'Did grandmother know?' Grace was stunned.

'Nobody knew, apart from two other girls at the home for unmarried mothers where you were born. I was going to tell your grandmother, but when you were born, you were so pale, nobody even questioned the colour of your father, although they wanted to know his name.'

'But why didn't you tell me about my father? Surely I had a right to know?' demanded Grace.

'You don't understand,' pleaded Marjorie. 'I wasn't trying to conceal anything. Or at least if I was, it was only to protect you. In 1958, nice, middle class sixteen-year-old girls didn't have illegitimate children, let alone mixed race ones. Since nobody could guess by looking at you, why make your life more difficult? My mother would probably have thrown me *and* you out if she had known. There was no Sidney Poitier in "Guess Who's Coming to Dinner" to say he would marry me. I didn't even know Erroll's second name.'

'But why didn't you tell me when I was old enough and had left home, or even after grandmother died?' asked Grace.

Marjorie's shoulders sagged. 'I thought it no longer mattered. You had made such a successful life for yourself. Why did it matter who your father was?'

Grace lay back on the ground and pillowed her head on her arms. She had a father out there, probably in America, who might still be alive.

'Did you love him?'

'I think I thought I did, if that makes any sense.' Her mother turned round and looked down at her. 'Does it matter very much?'

Grace thought about it. Did it matter anymore? 'Probably not.'

'I'm sorry I can't tell you much more about him. I wish I had a photograph or something to show you.'

'It doesn't matter. I like your description of him. Sometimes it's better to leave things to the imagination.'

Marjorie touched Grace's cheek. 'And I was the one who accused you of having no imagination.' She was silent for a moment. 'There is one more thing I can tell you about him. '

Grace turned to look at her. 'What? '

'His mother's favourite song was "Amazing Grace".'

THREE MONTHS LATER

A watery sun struggled to break through the clouds but could do little to pierce the lead-like gloom as Grace gazed out of her office window. She had arrived back from Greece to find she had been given a much larger office and Burgess & Burgess had also increased her salary. Her secretary, Libby, had almost crowed with triumph as she showed her into the new office.

'Bartle and Duncan had kittens while you were away. They just couldn't cope without you. I think it started them thinking about what would happen if you moved to another publisher. So they called a directors' meeting - that's to say the two of them and a huge Indian takeaway - and decided to give you a decent office and pay you more, although still not what you're worth if you ask me.'

Libby was probably right about the money, thought Grace, but she was happy where she was, especially in her new office whose gracious arched windows overlooked a small square surrounded by tall, grey Georgian houses. As she watched a chill gust of wind caused yet more golden-brown leaves to break loose from the plane trees outside and drift down to join those already carpeting the ground. Autumn had arrived.

Before turning back to the pile of manuscripts on her overcrowded desk, Grace briefly caught sight of her reflection in the window. Her tan had long since faded, but now when she looked at herself, she saw her face, not the fact that she did not look like a Hamilton. It was as though she had been gazing at one of those optical illusions that looked like one thing until someone pointed out that you could look at it in a different way, completely transforming the picture. It was all a question of seeing. Sometimes you only saw what you looked for, not what was there.

When she first came back from Greece, Grace had felt self-conscious, half-expecting that because she saw herself differently, other people would too. The strangeness was emphasised because she also had to adjust to being single again, although she had found that much easier than she expected. It had taken longer to adjust to her knowledge about her father, although after a while, she realised that it changed nothing - at least not on the outside.

For a while she had played with the idea of going to America to find him but had soon discarded the idea. Searching for a black jazz musician called Erroll who had slept with a white girl in Paris nearly forty years ago, was a mission doomed to failure. Besides, knowing who she was in the sense of being a person, was far more complex than just knowing who her father was. She had known who her mother was all her life and that had not helped in the least. In some ways, it had probably added to her confusion. However, she no longer felt angry. Marjorie had been little more than a confused child when she got pregnant. It must have taken a lot of courage to refuse to give Grace up for adoption.

That was not to say her relationship with her mother was any easier - just different. They had left the island together and travelled by ferry to Athens where they spent a few days enjoying each other's company. Since getting back to London, they had slipped into the habit of lunching together once a week. However, their new relationship had limits. Marjorie had moved in with Grace while her flat was being renovated, but after only one week, they both agreed that in the interests of remaining friends, it would be better if she moved out. This was achieved without rancour on either side, and in some ways, had served to strengthen their relationship.

The shrill tone of the telephone made Grace jump. She picked up the receiver. 'Grace Hamilton.'

'How is my darling child today?'

Grace smiled. Think of the devil.

'I'm fine mother, really I am. You don't have to keep checking on me like this.'

'I'm your mother, I'm meant to worry about you. Are you sure you're not feeling lonely?'

'I'm enjoying having the house to myself again.'

'And Roger?'

'We had lunch last week. He's looking for a house in what he hopes will be his constituency. All he can talk about is the next election. He's suddenly discovered he has an environmental conscience. I think it has something to do with a proposed motorway extension that comes a bit too close to some extremely expensive properties owned by his possible constituents. It seems they have been on their leafy streets demonstrating shoulder to shoulder with the very same 'tree-huggers' that Roger has spent years prosecuting,' Grace laughed. 'I don't think he misses me at all.'

'I'm sure he does, in his own peculiar way. But what about you? Do you miss him?'

'I miss his presence around the house, particularly in the morning, but that's not the same as missing him.'

'And Yanni?'

Grace looked down at the open manuscript her secretary, Libby, had put on her desk that morning. Written by a woman who had lived in Greece for a year, it was a part memoire, part travelogue. Even though she had a pile of other manuscripts that had priority, Grace had not been able to resist opening it.

Its opening words read: *"Greece has only three venomous creatures: scorpions, adders and men. To the bites of the first two there are effective antidotes, to the bite of the third, there is none."*

Grace looked out the window before replying to her mother's question. It was raining again, the drops splattering the glass like tears. When she stood in the dusty village square for the last time, her mother chattering happily to Savvas the taxi driver as he loaded their suitcases, she had barely been able to see through her tears. She had hoped, against her better judgement, that Yanni would come to say goodbye, and her judgement had proved right. Only Adonis had emerged from his kafenion to say goodbye, smiling shyly as he presented her with a leaving present of some feta his mother had made and a small bunch of flowers. He blushed when Grace hugged and kissed him.

She had resolved not to look back, but as the taxi climbed into the mountains, she could not resist turning round to catch one last glimpse of the village and the harbour far below. As she did, she felt as though she was being torn apart.

'No,' Grace replied, 'I don't think about him at all. I've got far too much on at work for that.'

'You know what they say about all work and no play,' said Marjorie, 'I don't want you turning into a recluse while I'm away. I shall call to check up on your progress. Mothers always know best, and this mother's recipe for your recovery is to find yourself a very sexy young man, forget about the nice part.'

For the first time in their telephone conversation, Grace became aware of background noises on her mother's end of the line.

'What do you mean while you're away? Where are you calling from?'

There was a throaty giggle on the other end of the line.

'Remember the flight back from Athens when I managed to get us upgraded to business class, but you were so exhausted you slept most of the way? There was this absolutely charming Italian sitting by himself who insisted I join him in a bottle of vintage champagne. Well, he's sent me first class tickets to join him in his villa on the edge of one of the Italian lakes. From the pictures I've seen, it looks more like a palace.'

For a moment Grace was aghast, then she thought about the transformation in her mother's appearance since she arrived back in London. All traces of Gaia the earth mother had been banished. She had lost a lot of weight and her hair had been cut very short and streaked blond to disguise the grey. She was looking not only younger and prettier, but also happy. Now Grace knew why. She should have guessed that there was another man around.

'Are you sure you want another foreign adventure? After all, you don't know much about him. He could be anybody.'

'Actually, I think he's some sort of Count, but I must rush, I think that's the last call for my flight.'

Grace couldn't help smiling. Her mother was incorrigible. 'No post cards begging for help this time. I'm far too busy to come to Italy to rescue you. '

'I rather think *I* was the one who did the rescuing, don't you?'

'All right, ' Grace laughed, 'but don't stay away too long, I need you.'

'You? Need me?' There was a pause. 'Darling...why on *earth* would you need me?'

'You're my mother aren't you?'

Printed in Great Britain
by Amazon